A DEATH IN PARIS

By Dean Fuller

Passage
A Death in Paris

A DEATH IN PARIS

An Alex Grismolet Mystery

DEAN FULLER

LITTLE, BROWN AND COMPANY
Boston   Toronto   London

Library of Congress Cataloging-in-Publication Data

Fuller, Dean.
   A death in Paris : an Alex Grismolet mystery / Dean Fuller.—1st
ed.
      p.   cm.
   ISBN 0-316-29603-1
   I. Title.
PS3556.U38D43   1992
813'.54—dc20   91-47637

10   9   8   7   6   5   4   3   2   1

MV-NY

Published simultaneously in Canada
by Little, Brown & Company (Canada) Limited

Printed in the United States of America

For Barbara

Note

The author knows of no one at the Préfecture de Police, the Sûreté Nationale, the Élysée Palace, the Musée Cernuschi, the Brazilian Legation in Paris, or the prosecutor's office in Bremen who bears the slightest resemblance to any character in this book, all of whom, virtuous or vile, are entirely imaginary.

Part One
THE LETTER

1

8 Rue Georges-Berger

Paris
Fri. 12 Nov. 1982, the old man wrote.

Darling Mims:

Trip left me pooped but gratified. NATO graybeards deeply divided on need for hardware superiority, even parity. None shares Wash's dark image of Cossack threat. Nevertheless, managed some compliance due, no doubt, to my greatly advanced age (and startling good looks).

He stopped writing. The gold Waterman, an anniversary present from his wife, was leaking again. He got up from the desk and walked to the bathroom, where he emptied the pen into the toilet. He flushed the blue water away, moved to the sink, and rinsed the bladder with fresh water. Returning to the desk, he sat down again, unscrewed a bottle of ink, dipped the old pen, and resumed writing.

Would have backed out of yesterday's Armistice Day festivities, but Zeke talked me into going. Glad I did for two reasons: (1) At Arc de Triomphe, saw Jules Poinsard, President's father, age ninety-two, struggle up from his wheelchair unaided and embrace Heinrich Loesser, his umpteenth victory nearly sixty-five years ago. And (2), after Élysée reception, had drink with Zeke and Jan Bollekens to celebrate first anniversary of my epiphany. Cheers!

Pop tomorrow. Home Sun.

Bless,
P

P.S. This letter and small birthday present from Musée C come courtesy Zeke who flies N.Y. in the morning. He'll deliver same on his way to Misquamicut. I'm off to parc.

X

He blotted the page, folded it, placed it in a matching envelope, sealed it, and wrote *Millicent . . . by Zeke's firm hand* on the front. He capped the ink bottle and the Waterman and, leaving both on the desk, got up to put on his vest and suit jacket. Checking to make sure he had his keys and wallet, he walked to the vestibule, struggled into his dark overcoat, and stuffed the envelope in a pocket. He turned off the lights, opened the heavy apartment door, stepped into the hall, and closed the door behind him. Holding on to the bannister, he carefully walked down the carpeted staircase to the marble-floored foyer below, stood beneath the dim chandelier for a moment to gather his thoughts, and let himself out into the darkening Rue Georges-Berger.

The Gardener

Joseph Poirier, age fifty-eight, of Rue Jean-Dollfus, Eighteenth Arrondissement, was employed by the Paris parc system. A man of average height, athletic build, and wholesome features, the greater proportion of his work took place in and around the parc greenhouses in Neuilly, where he raised plants from seedlings for the city nurseries. However, last May, he was temporarily assigned to the Parc de Monceau, a small metropolitan sanctuary of trees, shrubs, and statuary in the English style, pleasant promenades, and a shallow basin. Just off the Boulevard de Courcelles in the fashionable Eighth, Monceau, which is highly visible, was selected by the parc system superintendents to receive forty young arborvitae trees. Poirier, who had attended the trees from seed, supervised the transplanting.

The task took most of the month of May. It was a pleasant interval, enabling him to rise later than his usual hour of 5 A.M. and to spend more time out of doors. Too, it permitted him a glimpse of the heart of Paris in the spring and to enjoy, apart from the odd street riot, the romantic rituals for which the city is justly famous.

In mid-June, he returned to his regular duties in Neuilly. Never-theless, through the hot summer months and into autumn, he visited the parc regularly to view the progress of the young trees. These visits were usually in late afternoon or early evening on his way home.

On 9 November, after a moderate frost, Poirier decided the trees would require winter protection. Consequently, he filled out a requisition form for mulch and burlap to be picked up at the greenhouse in the Jardin d'Acclimatation on 12 November.

Twelve November was a Friday. Poirier was dressed warmly in homespun trousers stuffed into rubber boots, an alpaca vest under a blue smock, a brown canvas apron around his waist, and, on his head, a floppy old beret that had belonged to his father. He arranged to leave Neuilly a bit early so he could mulch and wrap perhaps a third of the young trees in the parc before dark, which, at this time of the year, occurred shortly after 5 P.M.

He placed the mulch and burlap in the back of his 2 cv truck—by his reckoning the oldest vehicle in the parc system, with nearly 400,000 kilometres—had a cigarette with the greenhouseman at Acclimatation, and drove to the parc, arriving there at 4:30. He turned into the Avenue Ferdousi, drove through the gate and onto the grass near the intersection of the Allée de la Comtesse-de-Ségur. It was cold, about two degrees centigrade, and the ground was hard. The parc appeared to be deserted. Even the refreshment kiosk was closed.

He unloaded what he needed from the truck and started to work on the trees to the south of the basin. There were four. He surrounded the base of each with bark to a height of twenty-five centimetres and double-wrapped the trunks with burlap up to the lower branches. This was to protect the root system from frost and the trunks from animals. He finished these by 5:15. He then moved the truck to the north end of the basin and began working on the trees there. Because of an overcast, it had already become dark. The sky was a dirty brown and the air smelt of coal smoke and roasting coffee.

About ten minutes before six he walked to the truck, got his electric torch, and returned to the last tree but one at the north end of the basin. Except for a few autos traversing the Boulevard de Courcelles and an occasional pedestrian in the vicinity of the Pavillon de Chartres, Poirier was satisfied he was alone in the parc. Until he heard the cry.

It was a weak, hoarse cry, like a seabird but pitched lower. It came from the south end of the basin, where he had worked less than an hour before.

He shone his light in the direction of the sound. But either the distance was too great or the darkness not yet deep enough to support his beam, for he saw nothing. He got to his feet and, continuing to shine the light, shouted "Ho là! Are you all right?" There was no answer. He shouted again. No answer.

Poirier was not an emotional man. While capable of some sentimentality, he relied largely on the principle of cause and effect for guidance in his daily affairs. This had made him an excellent gardener, a reliable husband for twenty-three years, and, in 1944–45, provided him a certain sangfroid during his brief service in the Résistance.

He extinguished his flash, picked up a trowel, and started in the direction from which the sound came, noting the time on the luminous dial of his watch: 5:52 P.M. He circled round the bottom of the basin, skirted the Allée de la Comtesse, and started up the promenade leading to the shallow pond, trying at the same time to keep his eyes on the spot in the darkness he imagined was the source of the cry.

As Poirier approached this approximate place, he stopped and listened. He heard a faint gasp ahead and just to the right. Dropping to one knee and transferring the trowel to his right hand, he switched on his torch again and shone the light at the sound.

The man was lying on his back about half a metre from the promenade. He was a large man of a certain age. Indeed, he was probably in his late seventies or early eighties, white-haired, and well-dressed in an expensive overcoat. He was just alive.

Poirier stood, quickly shone the light in an arc around the old man, and moved closer. The ground was softer here below the basin. He heard his boots suck. The old man opened his eyes and stared at the light.

"Can I help you, monsieur?" Poirier asked gravely. The man's chest heaved and he gasped a single word. Poirier thought the word was "Ta" or "Tant," although, in the circumstances, neither word seemed appropriate. Until that moment, Poirier had not noticed a wound. Now, the effect of speaking caused blood to pour from the old man's mouth. He closed his eyes and choked. After perhaps twenty seconds he made a prolonged sigh followed by a gurgling noise. He lay still. Poirier was certain he was dead.

The Musée Cernuschi, a small private museum containing a collection of rare antique Chinese porcelain, stands perhaps a hundred fifty metres from the parc basin, at Avenue Velasquez. Here there is a telephone that Poirier, having made the acquaintance of the museum custodian during the summer, occasionally utilized. He extinguished his torch and, placing the trowel in his smock, ran as fast as his legs and age would allow. He reached the museum, lungs bursting, just as the custodian was preparing to lock up for the night. The latter, a diminutive and rotund individual of remarkable fastidiousness, did not approve of running. He held the view that, except for participants in track-and-field events, people who ran were late. He nearly closed the heavy door in Poirier's face until he recognized his summer friend.

"There's been a murder in the parc!" Poirier gasped as he stumbled over the curb. "I must call the police!" The custodian admitted Poirier and immediately slammed and locked the door.

Inside was a small reception area. The receptionist, whom Poirier remembered as a tall, dark-haired woman, was not at her desk. However, he noticed a small parcel wrapped in silver paper near the phone that the custodian now dialed and handed to the gardener.

The Commissariat of Police at Quartier Europe answered on the first ring. They took Poirier's name, address, and phone number, told him to return to the site, to touch nothing, and to wait for the gendarmes, who would arrive within five minutes.

The Investigation Report

The city of Paris, like most major cities, has its own metropolitan police. The Préfecture de Police, housed in the baroque Palais de la Préfecture near Notre Dame, are the first to respond to city crimes, whether at the Commissariat or the Homicide Bureau level.

The Préfecture treated the Parc de Monceau nonnegligent homicide (code 010), robbery with firearm (code 030) immediately and professionally, if routinely.

Assigned to the case was the soon-to-be-retired Inspecteur B——, who arrived at the scene with a photolab crew, pathologist, forensics inspecteur, ballistics technicien, and a trio of inspecteur-trainees. In his report, filed the next day, he wrote:

Parc gardener POIRIER, Jos., leads us to murder site illuminated by Commissariat jeep headlamps. Victim is old man of perhaps 80 years but robust and sartorially impeccable, rosette of Légion d'Honneur in lapel, lies supine 20 metres south of basin near promenade. His wallet and ident are missing. However, single 1000 franc note, possibly dropped by assailant, is found nearby. Banque note, serial no. XX55742, series 1978, bagged for fingerprint lab.

Pathologist (Dr. Lupi) estimates TOD at approx 1750; COD, shock, blood strangulation, oblique frontal shot penetrated great vessels of media sternum. Passage of projectile pristine w.o. customary trauma associated with exit of soft-nosed bullet. Estimated calibre, 6.3 mm.

Forensics (Dr. Chartier) bags letter, written in English, white notepaper, ink Gironde Bleu No. 3; bags 2 doorkeys, French, 1 small stamped key (briefcase or bicycle lock), American, 1 handkerchief, no initial. Attempts to ident victim through clothing negative. However, clothing analysis reveals canine hairs embedded in suit fabric from fawn-coloured Welsh Corgi. Repeated brushings suggest valet service. Small samples of red clay on soles of shoes suggest victim recently abroad.

Blood type O (IV). Tissue exam at wound indicates presence of silica particles and petroleum derivative. No trace of gunpowder.

In absence of ballistics Chef-Inspecteur du Temple, ballistics lab technicien accepts pathology estimate of calibre 6.3 mm. Clean exit wound suggests steel or teflon-coated round. Weapon probably long-nose automatic with silencer.

Photolab chef and assistant measure and outline footprints in soft ground for plaster casts; trace victim silhouette as he lies. Majority of footprints adjacent to site are those of gardener. Unidentified are footprints within 2 metres of body, possibly made by woman's new high-heeled boot, size 10. Also unidentified, foot-prints of small, probably male, shoe, pointed toe, size 6.

Inspecteur-trainees question neighborhood residents.

We are hampered in our investigation for want of victim ident. While lack of victim ident frequently points to underworld killing, victim's demeanor, age and Order of the Légion d'Honneur seem to preclude such an association. We have no witnesses. No one heard a shot or saw anything remarkable in vicinity of parc between 1600 and 1800 Friday. Indeed, inspecteur-trainees have interrogated more than 100 individuals without result.

Usual informants in Eighth Arrondissement produced consensus that killing is simple mugging, one-shot piece of work by amateur. No professional, informants assert, would risk wasting old man in public parc, two blocks from Étoile, for few thousand francs.

Question gardener and release him on own recog. Permit one photo of victim, shrouded, by reporter-photog of LE QUOTIDIEN.

Victim's personal effects and letter, in translation, delivered this office by Palais de Justice.

There were seven homicides in Paris on Friday, 12 November. Five of these were domestic disputes solved, in each case, within twenty-four hours and accompanied by the sobbing, crestfallen, hungover confessions of husbands, wives, and lovers.

The sixth homicide, the one that drew the headlines, was the gangland slaying of a Corsican priest. For several months he had been under surveillance by the police for his activities in connection with a cocaine ring in the Eighteenth. Apparently set up by his associates, who feared he would turn informant, he was riddled by automatic weapons fire on the steps of the Basilique du Sacré Coeur in broad daylight.

The seventh murder of the day was the one in the Parc de Monceau. Except for the preoccupation of the Préfecture's unremarkable Inspecteur B——, and a single paragraph in the tabloid Le Quotidien, it went largely unnoticed. Until later.

2

Alex

ALEX GRISMOLET awoke from a childhood dream. He dreamt his ears stuck out. His mother was holding them flat to his head with her hands. "Be still, Alexandre," she said. "Do you want to go through life with flaps?"

He opened his eyes. The light by his bunk was still on. He felt the Walkman headset pressed to his ears. Mercifully the device had shut itself off automatically after he'd fallen asleep or Harvey Phillips would still be playing the Hindemith Tuba Sonata.

He glanced at his watch. Six-twenty A.M., Sunday, 14 November. Something about the date triggered a flutter of anxiety in his belly. Something about tonight. Philippa's debut! Philippa's first steps outside the Corps de Ballet.

Suddenly awake, he removed the Walkman and hung it on its hook. Alex never took the thing outdoors. He disdained the regiments of joggers and cyclists who, each morning and evening, swept silently up and down the quays of Paris, uniformly sweat-suited, earmuffed, and wired, cruising on automatic pilot, displaying no human sign except for the occasional head wag or finger snap. The portable, public cassette player seemed, to Alex, a poultice for the lonely or the painfully shy. The private Walkman, on the other hand, was something else. There were two aboard *Le Yacht Club*—one Alex's, the other Philippa's. To him, they were symbols of esteem and privacy between friends. When it happened, despite their divergent work schedules, that they were able to enjoy music together (anything by Stravinsky, Poulenc, Cantaloube, most Offenbach, all of Ellington, Bill Evans, Milt Hinton, or the Swingle Singers), they listened sprawled on the cabin sole before the tape deck in the main saloon. But if, late at night, he needed the Hindemith or she the Leap of Faith Rock Band, they slipped quietly into their earphones and stole away to private auditoriums.

Le Yacht Club is Alex and Philippa's home. Alex acquired the former canal barge ten years ago, the year he passed his exams for the Security Police and managed, finally, to break through the red tape that enabled him to become Philippa's guardian. Philippa was eight at the time, Alex twenty-four. Since then, as time, weather, and finances permitted, they steadily and extensively restored what was basically a derelict workboat to comfortable living quarters: there was now a large, airy saloon painted white with teak trim, a galley with refrigerator and paraffin stove, and, forward of amidships, two staterooms, each with a double-size bunk and private head.

Le Yacht Club is a ship without a sail, that is, a vessel with no means of propulsion. In the bilge, below decks, lurked a large Buda diesel tractor engine whose main bearing had long ago been immobilized by wear and indifferent lubrication. Alex's budget did not include replacement or repair of this Mesozoic chunk of rust. So, each year, his wintertime fantasy of running down the canal system of France to perpetual sunshine remained an illusion.

Le Yacht Club is moored at 12 Quai de la Charente, just inside the northwest extremity of the Nineteenth Arrondissement, a three-minute walk from the Porte de la Villette metro station and five minutes from the Pâtisserie Mariette, where the second batch of croissants leaves the ovens at 6:50 A.M.

Sunday is usually Alex's day off. Except for the ballet tonight preceded by a dinner with Claudine (make note: mend rip in old smoking jacket and call Claudine to confirm), he'll be free to work on the boat, practice his tuba, and later, sit in with a transient jazz band called Combo Passager made up of employees, business-people, teachers, stockbrokers, and government workers, most of them talented, all nonunion, nonprofessional musicians who meet once a week at the Pompidou Centre to play, with the blessing of the Minister of Culture, nonstop jazz from twelve to three. That is, unless the beeper summons. Every Sûreté inspecteur, like a doctor, carries an electronic pager, day and night. The device, though necessary, is a creation of the devil to Alex.

He unfolded himself from his bunk. He accomplished this, because of his remarkable height—just under two metres—in sections, rather like a camel or a giraffe. In fact, when he first reported to the Sûreté Nationale as a serious young inspecteur-trainee, Alex's colleagues called him The Giraffe. Later, when they learned he lived on a boat, they renamed him The Mast. Others, less charitable and noticing the Breton red-blond hair and beard shining like a beacon atop his spare frame so high above the ground, called him The Target.

He ducked into the saloon, opened the skylight hatch, took a few deep breaths, and started his stretches and bends. These were ballet exercises given to him as a thirtieth-birthday gift by Philippa a few years before. She was thirteen and a half at the time and enrolled in the Paris Opéra Ballet School. She had laboriously sketched them out in her own dance notation. There was a birthday card attached. On it she wrote, "To my beloved Papa. Do these exercises faithfully to remain forever beau."

He did the exercises more or less faithfully. This morning, he slightly cut short the prescribed fifteen minutes and dressed. He peeked in at the inert mound of pillows, blankets, and black hair that was Philippa, put on the coffee water, slipped the beeper into the pocket of his down jacket, and went ashore with five minutes still remaining before the second batch of croissants would be ready at Pâtisserie Mariette.

It was a soft morning. The joggers were already out in numbers. He bought a copy of Le Matin and read the police blotter while waiting in queue at the pâtisserie. The Préfecture had now two suspects in the Basilica murder. The mugging of an unidentified old man in the Parc de Monceau remained unsolved. The son of a Turkish diplomat was being held by the narcotics squad for the alleged possession of 450 single-gram pellets of opium packaged as cat food.

"So, Alex," Mariette said as she passed him the white bag of hot croissants, "you got a claque together for Philippa tonight? What's she dancing?"

"Red Riding Hood in Sleeping Beauty," Alex said. "And no claque. Too expensive." He held out a twenty-franc note.

"No," she said. "An opening-night present for my angel. Bring me a program."

*   *   *

There is no grander interior on earth than the foyer of the Paris Opéra. But the crystal chandeliers and diadems, the gilt pilasters, friezes, and cornices together with the great hazy space reaching up to the dim, vaulted ceiling above, need people below crowding the parquet to embellish the ornamentation and balance the opulence. When Alex and Claudine arrived ten minutes before curtain, the place was deserted. Alex was irritated. Tonight was Philippa's debut. The foyer should be jammed.

"Chéri," Claudine said, "would you pay to see a sports match if you knew the team manager was withholding his stars and playing his novices? Every balletomane in Paris knows from the program that this Sunday night is baby night. Nobody will be here except friends . . . and parents." This last remark was accompanied by a too patient smile. She excused herself and went to the ladies'.

The bitchiness was not characteristic of Claudine. To the contrary, it was her serenity, her cool good looks and even intelligence that had initially appealed to Alex. That she'd undergone a sort of reverse metamorphosis, from rare luna moth to garden-variety caterpillar, was entirely Alex's fault, and he acknowledged it by doing the penance of continuing to see her.

Their first encounter had occurred casually at the Hippodrome racecourse one autumn Sunday two years ago. Alex was there with Combo Passager playing between races. It was after the last steeplechase that Claudine, dressed in white riding breeches, white shirt, white vest, and white hard hat held on by a ruby red scarf, suddenly appeared, exercising a three-year-old on the flat. At about the clubhouse turn, the horse pricked up its ears at the music, broke from a canter to a walk, and came over to the bandstand. To Alex, born and bred on the coast of Brittany, the moment seemed uniquely, urbanely romantic. He never tired of the image: Claudine in white hat and red scarf, perched on the chestnut jumper not ten paces away, with the shadows of the Bois de Boulogne reaching across the racecourse infield behind her. He never tired of the image even after he tired of her.

She worked for the Globus stables as an exercise girl and apprentice jockey. She didn't look like a jockey. She was taller and slimmer than most of her male colleagues. And she didn't behave like a jockey, although Alex wasn't precisely clear how a jockey behaved, having never known one. He supposed they were all Spanish and temperamental. She seemed too calm and self assured—like an airline pilot.

"You don't look like a detective either," she said. "You're too healthy. You don't wear a trench coat. You don't even smoke cigarettes."

But though Alex was the easy romantic and Claudine the practical one, it was she, not he, who was falling in love. It was she who wanted their association to mature slowly, to avoid the potholes of desire and passion, to endure and develop into something fine and lasting. Had that occurred, had Alex been able to move at her tempo, the relationship might have survived.

Several months after their Hippodrome meeting, Claudine made dinner for him in her small, fourth-floor flat in the Rue de Navarin. She was an excellent cook and had prepared a luxurious Chicken Chasseur with new potatoes in their red jackets and a salad of endive. They were sitting on the floor in front of the couch, finishing coffee, when Alex reached over and stroked her hair. She stiffened. "Oh my God, Alex!" she whispered. "Not yet! Please!"

Too late, he took his hand away. Her carefully nurtured reserve had already collapsed. She began to moan. Whether it was physiological or psychological or both, he never learned, but it seemed there was scarcely a square centimetre of her body that wasn't erogenous. If he touched her she had an orgasm. If he kissed her she had an orgasm. And when he finally had an orgasm he didn't know if she was having another or was still on the same one she'd had twenty minutes ago. He utterly demolished her composure and realized that it was her composure that had appealed to him, that she'd been more desirable when she was still inaccessible. All of which, he supposed, made him exploitative, manipulative, and sexist. But there it was.

Claudine returned from the ladies' lounge with brave, new eyes. "Shall we go up?" she said cheerfully and led the way to the staircase. The evening, so far, had not been a success. They had dined at a restaurant (her choice) called Cave des Capucines, better known for its candlelit intimacy than for its menu, which consisted largely of cheese fondue. The waiters wore monk's robes and open sandals with wool socks. Alex felt ludicrous sitting at the tiny corner table surrounded by plastic rocks. There had been a few tears. She'd spoken again of Alex's courage, of his willingness to confront the criminal world but his inability to make a simple emotional commitment to her. He finally managed to change the subject. They talked about her employer, the stable owner Max Globus, how sweet he was to her and how she might, with his help, make jockey this winter. After they left the restaurant Claudine did her best to appear enthusiastic about Philippa's debut. But this was an almost insurmountable obstacle for her.

When Claudine first met Alex, she was stunned that, as a young man, he had actually become the guardian of an eight-year-old child and given her a home. This humanity, this nobility of spirit, set Alex apart in Claudine's mind. A man who could do that . . .

Then she met Philippa; long-legged, black-haired, blue-eyed, alabaster-skinned Philippa, at that time no longer a child but sixteen going on thirty; exquisite, watchful Philippa, auditioning her guardian's girlfriends.

It was then that Claudine sensed she would never reach journey's end with Alex.

Alex should not have invited Claudine to Philippa's opening. He should've driven to Douarnenez and fetched his mother; or asked Mariette from the pâtisserie; or come alone.

The evening's last heavy blow landed as they took their seats in the mezzanine. They found themselves surrounded by a ragtag block of mentally retarded adults from a state hospital who, with their attendants in green uniforms, had been invited by the management free of charge in an effort to fill the house. As the lights went down, Alex imagined he was part of a painting of purgatory by Hieronymous Bosch. But no performance ever had a better audience. They cheered and stamped their feet at the end of the overture, and when the curtain rose on the court scene, they whistled at the bad fairy and applauded the good. They watched gravely during the pantomime, some standing in the aisles, trying the movements themselves. Alex was so fascinated that he forgot to be nervous and was unprepared for Philippa's entrance.

Wild cheering and stamping. Philippa, without breaking her characterization, acknowledged the mezzanine. The costumier, or the ballet master, or Philippa herself, or a combination of all three had arrived at a more stylish-looking Red Riding Hood than Alex had ever seen before. The hood had an almost high-fashion look. Instead of hiding Philippa's face, it framed her large eyes and cheekbones and allowed a single, thick fall of black hair to pour over one shoulder. And the costume moved in a way that emphasized Philippa's strong, white stride and her fast, high-arched feet.

The Wolf entered. Piercing whistles. One whistle seemed higher than the others; a nonnote, somewhere between sparrow C-sharp and D-natural, continuing after the other whistles stopped. It was Alex's beeper. He switched off the signal and leaned over to Claudine.

"If I don't come back right away, meet me at *Le Yacht Club* after the performance. I shouldn't be long. And take a cab." He gave her 150 francs and a peck on the cheek, and climbed the steep aisle through a hillside of pale, reflected faces caressing the fairy tale with rapt, button eyes.

He called the Maison from the gentlemen's lounge.

The Assignment Desk answered. "Sûreté. Officer Brieuc."

Brieuc was an inspecteur-trainee from Alex's hometown. "Good evening, César. Alex Grismolet."

"Ah yes, Chef-Inspecteur. The Commissaire wishes you to meet him at the Ministry of Interior."

"When?"

"Immediately, sir. Where are you? I'll send a car."

"Don't bother. What's happened?"

"The Parc de Monceau murder. They've identified the victim."

"But that case belongs to the Préfecture."

"I am told, Chef, that since approximately five P.M., the case has belonged to the Sûreté. When the Commissaire learned the victim's identity, he informed the Minister of Interior, who immediately ordered the transfer. As the case is no longer a purely metropolitan affair, the Paris police have cooperated. Their Investigation Report is already at the Ministry. The Commissaire will meet you in the small reception room on the first floor. Are you certain you don't need a lift?"

3

Wilson

COMMISSAIRE Henri Demonet, Directeur of the Paris Sûreté, lit his pipe. The flame above the briar hovered and jumped and the small room slowly filled with an opaque cloud from his blazing mixture.

"His name is Andrew Wilson," the Commissaire said.

Alex had arrived at the Ministry of the Interior a few minutes after nine, where a bailiff directed him to the first-floor reception room. He'd signed a receipt for the Investigation Report delivered by the Préfecture and had read it through twice before his boss arrived.

Andrew Wilson. Alex's lips pronounced the name. He'd heard it before somewhere, probably from Varnas, his Lithuanian-born assistant who had relatives in Chicago and was always reading the *International Herald Tribune.* "American?" Alex said.

"American, yes," Demonet replied. "But not at all typical. He was a Chevalier of the Légion d'Honneur. He was Directeur Emeritus of W. W. Wilson and Company, the wine export firm. However, he was much more than a wine merchant." The Commissaire had a handful of matchbooks on which he'd made some notes. "He was a sort of unenfranchised ambassadeur, a nonpolitical practitioner of private diplomacy. His objective was"—the Commissaire read from a matchbook—" 'To make reconciliation possible between official enemies through unofficial dialogue.' At least that's what Stevenson told me."

"Stevenson?"

"David Stevenson, manager of Wilson's Paris office. It was Stevenson who identified the body this afternoon. Awfully nice chap. English. Ex-Army. Lost a leg in '43. I persuaded him to stop in here before driving home." Demonet waved at the air. "Be a good fellow, Alex, and open the door a crack. The smokescreen has become nearly impenetrable."

Alex got up and opened the door. The air from the corridor swirled the pipe smoke into fractocumulus clouds that chased each other around the chamber.

Demonet puffed for a moment then got up himself and began to stroll, hands clasped behind his back, pipe firmly clenched between his teeth. Alex sat down. This was the Commissaire's promenade, his ritual dance to develop preliminary strategies, to extemporize, to sort out his thoughts and get things started. With his round bald head, his round body custom wrapped in modish pinstripe above tightly trousered legs, he looked like a middle-aged Daumier solicitor setting out on the boulevard.

"I want you and Varnas to take this case for me, Alex," he said. "I have informed the case judge. The warrant will be made out in your name. I may rearrange the furniture from time to time, but I want you in charge. Why? First, you are a Breton and not as insufferably French as me, which will go down well with the Americans. Not to overlook your excellent English. And second, because of your assistant's remarkably fraternal relationship with every police informant in Seine-Marne. I have already arranged for the lab people and Inspecteur Varnas to meet you at the Wilson flat tomorrow morning at nine." The Commissaire knocked his pipe out in the wastebasket. "Well," he said, "have you seen enough of the report to form any opinions?" Demonet was already in harness.

Alex glanced at some scribbled margin notes. "I think the Préfecture's preliminary conclusion that Wilson was mugged is probably wrong," he said. "The weaponry that Pathology and Ballistics describe isn't consistent with a mugging. Your average mugger seldom carries a silencer-equipped 6.3 millimetre long-nosed automatic. And steel or teflon-coated ammo isn't mugging ammo. Looks to me as if Path is working backward from the clean exit wound and Ballistics is acquiescing for want of something better."

The Commissaire refilled his pipe. "You can disregard that Ballistics Report, Alex. Chef-Inspecteur du Temple is on holiday. The Palais de Justice sent a lab technicien to the parc."

"Where is Hippo this time?"

"At the Topkapi Museum in Istanbul, cataloguing a rare medieval falchion for his antique arms society. I've telexed him to return immediately."

"Hippo on holiday in Istanbul in November? Doesn't he ever go to the beach in August like the rest of France?"

"I don't think his pallor could stand it. Hippo is happiest in archives. What else do you have?"

Alex looked down at his scribbles. "Forensics wound serology is puzzling. They report finding silica particles and traces of a petroleum derivative. That's the sort of a mess I'd expect from a cheap lead round. But a lead round wouldn't exit cleanly. Whatever, Forensics doesn't square with Pathology."

"It won't be the first time. What else?"

"There's a banque note with serial numbers and a thumbprint on it. And a gardener who's the closest thing we have to a witness. We have dog hairs and footprints to chase down. And we have Wilson's rather oblique note to his wife. It may give us something. He mentions the names of two men, apparently close friends of his . . . someone called Zeke and a Jan Bollekens. And, of course, there's Madame Wilson herself."

Demonet frowned and struck a match. Alex recognized this as a signal to wait. He glanced at his watch. He must remember to call Claudine. The Commissaire applied the torch to his pipe and pumped the perfumes of Latakia once more into the tiny room. Alex, accustomed to this ritual delay, had long before decided that his boss used his pipe less as a pacifier than as a prop and tactical weapon to create suspense and secure undivided attention.

"I think," the Commissaire said gravely, "that it would be both improper and imprudent to question Madame Wilson so early in the investigation." He waved away a necklace of smoke. "Improper because she is so recently bereaved—I have in mind the Sûreté's manners, Alex—and imprudent because of her close friendship with the President's wife."

It wasn't like the Commissaire to be scrupulous about manners in a criminal investigation. Clearly, his solicitude was connected to the Élysée Palace. Alex said, "I was thinking about Demonet's Dictum: 'Learn all you can about the victim.'"

The Commissaire nodded. "To be sure. And, to that end, Madame Wilson may prove to be a valuable asset which we must not squander by acting . . . precipitously."

Alex shrugged. "As you wish, Commissaire."

Demonet smiled encouragingly. "I have every confidence in you, Alex." His attention was diverted to the open door. "Ah, David!"

A man of medium height, middle-aged but fit and robust, stood in the doorway swatting at the smoke with a paisley scarf. He had the look of a sportsman, Alex thought. "Hallo?" he said in English. "Are you in there, Henri?"

"Come in, David," exclaimed the Commissaire.

Alex stood as Stevenson limped into the room. He walked on an artificial leg and moved with an expansive, thumping sort of enthusiasm. Demonet introduced them. Alex bowed. Stevenson noted Alex's size, nodded pleasantly, and tossed his overcoat on a nearby chair. He folded his leg at the knee and sat down.

Alex guessed him to be fifty-five or sixty. He wore a brown suit, blue oxford shirt, and a red and brown striped bow tie. His short-cropped sandy hair was going gray but the regimental moustache was still blond. Alex wondered if he dyed it; a sunlamp, perhaps. His face was tanned and completely unlined. He waved his scarf again.

"Bloody hell, Henri," he said, still in English, his accent rather flat and nasal, "the air quality in this room is damn marginal." He waved his scarf a third time and switched to French. "Demonet, are you familiar with the incendiary properties of dried rabbit turd? Believe me, it burns with an aroma far superior to whatever you're smoking." He laughed a little longer than necessary at his own joke and winked at Alex.

The Commissaire grinned and put away his pipe. "Good of you to come, David," he said. "Bring Alex up to date as fully as you can. I know you want to get home."

Stevenson put on a pair of half spectacles and studied an index card he produced from an inside pocket. After a moment, he removed his glasses and, in excellent French, addressed Alex directly with none of the forced joviality that had characterized him a moment ago.

"Andrew Wilson was booked on the Concorde from Charles

de Gaulle to Kennedy at eleven this morning," he said. "At twelve
forty-five I happened to check the office answering service from
my home in the Sixteenth. There was a message from Madame
Roget, the propriétaire of the building where the Wilsons maintain
a residence. As I had luncheon guests and there was nothing in
the substance or manner of the message to suggest an emergency,
I decided to wait until my guests had departed before returning
Madame Roget's call.

"They left about two. However, before I could phone Madame
Roget, I received an overseas call from Wilson's granddaughter.
She'd been waiting for him at Kennedy in New York. When she
learned that her grandfather had not boarded the flight in Paris, she
phoned the Wilson flat. Getting no answer, she rang me at home.

"I contacted Madame Roget immediately. She told me that
Monsieur Wilson had not slept in his bed Friday or Saturday."
Alex started to make a note. Stevenson interrupted his narrative.
"I wouldn't place too much emphasis on that fact, Inspecteur. At
eighty-four, Wilson had the independence and energy of a man
half his age. He seldom told Madame Roget where he was going
or when he might be expected back. She, in fact, said she was not
at all alarmed until this morning when he failed to meet the limousine he'd engaged to drive him to the airport.

"Still hoping for a rational explanation for his disappearance,
I nevertheless called my friend, Commissaire Demonet, for advice.
He suggested I meet him at the Maison at four-thirty. In the time
it took me to get the car and drive from my home to Rue des
Saussaies, the Commissaire had established the possibility of a link
between Wilson's absence and the Parc de Monceau murder. Arrangements were made and, at five-fifteen this afternoon, we were
admitted to the city morgue, where I performed the saddest duty
of my life. I then performed the most difficult: to call Millicent
Wilson in Connecticut."

Stevenson removed his glasses and put away the index card.

Alex glanced sideways at his boss. "David," the Commissaire
began, "Chef-Inspecteur Grismolet has some questions. But they
can wait until tomorrow if you prefer." Demonet was minding
the Sûreté's manners again. Stevenson waved away the suggestion.

Alex withdrew a small white envelope from the report and

handed it across the table. "Wilson wrote this note to his wife before he left the flat Friday afternoon. Would you read it, Monsieur Stevenson, and tell us what it means to you?"

Stevenson put on his glasses again. He handled the envelope with a certain diffidence. Peering over the spectacles at Alex, he said, "I think I should mention that I am not an intimate friend of the Wilsons. I am their business associate. I believe Andrew Wilson was persuaded that friendship in the business environment, however well-intentioned, could be counterproductive to the decision-making process." He patted the envelope. "Under the circumstances, it might be inappropriate that I see his last, private words to his wife."

"My dear David," the Commissaire said, "I have seen the note. It is simply a memo of events and a brief outline of Wilson's travel plans. Nothing more. However, he mentions some names we have not been able to identify. Could you help us with those at least?"

Stevenson nodded and turned the envelope over.

" 'Millicent . . . by Zeke's firm hand,' " he read. He grunted. "I wouldn't wish to attest to the firmness of Zeke's hand."

"Who is Zeke?" Alex asked.

"An old friend of Wilson's. Lewis McKim. He was a pilot in World War One and, later, a newspaperman in Rhode Island. He has a home near the Wilsons in the States. I forget the name of the place."

Alex pronounced it carefully. "Misquamicut."

"Sounds right." Stevenson slipped the note out of the envelope. He began to read but stopped immediately. "Everyone, at least his close friends, called Wilson 'Pudge.' " I don't know how he came by that nickname. He called his wife 'Mims' or 'Mimsy.' They had some private thing about the jabberwocky that has always eluded me. They even named their boat *Brillig*, I believe."

Stevenson read on. He read the letter through to the end, frowning once or twice and rereading certain sections. Finally, he folded it carefully, inserted it in the envelope, and returned it to Alex.

"Monsieur Stevenson," Alex began. "Is there anything in the letter that you would connect to Andrew Wilson's death? His recent work with NATO, for instance?"

Stevenson turned to Demonet and smiled. "Henri, I thought your man was only going to ask me to identify a few names."

"You needn't answer the question, David," Demonet replied amiably.

Alex hardly recognized his boss. The Commissaire was flinging cordiality about as if he were a candidate for the Chamber of Deputies. Nevertheless, Stevenson responded.

"I suppose the question is reasonable enough." He considered his answer for a moment. "Are you asking me if I think the Danish ambassador to NATO popped down to Paris in a fit of pique over tactical weapons reduction or something and put a bullet through Wilson?" Stevenson seemed entirely serious. "If so, then no. I don't think there was that sort of connection."

Alex waited. "Another sort of connection, then?"

Stevenson removed his spectacles and rubbed his eyes. "It's no secret Wilson had enemies. Not personal enemies, that I know of; ideological ones. On the right he was flanked by conservatives, many of them Americans, who viewed his attempts at reconciliation politically reckless and commercially unprofitable. And, on the left, were the radicals, groups often committed to violence, who saw negotiation and reconciliation as hostile to their revolutionary struggle."

"Are you suggesting the murder was politically motivated?"

"No. Ideologically motivated, perhaps. Wilson was apolitical. I think it is possible that his death may have been connected to his activities as a private diplomat generally rather than to his work in NATO specifically."

The Commissaire broke in. "David, what was this Armistice Day thing with old Jules Poinsard embracing some Boche?"

"As I understand it, Henri, President Poinsard, at the urging of his father, invited the approximately eighty surviving air aces of World War One to Armistice Day ceremonies in Paris to honour their fallen comrades. I think about twenty-five of them were well enough to attend."

"Former enemies as well as allies?"

"As I understand it. The ceremonies took place on Thursday. Wilson had just returned to the city from his NATO trip and presumably did not plan to go. I guess Zeke changed his mind."

"Do you know any of the men mentioned in the letter?" the Commissaire asked. "Loesser? Bollekens?"

"I've met Jan Bollekens. His law firm has represented the Wilson family in Europe for years. Bollekens himself is, of course, retired."

"Is that a Dutch name?"

"Flemish. The firm is Belgian, in Louvain. I don't know Loesser, the German. Wilson did. They were longtime friends, members of the Old Eagles or something. As to what Wilson meant by—how did he put it?—celebrating the anniversary of his 'epiphany,' I have no idea. Perhaps Millicent will know. It's probably one of those private things, like the jabberwocky."

"What's 'Pop?' " Alex asked.

"Excuse me?"

"In the note he wrote 'Pop tomorrow.' What does that mean?"

"I expect it means Poperinge, in Flanders. There's a military cemetery there. Wilson often went there to visit old comrades, those who were less lucky than he." Stevenson cleared his throat. "I must say I understand that. Done it myself enough times. You don't forget."

Alex's generation had not gone to war. But, as a child, he'd been given a unique view of war . . . the Great War of 1914–18 . . . by his grandfather. Because of this exposure, Alex responded with more understanding and respect than his peers did when older men spoke this way. He now waited a decent interval before continuing. When Stevenson seemed ready to go on, Alex asked him about the postscript to Wilson's letter. "May I read it aloud?" Stevenson nodded.

" 'This letter and small birthday present from Musée C come courtesy Zeke who flies N.Y. in the morning. He'll deliver same on his way to Misquamicut. I'm off to parc.' "

Stevenson replied, "Musée C is, of course, the Musée Cernuschi on the edge of the parc. Millicent Wilson collects Chinese porcelain and spends rather a lot of time there when she's in Paris."

Alex nodded. "It fits. When Wilson said he was off to the parc he was probably on his way to the Musée Cernuschi to pick up her birthday gift."

The Commissaire asked, "Where did you get that?"

"Gardener's testimony. The gardener saw a gift-wrapped parcel

on the receptionist's desk when he ran there to call the police."
Alex turned back to Stevenson. "How well do you know this man
Zeke?"

"Not well."

"Can we assume he knew Wilson was coming with the letter
and the gift?" Stevenson frowned. "Because if he knew and did
nothing when Wilson failed to show up . . ."

Stevenson shook his head. "Inspecteur, Zeke McKim is a very
old man and nearly senile. I doubt Zeke knew Wilson was coming
or that an appointment was made. I expect that Wilson planned
to place the letter and gift in Zeke's carry-on luggage, pin a note
to his lapel, and hope for the best." Stevenson shrugged and smiled.
He looked at his watch. Demonet eyed Alex.

"While I have you here, Monsieur Stevenson," Alex said, "may
I ask, just for the record, where you were on Friday the twelfth
at approximately 6 P.M.?"

Stevenson thought for a moment. "Yes. I had a doctor's appointment. My physician is Roscoe Fielding, Avenue de Wagram.
He takes care of the old stump and related bones."

The Commissaire interrupted. "I think that's enough, Chef-
Inspecteur. Well, David," he said, "you've been very helpful. We
won't trouble you further."

The Commissaire got up.

"No trouble, Henri." Stevenson placed both hands flat on the
table and propelled himself to his feet.

Alex, still seated, assembled the material on the table before
him. "There is one more question, monsieur, if you don't mind."
Stevenson waited. "According to the gardener's testimony, Andrew
Wilson uttered a single word before he died. To the gardener, the
word sounded like 'Ta' or 'Tant.' Does that suggest anything to
you?"

Stevenson stared at Alex. "Well yes," he said. "The word must
have been 'Tom.' "

"Tom."

"Tom Wilson. Andrew Wilson's older brother."

"And where is he, Monsieur Stevenson?"

"Poperinge."

4

The Parc

ALEX remained at the Ministry to deliver an all-points to Commissariat and Sûreté bureaus describing the banque note found at the murder site. He took a few minutes to review the Investigation Report once more and, finally, phoned the Maison. The same trainee was on the desk.

"How much longer will you be there, César?"

"Until at least two, sir. My relief is ill."

"I want you to call the Army of the Air and get some phone numbers for me. One is for an American, Lewis 'Zeke' McKim, probably staying at a Paris hotel or pension. The other is for a Belgian, Jan Bollekens, possibly still in Paris but more likely in Louvain." He spelled the names.

"McKim. Bollekens. Done, Chef-Inspecteur."

"I'll be there in an hour."

Alex rang off. He placed the Investigation Report in a folder and his notebook in the pocket of his opera cape.

As he stepped into Rue des Saussaies, the bells of Église Saint-Augustin struck midnight. A lopsided, gibbous moon, scrimmed by low, stationary clouds, hung in the damp sky above the city. A dirty ring encircled the moon. He guessed it was already raining in the Bay of Biscay.

The Parc de Monceau lay less than a kilometre to the northwest. Alex wanted to walk over the murder site, to look at distances and listen to sounds while the Investigation Report was still fresh in his mind.

The parc, surrounded on three sides by residences, is openly visible to the pedestrian only from Boulevard de Courcelles to the north. From any other vantage it is literally seen as a refuge, a hidden surprise glimpsed now between formal buildings and then through magnificently lacquered fleurs-de-lis and coats of arms, milk-glass carriage lamps and gold-tipped grillwork. The first view of the parc seen this way, even in winter, is likely to be fanciful and indelible, like the memory of a beloved landscape.

To get a good look at the Musée Cernuschi, Alex approached the parc via Avenue Velasquez. The musée, number 7, was a former private villa of typical sandstone construction. It was very nearly the parc gatehouse. The entrance, set back from the cobblestone street, contained a pair of ornamental metal doors. The windows of the ground and first floors were formal and pedimented while the second floor above displayed a trio of equally spaced rectangulars. The entrance was dimly lit by a pair of gas lamps. To one side, a framed, glass-covered signboard announced the musée's hours of operation: Tuesday through Sunday, ten to six; Monday closed.

Closed tomorrow then. Alex studied the building for a moment and speculated again on the gift-wrapped parcel mentioned in the gardener's testimony. If David Stevenson had been correct in his suggestion that Zeke McKim was not expecting a visit from Wilson the night of the murder, could the same be said of the musée personnel? Were they expecting Wilson?

The answer to that question turned on the gift-wrapped parcel; whether, as Alex had assumed, it was indeed the birthday gift for Millicent Wilson. While the question wasn't one that justified obtaining a court order to open the place early, it was a question he wanted answered soon. He made a note to identify and contact the musée directeur.

Counting his steps, he moved on. In less than twenty paces, he entered the parc itself via the Allée de la Comtesse. Underfoot, cobblestones changed to white gravel, only marginally easier to negotiate in opera pumps. Ahead and to the right, he could see the gray marble columns of a replica Greek temple ruin gleaming faintly in the reflection of antique filament parc lights. This was the area of the basin. A pair of white-putteed gendarmes, standing next to a police barricade, studied Alex as he approached.

"Good evening," Alex said. He showed his Sûreté identification to the senior police officer. The city cop, no lover of federal police, glanced at the photo and compared it to the young giant standing before him in evening clothes.

"Your number, please?" the constable asked.

"89243832."

"You reside at number ten, Quai de la Gironde?"

"No. Number twelve, Quai de la Charente."

"Your date of birth is 15-4-48?"

"15-5-48. I am one metre, ninety-seven, eighty-eight kilos, blue, blond, and I have been to the palace to see the queen. Anything else?"

The gendarme handed back the ID and saluted. Alex nodded and moved up the promenade leading to the basin.

The prom itself was three metres wide and bordered by a low, iron wicket fence. He came to the still-visible silhouette painted on the ground, the crime-lab outline that exactly located the final position of the victim. The hackles at the back of his neck stirred. There was something about the style of the outline, like the drawing of a gifted child eloquently able to capture the essence of a subject with a single, unbroken line: the oblate head—without eyes, nose, or mouth—cocked slightly, arms flung, legs at rag-doll angles, one foot bent onto the promenade, the other stuck in the mud. Petroushka.

Alex looked beyond to a scatter of white-circled footprints.

The ground, frozen in some spots, was softer here. Poirier's sturdy rubber-boot prints were everywhere. The small, pointed-toe prints between the body and the promenade seemed disconnected from the haphazard pattern of larger, heeled boot prints above the body site. The depth of the woman's boot prints seemed to vary with the degree of frost in the turf. In some places the print of the left boot appeared sharper than that of the right. Police footprints were x-ed out.

Pathology had estimated projectile entry at ten degrees below the horizontal. Alex imagined this geometry vis-à-vis the victim's standing height. It told him nothing about range. The killer could've fired from a lower elevation on the promenade or point-blank. But there were no powder burns. As to trajectory, the shot, after penetrating the victim, probably described an arc over the gardener's young trees and ended in the dense foliage of the English garden.

Even in winter, with the garden cut back, an army of sappers would be needed to locate a slug in that space. Notebook: *quarter n.e. quadrant, index and bag debris.*

He walked the wicketed border of the graveled path above and below the site. The wickets, twelve centimetres high, were designed to confine pedestrians to the promenade. At some point, two persons had crossed the wickets onto the soft ground. Had they crossed together? Or separately? Had they left their tracks in the earth before the gardener arrived on the scene? Or after he ran to the musée? Or both? There was no shortcut, computer-simulated answer to those questions. During the days ahead, inspecteur-trainees would perform the dreary business of checking the plaster casts of these shoe and boot prints against every shoe outlet in Paris.

Alex moved above the site and climbed the stone steps to the bridge over the basin. The pond had been drained for the winter.

From the crown of the bridge, he could see the refreshment kiosk and the promenades leading to the north gate, the gate through which Wilson had entered the parc. There were four of them. Wilson had had four choices of route to the Musée Cernuschi. Yet he'd chosen the route across the basin bridge, by no means the most direct. Alex made a final note: *favorite hike?*

He pocketed the notebook in his cape, crossed the bridge, and circled to the left, to the row of arborvitae the gardener had been working on when he heard Wilson cry out. The wind before the rain had started. Branches of trees were beginning to move. The parc lights seemed to blink.

Alex looked behind him and to both sides. Something seemed wrong. Was he in the right place? He took visual cross bearings. Boulevard de Courcelles to the left, the allée to the right, the basin straight ahead. Okay.

He completed the circuit and returned to the basin promenade. The gendarmes leaned on the barricade and watched in silence. He took a last look round, nodded to the constables, and walked back to the musée. Rain began to fall. Leaving the parc, Alex had a strong feeling he'd misplaced something or that a detail had eluded him. Something was amiss. Whatever it was, it tantalized and remained out of reach.

César Brieuc, the young Assignment Desk officer, on duty way past his interior-clock bedtime, slept at his post. Alex hung his wet cape near the entrance radiator. Without disturbing César, he removed the memos he'd requested earlier and quietly climbed the stairs to his tiny first-floor office.

Alex shared a walk-in closet with his assistant, Inspecteur Varnas. This cell—square, windowless, and airless—contained a brown linoleum floor buckling beneath cracked plaster walls painted a shade of bureaucratic green that resembled cream of celery soup. The style of furniture was Early Devil's Island. There were two wooden desks with chairs, some cardboard filing drawers on the floor, and a small safe, seldom used. The only decoration was a framed print of a racehorse named Bicot, donated by Claudine. As Alex entered the darkened office, he spotted the horse and remembered he'd forgotten to call her. Too late to worry about it, he decided, and put her right out of his mind. He switched on his desk lamp. There was a perfunctory flash followed by total darkness. The filament of the blown-out bulb, etched on his retina, shimmered for an instant. He saw the murder site again. He saw the silhouetted trees. The missing detail fell into place. The parc lights!

He crossed the few metres to Varnas's desk, switched on the lamp, picked up the phone, and called Information for the number of Électricité de France, Paris, Bureau de Service. After a few rings, a woman answered.

"Arrondissement?"

"Eighth."

"One moment." Computer keys. "Address of complaint?"

"No complaint, mademoiselle. I want to know if there was a power failure last week in the vicinity of—"

"That's Monitor and Repair," she said. "I'll transfer you."

While Alex waited he focused on the detail. According to testimony, the gardener had been forced to use an electric torch after 5:30 P.M. Friday in order to mulch his trees and locate Wilson in the early darkness. In the Investigation Report, the Préfecture stated that the murder site had been illuminated by headlamps, the headlamps of the Commissariat jeep. Yet tonight, walking near the basin, Alex encountered no difficulty making out footprints and other details by means of the regular parc lights. So why the jeep headlamps on Friday? They wouldn't have needed them for Pathology. The Path van carried its own floods and generator. To be sure, street and parc lights burn out at intervals. But one at a time, not simultaneously in strings, like Christmas-tree lights. What then? Was there a blackout in the Parc de Monceau at or before the time of the shooting? And, if so, was it accidental?

The phone popped. A man with a dry, practical voice came on. "M and R. Technicien Tari."

"Chef-Inspecteur Grismolet, Sûreté," Alex said, rather loftily, to determine immediately if his listener was police cooperative.

"At your service," the dry voice replied, betraying neither enthusiasm nor indifference. Alex switched on the tape recorder.

"Monsieur Bari?"

"Tari. Thomas-Antoine-René-Isadore."

"Thanks. Routine inquiry, Monsieur Tari. Can you determine if there was a power failure last Friday, twelve November, Eighth Arrondissement, late afternoon, in the vicinity Avenue Ferdousi and Boulevard de Courcelles?"

"Stand by please," the technicien said after writing all the information down. Alex was put on hold. While he was on hold, which seemed interminable, he was entertained by taped mandolin music. There was something ludicrous about this. The time was nearly 2 A.M. and his police tape was recording taped mandolin music provided by the electric company. He tried to extract a metaphor from this experience, but before he could the twanging stopped in midphrase and Tari was back.

"Monsieur?"

"I'm listening."

"Speaking strictly," he said, "there was no power failure in Paris on twelve November." Alex waited. "That is to say, there was no dynamo failure. However, I have an arc out in the junction box at Pavillon de Chartres at approximately four twenty-two on Friday the twelfth."

"Arc out?"

"Short circuit. Unfortunately, the time is inexact. I have only the time the manager of the refreshment kiosk in the Parc de Monceau called to say she'd lost power."

"Would you say"—Alex posed the question carefully, hoping

his line of inquiry would not suddenly collapse under the weight of some technical detail—"that a short circuit of this type was unusual, in view of the redundance of your system, automatic fail-safes and so on?"

"Unusual?" Tari seemed puzzled by the question. "I couldn't say. Most failures come from overload during peak periods at dynamo or transformer stations. However, anything can fail—when humidity is high, when there are extremes of temperature, or when there has been improper maintenance, as was the case with the box at Pavillon de Chartres. The insulation had deteriorated."

"What time was it repaired?"

"The repair was not completed until after seven. Actually, the box wasn't repaired. It was replaced."

"Do you still have the old one?"

"No. Replaced equipment is cannibalized and serviceable parts reused."

"One more question, Monsieur Tari. Were there any other junction-box failures in Paris on the twelfth?"

"One moment." Alex heard him shuffle some printout. "No. No junk boxes out. We lost a condenser at the Heliport, a diode in the traffic lights at the intersection of Rue Étienne-Marcel and Boulevard de Sébastopol . . ."

"Well, thank you, monsieur."

". . . a resistor at Avenue Bosquet."

Alex hung up. He returned to his own desk and took the Investigation Report and the memos from César back to Varnas's desk. He placed the Investigation Report in the center of Varnas's old-fashioned blotter with a note: "Read before going to Wilson flat Monday." He then sat down and turned his attention to the memos.

Lewis (Zeke) McKim's Paris address was Hôtel Fleury, Rue de la Banque, Second. The memo listed the hotel phone number. Jan Bollekens lived at Limburg 4, Leuven (Louvain), Belgium, and the memo noted two phone numbers, one an office, the other his residence.

Alex dialed the Hôtel Fleury. He raised the night clerk. "Did one of your guests, an American named Lewis McKim, check out yesterday and return to the United States?"

"McKim? One moment, please. McKim. No, monsieur. Lewis McKim has not checked out. He is away for the weekend. Is there a message, monsieur?"

"No message."

Alex rang off and glanced at his watch: 2:15. He still had some time before the flower market opened. He picked up the phone again and dialed Jan Bollekens's residence in Louvain, Belgium.

5

Millicent

MILLICENT WILSON lay in the dark and listened to her heart. Incredibly, it was still pumping after seventy-eight years. It was a reassuring presence, thumping away, loyal despite continuous abuse. She lit a cigarette and glanced at the digital clock, a grandchild's gift, glowing from the side table. Ten minutes to ten. Children asleep in Stonington. Pudge dead in Paris.

She listened to her heart and tried to think of heart songs; anything to erase the memory of Stevenson's phone call earlier . . .

"Shot through the heart?" she heard herself say again.

"Through the media sternum," Stevenson said.

After her initial disbelief, Millicent's first thought was to ask Stevenson if Pudge had been armed. But she stopped herself. Stevenson might consider the question odd. Instead, she asked if the police had any leads. Stevenson wasn't sure. He said they were looking for Pudge's wallet. It had been stolen, which accounted for the delay in identifying the . . . um . . . body. The word dangled clumsily. She ignored it. Actually, it gave her a straw to clutch at.

"Stolen? Then the shooting could've been an unpremeditated, random sort of thing?"

"Possibly. The police have not ruled out robbery as a motive." He then mumbled some stock condolences about the world being poorer and, soon after, hung up.

At that instant, standing in her sun-drenched living room, surrounded by the familiar landmarks of her fifty-seven-year itinerary with Pudge Wilson, Millicent gingerly tasted the first seconds of her strange, new privacy. Suddenly and without warning, she felt an overwhelming force rise within her: a crushing, suicidal need for a glass of vodka; hundred-proof vodka, neat, no ice, no mixer, no garbage, just the straight fix down the oblivion tube, right into the bloodstream.

The thought that she might actually have a drink after ten dry years caused the pale face to flush crimson. A weirdly erotic heat raced through her body, promising mischief and adventure. She gasped and hung on to the phone. Closing her eyes, she could visualize the bottles in the unlocked liquor cabinet, untouched by her for so long: shelves of gleaming celebrants standing in ranks, all spit and polish like hussars or bishops.

She clung to the phone with both hands and remembered Daisy Dexter saying to Pudge, "But dearie, if she's *really* an alco*hol*ic"— Daisy spoke in italics—it's *mad*ness to keep liquor in the house in an unlocked *cab*inet!" Pudge bet Daisy a thousand dollars Mims would stay on the wagon. And knowing Daisy would not listen to swearing, he added, "Besides, the goddam booze belongs in the goddam liquor cabinet, Daize, not at the bottom of the goddam clothes hamper!"

Millicent clung to the phone with both hands and tried to remember Bill's phone number; Bill, her old AA sponsor, the homeliest, most boring man she'd ever met but the man who saved her soul and taught her to make iced tea twelve ways.

She concentrated on the phone. Hold on to the phone, Mims. As long as you hold on to the phone you can't go to the cabinet. One thing at a time. Liquor cabinet, apocalypse. Telephone, life raft. If you hold on to the telephone, help will come sooner or later and you'll be safe.

Bill's number. He lived in Mystic. 536-something. She couldn't ask information because she'd never known his last name. She wondered what would happen if she dialed the emergency number. She'd read a story somewhere, probably in *The New Yorker,* where this ditsy heiress, dining alone in her duplex, called 911 and asked them to send someone over to open the wine.

She clung to the phone and tried to trivialize her situation. And then, miraculously, help arrived. The phone rang under her hands. It was her granddaughter, Laura, calling from Washington. David Stevenson had phoned Laura from Paris and now the family knew.

Laura and her mother, Sara, Millicent's daughter, would be in Stonington in time for supper. Suddenly there were things to do. The crisis was over. The maid was off. Millicent spent the afternoon shakily making potato salad to go with the smoked ham that hung in the springhouse. The panic receded into her mind's attic like the faded memory of an old passion.

There were no tears when the women arrived. The Wilsons were not a weepy family, not demonstrative or even particularly affectionate, except for Laura, who was only half Wilson. She held her grandmother in her arms and simply would not let go. Sara looked on wistfully for a moment, then turned away and made herself a martini.

No men came. Sara's husband was a Baltimore internist on call. And her brother, Web Wilson, a failed composer, had left his wife and was playing cocktail piano on a cruise ship out of Port Everglades. Only God and the union knew where he was.

The three women spent a quiet, polite evening together. The murder was mentioned only once. Toward the end of supper, Laura interrupted the silence and said, "Why would anybody want to kill Grandy?"

Millicent put down her knife and fork, placed both hands on the tablecloth, palms down, and turned her hooded eyes on her granddaughter. She seemed on the verge of a solemn reply. Instead, her expression abruptly changed and she got up. She said, "Laura, stay as you are, dear. Don't move." She hurried into the front hall.

Laura gave her mother a puzzled look. "What was all that?" Sara, who was making a highball, said, "She wants to take your picture."

"Why?"

"She thought she saw something."

Millicent returned with a Leica. She came to the table and focused on Laura. After a moment she lowered the camera. "You moved," she said. She placed the camera on the table and sat down. The hooded eyes returned. "To answer your question, darling, I don't know anyone who would want to kill Grandy. Not anyone who knew him, that is, with the possible exception of Daisy Dexter, whom he left waiting in the Plaza Rose Garden in 1920 to take me trout fishing on the Beaverkill."

Sara giggled.

Laura looked soberly at her mother. "Under the circumstances," she said, "I don't think that remark was either appropriate or very funny." She turned to Millicent. "I love you, Gran'mère, but every so often I get this big chill. It makes me wonder sometimes where you're coming from."

Sara sipped her drink and watched.

Millicent took Laura's hands in hers. "I'll tell you where I'm *not* coming from, Laura dear. I'm not coming from bereavement. Perhaps the correct phrase is 'I'm not *into* bereavement.' Whatever. I've seen enough of it to know that I'm not into it. There will be no more mourning in this house. We can praise Grandy and celebrate him and criticize him. But we will not mourn him." She got up slowly. "Now, if you kids don't mind cleaning up, the old lady is going to bed. It's been a tough day."

She kissed Laura on the top of the head, patted Sara's shoulder, and said to her, "Don't get so bagged you forget to turn down the heat."

Millicent steamed in her bath for nearly an hour. It vaguely bothered her that she hadn't wept. She'd wept when her father died. And when her Airedale pup drowned. How many years ago was that?

Maybe the emotional reservoir finally runs dry. Or maybe, if she stayed in her bath long enough, the hot water would free up her tears the way it frees up the cap on a ketchup bottle.

She soaked and tried to remember what she'd just read about stress in a Government Printing Office pamphlet. Stress control in the face of a thousand condolences would be impossible, she concluded. Pudge had always said "delegate." Very well. She would delegate Sara and Laura to answer the phone tomorrow. Later she'd set up a defense perimeter of some sort, a secretarial buffer zone to take calls, to respond to letters and testimonials, to weed out the authentic from the self-serving expressions of sympathy from school, colleges, foundations, and charities hoping for handouts. ("The President and Governing Board of The Society for the Preservation of the North American Birchbark Canoe wish to convey their deepest sympathy at this time, and . . ." Enclosed would be a postpaid, return envelope.) She got out of the tub.

Millicent and Pudge had always slept in the same room, first in a double bed, later in twin beds placed close enough together so they could touch. She sat on her bed and brushed her short, shaggy hair. If she stood far enough from the mirror without her glasses and squinted, she could conjure up a pretty fair likeness of the Millicent Ann Henry that attended the American University in Paris over fifty years ago. Nobody had believed it then, but she was a real platinum blonde.

She turned down her bed, removed her robe, and shut off the bedside phone. Then, with scarcely any fuss, which was her way, she crossed over the space that separated the beds, climbed into Pudge's bed, and switched off the lamp. She lay in the dark, smoked, and listened to her heart. . . .

Finally the songs came: "Heart and Soul," "Be Still My Foolish Heart," "Young at Heart," "Be Careful It's My Heart," "Heartburn," "Wind Around My Heart," "The Heart Is Quicker Than the Eye," and "My Heart Stood Still," Pudge's favorite, that he could play by ear on the black keys.

The clock in the village church started to ring. Ten o'clock. The night was so still, the sweet, deliberate chiming could have been struck on the moonbeams outside her bright windowsill. At approximately the fifth bell, Millicent heard the phone ring downstairs. She guessed it was Sara's husband calling after coming off duty. But a moment later, a knock came at the door. Laura looked in.

"Gran'mère? Are you awake?"

"Yes, dear."

"The phone's for you."

"At this hour? Who is it?"

"Jan Bollekens, Gran'mère. Calling from Belgium."

Millicent experienced a flutter of fear and listened to the beat of her heart accelerate. After years of phoning between Europe and America she had learned not to expect a call from the continent after 5 P.M., 7 at the latest, except in an emergency. For Jan Bollekens, it was the middle of the night. Somehow he'd already heard about Pudge. But he wasn't calling at 3 A.M. his time to offer his condolences.

It came back to her then that it was almost exactly a year ago that she last spoke to Jan, just like this on the transatlantic phone, but during the day, she thought. It was Jan who'd given her the news that Pudge had found what he was looking for in Scotland. Suddenly the world seemed a brighter place and she'd been moved to exclaim—God forgive her—"Now maybe everything will be all right!"

"Gran'mère?"

"Yes, darling. I'm just collecting myself." She reached out and turned on the bedside lamp, an unfamiliar business from Pudge's side.

Millicent longed for a palliative. Spontaneity was not her strong suit. She wasn't ready for Jan this time. Jan, the former judge, Jan the patient, the compassionate. She got out of bed and, holding the cigarette in her teeth, slipped back into her robe.

"I'm on deck now, Laura," she said. Her granddaughter withdrew.

Like Pudge, Jan had flown in World War I, but with the Belgian Air Service. He was a tiny twinkling marvel of a man, fun to be with but married to a towering horror named Charlotte: awful Charlotte with a mouth like a howitzer, who made a career out of being forever and furiously on the verge of death. She was somewhere near ninety and spent all her time propped up in bed so that Jan had to wait on her. She was mean, manipulative, and ugly as mud, and there was no doubt in Millicent's mind that she would outlive them all.

Feeling shaky and ill-prepared, Millicent took a deep, lung-filling drag on her cigarette and turned on the phone. She lifted the receiver. "Hello, Jan."

"Mimsy." The resonant voice, which seemed to caress the French language, could have been in the next room. "Mimsy, I cannot console you, my dear, until I console myself."

Recalling her conversation with Stevenson, she replied, "I think it would be consolation enough, Jan, if we were to find that Pudge's death was the result of a haphazard urban crime, unrelated to . . .

anything. Actually"—she decided to press the point—"according to David Stevenson, the Paris police are nearly persuaded that robbery was the motive."

"Mimsy, I have already spoken to the police."

She noticed her cigarette ash. It had grown perilously long and now hung over the hooked rug between the beds. She carefully tucked the phone under her chin and tried to bring the table ashtray to the cigarette. But her hand trembled and the ash fell into the rug's pasture pond, soiling the water where the spotted cows drank.

"You called the police?"

"No. They called me."

She took a last puff and butted the cigarette. "But how weird, Jan. Why would the police call you?"

"They found my name on a document in Pudge's overcoat pocket."

"The overcoat he was wearing in the parc?"

"Yes."

"I see. What sort of document?"

"A letter to you, Mimsy."

She closed her eyes. A letter to me. Sweet Jesus, here come the tears. She felt a preliminary tremor in the chin, the beginning of the awful crumpled mouth. A letter to me! Sweet baby Jes— But alarm abruptly preempted tears. "Jan?"

"Yes, my dear."

"What did the letter say?"

"I can't tell you precisely. I can only surmise what Pudge wrote by the questions the police asked. I gather it was a short letter. A note really. He wrote briefly about his NATO trip, which was apparently successful. He mentioned the Armistice Day ceremonies at the Arc and the Élysée Palace reception in the evening."

Millicent really hadn't believed Pudge when he told her the French Army of the Air was going to play Armistice Day host to all those octogenarians, each with his special diet and medication, half in wheelchairs or walkers, all rheumy-eyed, stubborn, and intensely proud. And all probably needing to go to the john in the middle of reaffirmed allegiances. She asked, "Did Pudge go?"

"Yes."

"What about Herr Schumacher?"

"Excuse me?"

"I was kidding. Did Zeke go?"

"Yes, Zeke is another reason for my call. He was to fly home Saturday and hand deliver the letter to you."

Saturday was her birthday. "Where's Zeke now?"

"That's what the police want to know."

"I suppose it's possible he's still in Paris. Or at least still in France. And it's entirely possible he doesn't know about Pudge. Zeke has a fetish about avoiding the news. Jan, you might try to contact him."

"I will, Mimsy."

"When you spoke to the police, had they been to the apartment?"

"They didn't say."

"They didn't mention Madame Roget?"

"Who?"

"Clothilde Roget, our concierge."

"No."

"Well. I suppose it doesn't matter. What else did Pudge say?"

"After the Élysée Palace reception, he, Zeke, and I went to a bistro in Rue Bayard and drank a toast to Doctor Douglas."

"Dear God! Pudge didn't write that in the letter?"

"No. What he wrote in the letter was that we celebrated the first anniversary of his epiphany."

Millicent reached for another cigarette. "And what did the police make of that?"

"They asked me what the word signified. I told them it was not a word I had heard him use, that possibly it meant something to you. I told them that I recalled the moment as a somewhat nostalgic and sentimental one between old soldiers, and one which produced for me a notable hangover and several days of severe diverticulosis."

"Were the police satisfied with that answer?"

"Probably not. But they changed the subject. They asked me if I knew anyone who might want to kill Andrew Wilson."

She held the unlit cigarette between her lips. "And?"

Bollekens paused for an instant. "Millicent?"

He never called her Millicent. She waited.

"*Amor proximi,*" he said. " 'Love of neighbor.' Love of neighbor has compelled me to bend a principle for you from time to time up to a point. But there's a limit. Now, I must ask you this: If the police cannot identify Pudge's killer, what will you do?"

She'd been waiting for this. She'd known it was coming seconds after Laura told her who was on the phone. Nevertheless, she said, "I don't follow you, Jan."

"I will explain. Every year there are urban homicides that are deliberately made to resemble muggings. The modern killer knows that a big-city mugging without witnesses or without substantial physical evidence is virtually untraceable. Of course the police know it as well. Now. From their conversation with me, I gather the police do have some evidence that this crime was not motivated by robbery. However, if they can't turn up a suspect and have no other choice but to fall back on the robbery option—in other words, if the case remains unsolved—what will you do?"

She lit a cigarette. "Nothing," she said. "I'll fly to Paris Wednesday and collect Pudge. Aside from that, nothing." She exhaled.

"Mimsy. If the case remains unsolved, I cannot do nothing. There are ethical considerations as well as considerations of law."

She felt her jaw tighten. "Are you going lawyerly on me at this late date? We've kept this confidence for a lifetime."

"Yes. And I've always respected that confidence. But to keep it now may endanger the public. I cannot do nothing—unless the crime is solved within a day or two."

"I'm counting on that," she said without hesitation. "My God, Jan, wouldn't you feel a fool if you and Zeke went to the Sûreté prematurely and it turned out the killer was nothing more than some petty thief with a Saturday night special? You'd feel a fool and the press would have a field day. No. I intend to do nothing. I don't have your juridical conscience or Pudge's instinct for retribution. Very little matters to me except what I have left: my kids, their kids, and a few memories, both sacred and profane."

"The law will not be sympathetic to that view, Mimsy. The law was written to protect the public."

"Bugger the public," she said softly. "Bugger the law, and bugger you too, pal, if it comes to that. It's been a lot cozier for you and Zeke all these years than it has for me. I lived with Pudge. I listened to the nightmares. I'd like a nickel for every time I've stood in that goddam cemetery! I raised his children, terrified that at some unguarded moment the instinct would return and wreak havoc! I should've torpedoed his priorities right at the start!" She twisted the corner of the bedspread into a rope. "Then maybe we could've lived a normal life—free of ghosts!"

Bollekens was silent. Finally, he said, "Maybe."

"We'll never know, will we?" She slowly rubbed her forehead. "I'm sorry, Jan. You're the last person on earth I should growl at."

"It's all right, Mimsy."

She hesitated. "Let me ask you one favor. Please. Wait a little. Give the police a chance. Maybe in a few days, in a week, they'll find something . . . some substantial physical evidence."

"And if they don't?"

"I pray they will. Because the spectre of Saint Tom the Unavenged, standing forever between Pudge and me, is not something I want my children and grandchildren to learn about on the morning news. Good night, Jan."

She hung up. While she planned her next move, she lit another cigarette. After a few puffs she dialed the international code group, the prefix, and the number in Paris for Clothilde Roget.

The propriétaire of 8 Rue Georges-Berger, accustomed to tenants' emergency calls in the middle of the night, was not alarmed when the telephone rang at 4:30 A.M. But when she realized who was calling, she was immediately alert.

Millicent asked if the police had been to the apartment.

"No, madame. I am told they will come this morning at nine."

"In that case, Clothilde, you can do something for me."

"Yes, madame."

"In the center drawer of monsieur's desk, there is a large unopened manila envelope with English postage stamps on it. I want you to take it downstairs and keep it for me until I arrive Wednesday."

Madame Roget hesitated. "You wish me to bring it down before the police arrive?"

"Yes, Clothilde. The envelope contains nothing of value to the police; only information that, if divulged, would be valuable to monsieur's business competitors."

"I have understood, madame."

"I'm sorry to wake you."

"It's nothing." She sighed. "You have my profoundest sympathies, madame."

"Thank you, Clothilde."

Bollekens

Jan Bollekens drew the muffler tighter around his neck. He tucked the woolly ends deeper into his dressing gown to protect his chest. His first-floor study seemed colder than usual. He could see his breath. Hear it too, he thought ruefully, as he listened to the respiratory legacy of a million Sweet Caporales penitently discontinued a million years ago.

He might have been premature in calling her. After all, there was no proof yet. But he'd developed a strong instinct over the years. He'd trained his probes and sensors to align themselves with the truth the way a compass needle responds to the earth's magnetic field.

The intercom buzzed. Charlotte, from upstairs. He answered. "Yes?"

"Is there to be no sleep ever again in this house?" she keened in her vinegary voice. "First the police shatter the peace, followed by my husband's transatlantic dalliance with the merry widow at Christ only knows what cost! And since when is it 'Mimsy, *dear*' and 'I cannot console you, my *dear?*"

"What do you want, Charlotte?" he asked, imagining her eavesdropping with her extension mouthpiece muffled by a pillow.

"The pan," she said. "And quickly, unless you want me to wet the bed."

He tossed some soft coal and wood sticks onto the embers in the grate so that the fire would rekindle itself by the time he returned to his study. Certainly there was no point in going to bed now.

He climbed the unlit back stairs, guiding himself along the wooden bannister worn smooth by the hands of Charlotte's nannies and her family's army of servants, now long dead. The last stair but one squeaked and warned him to reach for the china knob on the door at the top. Charlotte's father, for whom he'd clerked, had insisted that the door be hung so as to prevent small children in a rush from falling down the stairway, which had never been illuminated.

He opened the door and emerged onto the second-floor landing. It was washed in fading moonlight from a west-facing window. Bollekens closed the stair door and walked up the chilly, dark hall to his wife's bedroom. Her door was shut to keep in the warmth. He could hear her rapping impatiently on her bedstand with a spoon. He entered and was assailed by the heat from four blazing electric reflectors aimed at the bed, and by the damp smell of camphor and pine steaming from a humidifier. The room reminded him of a greenhouse carefully controlled for temperature and humidity to prolong the life of some endangered jungle cactus. Charlotte had thrown the bedding aside.

"Sweet mother of God, Bollekens!" she cried. "I have to piss!"

The white porcelain bedpan lay on top of a pile of magazines that were stacked on a chair next to her bed. She could easily reach the magazines but refused to try for the pan. The pan, as well as the medicines, tablets, astringents, and emollients that stood on the bedstand nearby, were the diurnal and nocturnal eccentricities of her life and central to her utter dependence on Jan since the day he retired from the bench and she became certain that, with time on his hands, he would go off larking like the shadowy characters in her magazine stories. Jan had never gone off larking. Except when he was a scout pilot. But that was B.C. (Before Charlotte).

He placed the pan next to her on the bed, rolled her over, and pushed it under her cratered, purple buttocks. She said, "Now turn your back and don't listen."

He obeyed automatically. While he waited he gazed down at the magazines on the chair. The top one was called *Contemporary Romances*. The other titles were not distinguishable. However, near the bottom of the stack, he noticed the edge of an engraved letterhead sticking out. It looked familiar. He reached down, separated the magazines, and immediately recognized a letter from his Wilson file. Without a second's hesitation to wonder how it got there, he slipped the letter inside his muffler, beneath which he was now beginning to perspire.

"I'm finished," she said.

He retrieved the bedpan with its tablespoonful of liquid and bit of crumpled tissue, walked to the water closet, and emptied it into the toilet. He then rinsed and carefully dried it both inside and out so it would not soil the top magazine as it once had done due to an oversight of his that'd precipitated a howling half hour of recrimination.

"Now go to bed," she ordered, punching her pillow.

"No. I'm awake. I have things to do."

"Humph." She scrutinized him. "You may as well know that it was I who took the letter you so cleverly retrieved just now." She adjusted her bed-jacket tassels. "Since the letter opens with 'I beg you to reconsider my proposal,' I quite naturally supposed it was a love letter to Millicent."

"The letter opens with 'Dear Pudge.' "

"I guess I wasn't wearing my glasses. Don't be disagreeable, Bollekens. You know you shouldn't leave mail around." She folded her arms across her bony chest and squinted at him. "So what is this confidence you and Millicent have kept for a lifetime?"

He ignored her question and smoothed out the bedclothes. "The letter you took was in my file. I did not 'leave it around.' "

"Answer me, Bollekens! Are you in love with her or not?"

"Behave yourself," he said. "Pudge is dead. Mimsy is an old friend of mine. And an old friend of yours as well."

"Yes," she replied. "Too old to be showing her knees. Good night."

"Good night." He kissed the damp forehead and withdrew. He returned to his study via the front stairs. The fire in the grate had started to smoke. He poked it until the kindling ignited, added a small maple butt and watched as the young flame licked around the gray bark. He smelt the coal underneath. The smell of soft coal in winter reminded him of headlamps: the amber headlamps of switching engines in the railroad freight yards he used to haunt as a boy, when he lived on a poorer side of town and was obsessed by steam trains. That was before the Great War, before he transferred his obsession to aeroplanes.

He watched the fire for a moment, then moved to his desk and took out the letter. It was the one he'd written to Wilson in March, urging him not to publish in *Tarmac*. Why, he wondered, would Charlotte be interested in that? The question produced a premonition, not yet identified.

He returned the letter to his file cabinet and watched the day materialize through an extravagantly paned casement window. In love with Mimsy? Absurd.

The cloud lighting came slowly in the east, streaks of gray against black, pink streaking on gray, a wash of orange, maroon, flaming red. Red sky in the morning.

6

International Herald Tribune

THE OBITUARY was on page twelve.

Andrew Wilson, Dead at 84
By Henry Reif

Andrew Wilson served four American Presidents without compensation or portfolio. That's the way he wanted it.

His goal, all his life, was to bring antagonists together for private talks that might lead to reconciliation; private talks on neutral ground, away from the pressures of politics or publicity. Had he held an official position at State or in the Foreign Service, he would not have been able to accomplish this goal which, he said, was 'dedicated to the proposition that the greatest evil in the world is not Power but Powerlessness, the alpha ingredient of alienation and revolt.'

Among successful reconciliatory efforts in which Wilson played a role, were negotiations during the immediate postwar crisis in Berlin that led to the Berlin Airlift, exploratory dialogue between European economic ministers that formed a basis for the future Common Market, and the formation of unofficial meetings between representatives of Israel and the Emir of Qatar in the Persian Gulf.

Although not a scientist, Andrew Wilson was one of the organizers of a series of international conferences designed to steer scientific effort to constructive rather than destructive directions of purpose. In 1957, these became known as the Pugwash Conferences.

He was a member of the Brookings Institute (1962), a referee for the Organization for Economic Development (1968) and a member of the International Foundation of Human Rights (1977). From

1979 to the present, he acted in an unofficial role as negotiator with the Organization of African Unity (OAU) and NATO.

In the early 70's, Wilson became interested in the work of the Institute for Policy Studies, a group of political scholars of the so-called 'New Left.' Thus did the Chairman and Director-Emeritus of the W. W. Wilson Company, a conservative firm founded by his grandfather during the reign of Napoleon III, come under the scrutiny of the F.B.I. for the first time. This was a source of some amusement to Wilson who, before sitting down to dinner with guests at his flat in Rue Georges-Berger, would face the chandelier hanging over the dining room table and solemnly announce the menu to J. Edgar Hoover.

Andrew Spencer Wilson was born May 11, 1898, in Watch Hill, Rhode Island. The single greatest tragedy in his life was the death of his brother, W. Thomas Wilson, killed in action in 1916 with the Royal Flying Corps (later the RAF). Wishing to vindicate his brother's death, Wilson joined the Air Service of the United States Signal Corps immediately after graduating from preparatory school. He was trained as a pilot in Canada, Texas and Issoudun, France. In June of 1918, he was posted to the 149th Fighter Squadron on the Western Front where he destroyed 14 enemy aircraft in less than six months. In November of 1918, he was awarded the Distinguished Service Cross and the Croix de Guerre with palm.

Returning to the United States after the war, he entered Brown University where he excelled in football and ice hockey. He graduated with honors in 1921 and entered the family business.

In 1926, Wilson was sent to the Paris office of W. W. Wilson Company. For the rest of his life, this city, which he considered his second home, was his base of operations. In the years between the wars, he managed the rehabilitation of certain French vineyards that dated from the time of Caesar, developed a dozen new wineries including one each in Romania and Hungary. It was in 1926 that the Willoughby-Jones affair occurred.

Andrew Wilson had held the British Air Service partly responsible for his brother's death. In July of 1926, an intensively researched article by Wilson appeared in the Manchester Guardian. In it he charged RAF Squadron Leader Allerdyce Willoughby-Jones with dereliction of duty in wartime. Willoughby-Jones, who'd been a Major in the RFC and was Wilson's brother's commanding officer in 1916, did not hesitate to sue both the Guardian and Wilson for libel. However, Wilson's evidence presented in the court case that followed disclosed such an appalling tableau of misprision and squadron corruption—including the suborning of maintenance and medical personnel—that the suit was dismissed. In less than a year, Willoughby-Jones, already estranged from his wife and child, was discredited and asked to resign his Commission. A short time later, he shot himself. Wilson's capacity for compassion and generosity was noted at the time when he immediately established a trust for the widow with a principal sum well in excess of the amount named in the suit. In 1930, the widow emigrated to New Zealand.

During World War II, Andrew Wilson joined the Office of Strategic Services (OSS). He was 44 years old at the time but is known to have parachuted into occupied Europe and, on more than one occasion, visited his brother's grave in Belgium.

In 1952 he was made a Chevalier of the Legion of Honor by President Vincent Auriol, an award that was vigorously criticized by political figures of the French left.

Like other Americans living and traveling abroad, Wilson was reported to have been debriefed from time to time by the C.I.A., particularly after his trips to Eastern Bloc countries with which he did business. The W. W. Wilson Company denied this allegation and the C.I.A. declined to comment.

Andrew Wilson is survived by his wife, the photojournalist Millicent Ann Henry of Stonington, Connecticut; a son, T. Webster Wilson of New York; a daughter, Sara Wilson Armstrong of Owings Mills, Maryland; and three grandchildren.

Funeral plans were incomplete last night.

7

Philippa

PHILIPPA awoke. Without opening her eyes she rolled over, arched her back, and stretched. It was a dancer's stretch, sinuous but elegant, prolonged, unimaginable except in a cat.

She reached under the covers, grasped her right foot by the arch, withdrew it from beneath the bedclothes, and extended her leg ninety degrees to her body. She held it there for a moment, adjusted her turnout, and increased the extension by another forty-five degrees. At the top of the extension, her toes, arched into a single crescent, touched something wet and cold. She gasped, whipped her foot back under the covers, and sat up in a chaos of black hair and tangled eyelashes. Her foot had touched a chrysanthemum.

The stateroom was packed with fresh flowers: chrysanthemums, daisies, African violets, yellow roses, red roses, orchids, baby's breath, and a half dozen species Philippa could not name. She swung out of bed. Holding her thick, waist-length hair back with both hands, she leaned over and smelled every blossom in the room. They still had water droplets on them. Alex had been to the flower market.

She tied her hair back in a kerchief, brushed her teeth, washed her face, and, still wearing her nightgown—an old much-laundered work shirt of Alex's that came to below her knees—tiptoed across the passageway into his stateroom. She peeked first to make sure he was alone. This was merely a ritual. Alex never brought anyone back to *Le Yacht Club* for the night. Nevertheless, Philippa checked.

He was fast asleep on his back, snoring lightly; Zeus with mouth ajar. She placed a single finger on his forehead. His eyes flickered open instantly, as if triggered by a switch.

"Galvano," he said.

"What?"

He peered at her. "Silvano Galvano," he said clearly.

"What's that?"

"Electric."

"You're not awake."

He closed his eyes again. "Not," he said.

She kissed him on an eyelid. "The flowers are magnificent. For once I'm speechless."

"Rather at a loss for words myself," he grumbled and yawned. "Actually, I borrowed them from a church. They have to be back for the ten o'clock Eucharist." He opened his eyes. "What's the time?"

"Eight-fifteen and raining. You can stay in bed all day."

"Can't. Got to meet Varnas at nine." He reached down and picked the early edition of the *International Trib* off the floor. He handed it to her and tapped the Wilson item.

He skipped his exercises and showered. When he returned she was huddled under the covers, hugging his pillow.

"Will this one last long?" she asked.

"Don't know. Just started." He faced the mirror and combed his wet hair and beard. "Why?"

She propped herself on an elbow. "We'll be dark starting the twenty-sixth of December. I get two weeks off. I thought if you were free we might go somewhere."

He stopped combing and glanced at her reflection. "You want me to go on holiday with you? What's happened? You have a fight with Jean-Jacques?"

"No. But I've decided J-J has a death wish. I mean really, he's a dancer and he wants to go skiing! What *is* that? Besides, I want to go somewhere warm."

"Like Antibes?"

"Like Martinique."

He launched a stern, parental frown into the mirror. "Bit grand for us, isn't that?" She gave back her daddy's-little-darling smile. For a second she resembled her mother.

"It's seventy-five hundred francs airfare," she said. "The inn at

Anse Mitane costs six hundred a day. If we catch our own squid and langoustes we can stay for ten days without frills for thirteen thou, five hundred. What do you think?"

"Sounds wonderful."

"Alex, I'm serious. I'm even moonlighting to make extra. I'm teaching aerobics to a bunch of union ladies from the National Society of French Railroads. I've already saved a hundred forty francs and started a kitty. If we both feed the kitty we can make it."

"Order the tickets."

"Alex!"

"Look, if I catch my thief I'll get a bonus. If I get a bonus we'll go first-class and eat out. In the meantime there's grapefruit in the fridge. If you visit Mariette's for croissants, don't forget to take a program from last night. I promised her.

"Croissants? Are you mad? I eat tofu and gelatin for breakfast."

Alex was ready to leave. He sat on the edge of the bed and touched her face with the back of his hand. "I'm proud of you," he said. "I was already fairly proud when you were knobby-kneed and wore braces. But I'm extravagantly proud of you after last night."

The sloe eyes sparkled. She leaned against his hand. "Proud papa?"

"First in line. How did it go after your spectacular entrance?"

"Claudine thought I was divine. When I came here at twelve-thirty after the company party, she was waiting to tell me how divine I was."

"I'm sorry."

"She's annoyed."

"I'm sure."

"She left a note. It says"—Philippa used her mock-serious voice—" 'We must talk!' "

"When did she leave?"

"About twelve thirty-two."

"And what did you find to talk about in all that time?"

Philippa grinned. "I told her you'd screwed every girl in the company except me and were starting on the boys."

Stevenson's Wife

She and David had twin beds. They were Queen Anne four-poster reproductions; very English. The satin quilt on hers had not moved during the night. His bedclothes were entirely on the floor again. She'd covered him twice since midnight.

She turned on the bed lamp. His twenty-four-hour army clock showed 0714. Monday already. "David, it's after seven," she said softly so as not to alarm him.

"I'm awake," he mumbled, and sat up. He half twisted round, cleared his throat, and spoke to the air.

"I will call Agence-France Presse from the office this morning to confirm Millicent Wilson's arrival on Wednesday. Have you got your fur coat out of storage?"

"No, chéri."

"Do it, please. I want you to wear it to Charles de Gaulle when we meet Madame Wilson." With that he hoisted himself onto his good leg and hopped, farting, into the bathroom.

The name Millicent Wilson evoked some compassion in Stevenson's wife. She'd heard that Millicent Wilson was a recovering alcoholic. She wondered why. Andrew Wilson had seemed like such a nice person. Still, she supposed there were reasons for alcoholism in women other than difficult husbands. In Sweden, for instance, there was a lot of alcoholism in women because it was dark so much of the time. She guessed that if she were Swedish she might be alcoholic. But she was French and had decided a year ago to cut back her consumption because she was putting on weight. She'd restricted herself to beer and little splits of wine.

Then David started having his stress episodes. That they were probably war related didn't make it any easier on her. For the first time in their marriage, she felt apprehension. The beer and wine no longer did the trick. She began regularly to visit the pantry, where she poured off half of whatever she was supposed to be drinking and replaced it with Stolichnaya. The vodka assuaged her fear, armed her against unprovoked attack, and provided the illusion that she had the situation under control.

The irony was that she still loved him. Sometimes it made her weep.

8
0

Varnas

ALEX stepped out of the Monceau metro station into the rainy
morning. He wore his ancient and faded rain gear.

Under low cloud cover, Paris had turned umber, like a sepia
print. This photographic analogy occupied him as he paused to
gaze at the parc before continuing into Rue Georges-Berger. The
parc looked old: amber dots in a spiky thicket. The lights were
already on.

The gendarme outside 8 Rue Georges-Berger glanced at Alex's
ID and opened one of the heavy double doors. "First landing,
Chef-Inspecteur, top of the stairs."

"Anyone here?" Alex asked.

"Since over an hour," the constable replied, looking purposefully down the street to avoid any suggestion of criticism. Alex
was late.

On his way to the Wilson flat, he'd made an unprofitable detour
to the Maison in an effort to run down the directeur of the Musée
Cernuschi. File had had no information. He was finally able to
locate the directeur's residence (in Issy) through an acquaintance
at the Ministry of Culture, only to find, from the heavily Slavic
cat-sitter who answered the phone, that Madame Seńkowska was
away and would not be back until tonight.

Alex entered the building, crossed the marble foyer, and climbed
the carpeted stairs as the diminutive Forensics Chef-Inspecteur
Chartier emerged from the Wilson flat. Chartier, as usual, had arrived first and finished first. He did everything first. In his middle
forties, he still seemed a proper and punctilious schoolboy, first
to finish his homework in study period, first to complete the final
exam, first to stride from the classroom into summer's freedom,

oblivious to the brackets of hostile glances pursuing him. Chartier viewed most of mankind, especially operational police inspecteurs, with that special disdain the pure scientist reserves for his less precise brethren. He gazed reproachfully at Alex's rain gear, so dissimilar to his own meticulous dark blue impermeable, matching fedora with removable waterproof cover, and shiny black overshoes. He carried a large leather case containing his file, lab equipment, and microscope. It too wore a removable waterproof cover.

"Good morning, Raoul." Alex knew Chartier well enough to call him by his first name and well enough to realize he was sensitive about his height. They did not care for each other.

"Yes," said Chartier with a curt nod. "The Corgi dog belongs to the propriétaire, Madame Roget, and I've traced the red clay on the victim's shoes to a deposit of hydrous aluminum silicate in the Arno valley near Arezzo. Your . . . ah . . . Lithuanian lackey has it all." With that, he stepped around Alex and glided down the stairs, swift and silent as a ferret. Alex watched him go and speculated on the risks and rewards of, someday, crowning the obnoxious little son of a bitch with his own microscope. *Lithuanian lackey!* He removed his oilskins on the landing and entered the Wilson flat.

The front door opened on a small, wood-paneled vestibule floored in gleaming black-and-white patterned tile. A brass coatrack stood in one corner beside a small provincial appointment table. Over the table, Alex saw his reflection in a gold-framed mirror. To the left of the mirror, a paneled door, half open, led to a study. Next, through a small arch framed by Doric columns, stretched a long, chandeliered and carpeted corridor, the central passage to the rest of the flat.

Alex paused a moment to reconnoiter his first impression of Andrew Wilson's Paris home. There was a purity about the place, a kind of spotless refinement, pleasant, cultivated but, at first glance, impersonal.

He started down the corridor. The elegant air was suddenly shattered by a burst of profanity followed by the flash of a photocell from the direction of the living room. Alex looked in. The well-upholstered figure of Chef-Inspecteur Crusson of the Dactyloscopy lab seemed to fit the room physically. Everything in it was up-holstered except the Aubusson rug and the Steinway. The portly chef of fingerprinting stood in the curve of the piano like a diva about to embark on a song cycle. Across the room, a technicien and a man with a Rollei camera were finishing up. Crusson jerked his thumb over his shoulder at the piano, covered with photographs.

"Deliver me from society homicides!" he cried. "There are twenty-nine framed photographs on this piano, twenty more in the bedroom, and ten in the study. That's fifty-fucking-nine framed photographs to dust for prints, never mind the dining room with the fucking Chinese porcelain. Gimme a nice proletarian killing in Ivry where four outta five prints are on file and where we can dust in ten minutes because all they got is a TV and a fucking bidet!" The big man came over and shook hands. "Pardon my French," he said and grinned.

"Good morning, Claude," Alex said. "Where's Varnas?"

"Downstairs with what's-her-name. The propriétaire."

"Madame Roget."

"Yeah. She was waiting here when we arrived. I printed her while Chartier was doing his thing. Christ! What a tantrum! You'da thought I asked her for a blow job instead of a thumbprint! She hollers she can't go to mass and take communion with police ink on her fingers. I sent Varnas down with a bottle of acetone." Crusson opened a can of mentholated snuff and placed a pinch in his cheek. "You got anything yet, Alex?" he whispered, his tobacco breath newly minted.

"I got faith in you, Claude," Alex whispered back.

Crusson muttered, "You'll be here till fucking spring!" One of his men came in from another room.

"All done in back, Chef."

"You get the maid's room?"

"Yes, Chef."

"Kitchen, pantry?"

"Everything, Chef."

"Okeh. Pack up." He turned to Alex. "It's all yours. I'll tell Varnas you're here. By the way, that woman's prints are all over this place."

Alex thought that odd. Normally, a propriétaire wouldn't attend to the personal needs of her tenants except in repair or emergency situations. "What do you make of it?" he asked.

"I'm not sure. Maybe she cleans the place. One thing you can be certain of. She wasn't his mistress. You'll find the fingerprints of a rich man's mistress on his pocketbook and his pecker but never his vacuum cleaner. Well"—he picked his overcoat off the floor—"you're the detective."

Crusson rumbled out, leaving Alex alone in the living room with its rotund, slip-covered chairs, piecrust tables, and piano load of photographs.

Alex wanted a look at the photographs. He expected wedding portraits, baby pictures, vacation pictures, grandchildren; a long, sweet chronicle of filial love and devotion. Not a bit of it. The photographs on the piano were all professional, the work of Millicent Ann Henry. Alex had seen some of them published in magazines years ago. Now he was looking at the originals.

There was the photo of de Gaulle, haughty as a camel, returning to Paris after the liberation; an oriental child, squatting in bomb rubble, weeping; Picasso in a bathing suit and dark glasses. There were, as well, a number of photographs of noted people in which Andrew Wilson appeared: Wilson with Roosevelt on a sailboat, Wilson receiving his Légion d'Honneur from Auriol, Wilson with Kennedy, with Lord Mountbatten, with Jomo Kenyatta. The gallery was an impressive display of the photojournalist's art but added nothing to what Alex knew of Wilson.

He left the living room and moved down the corridor to the dining room.

A year or so ago, on a visit to the flea market, Claudine had said, "There'll always be something somewhere that someone wants as long as it's old." The maxim came echoing back as Alex switched on the dining room chandelier. Antique oriental porcelain gleamed from nearly every corner. Sideboards contained blue and white bowls, peach-bloom bowls, monochromatic bowls, bowls decorated with Mongol horsemen, dragons, clouds, petals, trees, fish. There were cups, saucers, plates, flasks, horse heads, decanters, a trumpet-shaped vase, and a tureen delicately painted with the figures of children in a garden. It was a dazzling and probably priceless display. But apart from the fact that a family dining room seemed a curious place to exhibit an antique oriental porcelain display, the collection itself meant little to Alex. He was not equipped or disposed to judge it. Rather, it was the porcelain link to the Musée Cernuschi, Wilson's last destination, that Alex wished to examine. He turned off the chandelier and walked next door to the master bedroom.

Punching the light switch there, he saw what he thought he might be looking for. Between the twin beds, the twin dressers, the chaise longue, and a small writing desk, tables and bookshelves were crammed with family snapshots.

During a lecture on Investigative Procedure years before, Alex had been warned by an instructor never to trust a photograph except for purposes of identification and then only with scepticism. He'd never taken that counsel. Photographs fascinated him. At the flea market he spent all of his time leafing through old photo albums of families he didn't know, to see what the pictures could tell him. He even bought several, for browsing. Now he looked forward to browsing through the Wilsons' lives the same way. He was immediately disappointed.

Each generation of Wilsons appeared to have been arranged in front of the camera at attention. And always smiling. No one roughhoused or waved. Everyone stood right there and smiled. There were no photos of Andrew Wilson at all; probably because he was the photographer and, unlike his wife, an indifferent one.

There were a dozen pictures of Millicent, patrician and heavy-lidded, taken at Christmas; Millicent, with her two children, a boy and a girl, always in front of a Christmas tree. This catalogue began, judging from her blond, bobbed hair and the age and clothing of the children, somewhere during the twenties. It finished years later, still in front of the Christmas tree, with still-beautiful Millicent now a matriarch surrounded by a collection of nieces, nephews, and grandchildren, her virtually unrecognizable middle-aged son and daughter, and their spouses.

The later photographs, taken by automatic color camera, were of a better quality than the early black and whites. However, nothing else distinguished these pictures except the size, age, and numbers of the subjects and the more or less chronological shifts in clothing and hair styles. The relentlessly agreeable expressions never varied. Here were no dissenters. The only sign of life in this cheerful American waxworks was the pinpoint of light in the iris of each eye as the flash went off.

It seemed curious to Alex that Millicent Wilson, the remarkably gifted photo-artist, would participate in such a pale performance, even as a snapshot subject. (Did Steichen, visiting Disneyland, turn and smile as Madame Steichen said, "Cheese, Edward," and pressed the shutter of her Instamatic?) Indeed, of all the noncommittal Wilsons, Millicent's expression seemed the most noncommittal, the most impassive and ambiguous. Alex had no idea who she was or what to expect when he met her.

He turned off the bedroom light and walked slowly up the narrow hallway with its three small brass chandeliers illuminating leafy yellow wallpaper. Across from the living room, behind a closed door he hadn't noticed before, he heard the floor creak and the sound of someone whistling "The Passing Lighter," a sentimental ballad popular before Alex was born. Only one person he knew whistled that song. He opened the door and found himself in Wilson's parquet-floored study, gazing down at the joyful visage of Inspecteur Alphonsas Varnas.

"Good morning, my dear," Varnas said, placing a small bottle of acetone into an open satchel by the door. "So, Alex, how is my Philippa's debut?"

Varnas (no one called him Alphonsas) spoke French in the present tense only. This had occurred because of a complex politico-linguistic situation. Varnas spoke five languages ("If you are Lithuanian, Alexei, you got to do something!"). His Litvak and Russian were entirely fluent. He spoke prisoner-of-war German; that is, he spoke a fairly fluent low German with most of the correct articles and endings. But when he came to learn French and English, he seemed to have been overcome by euphoria.

Liberated in 1945 from the doctrinaire East, and breathing, for the first time, the heady, permissive perfumes of freedom in the unstructured and chaotic West, he learned French and English in the present tense only, and without articles ("I don't see you yesterday, Alex, when I come to Maison").

Alex loved him. Varnas, twenty years older, provided the warm, mature, dependable male figure Alex had never known as a boy. Alex's father, an eccentric and domineering professor of archaeology, had seemed as cold and huge to his son as the megolithic stones he studied in a hopeless effort to prove the existence of a race of pre-Celtic Breton giants. His father was always distanced, towering against the coastal sky like a tree Alex could never climb. Varnas, on the other hand, diminutive as a gorse bush, was always there, listening, counseling.

That Varnas was senior in years to Alex but junior in rank was not an accident or a bureaucratic oversight. During his internment, first by Germans then by the Russians, Varnas had seen enough of rank. The thought of exercising rank enfeebled him. Now that he had freedom, he wanted it all: freedom to act, to hypothesize, to kibitz, to complain, to snoop, even to disappear occasionally. Let someone else assume the responsibility of rank. Alex was willing. And the system worked well.

Alex grinned down at his friend, correct as always in his dark, vested suit, gold watch chain, and black homburg. The hat, as far as Alex knew, never left its accustomed place except during sleep and during the Commissaire's Monday-morning briefings.

"Philippa brought the house down," Alex said.

"She is enchanting young woman, Alex. Also the fine dancer."

While he dropped most articles, Varnas sometimes inserted them where they were not needed or inserted the wrong one. "If I am thirty years younger, I take her to Tour d'Argent for the dinner."

"They'll love her there," Alex said. "She eats blue-green algae and plankton for dinner."

"I call ahead," Varnas replied. Alex noticed a rolled newspaper in Varnas's jacket pocket.

"You've seen the obit?"

"Yes," Varnas said, removing the paper and scanning it briefly. "I see obit and also Investigation Report you leave for me." He moved over to the large mahogany desk. "So. Andrew Wilson. I hear already about Andrew Wilson from philosophical cousin named Katiunas in Chicago. Man of private diplomacy. Conciliatory man. Man of Peace." He placed the newspaper on the desk next to a box of police-issue, one-size-fits-all white cotton gloves left by Chef-Inspecteur Crusson.

Varnas put on a glove and opened the top right desk drawer. "Gentle man, Andrew Wilson," he said. "But I am little bit disappointed to find that, when effort at reconciliation fails"—Varnas reached into the drawer—"Man of Peace resorts to conventional alternative." He withdrew a large handgun in a shoulder holster. "Very serious gun, Alex. Browning nine millimetre automatic. Big firearm. And shoulder holster is stained from sweat. Weapon does not always remain in drawer."

"Is that where you found it?"

"Not in desk. In bedroom bureau drawer. With socks."

"Questions and answers."

"Yes, my dear."

"Sporting gun?"

"Negatarian."

"Defensive weapon?"

"Mmm . . . I think not nine millimetre."

"Eighty-four-year-old man of wealth, vulnerable to haphazard attack, fears robbery of priceless porcelain pieces in apartment, keeps handgun in drawer for protection."

"Negatarian. Maybe yes if gun is Webley twenty-two. Not cannon like this. And Alex, Man of Peace carries gun. Outside. In street."

"But not, apparently, in the parc," Alex added. He put on a pair of gloves and took the weapon from Varnas. "Did Crusson check it for prints?"

"No. I wish you to see gun first."

Alex sniffed the holster. It smelt of mothballs and wool. "Smells like bureau drawer. I wouldn't say this had been worn recently."

He removed the automatic from the holster and popped the clip. It was well oiled and fully loaded. He removed and pocketed the bullets, opened the breech, and examined the interior of the barrel. The rifling was clean but worn. However, the firing pin was like new. Alex snapped the breech closed and reinserted the empty clip. He replaced the gun in its holster and handed it back to Varnas. "Bag it for the lab," he said. "Is there a license?"

"Yes, Alex. In file drawer of desk."

Alex watched Varnas seal the automatic in Plasticene. He recalled again the Maison doggerel attributed to the Commissaire:

Here is Demonet's Dictum:
Learn all you can about the victim.

The rationale behind this was as old as crime. You looked for
something in the victim's background—a weakness, an obsession,
a contradiction sufficiently remarkable to suggest a motive for
murder.

Demonet was fond of saying "No one ever murdered a man
because he loved his wife and kids." To be sure, the gun seemed
out of character for Wilson.

"What else have you skirmished this morning?"

Varnas had already bagged some documents. "I find couple
periodicals, couple folders with magazine articles Wilson is working on, file of business correspondence, report of Romanian wine
production of cabernet sauvignon, checkbook, bank statements,
receipted bills." Varnas picked up an elaborate blue, white, and
red program, big as a three-star restaurant menu. "This is invi-
tation and program to Élysée Palace reception dinner for air aces
of First War. Aces are listed in back with photos." He returned
the program to the desk. "But mostly I find names, Alex. Beginning
of Laundry List. I have detailed itinerary and agenda of Wilson
trip for NATO with names and short bio of ministers in London,
Copenhagen, Amsterdam, Bonn, Lisbon, Florence-Arezzo, and
Paris. I bag all this for file inspecteurs, poor sweet bastards, except
postcards."

Alex sighed. The Laundry List, basis of nearly all police work,
was the list of persons who had been in any way associated with
the victim, especially during the last months of his life. Each name
on the list could become a file and each file a dossier, depending
on circumstances. Despite microfiche archives, computers, and
electronic communication systems, the checking process was still
time-consuming, especially if, as in this case, the Laundry List was
international.

"No diary?" Alex asked. "No journal?"

"Negatarian."

"No address book?"

"Negatarian."

"Seems peculiar for a busy man."

"Maybe not," Varnas replied. "Maybe, when you are over eighty years, very many old friends in address book are gone. The few who are left you know by heart. Still, I find three names and numbers penciled inside phone-book cover. Handwriting is not Wilson's. Maybe madame's. First name is 'Musée Cernuschi.' Second, 'Anna,' with phone number in Sixth Arrondissement. And third is 'Clothilde.' I don't know who is 'Anna,' Alex, but Clothilde is Madame Roget, propriétaire of building whom I take liberty of asking couple questions while removing fingerprint ink."

"Crusson said she was annoyed."

"Annoyed?" Varnas leaned against the desk. "I think better word is 'outrage.' She is very protective of Andrew Wilson, Alex. I think she is in love with him."

Alex sat down. "In love? What about her husband?"

"Killed in war of 1940," Varnas said quietly. "When he is twenty. She is sixteen."

A war widow at sixteen. Younger than Philippa. Walk home, child, and tell your dolls their papa is dead. "Did she remarry?"

"No."

"Family?"

"Peasant."

"And she's in love with Wilson?"

"Not like that, Alex. Listen. I go downstairs with acetone. Doggie meets me at door. Very much barking. She comes to door, says, 'Chute, Étienne!' Doggie shuts up. She opens door. I ask to come in. She looks at my hat. Way she looks at my hat, Alex, could be whirly-beanie. I got to take it off before she lets me inside loge.

"She is very correct," he went on. "It is not appropriate that I touch her fingertip. I hold bottle, moisten rag; she herself performs task of removing ink. While this goes forward, I ask couple questions. She says she does nothing for tenants except collect garbage. No cleaning, cooking, nothing. Once, long time ago, she does a small dress making for Madame Wilson. But nothing for monsieur. Never. She treats him same like other tenants.

"When I hear this I say, 'But Étienne does not treat monsieur same like other tenants.' She stops scrubbing thumb. I see small vein appear in forehead already.

" 'Monsieur Wilson loves little doggies,' I say, 'especially Welsh Corgi, which explains why police microscope finds very many Étienne hairs on Wilson's suit even though you brush them off pretty good.' She hands me rag and walks to door. 'You may go now,' she says. Then I tell her about fingerprints in kitchen, on vacuum, on toilet bowl.

"She looks back slowly from door and regards me. Not angry. She looks me over and finally she says, 'There is no impropriety, Inspecteur. When Monsieur Wilson goes for walk, he often takes Étienne. As to fingerprints . . .' She looks down at her hands as if they betray her, and she says, 'When Madame Wilson leaves Paris in autumn and takes maid back to America with her, she relies on monsieur to engage temporary housekeeper. But monsieur cannot be bothered. His mind is too full of important things. He has no time for unimportant things.' She stands very straight, Alex, and says, 'It is my honor, my joy to do unimportant things for monsieur.' She is grand now, Alex. Proud. 'There is no impropriety,' she says again and returns to door. 'Now . . . please let me go to mass.' "

Alex got up. "Why do you think she denied taking care of Wilson until you mentioned the dog hairs?"

Varnas considered this for a moment. He fingered his watch chain. "To keep feelings secret," he said. "If she has love for Wilson, it must remain"—he searched for the word—"immaculate. Also, Alex, whole thing could be traumatic fantasy. Boy she marries is shot. Then man she cares for is shot. She loses husband all over again."

"What is that? Baltic-Freudian insight?"

"Not insight. Madame Roget wears black hat, black veil, black stockings and shoes. Madame Roget is in the mourning, Alex."

Alex was silent. If Varnas's characterization of the propriétaire was accurate, if she was emotionally protective of Wilson, she could just as easily prove to be hostile as helpful. Alex decided to assign Varnas to her.

"Project, Varnas."

"Yes, Alexandre."

"To gain the confidence of Madame Roget with the object of learning Wilson's daily activities before his death, particularly his walking habits. Was his routine regular enough to be predictable? Was it his habit to go to the Musée Cernuschi via the basin promenade? If so, who, besides Madame Roget, may have known about it?"

Varnas nodded. "May require few days, Alex, maybe more. She is very closed right now. I try." He started to collect the handgun and other bagged material.

"I have something else for you," Alex added. "Something you can start on right away. I need a profile."

"Who?"

"Silvano Galvano."

"Galvano. Sicilian, ex–Italian Navy wireless operator, electrical genius, once opens banque vault by remote radio-magnetic device, jams Préfecture police transmitter with voice of Italian tenor Gigli singing 'Rigoletto.' What about him?"

"The parc lights at the murder site were shorted out a little over two hours before Wilson was shot."

Varnas whistled. "Very good, Alexei!"

"Of course it could have been accidental."

"Of course. Where does this happen?"

"Junction box at Pavillon de Chartres."

Varnas whistled again. "A hundred metres away. Very, very good, Alex. But I think not Galvano."

"Why?"

"Préfecture repatriates Galvano to Palermo couple years ago. I don't hear his name since that time."

"What about other geniuses?"

"Okeh. There is Constant Sabatier, also called 'Sparkles.' His speciality is illegal fireworks and detonation. Then there is Dieudonné. Simon Dieudonné, also know as 'Simple Simon,' and 'Simon the Électricien.' But I hear he goes straight after last time in the pen. Also there is Marius . . . I don't know his surname. He immobilizes alarm system at Troyes penitentiary in '56 and escapes. But he is older now, in seventies. There may be more." Varnas gathered up the Plasticene bags again. "I check with master file at Palais de Justice, Alex, then make few inquiries at Café Ajaccio and Chez Suzanne, to see if any unusual électriciens come to town lately." Varnas produced an umbrella. "You wish to walk back to Maison?"

Alex glanced at his watch. Nearly eleven. He wanted a few minutes to himself before returning to the office, where choleric file inspecteurs and inspecteur-trainees would be standing about in hostile little clusters waiting to be assigned. "No," he said. "You go ahead."

Varnas left Alex at the flat and returned to Rue des Saussaies.

Alex moved over to Wilson's desk. Between heavy glass book-ends bearing the coat of arms of St. Paul's School were several leather-bound volumes: *The Wines of Provence, Yeasts and Moulds, The Wartime Diary of V. C. Moissinac* (1922), and *Mirror and Shadow,* a medical biography of Richard K. Douglas, M.D., D.S.O., O.B.E., by M. A. Robertson (University of Edinburgh, 1980). The bindings, slightly worn, were identical and gave the disparate little collection a clubby, customized look of elegance and permanence.

Alex turned to the phone directory and, into his notebook, copied the names and numbers Varnas had found written inside the cover. To satisfy himself, he dialed the Musée Cernuschi. A taped female voice, cultured and carefully cadenced, answered and told him what he already knew: that the musée was closed Monday. He hung up and dialed the number for 'Anna.' There was no answer. He hung up again and found himself inspecting the third collection of photographs Crusson had complained of. These pictures, on the wall and on the desk, were in sharp contrast to the genial family portraits in the bedroom and the slick parade of celebs on the piano. These photographs had not been assigned. They'd been chosen.

On the wall, somewhat in the style of old silent-film glossies, were photos of aviators. The first to catch his eye was a wildly improbable shot of a very young Jan Bollekens, perched in the cockpit of a biplane, holding a puppy. The caption read "Solicitor as pilot, Thistle Escadrille, Aug. '18." It was signed "Boli." Beneath this was the dark and handsome Dieter Preuss, his luxuriant hair parted in the middle, the four split points of his Blue Max medal showing under the high collar of his German Air Service tunic. The photo was inscribed, "To P. Wilson, a true fine gentleman!!"

Next to Preuss appeared the blond, clear-eyed Heinrich Loesser, gazing off into the clouds, signed "Thanks for everything, 'Hank' Loesser." There were photos too of Basil Cottrell and Donald Benedict, both in RAF helmet and goggles, both debonair with cigarette holders, one signed "All the best, Wilson," and the other, "Cheerio, Pudgio!" None of the men looked over twenty.

On the desk in a wallet-size Florentine leather portfolio were three faded snapshots: one of a bearded old man seated in a white wicker rocker, wearing a linen suit, bow tie, and panama hat; another of a fine-boned, sad-eyed, faintly smiling woman of a certain age in a shirtwaist, a wisp of hair escaping her bouffant coiffure; and the third of a handsome blond woman surprised by the camera while standing chest-deep in water, a trout rod in her hand. Alex guessed the old couple to be Wilson's parents. The young woman was Millicent, caught in a charmingly unguarded moment long ago.

But it was a pair of enlarged photographs, yellow with age, that dominated the display on the desk. The first showed two boys holding a string of fish between them. The tousle-haired, nearly identical brothers are grinning and squinting at the photographer, whose head shadow can just be seen in the foreground. The other picture, taken in a portrait salon in Toronto in 1915, shows a young officer in the uniform of the Royal Flying Corps.

Alex sat at the desk and carefully studied the sixty-five-year-old portrait of the nineteen-year-old boy.

Tom.

What anguish forced that last, gasped word from Andrew Wilson's throat as he lay dying below the parc basin in the beam of Poirier's electric torch?

Alex shut his eyes for a moment. In the darkness, the haunting memory of Grandfather's scrapbook returned, images materialized; the smiling Zouaves in their absurd pantaloons, marching innocently off to glory and slaughter in Belgium, the lone biplane in the empty, white sky. And Grandfather. Grandfather, moustachioed, florid and sniffing, puffing on his inextinguishable calabash, showing the neighborhood children how to bayonet a Boche.

Feeling slightly bewitched, Alex rubbed his eyes and got to his feet. He yawned and stretched and leaned across the desk to turn off the lamp.

The phone rang. It startled him. But then he realized the Maison knew where he was. He picked up the receiver.

"Allô?"

"Pudge?" A scratchy old American voice. "Pudge? It's Zeke. How about lunch?"

9

Chez Suzanne

VARNAS knew that espionage, like corruption, was part of life. It occurred at every level, from the village keeper-of-morals, vigilant behind her parlour curtain, to the foreign agent, scuttling into the country with a visa to study Sumerian cuneiform at the Sorbonne.

Early in his career, Varnas reconciled himself to this circumstance. He was therefore neither surprised nor squeamish when he first encountered the reality of the police informant.

He learned that the hard-core criminal, the mafioso or Milieu member, seldom becomes an informant. The gangster's oath of fealty and silence precludes it, or he dies young. It is usually the petty crook—the forger, fence, or pimp—who, when apprehended, is given the opportunity to choose between prison or conditional liberty as a police informant. If he chooses to become a police informant, he becomes, in a sense, a double agent, repeatedly required to distinguish between loyalty and betrayal, and to avoid the consequences, as necessary. While sometimes profitable, it is not an easy life. Police officers are sensible to this and handle their charges cautiously. If they do not, the entire informant network can disappear overnight and, with it, a vital source of police intelligence.

Within a block of each other, nestled in the foothills of Montmartre below the funiculaire to Sacré Coeur, are two cafés known as recreational centres for low-level crooks of various stripe. The cafés are Ajaccio and Chez Suzanne. Each provides a measure of privacy (poor lighting, overcrowded), tables and setups for cards, dice, and other games, and a continuous supply of alcohol in some form. To augment the bar, Ajaccio serves sandwiches and plates of raw onions and Greek olives. From a kitchen the size of a closet, Suzanne produces authentic provincial dishes, a different one each day. For this reason, Chez Suzanne is Varnas's favorite. But as he was early for lunch, he walked first to Ajaccio in Rue des Abbesses. The rain had stopped but the air was chill and brittle.

Ajaccio, named after the capital city of the island of Corsica, is owned by a sooty-bearded Bulgarian judo expert widely believed to have strangled a common-law wife with his black belt. That the story was probably apocryphal is beside the point. It's just the sort of tale that makes Ajaccio Ajaccio: an authentic Pigalle dump, two rooms, the front one always jammed, the back one less so because it is unheated and far from the bar. This is a hangout for bookies, publishers of pornographic comic books, and small-timers who push illegal amphetamines, pep pills, and black-market cigarettes.

Varnas edged through the crowd, stood near the bar, and ordered a vermouth. For the next hour, the names of the illicit électriciens he'd obtained from the active file at the Palais de Justice were quietly passed around with the drinks, the dice, and the plates of olives and onions.

As the hour of luncheon approached, Varnas excused himself from his companions and threaded his way to the miniature plastic palm tree situated across from the entrance to pay his respects to the owner. This was the spot where the Bulgarian always stood. From here, by means of carefully placed advertising mirrors donated by Dubonnet, Gaulloise, Byrrh, and a dozen other suppliers, he could keep both rooms more or less under surveillance.

"Glad to see you are patronizing Ajaccio, Inspecteur," the bearded propriétaire rumbled, his dark eyes slowly cruising. He rolled his r's like a Toulousien. "When it is raining or otherwise too unpleasant for us to go out and play, we feel a whole crock of shit safer in here with you to protect us."

Varnas thanked him, made his way out of the crush, and walked back down Rue des Abbesses to Chez Suzanne.

This café, run by an ex-madame from Limousin whom Varnas protected from the vice squad a decade ago, resembles a large, dark lavatory. Its walls and floor are covered in brown tile while the ceiling is square-patterned tin, painted black. A full-length, floor-to-ceiling window presents its soiled face to the street, bottom-curtained against the curious.

Chez Suzanne is quieter and, because its owner is a woman, is considered a bit more refined than Ajaccio. Most patrons eat, drink, and play dice or cards wearing their hats and overcoats. Varnas is not sure if this custom exists to enable them to depart the premises on short notice, if it is an expression of Pigalle indifference to the canons of bourgeois decorum, or if they're just cold.

All the tables were occupied. Varnas, wearing his overcoat and homburg, took his meal at the tiny bar under Suzanne's personal scrutiny. She was about Varnas's age but twice his size. When she leaned on the bar, she had to do so sideways to keep her huge bosoms out of his Veau á la Crème.

As Varnas ate, Suzanne watched some men at a table by the window playing bezique. "That filth has been in here since I opened!" she exclaimed. "Two pastis and a Perrier in two hours! I give them ten minutes more!" She looked at Varnas's plate. "How's the veal?"

"Superb."

"Eat your watercress, chéri. It will keep the lead in your pencil." She winked and waddled into the kitchen.

Varnas finished the last of the veal and mushrooms, wiped up the crème sauce with a chunk of bread, and deposited his plate in the dumbwaiter. He ordered a vodka from the barmaid and joined the bezique players, three pimps who supplemented their income fencing stolen baby food.

In the next few hours, Varnas arranged to lose 140 francs and to buy several rounds of pastis for the table. At the same time, he carefully solicited the information he sought concerning the électriciens in the Justice dossiers. He did this with delicacy and nuance, as if he were floating a needle on water. It was a ritual expected and enjoyed. Varnas was well liked among stoolies. They knew that if a nephew got in trouble they could usually rely on him for help. For his part, Varnas owned the longest list of useful police informants of any inspecteur in Paris.

After a few games, he returned to the bar, selected a toothpick, and paid his bill. Suzanne gave him his change and stepped from behind the cash register. She took one of his hands, slipped it inside the bib of her apron, and placed it alongside one of her giant knockers.

"Listen, Inspecteur," she whispered. "If you ever get lonely one of these long afternoons, you have only to drop in after la soupe. I'm always here." She smiled. Gold and silver stars sparkled in her bridgework. "You know what they say: a big woman keeps a man warm in winter and provides shade in the summer."

10

Zeke

AT a few minutes before noon, Alex removed his foul-weather gear beneath the porte cochère of the tiny Hôtel Fleury and walked through the bronze front door. He crossed the lobby and picked up the house phone next to the reception desk. A young woman came on.

"Service?"

"Lewis McKim, please."

"Room 304, m'sieur. One moment." Alex counted eight rings. Finally the scratchy old voice answered.

"Yeah?"

"Sûreté, Monsieur McKim," Alex announced.

"Come on up, Lootenant."

The small hotel's sole elevator, a brass and glass cage that rose from the centre of the lobby inside an ornate shaft of black and gold grillwork, had just begun its sedate climb, carrying a cargo of elderly ladies recently back from a tour of Notre Dame. Alex took the stairs. Without hurrying, he reached the third-floor landing in time to see their pious faces ascend and disappear through the ceiling.

There was no need to search for room 304. Across from the elevator shaft, a bandy-legged old terrier of a man stood with his hands on his hips, guarding an open door. He was rumpled and his color was battleship gray: baggy dark gray trousers, gray cardigan over a faded gray turtleneck. And the deep-furrowed face and close-cropped hair were gray as well. Alex approached. "Monsieur McKim?"

McKim stuck out a gnarled hand, fingers mahogany stained from nicotine. His grip was surprisingly strong. "Don't Monsoor me, Lootenant," he said, scowling. "Call me Zeke like everybody else does. And if you don't mind, we'll stick to English. I never learned to parlay-voo anything more than Doughboy French. Come on in." He turned and led Alex into his room with the short, pigeon-toed strut of an old fighter.

"Doughboy French?" Alex asked, switching to English. "Is that similar to G.I. French?"

"Yeah, but first edition. 'Polly-wolly ding-dong wee-wee manure.' What'll you drink?"

Alex glanced quickly around the room. While Zeke's Hôtel Fleury enjoyed a good reputation among foreign tourists, this room was surely the irreducible minimum accommodation: single bed, phone, two wooden chairs—one a rocker—a standing lamp, a single Watteau reproduction on the wall, and a table in front of a curtained window holding the cold remains of a breakfast tray. On the table was an ashtray, a copy of the *International Trib* that Zeke had sent for after speaking to Alex (this was folded under a magnifying glass), a half bottle of whiskey, and two water glasses. Zeke uncapped the bottle.

"Not for me, thanks," Alex said.

"Probably just as well," Zeke grunted. "This is PX bourbon. 'Old Armpit' or somethin'." He poured himself half a tumbler. "Have a seat."

Alex took the straight chair. Zeke remained standing, his knees slightly bent. He made a toast. "To Pudge," he said, and drained the glass. He stood for a moment, blinking at the empty tumbler. Finally, he placed it on the table and lowered himself carefully onto the rocker. He coughed and scowled at Alex.

"Don't expect too much from me, Lootenant," he said, his voice raspier than before. "Pudge and me been cheatin' the undertaker for so long it don't much matter to us if we croak in bed or some other way. Dead is dead. I'm not real sure I care a whole hell of a lot who killed Pudge Wilson. If the camels don't getcha the mosquitoes must. Mimsy'll feel the same. Main thing is he's gone and won't be back. And that's a piss-poor state of affairs. Piss-poor obit in the *Paris Trib* too!"

He reached into the pocket of his sweater, brought out a pack of Lucky Strikes, and offered one to Alex. Alex declined. Zeke took one himself and tossed the pack on the table. "Don't smoke! Don't drink! What's happened to you people? France is goin' straight to hell in a Coke bottle!" He tapped the unfiltered cigarette repeatedly on the back of his bony hand. "Pretty soon," he said, "you won't be able to tell Paris from downtown Woonsocket."

He lit the Lucky and inhaled so deeply the smoke didn't reappear until he spoke again. "Of course I haven't had time to sort things out in my head," he said, leaning back in the rocker. "In my head, Pudge's only been dead an hour . . . since I talked to you on the phone." He rocked slightly. "Well, never mind that. What do you want to know?"

Alex put his pocket tape recorder between them. "All you can tell me about Andrew Wilson," he said. "And a few related things."

Zeke picked up the tape machine and examined it. "Cops didn't have these gadgets in my day," he growled. He put it back on the table.

Alex rolled the tape. "How is it you didn't go home on Saturday as planned?" he asked.

The old man frowned. "Was it Saturday?"

"According to a note Wilson wrote his wife, you were to return to Misquamicut on Saturday."

Zeke coughed and poured another finger of whiskey. "Lootenant, you ever hear a song called 'The Last Time I Saw Paris'?"

"Sure."

"Well, I had a strong feeling after the Armistice thing—" He interrupted himself. "When was that?"

"Thursday."

"I had a strong feeling Thursday that this was going to be the last time for me. So I decided to hang around a little while longer. I hired a car and driver for the weekend and went out to Château Thierry and Chaumont and down to Issoudun for a last look. I guess I came back yesterday."

"You don't remember Wilson asking you to deliver a note and small gift to his wife?"

Zeke shrugged and swirled the whiskey in his water glass. "I can remember every detail of what happened to me sixty years ago, Lootenant. But don't ask me to remember what the hell happened last week." He tossed off the whiskey.

Alex watched the old man smoke. He held the Lucky like a cigar, between his thumb and forefinger. "Maybe I can help you remember," Alex said. "Wilson mentioned in the note that you and he had a drink with Jan Bollekens after the Élysée Palace reception. He said you celebrated the first anniversary of some occasion. Do you recall that?"

"I don't recall drinkin' with Bollekens."

"Did Wilson mention what he was celebrating?"

Zeke chuckled. "Christ, maybe he was celebratin' the day he switched from gin to vodka."

Alex smiled. "Would you call that an epiphany?"

"Well, I'd sure as hell call it an improvement! I don't know, Lootenant. Coulda been anything. Pudge was always celebratin' somethin'." Zeke rubbed his hands together and suddenly leaned forward. "Say. How about some lunch?"

The suggestion was so abrupt, Alex couldn't tell if Zeke was really hungry or just anxious to change the subject. His expression gave no clue. Alex glanced at his watch. It was twelve-thirty.

Struggling to his feet, Zeke said, "How many times will you get the chance to have lunch with the only *Providence Journal* reporter from Washington County, Rhode Island, to win the Pulitzer Prize for a farm and garden piece?" He poured a little more whiskey. "I'll make you a charter member of the Pudge Wilson Annual Room Service Memorial Luncheon Committee. That way, if I'm not here next year, you get to conduct the meeting." He emptied the glass.

Alex acquiesced. Zeke insisted on calling room service himself. He ordered minute steaks, fried potatoes, salad, a bottle of Beaujolais Nouveau, and café filtre—all in his more or less fluent Doughboy French.

Alex helped him clean off the table; that is, they moved everything from the table to the bed. Zeke opened the curtains in front of the window. This let more light into the room—gray light, as it happened. It also enabled them to enjoy the view of the back of the Banque de France. After these exertions, Zeke went to the bathroom.

Alex stared out the rain-soaked window. He decided David
Stevenson's characterization of Zeke as "almost senile" was premature. Old people, Alex knew from experience, usually sorted
out the recognizable signals and landmarks of their long lives and
discarded the rest. Grandfather had done that. At eighty-five,
Grandfather could remember precisely the name of every man in
his infantry regiment of 1914, but years later would instantly forget
why he was on an errand for his daughter. Zeke wasn't senile.
Zeke was simply away, remote as the mountains of the moon, but
distanced by time instead of space.

The old man returned from the bathroom with his short hair
freshly combed. He leaned on the table and peered at the rain
outside. "I wonder if we'll be allowed to pick the age we want to
be when we go to heaven. I'd hate to think of bein' eighty-six for
the rest of eternity, with heaven a kind of celestial nursing home
where everybody's on a special diet." He blinked and cleared his
throat. "And somethin' else: I hope they got a trout stream up
there. Because if they do, that's where you'll find young Tom
Wilson waitin' for his brother to show up." He shook his head,
turned slowly, and again lowered himself into the rocker.

He was blushing. He seemed embarrassed, as if he'd betrayed
some old newspaperman's oath against sentimentality. "Hell! This
hotel's takin' a terrible long time to get that food up!" he grumbled,
glaring at his fingers.

Alex sat down across the table from him. "The photograph on
Wilson's desk," Alex began. "The one with the string of fish."

"Yeah?"

"I couldn't tell which brother was which."

Zeke hesitated. Alex wasn't sure if the old man was woolgathering or being vigilant. He guessed vigilant. And trying to
make a choice between his duty to protect Wilson's privacy and
his desire to tell Wilson's story. For an old man, to relate an old
story to a new audience is an overwhelming temptation: one more
chance for undivided attention, once more for self-esteem.

"You couldn't tell which was which," he finally said. "Not
from a reasonable distance, you couldn't. They had the same build,
the same coloring, the same cowlick. They had the same slow,

careful walk, goin' up on the balls of their feet with each step. When they talked they gestured and nodded their heads the same way. I don't know where they got it. It wasn't from their parents. Folks said they were fed off the same placenta even if they missed bein' twins by two years."

Zeke shot Alex a glance that seemed almost hostile. "You know what innocence is?" he asked. "You probably don't, you bein' French. I always swore that the average six-year-old French kid knows more about what the hell's goin' on than any full-grown American." He tapped another cigarette.

"To understand Tom and Pudge you got to understand innocence." He lit up. "How old are you?" Smoke floated around his nose.

"Thirty-four."

"Humph. You won't understand. The innocence I'm speaking of comes from away back, from the Nineteenth-Century Victorian Virtues. The virtues were Loyalty, Duty, Honesty, Patriotism, Thrift, and Hard Work. A man could go blind lookin' for those virtues today. Tom and Pudge grew up with 'em. So did I. Except the Wilsons lived in Watch Hill and I lived on the mudbanks of the Pawcatuck River."

Zeke relaxed his militant expression. "People from Watch Hill don't exactly associate with folks from Pawcatuck, even today. Back then it was unheard of. But boys have a way of breaking down those barriers. I worked summers in my uncle's bait shack near Napatree. The boys bought their squid from me. Pretty soon we became friends, although I wasn't in a helluva hurry to admit it because I was older and naturally tougher. One Sunday they invited me up to their place to make ice cream. Now ice-cream making is not proper work for an older, tougher kid from Pawcatuck. But I made an exception because I wanted to see that big shingled house on the hill.

"Peppermint ice cream with chocolate sauce!" Zeke almost smiled. "I'd never tasted anything like that in my life! And I never seen anything like the contraption Webster Wilson, the boys' father, rigged up to freeze the cream. He jacked up the hind wheel of his Marmon automobile, took the tire off, and ran a belt from the drum to a larger drum on a separate axle that somehow turned the freezer. All we did was to keep the ice and salt comin'! There was always something goin' on up at the Wilsons'.

"I guess the boys got their feeling for adventure from Webster. He taught them to fish, freshwater and salt. He taught them to shoot. And to build things.

"Tom was the best fly-fisherman I ever saw. Even when he was a boy he could cast a dry fly clear across a stream and drop it under a bush sixty feet away without snaggin' the bush or spookin' the water. And the thing of it was that Pudge was as proud of Tom's casting as if he done it himself. There was no jealousy between them. Pudge was a better shot than Tom, though. Better shot than anyone. He could do somethin' I never seen before or since. He could bring down a duck on the wing with a single-shot rifle. Not a shotgun. A rifle. I seen him do it with a pistol too."

"Is that why he kept the pistol in his sock drawer?" Alex asked. "To shoot ducks?"

Zeke scowled. "You mean the Browning?"

Alex nodded.

"No. He had that to keep Mimsy happy." He shrugged. "She thinks everyone should carry a gun."

"Excuse me?"

"Mimsy thinks that the only way to stop crime is to arm everyone. She has her own statistics to prove that disarmament breeds war and that there was less per capita crime in the Eighteenth Century, when everybody carried a piece."

Alex recalled the snapshots in the bedroom. Did an authentic zealot lurk behind those patrician features, or had she turned into a scattered old lady? Or was this a smoke screen? Alex asked, "Did Wilson agree with her theory?"

"No. Just the opposite. But he liked guns. He was a real sportsman."

Lunch arrived. The waiter turned on the overhead light and wheeled the linen-covered table into the centre of the room. The plates with their domed warmers and the silverware jingled pleasantly and gleamed under the reflection of the ceiling fixture. The waiter started to extend the leaves of the mobile table, but Zeke wanted lunch served at his own table by the window. Without a word, the waiter spread a fresh tablecloth and transferred the settings. He displayed the label and opened the wine, leaving the bottle with its cork next to Zeke to breathe. He placed a tiny bud vase with a single pink rose on the table, followed by a small serving dish containing the bill, facedown. He then withdrew to a discreet distance. Zeke studied the bill carefully. His thin lips moved as he checked the addition. Finally satisfied, he signed at the bottom. Alex couldn't help seeing the amount from across the table. Zeke reached into his pocket and pulled out a handful of bills. Alex guessed the tough old man would overtip. He did: fifty percent. The waiter bowed and left.

Zeke tasted the wine and poured, his hand as steady as Alex's. They began lunch.

"That snapshot of them with the string of trout was taken on the Farmington River in 1907," Zeke said. "Tom was eleven and Pudge nine. Those boys took on every day as a unit. When they worked on somethin' together—and they were always together until Tom went away to school—you were lookin' at a two-headed, four-armed, four-legged individual creature. Reminds me. Their mother, Emilie, claimed that when she was pregnant with Pudge, Tom, who wasn't yet two, knew he was gettin' a brother and used to pat her stomach and talk to him.

"The year after the Wright brothers flew at Kitty Hawk, Tom and Pudge built the first underground clubhouse in Watch Hill. They dug a six-foot-square hole in the ground about four foot deep with a trench leading to it. They covered the hole and most of the trench with boards, covered the boards with earth, and planted grass seed. In a couple months you couldn't tell the clubhouse was there unless you seen smoke comin' out of the stovepipe.

"They built a treehouse forty foot up in a big maple at the top of their property. You got there by ship's rope ladder to the lower limbs. Then you pulled the ladder up and climbed the rest of the way. The house had two bunks, a table and chairs, a water bottle, a kerosene lamp, and a spyglass. With that glass you could see people walking around on Fishers Island on a clear day. One day we seen a woman on the east end squat down behind a bush to go to the bathroom. We snapped that glass shut quicker 'n it takes to tell it and waited until she was finished. That's what I mean by Victorian virtues and innocence.

"Old Webster claimed there was nothing a man couldn't have if he was willing to build it himself. In 1909 he bought a half-rotted lifeboat and, with the boys, restored it and converted it to a cruising sailboat. She was the first *Brillig*, a gaff-rigged cutter. She had two bunks, a coal stove, an oak bucket for a toilet, and, of course, no engine. She'd do about six knots with the wind aft, about three with the wind close aboard—most of it sideways— and if the wind pooped she had to be anchored or sculled home. Tom and Pudge sailed that boat everywhere: to Block Island, to Newport, Cuttyhunk, the Vineyard, and once to Nantucket. Alone. Tom was just fifteen and Pudge thirteen. Says a lot for Webster's confidence in them.

"Besides the cutter, they built an iceboat, a toboggan, model airplanes, dozens of kites, and a crystal radio set using a Quaker Oats box to wind the coil. Always something goin' on."

Zeke poured more wine for Alex and gave him the rest of his potatoes. He was finished, his steak only half eaten. He put his fork down and tapped a cigarette on the tabletop.

"Always somethin'." He lit the cigarette and inhaled. "Of course, it had to end some time. And it did, in the fall of 1911, when Tom was sent off to boarding school. He was fifteen and, like his father and grandfather, was expected to spend the last three years of his schooling at St. Paul's before going to Brown.

"At the end of the first week of September, Webster and Emilie accompanied Tom to Concord, New Hampshire, on the train. It took several days, as I recall. Pudge, whose local school had already started, couldn't go.

"The night before Tom's departure, it was agreed the boys could spend the night in the treehouse, provided they were up by six. Breakfast was to be at six-thirty. The train left Providence at half past eight.

"Pudge told me they talked until almost dawn. They talked about God and duty and luck and what was expected at St. Paul's, where the prospectus listed such dark subjects as solid geometry, physics, Latin, and Greek. They made plans to do some blue-water cruising in *Brillig* the following summer with a view to sailing around the world someday—like Joshua Slocum—perhaps by 1920, when Pudge would be finished with college.

"Next morning, I went up to the Wilsons' after breakfast to say good-bye. That interval, just after breakfast, was the most difficult for Pudge. Since he wasn't needed around the house, where Tom's packing was being finished up, he thought he'd go down the hill to the dock and pump *Brillig* dry, just to stay busy. I walked down with him. I guess the heft of the wooden bilge pump he and Tom had built, the familiar sound of the sucking and drawing, and the smell of the bilge water were all too much for his thirteen-year-old heart. He began to sob. I'd seen it comin' and pretended to be busy on the other side of the wharf. But Pudge kept pumping. He was pumping and sobbing when his father called down from the house. Tom was ready to leave.

"The Wilsons had a new Hupmobile. It was parked in the driveway. That thing had seven spare tires! Pudge helped his father load Tom's trunk and suitcase onto the roof and secure them with clothesline. Tom's tennis racquet, skates, and fly rod went inside. The whole household, plus the dogs and me, were gathered on the front porch for good-byes.

"There was Gracie, the Scottish housekeeper who'd helped raise both boys. Her eyes were the color of sky; 'Eyes that could spot a lie in the dark,' Pudge used to say. She was smiling, but her chin was trembling. She held an embroidered hanky, just in case.

"There was Mary, the disagreeable Irish cook, who said little—especially to Gracie—but was a good plain cook as long as it was lamb. She went to Mass three times a week, never laughed, and never cried. But when Tom offered his hand to say good-bye, she threw her arms around his neck and bawled.

"Hector, the gardener-handyman and former coachman turned chauffeur-without-livery, waited by the car he was to drive to the station. He seemed sobered by responsibility and respect for the moment. He wore his best suit and hat.

"The Wilsons got into the car, Tom in front and Webster and Emilie in back. Hector cranked the Hup and the thing started with a roar. I saw Tom reach over to retard the spark and advance the throttle. Gracie commenced to cry. The dogs barked. Hector climbed in behind the wheel. There was a grinding of gears. The

Hup moved off down the gravel driveway, putting up a flock of pigeons that'd been feeding on grass seed. Gracie and Mary waved their handkerchiefs. Hector tooted the horn. Pudge and I waved as the car turned into Ocean Avenue. We caught a glimpse of Tom wavin' back. Then the car disappeared behind the neighbor's hedge and Pudge began countin' the days to Christmas vacation.

"Because of America's reputation for egalitarianism, you might be surprised to learn, Lootenant, that the difference between a public school kid and a boy from St. Paul's in 1911 was the difference between a dustman and a duke, if not intellectual, then at least social." He lit a new cigarette from the old one.

"When Tom Wilson came back from St. Paul's in the summer of 1912, I expected to see a change in him. And I expected Pudge would too, one that might affect their closeness. I was waitin' for the patronizing glance, the reference to some highfalutin item of scholarship I never heard of. Thucydides or somethin'. I needn't have worried. He hadn't changed at all, except that he was smarter. He was the same gracious, funny, enthusiastic—even more enthusiastic—young man who'd gone away nine months before. The only difference was he told a couple of mildly ribald jokes that had us rolling on the ground and kickin' our feet.

"I don't just know what it was that made Tom the way he was. Or Pudge the way he was. Or them the way they were together. Certainly, it had something to do with their parents. Emilie and Webster never set the boys against each other the way some parents do for their own short-term convenience. And so the boys were never humiliated. Yes, I'd say it had somethin' to do with the parents. But—and I'll bet my last pack of Lucifers on this—it had a lot to do with innocence."

Zeke leaned toward the bed for the whiskey bottle. It was just out of reach. Alex got up and handed it to him.

"Thanks," he said and poured a finger into his wineglass. Alex sat down again. "Two years later, Pudge followed Tom up to Concord. During the year the Wilson boys were there together, St. Paul's School never lost a hockey game. Then came August, 1914, and the Germans walked into Belgium."

Zeke took a sip of the purplish whiskey. "A month later, or

about a week after your grandfathers stopped the Germans at the
Marne . . ."

Alex thought someone had poked him in the ribs. "How did
you know my grandfather was at the Marne?"

Zeke blinked and blew smoke through his nose. "I didn't," he
said. "I was speaking generationally."

"My grandfather was there."

"Did he live through it?"

"Through the Battle of the Marne? Yes. He was wounded."

"Is he still alive?"

"No."

"Did you know him?"

"Very well."

"Did he tell you about it? The Marne, I mean?"

"Yes. And the Aisne too."

Zeke looked at Alex. "And did you understand what he told
you?"

Alex stared. Understand? Understand Grandfather? Dear God,
what a question! Still, he realized Zeke deserved a respectful answer. "No. I didn't understand at first. The war of '14 seemed a
myth, no more real than the campaigns of Caesar or Napoleon.
It seemed a museum war: old uniforms in glass cases, rusty bay-
onets, aeroplanes hung from the ceiling. Then, when I was about
ten, Grandfather started walking me over his old battlefields. And
now . . . yes. I understand what he told me."

Zeke sniffed and butted his cigarette. He scowled at Alex as
usual. But the eyes above the scowl showed a trace of interest.
"Well, as I was about to say, the week after your granddad routed
the Kraut, Tom Wilson started his freshman year at Brown
University.

"Most American families, mine included, didn't pay much attention to the war. The Wilsons were different. Emilie was half
Belgian. She had relatives in the war zone. And Webster'd been
touring the French wine country when hostilities broke out. He
was at the W. W. Wilson office the day your grandfather fought
on the Marne, certain Paris would fall by evening.

"All these details weighed heavy on the boys, particularly Tom.

Until his father returned safely in December, Tom borrowed a motorbike and rode the forty miles of dirt and gravel between Providence and Watch Hill just to be with his mother on weekends.

"Sentiment in the U.S. was generally pro-Allied. A lot of youngsters at eastern colleges, that fall, were filled with romantic indignation. A few left school and joined the Foreign Legion. One of Tom's roommates, a Canadian boy, went home to join the Royal Flying Corps.

"By the spring of 1915, Tom was itchy and decided he had to do something. He wrote Pudge, declaring his intention to become a pilot and asking Pudge's opinion. In his letter, Tom enclosed an early war poem of Rupert Brooke. Pudge wrote back that Tom's plans sounded 'excellent'—I believe that's the word he selected— a word I notice has returned to usage among the young today. It all sounded 'excellent,' he said, but hoped Tom would consider postponing at least until Pudge was old enough to go too.

"In the end, of course, Tom went. He took a train to Toronto and joined the Royal Flying Corps. It was the first time he'd ever gone against his parents' wishes. But he had the fever that burns only in the innocent. I suppose Webster understood. Emilie never did. You know the rest."

Zeke glanced over at Alex. "Lootenant, if you slide the table your way, I can get up. I'm afraid if I don't get up from time to time I'll be stuck in a sittin' position and they'll never find a box to fit me."

Alex moved the table and helped Zeke to his feet. Like men who automatically gravitate to the fireplace after dinner and stand with their backs to it, even if it's unlit, both men now took up positions facing the window and sightlessly stared at the back of the Banque de France. The rain had stopped.

"I don't know *all* the rest," Alex said. "I know that Tom Wilson was killed. From the obit I know Andrew Wilson joined the American Air Service to vindicate his brother's death. Also from the obit, I know that Andrew Wilson was sued for libel by Tom's former commanding officer." Alex faced the old man. "Tell me something, Monsieur Zeke. Did Andrew Wilson vindicate his brother's death to his satisfaction?"

Zeke didn't hesitate. "Hell yes. Pudge took fourteen of their best in exchange for Tom."

"And that was enough?"

"Sure."

Alex chose his words carefully. "If it was enough," he said, "why, ten years later, did he go to such an extreme to humiliate and indirectly contribute to the death of Major Willoughby-Jones?"

Without a word Zeke stepped over to the room-service table and rolled it toward the door. In a moment, he turned back. "Pudge didn't set out to humiliate Willoughby-Jones. Pudge set out to discover the mystery of Tom's death. In solving the mystery, he exposed the muck surrounding Willoughby-Jones."

"But monsieur, Tom Wilson is buried in the military cemetery at Poperinge. He was a pilot. He was shot down. Where's the mystery?"

Zeke scratched his chin and stepped slowly back toward the window. "There's fifty kilograms of fieldstone in that casket at Pop, Lootenant. Nothin' else. Not even a belt buckle. But to return to your question. Pudge didn't set out to destroy Willoughby-Jones. And I'll tell you somethin' else. If the Royal Flying Corps had known the truth about that officer in 1916, they would've saved him the trouble of shooting himself." Zeke turned away from the window. "Willoughby-Jones was addicted to morphine. He was a man of charm and persuasion who managed to support his habit nicely by selling replacement aircraft engines and spare parts to the French. This involved suborning a depot supply officer, a hungry Liverpool ranker who'd earned his pips the hard way, and the squadron medical officer.

"In the five months Willoughby-Jones commanded the squadron, Pudge reckoned that eighty percent of all pilot casualties were as a direct result of engine malfunction . . . that is, power loss in flight causing the airplane to break formation, or outright engine failure requiring a forced landing or crash.

"The technical sergeant-major responsible for squadron maintenance, a man of courage as it turned out, finally realized what was going on and blew the whistle. The medical officer, who'd supplied the morphine, was dishonorably discharged and stripped of his civilian license. The supply officer was shot. Willoughby-Jones was sent home on sick leave."

"Sick leave?"

"Aviator's neurasthenia. Combat fatigue."

"How was that possible?"

"Pudge called it 'Swagger Stick Diplomacy.' You don't see it now. But in those days, unless a member of the British officer class turned and ran from the enemy in front of a dozen witnesses, he was pretty safe."

"And all this came out in court?"

"Yeah."

"After the trial, was there any resentment or ill feeling against Wilson from the RAF?"

"Some. They'd fought Jerry for four years and Pudge'd only fought him for six months. Some were angry. Some were just embarrassed. Still, no one could really fault Pudge after what he did for the widow."

"Wasn't there a child?"

"Yeah. Grew up just in time to die in the second war. New Zealand Expeditionary Force, either the ETO or the Far East. I forget which. Damn unlucky family." Zeke chugalugged the whiskey in the bottom of the wineglass, made a face, and settled back in the rocker. Alex remained standing.

"Did Wilson ever solve the mystery of his brother's death?"

Zeke nodded. "Finally. You know how to fly?"

"No." Alex sat.

"It takes practice. Ridin' a bike takes practice. You wouldn't put a kid on a bike one day and stick him in the Tour de France the next, would you?"

"No."

"Well, that's more or less what they done to Tom. Of course, a lot of replacement pilots in those days only had a few hours' solo time before they were sent up against the likes of Udet or Richthofen. But if they were lucky they got a better airplane than Tom got. He hoped for a Sopwith Pup squadron. But they sent him to Willoughby-Jones's outfit, north of the Somme Valley, where they flew BE-12s.

"The BE-12 was a slow, obsolete, single-seat biplane developed from the Royal Aircraft BE-2, a two-seater that'd been in France since 1914. The German's loved 'em. You could shoot one down with a bow and arrow. Brand-new, in level flight, they could do about ninety-five. They were as maneuverable as a cow in tall grass and climbed like a rock. They had a single machine gun on top of the upper wing, so far above the pilot's head he had to stand on the seat to change the drum. Presumably, the enemy was a sporting fellow who would do a bit of sight-seeing while waiting for this to take place. Worst of all, the BE-12 had a gas tank big as a bathtub under the upper wing. The enemy always went for it. Every aircraft the Germans had, including their barrage balloons, was better than the BE-12.

"Tom was sent up on November twenty-second, 1916, flyin' the oldest BE-12 in the squadron. The engine of his airplane had been due for its one hundred hour off-aerodrome overhaul for two months—or since Willoughby-Jones had been in command. Tom had never flown the airplane. Nor had he received any training in formation flying, enemy recognition, or fighter tactics, techniques that were the responsibility of each squadron to teach. He was accompanied by five other BE-12s. Their assignment was to provide cover for a flight of Martinsydes bound for Courtrai.

"After climbin' to three thousand metres, Tom's engine began to overheat. Unable to hold formation, he dropped back and lost altitude. Near the village of Menen, over enemy-held territory and separated from his flight by a mile or more, he was attacked by a headhunter out of the sun."

"Headhunter?"

"Enemy scout pilot. Hides in the clouds or in the sun, waitin' for stragglers. The Germans weren't the only ones who had headhunters. We had 'em too."

"And?"

"The first attack disabled Tom's airplane. Whether Tom was hit or his controls were shot away, Pudge never discovered. But the airplane began to spiral down. The enemy followed closely and continued to fire through a thousand metres. The tail group was shattered and a lower wing shot away. A tracer bullet struck the fuel tank and what was left of the aircraft exploded. Only the engine reached the ground. It was the engine serial number, reported by the Germans through the International Red Cross, that identified the airplane as Tom's. No part of him was ever found.

"When the Wilsons got word, Pudge was home from St. Paul's for Christmas vacation. From the moment the telegram arrived, Tom's name was never mentioned again in his mother's presence. Not for as long as she lived. She had every trace of him removed from the house: clothes, books, furniture, toys, photos, fishing tackle. Everything. And this job of housecleaning went to Pudge.

"The big maple that held the treehouse was cut down and sawed up. She wouldn't allow it to be burned for firewood. The boat was sold down east and never seen again. By the spring of 1917, Tom Wilson ceased to exist." Zeke coughed and sat back in his rocker. The curtain seemed to have come down.

Alex checked the tape. There was half a spool left. The old man bounced his cigarette pack on the tabletop and stared out the window. Certainly his story had poignancy enough. If it had become embellished over the years, the fact remained that Andrew Wilson's affection for his brother was remarkable. But was that all Zeke was going to tell him about the murdered man who was his close friend? That Wilson loved his brother? Alex asked, "Who was the German pilot?"

"Say again?"

"Did Pudge know who the enemy pilot was?"

"Yeah. He found out later. Some guy named de Clovis. Why?"

"Well, if he was so interested in the man who sent his brother up, I'd expect him to be interested in the man who shot his brother down."

Zeke turned in his chair. "Wait a minute, Lootenant. You're talkin' about two different things. The Englishman was a murderer. The German was just doin' his job. Pudge understood that."

Alex pronounced the name. "De Clovis. Sounds French."

"Yeah. But you can't go by names. The Germans had another ace with a froggie name: Beaulieu-Marconnay. The Limeys had a flyer named de Crespigny and the French had one named Waddington." Zeke studied the backs of his hands. "Well," he said, "I think that's about it. Anything else you want to know you can ask Mims." He looked up. "But don't expect too much from her."

"So you said before," Alex replied. "Doesn't she want to see justice done?"

Zeke focused on his hands again. "Mimsy isn't much interested in justice with a capital 'J,' Lootenant. Oh hell, in the abstract she might be. But when push comes to shove"—the old man's gaze flickered past Alex—"she's liable to be more interested in privacy than anything else."

Alex waited. But there was no more. "Well, thank you," he said and got to his feet. "I'm glad you were on our side during the war." The old man looked up and, this time, actually smiled. Alex added, "I do have one more question, if you don't mind. It's a standard police question."

Zeke nodded. "I know. Can I think of anyone who would've wanted to kill Pudge Wilson?"

"Yes. Or was it a haphazard crime? A mugging?"

Zeke took a deep, rattling breath, reached for a cigarette, and thought better of it. "I don't know, Lootenant. He's been shot at before."

"When?"

"In '51. In Riyadh, Saudi Arabia, on his way back from the Persian Gulf. He was tryin' to get the Hebrews and the Arabs together to talk business and some Moslem thought it was a punk idea. They never caught the guy. The same year, a shot was fired in Pudge's direction at Tempelhof. But whether the bullet was meant for Pudge or the Air Force general standing next to him was never determined. Then back home, in '53, he got a letter bomb from some flaky Bible Belt fundamentalist group because of an article he wrote for *The Nation*. The letter was delivered while Pudge and Mims were away on the boat durin' the hottest August in fifty years. It sat in his rural delivery mailbox for a week, melted, and finally went off, wipin' out most of R.D. Number One, Stonington, Connecticut. When Pudge and Mims came home a couple days later, there were still a dozen charred L. L. Bean fall catalogs hangin' in the hemlocks across the road."

Zeke rubbed the small of his back. "Hard for me to believe he got mugged. Pudge gettin' mugged in a parc in Paris is like . . .

Ulysses slippin' in a bathtub in Philadelphia. It's too bland. It's not his style. If I write his biography and it turns out he was mugged, I'll change the ending."

"You won't have to," Alex said, turning off the tape recorder. "He wasn't mugged."

Zeke held out both hands for Alex to help him up. On his feet he pumped Alex's hand, firm as ever. "You're okay, Lootenant. For your sake, I hope you get your man."

Zeke led the way to the door with his scrappy little walk. He opened it and pushed the room-service cart out of the way.

Alex thanked him for lunch. "You'll let me know, Monsieur Zeke, before you return to the States?"

"If I remember."

They both laughed. "And no last-time-I-saw-Paris," Alex said, towering over the older man. "Next year, when you come back for Armistice Day, lunch is mine."

"We'll see! We'll see!" Zeke nodded and patted Alex's arm.

"Speaking of Armistice Day." Alex stood in the hall. "This meeting of Old Eagles . . ."

"What about it?"

"Well, there you are, face to face with former enemies."

"So?"

"Do any of you, or any of them, still feel anger or hold a grudge?"

Zeke shook his head. "Hell, Lootenant, we were only enemies for a couple years by act of Congress. Here we been buddies for more than sixty. Look at the signed photos in Pudge's study. Half of them are Germans and Austrians he met at air shows during the twenties and thirties. Hold a grudge? Hell no. We're all members of the same old-farts' club, lucky to be alive and happy to meet every couple years for a drink. We get a little oiled and sing the old songs. The Limeys sing 'Roses of Picardy,' the Jerries sing 'Die Wacht am Rhein,' we sing 'There's a Long, Long Trail a-Windin',' and your guys sing 'C'est l'Alsace et la Lorraine.' "

Alex, standing in the hotel corridor, caught a glimpse of something then, a flickering image connected to a sliver of melody: Grandfather walking again the plowed field outside Vailly-sur-

Aisne, singing in his eerie, cracked baritone; Grandfather, who never forgave the Germans, singing

> C'est l'Alsace et la Lorraine,
> France's glory long ago!
> Oh . . . Oh . . . Oh . . . *Oh!*

Zeke shook his head. "Hold a grudge? Hell no! We're all refugees from another time."

Part Two
THE FLÉCHETTE

11

Hippo

THE Istanbul-Paris Express, an express in name only and no relative of the famous old Orient, crept ignominiously into Zagreb behind a tiny, mud-coloured switching engine. The train, its inert diesel locomotive victimized by contaminated fuel, was four hours late. A new engine was being dispatched from Trieste or Belgrade or someplace. No one knew for sure. And no one knew when the journey would resume, let alone when the train would reach Paris. The shivering passengers, shivering because the train's heating system had expired with the locomotive, found themselves in Zagreb, Yugoslavia. Zagreb, on a cold, overcast Tuesday morning in November.

Paris ballistics Chef-Inspecteur Hippolyte Maurice Ludovic du Temple peered through his round spectacles at the conductor who had just handed him a small blue ticket.

"Not to lose," the conductor said in a sort of French. "You get off those train, you need ticket for back."

Du Temple's black button eyes twinkled. "Very kind of you," he said in his soft, ecclesiastical voice. "Actually I had not planned to disembarque."

"Stays to you," the conductor said and moved along.

Du Temple tucked the blue ticket into the silk band of his brown felt businessman's hat with the upturned brim. It gave him a jaunty look, not at all in keeping with his ascetic, contemplative countenance.

Most of the chef-inspecteur's colleagues thought he resembled a Benedictine monk more than he did a crime-lab cop. Indeed, he seemed to bring an almost monastic piety to his ballistics work, while the devotions he performed in behalf of his beloved E.S.A.W.

(European Society of Antique Weaponry) approached the beatific. Baptized "Hippolyte" for his great uncle sixty-three years ago, he inevitably inherited the sobriquet "Hippo" in school, where he was the smallest boy in his class. It was a difficult antonym for a slight, dignified older detective shaped more or less like a pipe stem with a pot belly.

He pulled the muffler higher around his neck and looked out the train window. A line of steamy-breathed passengers moved slowly across the station platform toward a waiting room of sorts. Perhaps it was a detention room, he thought. There were a lot of impassive-looking police about, keeping an eye on things.

A large, swarthy woman with a runny nose entered the far end of his carriage. She moved slowly up the aisle, hawking newspapers from a stack she balanced on her head.

Du Temple attempted to relax. He had not slept well. Commissaire Demonet's telex to the French Consulate in Istanbul, picked up yesterday, had kept him awake most of the night as the express rumbled westward through the noisy Balkan mountain tunnels. "Return Paris immediately!" was the peremptory message. In the telex, the Commissaire had included some details of the parc murder: no shot had been heard, yet the calibre was said to be 6.3. It made little sense from a ballistic standpoint. Perhaps Emilio, the pathologist, who disliked working on weekends, had rushed his examination. Well, Hippo would have to examine the wound himself. When that might be, he thought, peering out the window at some railroad workers standing about with lanterns, was anybody's guess.

The newspaper vendor approached, advertising her wares in indistinguishable syllables. She stopped before du Temple. Uncertain of his nationality, she reached over her head with both hands and, miraculously, without disturbing the stack, produced two papers, one Viennese, the other French. She dexterously folded each twice before presenting it. Du Temple made out half a headline:

——ES TO WILSON SLAYING!

He gave the vendor a handful of dinars and opened yesterday's *Paris Soir*. In the center of page one, he read

ARAB CONFESSES TO WILSON SLAYING!
Sûreté Credited

Paris, 15 November

At 4 P.M. today, after round-the-clock interrogation of a Libyan seaman arrested early Sunday evening in Marseille, Commissaire Henri Demonet of the Sûreté Nationale announced, 'We have Andrew Wilson's killer. The case is closed.'

The Commissaire told Paris Soir that Shafik-al-Wadi, 18, of Homs, had been interrogated at Troyes prison. 'When he became hostile under questioning,' Demonet said, 'we informed him we would not keep him in solitary. At that point he agreed to cooperate.'

Shafik was arrested in the Port St-Jean section of Marseille while trying to purchase a forged passport with stolen banque notes bearing the same serial numbers as the one found near Wilson's body in the Parc de Monceau. Searching the suspect's hotel room near the waterfront, police recovered the murder weapon, a 6.350 millimetre Czech Stráźnice long-barreled automatic with a silencer. Trial is set for 14 December.

Du Temple dropped the paper on the seat and pulled his luggage down from the overhead rack. He had to get to Paris at once, which meant participating in the single activity he most disliked next to physical exercise. It meant he would have to undergo an aeroplane.

He left the train at Zagreb, bought a pint of cognac to settle his nerves, and caught a J.A.T. turboprop to Salzburg with a connection to Paris.

Hours later, as the police pathologist, Emilio Lupi, greeted the bleary-eyed ballistics chef-inspecteur on the echoing metal stairway that led to the subarctic basement of the Paris morgue, he decided Hippo looked rather jolly with the little blue whatnot in the headband of his hat.

Stevenson

The pocket FM radio in the remote and sealed-off mailroom of W. W. Wilson and Co., Paris bureau, played rock and roll more or less continuously, day and night: by day to maintain the cultural currency of its sole tenant, the teenage mailgirl, and by night to keep away the mice. As the office was closing Monday evening, a news bulletin interrupted *Les Puits* briefly to announce the capture of Andrew Wilson's killer.

Even as lights were flickering off in the passageways, the news proliferated. Stevenson, tweed-capped and camel-haired, stood at the lift, rhythmically pressing the down button with his walking stick as his secretary burst into the foyer.

He seemed stunned when she told him the news and immediately went back into his office to call New York.

Everyone in the New York office, except for a few stenographers and some people in bookkeeping, seemed to be either at lunch or working out. He left his message with the standby receptionist, an older woman. "The police have arrested a Libyan seaman," he said. "There appears to be no political or ideological connection. The motive, it seems, was robbery. Please inform Mrs. Wilson."

He rang off, waited a short interval, and dialed Commissaire Demonet's private line at the Sûreté. After several rings, a secretary picked up. The Commissaire was at the Ministry of the Interior.

"Tell him David called."

"Any message, Monsieur David?"

"Certainly. Give him my felicitations."

Bollekens

Jan Bollekens had lost patience. He reflected on this as he waited in his study for the taxi to take him to the airport.

Charlotte lay upstairs in an imitation coma. When, several days earlier, Bollekens had told her he planned to join Zeke in Paris for Mimsy's arrival, and to provide Mimsy support and counsel if and when she faced the police, Charlotte's response had been predictably violent. But it was nothing compared to the fit that seized her last night when she read of the Arab's confession in the newspaper. Now, with the case solved, she cried, it was an incontestable fact that Bollekens had no excuse to go to Paris except for devious purpose. Like an ancient soothsaying crone who can foretell the future by examining the entrails of freshly killed fowl, Charlotte poked and prodded herself for omens and declared that Bollekens was off to Paris not for the reasons he stated but to gambol in the Luxembourg Gardens with his girlfriend. "Now, with Pudge dead," she shrieked, "the coast is clear!!"

That was when he lost his patience and she went into her fake coma. He could tell when she was in her fake coma because she always left one eye partly open.

The only daughter of a lawyer and judge, Charlotte knew better than to ask her lawyer-judge husband to divulge professional secrets. Except when it came to the Wilsons. The Wilsons fascinated and scandalized her, particularly Millicent, whose beauty and uninhibitedness she'd always envied, loved, and hated. Her jealousy of Millicent amounted to an obsession.

With this in mind, Bollekens moved his private Wilson file out of harm's way and into a small hand trunk he intended to take with him to Paris.

There was a lot of stuff. He knew Charlotte had seen the one letter to Pudge, but he couldn't be certain she'd gone through the rest of the file. Much of the material was in German and English, neither of which Charlotte read fluently. The medical reports from the *Bundesarchiv* were in German, while the excerpts from the Douglas biography ran to nearly one hundred pages in English. Still, she might've been able to learn something just from reading his correspondence with Pudge. The question was, how much might she have learned, and how did she intend to use the information, given her jealousy of Millicent and her instinct for mischief?

What had chilled Bollekens on the night he called Mimsy—and bothered him still—was that Charlotte chose to pull that particular letter from the file and conceal it in a deliberately clumsy fashion so that he could not fail to notice it. Why? Had she acted on a whim? Or had she understood the significance of the letter and wanted him to understand that she understood?

He vowed to exercise extreme caution while he was in Paris, to remain always within Charlotte's reach by telephone, to indulge her continuously with acts of affection and admiration, to coddle her with gifts, gossip, and hourly messages of reassurance and homage. If he did not do this he could only expect the worst. She was at her most destructive when left alone and playing at catalepsy.

The practical nurse, hired by Bollekens to attend Charlotte during his absence, came into the study without knocking. She was a small, immaculate woman of perhaps fifty years, who'd spent her entire working life caring for the enfeebled rich. She came into the study with traces of wet oatmeal in her hair.

"Madame does not care for her breakfast," she said with restraint.

Bollekens, standing by the window, turned and watched the airport taxi move slowly up the long driveway. "I'm sorry, mademoiselle," he said. "You will receive extra compensation for service in the zone of combat."

The Maison

Alex had taken the call from the Marseilles chef du bureau describing the Arab's capture. After the bit about the thousand-franc notes and the forged passport, the chef said, "He's only a kid, Alex."

"But was he armed?" Alex asked.

"No."

"Nothing under the mattress?"

"No. He was staying at the local Red Cross–Red Crescent shelter. No alcohol, no smoking, no radios, no weapons, no jerking off. All we found was a used bus ticket from Paris to Marseilles."

"What do you think?"

"Any finger can pull a trigger."

.

Shafik-al-Wadi was flown to Orly Monday afternoon and transferred to the federal pen at Troyes, eighty kilometres southeast of Paris, where Alex and the Commissaire waited.

The Commissaire, his jaw swollen from emergency root-canal surgery earlier in the day, was not in a sanguine frame of mind for this meeting. As for Alex, he was completely unprepared for the encounter with the Arab. He had expected, at the very least, a defiant, criminal countenance. Instead, what stood before them in the interrogation room was a trembling, terrified slip of a boy whose voice had not completely changed, a child, scarcely out of puberty, who would have been entirely believable as the Third Shepherd in a Christmas pantomime.

Through an interpreter they questioned him for less than fifteen minutes.

"The footprints found in the park were made by the shoes you are wearing, Shafik. Do you understand?"

"Yes, excellency."

"And the thumbprint on the banque note found in the parc is your thumbprint."

"Yes, excellency."

"Who was the woman with you, Shafik? There are a woman's footprints in the parc next to yours."

"There was no woman with me, excellency."

"So you alone stole the money from the old man?"

"Yes, excellency."

"Was that before or after you shot him?"

"No, excellency. The old man was already dead when I came upon him."

Commissaire Demonet, possessed of a finely tuned understanding of politics and the art of misdirection, reached a conclusion long before the interrogation was over. He gave orders that the boy be held in solitary confinement in the women's wing, isolated from other prisoners, the police, and, above all, the press. From a secure phone in the warden's office, he spoke for five minutes to the Ministry of the Interior. He then called the editorial office of *Paris Soir* and delivered the press release that subsequently appeared in the Monday evening edition.

On the way back to Paris, he explained his strategy to Alex. "I told you I would move the furniture from time to time. The Minister has stated, as I anticipated, that the Arab's confession to the murder of Andrew Wilson will, by itself, not be acceptable, that the Sûreté will be required to provide evidence, independent of the suspect's confession, which will prove his guilt beyond a reasonable doubt."

Alex interrupted. "Commissaire, he's confessed to stealing the banque notes. No problem! We can prove that beyond a reasonable doubt. But to pin a murder charge—"

"Alex—"

"Commissaire, this isn't Algiers in the forties. If that kid gets a lawyer—"

"My dear Alex, he doesn't want a lawyer! He thinks he just

won the national lottery! He's safe and happy in a nice, warm French jail! In Tripoli they'd chop off his right hand and send it to his mother! Alex, this is the real world. The boy will never stand trial for the murder of Andrew Wilson. But in the meantime, we have the opportunity to exploit his presence. Don't you understand? The *fact* of the Arab, in prison as the prime suspect, God bless him, means we can conduct our investigation without interference and on *two* levels: one to be conventional with conventional evidence—footprints, banque notes, and the like—to satisfy the public, the press, and Wilson's killer, whoever he is, that the Sûreté is on the job; the other to be covert, to keep the public, the press, and Wilson's killer, whoever he is, in the dark as much as possible and for as long as necessary.

"Our rationale for continuing the investigation is that while the 'confessed' killer of Andrew Wilson awaits trial in prison, the Sûreté Nationale will pursue evidence that suggests the murderer may have had an accomplice, possibly a woman. Any more questions?"

Exhausted by a twenty-six-hour day, and short-tempered, Alex complained to Varnas. "Case is already frozen in fucking aspic! We won't be permitted to question Madame Wilson when she gets here because, he says, it might ruffle the Élysée Palace. Then he rubs the magic lamp and produces this baby Arab who isn't the murderer and a fenced long-nose Strážnice automatic that isn't the murder weapon!"

Varnas observed Alex serenely. "Commissaire's game is chess, Alex, not football. To be patient. What do you learn from conversations with Bollekens and Zeke?"

"Nothing. One, an ex-magistrate in the Belgian Superior Court, is skilled at evasion and persiflage, and the other, a retired newspaperman, gives me a sermon on innocence, brotherly love, and the virtues of privacy over the ambiguities of justice."

"Never mind. We have parc lights to look forward to."

"Yes. And the parc cleanup to look forward to and the Laundry List and old age."

Varnas moved to the door. "Excuse me. Do you or do you not wish to give instructions to Assignment Desk for tomorrow?"

Alex stared at the floor. He rubbed the back of his neck with both hands. "I tell you," he said quietly, "there is something not on the Laundry List about this case. Something other." He looked at Varnas. "Instructions for the Assignment Desk. Sure. All departments to proceed as if nothing has happened. Except I want the gardener, Poirier, in this office by nine, and the Musée Cernuschi file on my desk by nine-thirty."

"Get some rest," Varnas said and left.

Alex blew his dinner money on a cab back to *Le Yacht Club*. He dropped the few francs he had left into Philippa's vacation kitty. Unfed and fully clothed, he fell onto his bunk. Immediately, the phone rang. He could tell by the peremptory ring that the call was from Claudine. If he answered he knew he'd expose himself to a full gale of recrimination for his failure to explain Sunday night. He'd had a long day. He was beyond exhaustion. He did the sensible thing: he allowed the phone to stop ringing, waited a short interval, and called her.

"Where are you?" she asked.

"Opéra metro," he replied. With consciousness fading fast, he launched a preemptive apology before she could mount an attack. When she spoke she was small-voiced and wary. A few seconds before the operator would've interrupted, he said, "Listen, my train's coming. How about dinner Friday?" She was agreeable. He rang off and was instantly asleep.

Grandfather

At some point in the night he dreamed. In this dream Alex was a boy again and watching the saucer eyes of his childhood friends as Grandfather demonstrated, with a bale of straw, the proper use of the bayonet in hand-to-hand combat.

"Parry! Kick! Rifle butt to his chin! Put him on his back! And THRUST! Ahhh! Foot on his chest! WITHDRAW! Ahh! And THRUST again! Ahhh! Twist the blade! Ahhh! Withdraw and wipe! Eeeehhh!!" It was wonderful.

"Citizen soldiers, to arms!" Grandfather cried. "Defend the honour and glory of France against the barbarian invader, violator of your mothers and sisters and devourer of babies!" They believed it all: the bayonet charge at Onhaye, the fusillade at Vailly-sur-Aisne, the furious assault on the Saxon front across the Petit Morin, where Grandfather is said to have impaled a Boche to a tree on his blade. He showed them the bloodstain on the bayonet. No one imagined the blood might be rust.

Finally, in the dream, Grandfather turned to Alex and came close. He was so close Alex could see the hairs in his nose. With an expression of special understanding, camaraderie, and affection, Grandfather stood at attention and whispered "To the brigade, Alexandre!"

"To the brigade," Alex said aloud and woke up. He shivered and looked at his watch. Four-thirty; suddenly wide awake. He hadn't experienced a Grandfather dream in years. A war dream. All his childhood dreams and remembrances of Grandfather were connected to the Great War. To Alex, Grandfather was the Great War.

Grandfather's seventeen days of furious combat in late August and early September of 1914, during the long retreat from Belgium to the Marne, marked the pinnacle of his life's achievement, the *ne plus ultra* of glory and honour in an otherwise unexceptional career as a greengrocer. He glorified, esteemed, cherished, and celebrated with ferocious pride those seventeen days out of eighty-five unremarkable years.

But what had triggered the dream? Zeke McKim talking about Wilson? The memory of Grandfather singing "C'est l'Alsace" in the field outside Vailly? Vailly-sur-Aisne . . .

In April of each year, during the spring plowing, Grandfather traveled to his old battlegrounds to see what the ploughshares had turned up. He always came back with something: an empty cartridge, a shell casing, metal fragments, a rotted puttee. In 1958, Grandfather took Alex with him for the first time. Alex was ten, Grandfather seventy-seven.

They traveled by train and bus from Douarnenez to a cousin's house near Soissons, nearly six hundred kilometres away. It took a whole day. The cousin, who was a harness maker by trade, let them spend the night in his barn, where the raw hides were hung. To Alex, the Great War smelt strongly of hide, hay, and horse manure.

In the morning, they arose before dawn, washed in a basin of cold water, and breakfasted on bread and saucisson that Grandfather had brought in his knapsack. After breakfast, Grandfather shouldered the sack, put on his three medals with their faded ribbons, and led Alex down the road to the bus stop. This bus would take them to the village of Vailly, the scene of the great fusillade on the Aisne River in 1914. It was less than twenty kilometres away.

While they waited for the bus, Grandfather set the scene for the battle that had taken place forty-three years earlier. He made a sketch in the dirt with a stick. Here is the river, here is the village, here the bridge over which the Germans must come, here the fields they traversed on their way to the bridge, here, here, and here where we of the brigade were dug in, waiting for them.

The bus arrived in a cloud of dust. The driver recognized Grandfather from the year before and said, "Good morning, Corporal." It was a grand moment. Grandfather gave him a flat-handed salute and slowly climbed aboard with Alex scrambling behind. While Grandfather paid the fare, Alex selected a seat for them on the left side of the bus.

"No, no," Grandfather declared when he came back. "Sit on the right side, the river side of the bus. The French side. You are on the Boche side." Alex was never again comfortable on the left side of a bus, train, or aeroplane.

The road ran along the north bank of the Aisne. Grandfather seemed mesmerized by the muddy river, swollen with spring rain and the runoff from the Ardennes. "The river is clear in August," he said.

Alex looked out the "Boche" windows on the left. As the houses and commercial establishments began to thin out, he caught glimpses of sugar-beet fields being prepared for planting. The plows, great snorting yellow beasts, hugely tyred, didn't seem capable of creating the gently radiused curves that graced the rolling black earth to infinity—that is, to the top of the next wavy rise where the furrows abruptly disappeared, to reappear a moment later climbing a further rise in a cross-patterned geometry that made Alex dizzy. He turned back to the river. A stand of poplars flashed by. Grandfather tapped the bus window.

"Over there," he said, "behind that church, the first company of Percin's regiment anchored our left. From there to the bridge we stretched what was left of the brigade. One kilometre, a thousand metres, a thousand men, one man to the metre. The Boche had ten men to the metre."

The bus slowed. Farmhouses appeared. On a small patch of land on the "Boche" side, a boy no older than Alex plowed behind a horse. "Vailly," the bus driver called out.

"Come on, then," said Grandfather. They got up. Alex held on to the old man to be sure he didn't lose his balance when the bus stopped.

They disembarqued in a cobbled square with a fountain at its centre. Grandfather again saluted the bus driver, who tooted his horn, shifted gears, and rumbled off. Vailly smelt of wet earth, damp masonry, and dung. Grandfather gazed sharply around the square, looking for harrowing machines, for once the harrows took over from the plows, breaking up and sifting the earth for sowing, the farmers permitted no one on their land, least of all souvenir hunters. But Grandfather had timed their visit perfectly. The harrows, he was told, were two days away.

The Aisne Valley was not as popular with military buffs as the Somme, nor as dangerous. Spring plowing in the Somme Valley, the scene of four years of trench warfare and thousands of artillery barrages, still turned up the occasional unexploded shell, which, if it did not detonate on contact with the ploughshare, adding a tractor driver to the appalling list of casualties of three generations ago, often required an emergency call to someone at Army Bomb Disposal in Paris whose father was not yet born when the shot was fired.

Alex followed Grandfather out of the square. They walked toward the bridge. As the sound of the river filled the air above the cobbled street, Grandfather said, "Quite naturally, the town changed after '14. Originally, there were no houses this close to the river. The Boche cavalry, accustomed to an advance of thirty kilometres a day and thinking itself secure from attack, moved openly along this road in echelons of four followed by foot soldiers marching six abreast and singing at the top of their lungs."

Grandfather reached the bridge. He stopped in the middle of the road and placed his hands on his hips, like a general. "We took them completely by surprise. We had a regiment of infantry concealed across the river behind a rise in the terrain. The rise is no longer there; you will have to imagine it." He pointed to the opposite bank. "There, to the left, in a small copse—also no longer there—was our heavy machine gun. And there"—he pointed to the right—"our single mortar." Alex followed Grandfather to the centre of the bridge. "We allowed the Uhlans to reach this spot before opening fire: infantry barrage against mounted cavalry, machine gun and mortar fire against singing foot soldiers with their rifles slung. I will tell you, Alexandre, the concert ended abruptly. The chaos was unimaginable. Terrified horses reared and plunged: some leapt riderless into the river. In less than a minute the bridge was piled deep with dead men and animals. The machine gun and mortar decimated their infantry on the far shore. A few fled across the fields and were cut down. The only survivors were a handful who got back into the village."

Alex had heard the story before. It was nearly indistinguishable from the others and held no more real immediacy for him than the myth of Abelard and Éloise. But he thought he should say something. He said, "So after that, the war was over, right, Grandfather?"

"My God, Alexandre," the old man muttered, "the war is still not over." Alex remembered that remark years later.

They recrossed the bridge, skirted the village, and made for a plowed field just to the east of the last houses, the field over which, Grandfather said, the remnants of the German infantry tried to escape the furious assault. "There are hundreds of bullets in that field," he added. "We'll see what we can find." But as they reached the perimeter of the plowed earth, Grandfather stopped short and exclaimed, "Son of a whore in pig shit!" He glared across the field. Alex followed his gaze and saw a man fifty metres away wearing earphones and swinging a long metal pole with a sort of bell at the bottom. The man moved slowly along a furrow swinging the bell from side to side. Grandfather pulled at his moustache. "We will not associate with that excrescence, Alexandre. The filth does not search for artifacts. He looks for metal, for lead, scrap iron, steel coins, anything he can sell. He desecrates the ground," Grandfather said and walked away.

Alex followed him to a section of the field that ran roughly parallel to the Soissons-Neufchâtel road. Grandfather walked the first furrow from the road and Alex the next. "Move slowly, Alexandre. Focus your eyes on a spot one half metre in front so that you will not trip or fall. Curb any temptation to dig or break up the clods. What the plow has not turned up we will not find this year. Above all, touch nothing until I have examined it." With that, Grandfather established his deliberate, processional pace. Alex followed.

At first, the anticipation of finding a German machine gun or a rifle or the barrel of a cannon had excited Alex. It was the same sort of excitement he felt when Grandfather took him fishing: lower the baited hook until the sinker touches bottom, then reel in a bit; watch the tip of the rod ("What would you do if I caught a whale, Grampa?"). Shhh. Concentrate, watch the tip. And he did. But after twenty minutes without result, his excitement flagged and the urge to eat lunch at 7:30 A.M. became overpowering. It was now nearly nine o'clock and Alex, already bored, resorted to counting his footsteps. Slow march to the east end of the field, stop, move over two furrows, about face, slow march in the opposite direction. He calculated there were between 990 and 996 steps per furrow. He decided to take smaller steps so he could reach one thousand. He'd never counted to a thousand.

The monotony was temporarily relieved when Grandfather stopped to urinate. Alex had never seen Grandfather's pecker. He'd seen his father's, of course, because they used the same toilet at home. He'd been impressed with the length and breadth of his father's instrument and concluded that pecker size increased with age, like the trunk of a tree. The older you got, the bigger your pecker became. Quite understandably, then, he was anxious to have a look at Grandfather's great hose, that he guessed hung down to the old man's knees.

Grandfather unbuttoned and, without reaching in very far, produced a wrinkled, leathery appendage about the size of a sore thumb. Alex was bitterly disappointed. If that was all Grandfather could manage after seventy-seven years, what did Alex have to look forward to?

The procession continued. Grandfather found a bridle buckle with a bit of rotted leather still attached to it. But whether the buckle came from a Uhlan bridle or from a latter-day plow horse, he couldn't say.

At ten o'clock, Alex heard Grandfather's stomach proclaim lunch. They finished the furrow they were on and stopped in the lee of a natural windbreak made by a large boulder and a thicket of shrubs at the edge of the field. Grandfather unslung the knapsack. He sat on the ground and, leaning against the sun-warmed boulder, served up bread, saucisson, cheese, and red wine in tin cups. Alex felt enormously grown up because of the wine. His mother would not allow him wine, even diluted.

"To the brigade!" Alex said, raising his cup in a toast to Grandfather's war.

The old man peered at his grandson. "Thank you, Alexandre," he said huskily. "To the brigade!" The two men drank. Grandfather blinked and looked away.

Had this day on the battlefields of Vailly ended right there, Alex would have retained nothing more than the bittersweet memory of his first slight hangover, and his feelings of fellowship and affection for his grandfather. His young mind would not have been opened to the awful possibilities of life or reflected on some of the real consequences of glory and honour.

After lunch, Grandfather lit his pipe and studied the windbreak behind which they were installed. "I don't recall this clump," he said, getting to his feet. "I don't remember the enemy having any cover here." And he ambled off to investigate the little island of shrubbery and rock.

The moment Grandfather was out of sight, Alex, warm and somewhat lightheaded, reverted to childhood. There were straws and bits of tuber clinging to the clods of earth in the furrow near where he sat. A light breeze blowing across the windbreak created an eddy that lifted some of the loose straws skyward for a moment and deposited them in a furrow a few metres away. Alex improvised a game. He began tossing straws. The higher he tossed them the farther the wind carried them. He picked up a tuber that was shaped like a boomerang and sent it spinning. It seemed to soar by itself. Now he could have a contest between straws and tubers. At the end of four tosses, the score was Straws three, Tubers one. Wishing to make the contest more even, he selected a large tuber and lofted it. It went straight up and fell straight down. Too heavy. Somewhere on the other side of the windbreak, Grandfather began to sing, "C'est l'Alsace . . ."

Alex spotted the tip of a smaller tuber stuck in the crest of the next furrow. He trotted over, reached down, and pulled. It resisted. He dug around it to get a better grip and tugged. It broke loose. Something white came up. Alex screamed and dropped the skeleton of a human hand.

As the porthole beside his bunk faintly materialized in the darkness like a suspended lozenge, he made an effort to place this unsolicited recollection into some sort of rational frame. But as daylight brightened the porthole, chasing phantoms, the recollection faded. The recollection became a diversion without agenda, unlike the more pressing matters awaiting him: the gardener Poirier and the Musée Cernuschi.

The Maison

Despite the news of Shafik's arrest, a brigade of Police Academy cadets and a CRS squad again reported to the Parc de Monceau to quarter and bag the northeast quadrant. It was difficult. The ground was frozen.

At Sûreté headquarters, file inspecteurs, archivists, and computer programmers continued the monumental task of assembling the civil dossiers of eighty NATO ministers from fourteen countries, including their staffs and employees, twenty-four World War I aerial aces from eight countries, several hundred residents and service personnel from Wilson's Paris neighborhood, as well as the staff of W. W. Wilson and Co. and the directeur and employees of the Musée Cernuschi. Elsewhere, a band of inspecteur-trainees, equipped with plaster casts, set forth to visit the boot shops, department stores, and shoe-factory outlets of Paris.

"Time for coffee," Varnas said.

Alex stopped at the Assignment Desk while Varnas went into the street to buy café au lait and pastry at Á La Cart, a vendor-on-wheels with a striped canopy.

On the stairs to his office, Alex encountered the Commissaire, whose mood seemed to have improved since the evening before. Demonet stopped and made a magnanimous expression. He said, "I have, this day, transferred my Citroën TEA to you and Varnas for the duration of the case."

The Commissaire's Citroën was fifteen years old and handled like a tank. But Alex said, "Thanks. What will you drive?"

"The Minister has awarded me a new Simca," he said conspiratorially, and continued down the stairs.

Alex and Varnas breakfasted at their desks.

At one minute past nine, the parc gardener, Joseph Poirier, appeared in the doorway holding his beret. He was windburned and looked ill at ease in what appeared to be his only suit, an old blue serge, baggy at the knees from years of kneeling during the Kyrie. Poirier apologized for being late. He'd stopped in the parc to look over his young transplants but the place had been crawling with police. He had tried to work on the trees a few days before, but there was a police line and the flics had sent him away.

Alex wrote him a laissez-passer. The gardener took the paper and placed it in his beret. "Thanks, Inspecteur. Actually, now the case is solved and you have the murderer, I guess the police line will be removed."

"The case still has a few loose ends," Alex replied. "Be seated, Monsieur Poirier." The gardener preferred to stand. Alex got up, came to the front of the desk, and handed Poirier a copy of his testimony. "Look this over, Joseph, and tell me if it accurately represents the facts as you remember them."

The gardener put on a pair of dusty spectacles and, standing with his feet wide apart, read slowly through the pages, his chapped lips silently following the words.

It was possible, Alex knew, that a man like Poirier, a man who had trod the straight and narrow all his life, might be tempted to make the most of the temporary celebrity thrust upon him by circumstances. Since his name had appeared in Le Quotidien, he might now imagine himself an authority and choose to expand his testimony to match his new eminence. Alex waited.

The gardener finished reading. He removed his glasses and handed the document back to Alex. "Yes," he said. "That is the way it happened."

"You have nothing to add?"

"Nothing."

Alex sat on the edge of his desk. "When you were working near the basin Friday evening, Joseph, did it occur to you that the lights in the parc were out?"

Poirier thought for a moment. "I don't remember. Perhaps. Yes, come to think of it, I had to use my torch."

"But you didn't consider the fact significant enough to report?"

"Significant?" He puffed out his cheeks. "A blackout in the parc is no big thing, Inspecteur. It happens all the time."

Alex looked at Varnas. To Poirier he said, "After you reached the parc and for an hour afterward you mentioned you were conscious of an occasional pedestrian walking near the Pavillon de Chartres."

"Yes."

"Did you actually see the pedestrians?"

"No. It was dark. I was busy."

"So if I said that one of them might have been a woman large enough or tall enough to wear a size ten high-heeled boot, you wouldn't be able to corroborate my statement?"

"No."

Alex returned the photocopy to the desk. "Now, Joseph, describe for me what took place at the Musée Cernuschi."

"I went there to phone the police. It was not yet six but the custodian was ready to close. We called the Quartier Europe. They told me to return to the basin and touch nothing. That's all."

"You said there was a gift-wrapped parcel on the receptionist's desk."

"Yes. A small parcel."

"But the receptionist had left."

"Yes."

"Even though it was not yet six o'clock."

"Ah, Inspecteur, I can't say if she had left the building, she could have been in the coatroom or making pee-pee." The gardener suddenly frowned. "I just thought of something."

"Yes?"

"It may be nothing, but you mentioned a tall woman before. Are you looking for such a woman?"

"Maybe."

"The receptionist at the musée is tall. Not as tall as you, but very tall for a woman."

"Do you have her name?"

Poirier blew out his cheeks again and shrugged. "Ah no, Inspecteur, I don't recall her name."

Alex made a note and stood up. "Okay, Joseph. Thanks for coming in. Let us know if you plan to leave town for any reason."

The gardener shook hands with both men, secured the laissez-passer in his beret, and excused himself.

Just before ten o'clock, a harried File Section clerk delivered a list of four names that constituted the entire staff of the Musée Cernuschi. File said the list was over a year old. No individual dossiers had yet been assembled. It wasn't much. Alex brushed the pastry crumbs off the desk and stared down at the single sheet of paper. Varnas looked on.

The musée was administered by a Polish-born aristocrat of French citizenship. She was Wieska Seńkowska, age sixty. She had three employees: a conservator-artist, Monsieur Lucien Violet, age thirty-two; a receptionist, Thérèse Cabanal, age sixty-four—Alex circled the name—and a custodian, Arnaud Hamot, age forty-five. Various bonded guards from a local security agency were not counted as employees.

"Anyone here you know?" Alex asked.

"Negatarian."

"Not even the towering Thérèse Cabanal occupies a niche in your photographic memory?"

"Never heard." Varnas swallowed the rest of his cold coffee. "So. Do you wish to walk or ride to musée?"

"Ride."

"Then I go now to transport pool for ancient Citroën." He adjusted the brim of his hat and left.

Alex waited until a few minutes past ten before phoning the musée. A man with a bluff Pyrénées accent answered. "Aha, police!" the man exclaimed, as if he'd just won a wager. "One moment."

Alex made certain the recorder was working. It bleated intermittently. After a short interval, a woman with a pealing, bel canto voice came on. The accent was refined but contained echoes of a Slavic girlhood. Madame Seńkowska, the directeur.

Alex introduced himself and explained the circumstances of the continuing investigation. She did not seem surprised.

"But of course we will cooperate, Chef-Inspecteur! My God, what a catastrophe! We are still in shock! Especially Madame Gutierrez!"

"Madame . . . ?"

"Gutierrez. My receptionist."

Alex looked at his list. "What happened to Thérèse Cabanal?"

"Retired. Madame Gutierrez has been with me since April."

Alex wrote the name in his notebook. "Gutierrez. What's her first name?"

"Anneliese."

He leafed backward through his notes and came to the name copied from the Wilson telephone directory. "And do you call her Anna?"

"Anna, yes." She lowered her voice. "Monsieur, I do hope you will go gentle with her. She is a close friend to the Wilsons and is badly upset by all of this."

Alex said, "I see." But of course he didn't see at all. Not yet. The name from the Wilsons' phonebook had become flesh and blood so suddenly, and from such an unexpected quarter, that he was momentarily adrift. He thought back to the gift-wrapped parcel the gardener had seen on the receptionist's desk. "Madame, before I interview Anna Gutierrez or any of your employees, I have a question for you."

"Yes?"

"Last Friday evening—the evening he was murdered—were you

and your staff expecting Andrew Wilson to come to the Musée Cernuschi?"

Madame Seńkowska uttered a small sound of helplessness. "I was in London," she replied. "But . . . yes. I am told he was expected. That's the thing, you see. That's why Anna is so distraught. She feels she could have saved him."

12

Anna

THE cold front that scoured the Paris sky of rain clouds brought brilliant sunshine with it but cold and gusty winds as well. These tore the last, tenacious leaves from the city's trees. Muffled to the eyes, a few pedestrians stayed low and close to buildings.

Varnas, who disliked driving, gripped the steering wheel of the Citroën with both hands in a futile attempt to correct the old car's erratic, wind-buffeted course up Boulevard Malesherbes.

Alex looked over at his friend. "It doesn't help to hold the wheel so tight."

"It helps me," Varnas said.

Conditions improved when they turned into Avenue Velasquez and parked the car next to the musée in a windless pool of buttery sunshine. They got out and walked toward the entrance. As they did, Alex thought he detected a movement in one of the second-floor windows. It could have been a trick of sunlight. When he glanced up just before they reached the door, he saw nothing there but a half-drawn curtain.

The heavy door was opened by a paunchy, middle-aged man wearing a shiny auburn-coloured hairpiece. He was dressed in dark slacks, a spotless white shirt, and a polka-dot bow tie. Alex and Varnas entered a marble-floored reception area. Across from the entrance stood a dark, delicately carved desk backed by a scarlet oriental fire screen. Except for a phone and Rolodex, the desk was unoccupied. Next to the desk, a tall, luminous vase, dragon-decorated, shone blue and white. Opposite, a narrow flight of stairs led to the floor above.

Huddled on the first step of the stairway was a man of inde-terminate age wearing a wool ski cap, a heavy wool sweater, muffler, and woolen mittens. He appeared to be albino. He had the pale seamless face of a young man, but his hair, what could be seen of it, was pure white. He wore tinted glasses to shield his squinting eyes from the light. He could have been smiling.

A few steps above him on the stairs stood a pleasant-faced matron in an artist's smock. Her thin gray hair was brushed back in a chignon. The still air of the reception area carried the felicitous scent of sachet. Varnas removed his hat.

"Well, my God!" the woman said, smiling. "That didn't take long!" She came off the stairs and approached Alex and Varnas, her hands clasped in front of her hospitably. "I am Wieska Seńkowska. Is it too warm in here for you? I have to keep the heat up for Lucien. Arnaud, take their coats."

Alex and Varnas removed their outer garments and handed them to the man with the toupee. Madame Seńkowska lowered her voice to Alex. "I assume you will wish to see us individually?"

"Yes, madame."

"Then would you see Anna first? I want to send her home as soon as possible. She's upstairs in my office."

Varnas remained on the ground floor to interview the two men. Alex followed Madame Seńkowska up the stairway.

The windows of the large, cluttered room faced the street where the Citroën was parked. Another window, facing east, allowed the morning sun to pour in.

The directeur's desk, a large wooden table in the center of the room, was hidden under a mass of debris: pieces of glass, a mound of unpainted boxes, bits and pieces of ceramic, and piles of papers. The desk chair had a cardboard file on it. Other files lined the baseboard. An armchair, the only other chair in the room, contained a stack of lacquered trays and an electric clock with a broken plug.

"Excuse the mess," Madame Seńkowska said. She called out, "Anna, dear. The Chef-Inspecteur of Police is here."

Alex hadn't seen her. She was kneeling at the far end of the room, gazing through the window toward the parc entrance. She stood and turned. His first impression of her was that she was oriental. She was very tall and slender. Her skin color was light copper, and her thick, black hair was shoulder length and square-cut, in the Chinese manner. Her eyes were hidden behind large designer dark glasses, but the wide cheekbones beneath were manifestly oriental. She was simply but elegantly dressed in beige wool pants and a black silk sweater with the sleeves pushed up on her forearms. She wore a jade bracelet on each wrist and several long loops of gold chain around her neck. Alex glanced at her feet as she approached. They were tiny—size five or six at the most, and clad in delicate, red leather pumps with a half heel.

She nodded gravely to him when they were introduced. Madame Seńkowska took the file from the desk chair and bulldozed a clearing on the table. Alex emptied the armchair. The older woman smiled and withdrew.

Anna lowered herself into the armchair. She sat like a man, with one foot crossed over the opposite knee. She took up a large purse that had been on the floor next to the chair. It was a hopsack linen bag decorated with green and gold embroidered monkeys. "Do you mind if I knit?" she asked, in the same carefully modulated voice Alex had heard on the musée tape.

"Of course not." He placed his pocket recorder on the table and took the desk chair. She pulled a nearly completed sweater from the bag. It was extravagantly patterned in jungle colors. She gathered it in her lap, arranged the needles and wool, and began to knit. If she was distraught, she was handling it very well.

Alex started the tape. "Madame Seńkowska tells me you are devoted to the Wilsons."

Without looking up—"Yes. Millicent is my best friend in Paris. And Pudge was . . . well, like a parent." Her French seemed about perfect and was unaccented except for a certain international cadence. It was the carefully correct French spoken by diplomats but seldom by the people themselves.

"Madame is not French?"

"No. Brazilian."

Surprise. Brazil. Coffee. Nuts. Green and gold monkeys. Like the rest of the Americas, Brazil was probably racially mixed, which would account for her dauntingly exotic features. There was a patrician strain in there somewhere, though, Alex guessed. The walk, the carriage of the head. He asked to see her passport.

She put down the knitting and rummaged through her bag. After a moment she produced a passport and handed it across the table.

"Thank you." He opened it to the first page. Name: *Anneliese Maria Dolores Gutierrez*. Born: *5 June, 1949, São Paulo, Brazil*. A year younger than he. He examined the face in the black-and-white passport photo. With her dark glasses removed she looked . . . well, not Chinese. She had the wide, pale eyes of a cat. Pale green or blue, he thought. Opposite the photo page, under "Wife/Husband," he read *Jõapedro Santiago Gutierrez,* followed by an address. "Is your husband in Paris with you, madame?"

"No." And no elaboration.

He checked the visa pages. "I see you were in West Germany in March."

"Yes. For a few days. To see a friend I knew at school in Montreux."

"And you've been in France since April?"

"Yes. For seven months."

He handed back the passport. "Madame, how is it you were able to obtain a work permit so quickly?"

"I have no work permit," she said. "I am not paid for the work I do at the musée."

"You put in a five-day week without compensation?"

She looked up for the first time. "Not entirely. In return for my work here, Madame Seńkowska instructs me in recognition and appraisal, and Monsieur Violet in the care and restoration of antique oriental porcelain. At present, I am learning the vitreous enamels. And Lucien is teaching me Chinese brushwork and calligraphy."

"Lucien Violet. The conservator? Did I see him downstairs?"

"Possibly. Was he swathed in wool?"

Alex smiled at her word choice. "Yes."

She returned the smile slightly. There was a small space between her teeth. "That was Lucien." She went back to her knitting. "Lucien is . . . retarded metabolically, but in every other way a genius."

Alex leaned forward on the desk and placed the tips of his fingers together. "Then you're in Paris, away from your husband

and family, for the sole purpose of learning antique oriental porcelain?" He hadn't meant the question to sound quite so pompous. The morally censorious phrase "away from your husband and family" seemed to hang in the air between them like a stuffed shirt.

"I'm not here to learn porcelain art for myself, monsieur," she said. "I am here on behalf of the Trust Department of my father's bank in São Paulo. The present economic climate in my country precludes most Brazilian banks from creating a conventionally broad earnings base, consequently—"

He interrupted. "Excuse me. Am I to understand that you're a banker?" It was not a question he would've asked a man so abruptly.

She leaned over her purse to consult what seemed to be knitting instructions. Then she counted rows, counted them in Portuguese. When she finally replied to his question, she did it slowly and with forbearance. "Not a banker. A Trust Officer. My department is examining alternative investment opportunities for some of our larger depositors. I speak of paintings, sculpture, antiques, things of long-term real value that can be counted upon to appreciate. It's an investment sector that requires a high degree of expertise. That's why I'm here." She barely paused. "Now . . . can we get on with it? I can't imagine that my vocational skills are of any interest to you."

"Your credibility is of interest to me," he said pleasantly.

She glanced up. "Did Madame Seńkowska tell you to take it easy with me?" Alex nodded. "Well, you don't have to."

He sat back. "Good. Then suppose you tell me where you were at six o'clock Friday evening."

"At the Brazilian Embassy."

"For what purpose?"

"I hosted a reception for our delegation to the International Monetary Fund."

"I wasn't aware that the IMF met in Paris last week."

"They didn't. My group was here for a few days en route to Zürich."

There was something expert about the way she pronounced "Zürich." "How many languages do you speak?"

"Six." Alex stared. She did her slight smile. She said, "Does that fact alter your stereotype of a Latin American housewife traveling abroad without her husband?"

"Somewhat."

"Actually, I have been known to drink a banana daiquiri from time to time and dance the bossa nova in my bare feet on the beach at Ipanema."

At that moment, although he knew he was being patronized, Alex fell a little in love with Anna Gutierrez. Nothing alarming, just a warm, summer zephyr against his autumn cheek. "What time did you leave the musée to go to the embassy?"

She concentrated for a moment. "About twenty to six."

"By car?"

"Yes."

"Did you drive yourself?"

"No. An embassy car picked me up."

"Weren't you expecting Wilson at the musée between five-thirty and six?"

"Yes."

"But you didn't wait for him?"

"I couldn't."

"So you were at the Brazilian Embassy when he was murdered?"

The needles stopped. She looked across the table at him. "Yes."

"Then how could you have saved him?" She tilted her head as though she hadn't heard. "Madame Seńkowska said you felt you could've saved him. What did you mean by that?"

She folded the sweater around the needles and left it in her lap. She glanced at the windows. "If I'd delivered Millicent's birthday present to the Wilson flat on my way to the embassy, Pudge wouldn't have gone into the parc." She looked back at Alex. "That would have saved him."

She put the knitting back in her bag and sat quietly for a moment. "Perhaps I should explain that a couple of weeks ago, Pudge asked me to look for a birthday present for Mimsy. I found something in one of the flea markets. It wasn't very valuable, quite cheap really, but charming . . . one of the pieces that the Chinese manufactured for export in the twenties. It's a white porcelain snuff bottle with a portrait of Sun Yat-sen on it. It needed cleaning and the glaze was poor, so I gave it to Lucien to restore.

"Lucien thought he could have it ready in time for Mimsy's birthday. Actually he had it ready Friday. I called Pudge and told him. He was delighted and said he'd pick it up at the musée just before closing. When I mentioned that I might not be here, he told me to leave it for him on the reception desk.

"After I hung up the phone, something made me want to call him back and offer to deliver it. But at that moment, people came in. I got busy. When Lucien brought the bottle down from the studio about five, I was dressing for the reception. He'd wrapped it in tissue and brown paper. I didn't think the brown paper festive enough for a birthday present, so I took a few minutes to gift wrap it. I suppose I did that as a kind of penance."

"What was it that made you want to call him back?"

"I don't know."

"Premonition?"

"No. I don't have premonitions. I guess it was guilt. I'm not well known for my good deeds. But every so often the girl scout in me stands up and complains." She sighed. "I don't know how I'm going to face Mimsy."

"You gift wrapped the snuff bottle and left it on your desk downstairs."

"Yes."

"Did you tell the custodian to be on the lookout for Wilson?"

"No. The custodian and I are not on speaking terms."

"Why not?"

She shrugged. "He's jealous. He thinks I spend too much of my time with Lucien."

Alex wasn't sure she was serious. "Jealous? Why? Is the custodian in love with you?"

"No. He's in love with Lucien. But perhaps you didn't know. Both he and Lucien are—to use a trendy euphemism—gender distorted."

"What's that mean?"

"It means they're homosexual. And if I were Lucien's sainted mother, I would not approve of the match. Lucien is too young

and brilliant and Arnaud too old and boring. I suppose my problem
with Arnaud began when I started the sweater. Lucien had admired
the pattern of a cardigan of mine, so I said I'd make him one.
When Arnaud heard about it, he stopped emptying my wastebasket. No. There would have been no point in my telling the custodian to be on the lookout for Pudge. Madame S is the only one
he'll listen to, and she wasn't here."

"So we are to attribute to *temperament* the fact that no one at
the musée questioned the identity of the man murdered in the
parc!"

"I suppose. If by 'no one' you mean Arnaud."

"Where was Lucien?"

"On his way home. I gave him a lift to the Madeleine metro."

"Where's home?"

"Bagnolet."

"Does he live by himself?"

"With his sainted mother." She removed the glasses and dropped
them in the bag. Her eyes were green-gold, very large and diamond-
shaped—lioness eyes. There was some smudged mascara on the
lower lashes and a trace of puffiness around the cheekbones. But
even in semi-ruin, she looked magnificent.

"When you came into work on Saturday, was the package still
on your desk?"

"If I'd come in Saturday and found the package still on my
desk, I would've called Pudge or Madame Roget. Or you." She
got up slowly and stood before him, hugging her elbows. "I didn't
come in on Saturday. And I didn't come in on Sunday either."

"Why?"

"I went to the country."

"Where to the country?"

She explained that she'd driven to the village of Conques, four
hundred kilometres south of Paris for a weekend walking trip
through the Department of the Aveyron. She'd planned the trip
over a month ago and had made reservations in Conques at the
Auberge St.-Foy. "You can confirm that," she added.

"Did you go alone?"

"No. Lucien went with me. We drove to Conques Saturday
evening. We spent Sunday and Monday walking and sketching. It

rained Sunday. The inn put up box lunches for us. We didn't see a newspaper or TV or hear a radio."

"You went to the right place if you wanted to be out of touch. When did you get back?"

"About ten last night. At ten o'clock last night I still didn't know Pudge was dead." She turned away and walked slowly toward the street windows.

To keep her in range, Alex put the recorder in his breast pocket and followed. "What about Lucien? Did he come into work Saturday morning?"

"Yes."

"When you drove down to Conques that evening, didn't he mention the murder?"

"No."

"But he must have known about it."

"Not necessarily."

Alex crossed to where she stood at the window. "Madame Gutierrez, the conservator of the Musée Cernuschi worked most of the day Saturday not three hundred metres from where a crime was committed the evening before, and you're telling me he didn't know about it? I find that incredible."

"Do you? The only person who could have told him was Arnaud. And Arnaud was in a snit because of our weekend. You say you find it incredible. But Lucien is incredible! I told you. He's a genius! And like most geniuses, he's totally absorbed in his work. Not absorbed. Obsessed! He cares for nothing else. He lives in a trance. A murder has no meaning for him. A man could be killed in front of him and he'd take no notice . . . unless the man had a cormorant on a string, or carried an armful of peach blossoms. Nothing has meaning for him except his art. I've never known him to read a newspaper or attend the theatre or the cinema."

"But he goes hiking with you?"

She acknowledged this with a perfunctory glance. "Yes. He goes hiking with me. We find leaves and blades of dead grass to sketch or paint. There are bare poplars and linden trees in the Aveyron, trees to look at from a distance, from close up, from different angles, in different light. He sketches them all. He sketched a carp frozen in the ice. That's how Lucien goes hiking with me.

And in the evening we talk about porcelain. We talk about Kaolin, quartz and feldspar and enamels." She faced Alex. "No. At ten o'clock last night I still didn't know Pudge was gone. After I took my bath, I received a phone call from Madame Seńkowska. She'd just returned from a week in London on business." Her voice began to break. "On the flight home, she said an attendant gave her the Monday newspaper . . . and on the front page . . . "

She lost it there. The pale green eyes suddenly filled. The brimming tears refracted particles of morning sunlight like prisms. This shining lasted barely a second. She abruptly turned away from Alex toward the window and stared up the street past the parc entrance.

Anna was sent home. While Varnas finished questioning the two men, Alex spoke with Madame Seńkowska. She confirmed the circumstances of Anna's position at the musée. "Of course," she added, "now that she's become practically indispensable, I'm afraid I'm going to lose her."

"Where is she going?"

"To the States. Flying back with Millicent Wilson at the end of the week."

"That will not be possible," Alex said. While they waited in the reception area for Varnas, he asked her about Anna and Lucien's recent weekend.

Madame made a little tinkling laugh. "But my God, Chef-Inspecteur! They go somewhere every weekend! They're like sisters!"

Alex drove. Varnas gazed through the window and ruminated. "Do you think that because Anna has the small feet, she cannot wear size-ten boot?"

"Doesn't matter. While bigfoot was in the parc, Anna was at the embassy."

They drove down Malesherbes. Varnas's evaluation of Lucien and the custodian, while agreeing in substance with Anna's characterization of them, was more charitable. "I see them like father and son," he said, "or mother and son, if you prefer. I think custodian worries that Anna spoils Lucien, not that she steals him away. Lucien is very delicate. Like androgynous bird. Or neuter bird, if there is such thing. The way he speaks, in alto voice like castrato, you can't believe."

"She says he's a genius."

"Possible. I see some of his brushwork. Very excellent. But he is bizarre, Alex—bundled up like that in wool hat and mittens, indoors. When I talk to him he sits in lotus position, humming oriental tune like Chinese canary." They drove in silence for a while. "One thing occurs to me, Alex."

"What's that?"

"This walking trip in Aveyron."

"What about it?"

"She has reservation at inn since one month. Is it coincidence that reservation is for same weekend Wilson is murdered? Or is it part of plan?"

"What plan? She wasn't in the Aveyron when Wilson was murdered. She was here, in Paris. And she can account for every move she made from Friday evening through Monday night. Plus, she was always with someone, so we don't have to take her word for it."

"I know."

13

Claudine

BACK in the office, Alex stared at the memo on his desk. It read, "Call Claudine. Urgent" and gave the time her message had been received: 10:50—almost exactly the moment Alex found himself responding to the odd charms of Anna Gutierrez. He concluded that Claudine was probably telesthetic. How else explain the timing? Perhaps Anna had caused him unintentionally to give off some sort of rutting signal, some telepathic musk that Claudine's rotating antenna had intercepted and locked on.

Varnas came in with a telex blank. Together they composed an inquiry to the French Consulate in São Paulo requesting information and background on Anneliese Maria Dolores Gutierrez. It was routine. Varnas dropped a pair of Comcentre memos, fresh from the computer room, on the desk and took the telex form down the hall to the teletypist.

Alex glanced at the memos. The first referred to the Zeke McKim transcript of yesterday. The Error box was checked and the memo read: *2nd Lt. W. Thomas Wilson. 13 Wing RFC. Received 1916 flight training Hooten Park, Cheshire (England), not Reading as stated.* Sources for this pressing piece of news were (1) the Imperial War Museum, London, and (2) the London Public Records Office. Alex sighed. Computers were supposed to reduce the paper load.

He turned to the second memo. It referred to a receipted bill to *A. S. Wilson,* submitted by the *Cercle Caribine Sportif,* a gun club outside Paris. The bill was for *Replacement, firing pin, Browning FN automatic pistol* and listed the serial number.

Varnas returned from Telex wearing his overcoat. "If you don't need me, Alex, I go now to Parc Monceau. Cleanup is very slow because of frost, and César says cadets are being harassed by intransigent pigeons. If there is time, I pay social call on Madame Roget." He left.

Alex delayed calling Claudine so he could play back the Anna tape. His rationale for this was that there were details in her testimony he would later have to confirm: the embassy car, the IMF reception, the Auberge St.-Foy in Conques. He started the tape and put his feet on the desk. The thrilling voice had just uttered the words "I am learning the vitreous enamels" when the phone rang. It was Claudine. Reception on her wavelength seemed especially keen today.

"Alex?"

"Hi."

"Alex, I'm desolate! I can't have dinner with you Friday. Max has bought a new two-year-old he wants me to ride at Pau and we have to take the horse down tonight."

Alex tried to sound pleased without sounding relieved. "But that's marvelous! It'll be your first ride as a jock!"

"Yesss," she shrilled and made a little looping cry of anticipation and triumph. "It's finally happened! But Alex, I must see you! There are things we have to discuss. Can you come to lunch! Now? At my place? In half an hour?"

It sounded ominous. Even confrontational. "I'm pretty busy."

"Alex. I won't do my best in Pau if I can't see you before I leave!"

He felt a faint flutter in his stomach as he climbed the stairs to Claudine's tiny fourth-floor flat in the Rue de Navarin. A statement like "there are things we have to discuss" usually meant a quarrel. The last time they quarreled there were recriminations and reproaches followed by denials, tears, reassurances, kisses, and, ultimately prolonged lovemaking. The last time she was all luminous vulnerability. It was July. She was barefoot and softly pliant in a white cotton camisole. He wondered if she didn't precipitate these altercations precisely because she so enjoyed the reconciliations.

He reached the fourth floor slightly out of breath. The apartment door was open. Claudine appeared in faded jeans and paddock boots, smelling of hay and horse manure. He leaned down to kiss her. She averted her lips at the last second, which left her with a small, damp spot on her cheek. She smiled and patted Alex's arm.

"I've got to be back at the barn by two," she said. "How does a glass of blanc de blanc and a spinach omelette sound?"

"Perfect."

Alex hung his coat on the back of the door. She handed him a corkscrew and the wine and went to the stove to pour the eggs. She seemed temperate and easy. He sat at the kitchen table and started to open the wine.

She had just finished making a path of chopped spinach across the plateau of egg in the pan when she said, "Alex, Max has asked me to marry him."

He split the cork. Claudine folded the omelette expertly and slid it onto a serving plate. She divided it and gave Alex the big piece. He poured the wine through a paper napkin to filter out the fragments of cork. "I hope you like your omelette rare," she said after taking a test bite. They sat down.

The ordinary, domestic sound of silverware against plates seemed louder than usual. Claudine put her fork aside. "I'm not in love with him," she said. "He knows that. He also knows about you. And it's a measure of his honesty that it worries him. I told him he needn't worry because, after today, I wouldn't be seeing you again."

As Alex poked at his food, he experienced a tumble of conflicting emotions. He felt relief that the affair was over, annoyance that it had been her decision alone, and, damnably, some slight spark of renewed interest in her now that she was inaccessible again. He saw the white hat and red scarf once more. But he quickly caught himself: May your poor mother die in awful agony, Grismolet, if you interfere with this. "Max is a nice guy," he said, with his mouth half full. "You have a lot in common. You're good friends. That's important. Friendship is a better basis for marriage than most I can think of."

"Yes. So Philippa says."

He stopped chewing. "What?"

"Philippa says that friendship is a better basis for marriage than sex."

He put his fork down. "How did Philippa get into this?"

She shrugged. "She's been in it all along, Alex. Only I, being a little retarded, have taken two years, eight months, and sixteen days—or, specifically, until last Sunday evening—to realize it."

"Claudine, this is a happy occasion. Let's not spoil it by quarreling."

"But I have no quarrel with you, chéri. Everything became clear to me Sunday when I waited for you at the barge with Philippa. I completely understood, for the first time, that there is room on your boat for only one woman. And that woman is Philippa."

He groaned and drained his wineglass. "The boat's her home! She's my child!"

"*Was* your child. Of which I was reminded interminably when she trotted out the photo albums. All six of them! I was able to trace Philippa's development from homeless waif to apple of her papa's eye, from young adolescent at the beach in her first bikini to member of the corps de ballet, to soloist hurtling through the air in a grand jeté. I finally understood why you can't commit yourself emotionally: you're already committed! You've been committed to her from the beginning and will be forever! And now that I know that, I have no quarrel with you, Alex!"

This was an approach she'd never used before. He got up and carefully put his plate and glass in the kitchen sink. "What an absurdly romantic notion!" he said, trying to hang on to his composure.

"Alex, she's in love with you! I think you're in love with her!"

"And I think you're being obscene! Unless this is just a cheap shot at Philippa because you are not sure about Max!"

"Bastard," she said quietly, and went to the door for his coat. She took it off the hook and flung it at him. "Perhaps you will be interested to know that Philippa has applied to the civil court in Douarnenez to discontinue your guardianship. Do you want to know why? I'll tell you why! Because she's of age now and doesn't want you to be her guardian anymore! You've been her guardian for ten years! You've been her father and mother! Next comes lover and husband!"

He walked west. It was colder and the drop in temperature had thinned his anger. He surprised himself by losing his temper. Claudine had triggered a response in him for which he'd been unprepared, although this was not the first time he'd faced the issue of Philippa growing up. In his mind, that had occurred several summers ago when she appeared at the Maison to pick him up before an evening concert they were to attend at the Palais de Chaillot. She had just turned sixteen, and, until that moment, few of his colleagues, except Varnas, had set eyes on her.

She materialized in the open doorway of HQ, silhouetted in the long shadows of the setting sun, lithe, barelegged, wearing a tiny linen sheath and linen pumps, her thick, black hair pouring down her back like an ebony cataract. She hesitated a moment in the doorway, then, scarcely seeming to touch the floor, moved across the room to Reception with that slightly turned-out, extravagantly curved and long-muscled grace that sets the female dancer's fluid movement forever apart from the normal citizen's predictable gait. The Maison took one look and heaved a collective sigh. After that came the badinage, and the clichés.

Alex had no idea how many guardian-ward relationships in history had ended poorly, or, conversely, in a roseate glow bearing the official stamp of happily-ever-after. But the consensus among his associates and friends after that evening favoured the mythic platitude in which the young maid, growing up while everyone's back is turned, undergoes a glorious hormonal metamorphosis that produces not only a creature of rare beauty and lubricity but one who emerges with new and astonished eyes through which she suddenly sees her kindly benefactor as the perfect paramour with whom she will dance down the Champs-Élysées of life, like Gigi.

Alex was embarrassed by this scenario. Indeed, his response to it was that Philippa worked and played within her own peer group, and that when she decided to dance down the boulevard, if she decided, it would be with someone her own age. But even his mother had sounded a warning years earlier. On a blustery fall day very like this, as they were walking home from the courthouse in Douarnenez with the child between them, she turned to him and said, "It is a good thing you are doing, Alexandre. I only hope you have considered all the consequences."

He stopped for a traffic light. The consequences. He thought of the cottage at Plouescat, and the gale, and the damp, salt air, heavy with the odour of kelp. . . .

Philippa

At university, because it was his father's dying wish, Alex concentrated on a course of study prerequisite to a career in marine biology. After graduation—it was the year before he changed his mind and took the Sûreté exam—he worked for a summer as a toxologist in the Department of the Atmosphere, monitoring oil spills in the Bay of Biscay. The Atmos facility was located in the coastal town of Brest on the easternmost tip of Brittany. Nearby, a recreational sailing school called Sails of Finistère was installed with its moorings, docks, and living quarters. The school was known locally as SF. Alex, who'd grown up on this coast, taught there on weekends and in his spare time. It was an interesting and healthy life. The government had given him the use of a Renault 4 cv and a small living allowance that enabled him to rent a cottage on the seacoast near the village of Plouescat.

To this cottage, one late-July afternoon, and quite unannounced, came a pretty, taffy-haired young Englishwoman with a perfect Pears soap complexion. Alex recognized her as a recently enrolled student at SF. He guessed she was a year or two older than he. She had strapped an easel, a box of paints, and a sketch pad to her Kawasaki moped. She spoke no French.

Dressed in a white pleated skirt, light blue tank top, and sandals, she asked Alex if she might set up on his strip of beach and paint the pink granite rocks whilst the tide was out and the shadows long. He lent her a straw hat and an old white shirt. Her fair skin hadn't a good start on the Brittany sun, which, descending in the southwest, was deceptively fierce, even late in the day. The shirt came to her knees.

She finished painting about six and slowly climbed the steep path through the rocks to the terrace in front of the cottage. Twice she stopped to rest and to gaze out on the ocean. Alex had rummaged around in the kitchen and found some tea.

"How lovely," she said softly, removing the shirt and hat, "but I think I'm the only Englishwoman alive who abhors tea. I view it as a kind of punishment." She had to be going. Having said this, however, she made no move to leave. She stood in the middle of the kitchen, gazing out the window. For a moment Alex thought she was going to change her mind and stay. But she sighed and began gathering up her things. He helped strap the easel to the Kawasaki.

"Does the artist exhibit works in progress?"

"Horrors!" She smiled and climbed onto the bike. "Thank you," she said and held out her hand. "My name is Angela."

"Alex." He took the hand. "Please come again."

She did. Every day for a week. She would arrive in the afternoon, after her last sailing class, and stay until just before dark. Quite soon, she discontinued bringing the easel and paints. When Alex returned from work, he'd find her walking the beach or on the shingle or perched on the rock cliff, staring out to sea. Once he found her fast asleep in his bed, her clothes and underwear in a heap on the floor. This, however, was not meant as a seductive gesture. Indeed, at no time did he detect a sign that she was physically attracted to him.

Finally, one evening, when she seemed more reluctant than ever to leave, she gazed out the window as usual and said, "Alex, would you be my protector?"

It sounded interesting. "Protector?"

"Yes. I don't want to stay in town alone. The place is crawling with worthies interested only in plundering my knickers. That's why I fled out here to you. For sanctuary."

"What makes you think I might not be interested in your knickers?"

She turned up her saucer blue eyes for an instant. "Are you?"

He made a stab at looking debonair and succeeded in blushing.

She smiled and moistened her upper lip with the tip of her tongue. "How old are you?"

"Twenty-four."

"Really?" She arched her eyebrows. "If I'd known you were that old I might not have picked you so impulsively. You look a tall twelve." She touched his arm. "Seriously, will you look after me?"

He decided that this would develop into something alluring. He smiled and invited her to move in.

"Thank you," she said. "That will help me keep my promise."

"Promise?"

"My promise to Philippa." She faltered. "Well, not actually to Philippa. I made the promise to myself because of Philippa."

"Who's Philippa?"

"My daughter. She's coming tomorrow."

Straight down the garden path and into the minefield. It had never occurred to him that Angela was married.

"I'm a widow," she replied to his not-asked question. There were other reassurances: Philippa was bright, Philippa was house-broken, Philippa was no trouble.

"What does she eat?"

"Everything."

"Angela, who will take care of her when you're in class and I'm at work?"

"Philippa is used to roughing it," she said rather mysteriously. And inconsistently, Alex thought later, when she described Philippa coming off an elaborate month in the country at the family manse that belonged to Angela's parents, Lord and Lady Watten.

"Are you a Lady, too?"

"Technically."

Alex moved out of the bedroom and set up a cot under the kitchen window.

The next day was Saturday. It poured rain. Angela borrowed the Renault to meet her daughter at the Portsmouth Ferry slip in St.-Malo. Alex offered to drive her. "No," she said, "I want to do this myself. I want her to have my undivided attention for a change. We'll meet you back at the school." She drove off. He put on his oilskins and rode the moped into town.

Because of the weather, the day's water activities were canceled. Toward noon, when it became oppressively hot and the entire SF student body was gathered in the dining hall to watch training films, Angela returned from St.-Malo. Alex's first impression of Philippa, as she entered the hall clinging to her mother's hand, was of an immigrant child. She was dressed in an old-fashioned brown wool jumper that looked like a school uniform. She wore a dirty straw hat with a black grosgrain ribbon and galoshes. Angela caught Alex's eye and waved him over. The child smelt of boiled cabbage.

"She hasn't a stitch of summer clothing, for Christ's sake!" Angela said irritably. "Can you lend me some money?"

He drove them downtown to a popular bazar. Angela bought blue jeans, shorts, T-shirts, a bathing suit, and a pair of sandals. Philippa stood in front of a full-length mirror and gravely studied her new clothes. While Angela was fair-haired and the quintessential English beauty, Philippa was striking in an entirely different way. Her thick black hair had been chopped off more or less peremptorily, but she had lovely slanted blue eyes set over high cheekbones. She had a fuller mouth than her mother and a trail of freckles across the bridge of her nose.

"It's the black Irish," Angela said when Philippa went to the dressing room to change. "Her father was a Derry man." She volunteered no more and Alex didn't ask.

It rained through the weekend. Alex kept to himself to give Angela and the child time to get settled. But he was curious. He couldn't believe that Philippa had come from a month in the country unless she'd spent the entire time indoors. She was pale as opal. And what sort of grandparent would send a child to Brittany in July in a tatty wool uniform with no summer clothes? He found the answer to that question Monday, on his way to work.

Under the front seat of his car, he discovered a large rain-sodden cardboard tag with the twine torn out of it. Printed in English and French across the top were the words CHILD TRAVELING ALONE. Under this, in indelible ink, appeared transport information: Eastern Coach, Bristol Bus, Brittany Ferries, and so forth. At the bottom of the tag appeared "WOLD MANOR, Horncastle, Lincolnshire." Through a friend in the import-export business, Alex learned that Wold Manor was a home for indigent children awaiting adoption. It was administered by the Methodist Church.

So Angela had lied every step of the way, from the moment she appeared on his doorstep with the box of paints right up to the fabrication of Philippa's romp in the country with Lord and Lady whatsis. She was probably broke. And obviously all she wanted from the beginning was a room with a view and a place to park the kid. Still, while it was annoying to be deceived, he had only himself to blame. He had demanded no credentials or declarations of intent. Moreover, the consequences of her lying were likely to be short-lived and only mildly inconvenient since she and her daughter would be gone within ten days when the next crop of students arrived at SF.

So the cottage temporarily became Villa Philippa-by-the-Sea and the three of them some kind of family. Alex decided to disregard Wold Manor for the moment and to give the little girl plenty of space. She was wary of him in the beginning, particularly when Angela suggested she call him "Uncle Alex."

Their nearest neighbor, Madame Arthur, the banker's wife, was predictably scandalized by the living arrangements and did her Christian duty to the community by keeping the cottage and its tenants under constant surveillance through an enormous spyglass that had belonged to her seafaring father.

Weekdays, Alex drove to work very early. Angela, whose first class didn't begin until nine, trouped Philippa into SF on the back of the moped. The child was permitted to sit in on the lecture sessions but had to stay ashore when her mother went off sailing. During these intervals, which sometimes lasted up to six hours, Philippa sat alone on the veranda overlooking the moorings, practiced the two knots she'd learned (reef and bowline), and waited for her mother to come back.

After a few days of watching this, one of the young women employed in the school office came out on the veranda. "Did you bring your lunch, chérie?" she asked Philippa in French.

Philippa, who as yet spoke no French, rose obediently and looked blank.

"Aren't you hungry?" the woman then asked in English.

"No, mum, thank you."

"Would you like something to drink?"

"No, mum, thank you."

The young woman smiled. "Well, perhaps you'd care to come inside and chat with me for a while?"

"No, mum, thank you. I'm to wait 'ere."

The woman went back into the office and called Alex. Which is how Philippa came to experience her first government cafeteria lunch with a choice of three desserts, elsewhere to taste her first cheeseburger and her first langouste. And it was how Alex learned that one didn't ask Philippa if she wanted something (the answer was always "no, thank you") but took her by the hand, an experience that had no precedent for her and for which she had no learned response.

One evening, when Philippa was describing lunch to her mother and everything she'd learned about the periwinkle, Angela yawned and said, "Well, I'm glad you two are getting on so well."

Not long after this, Angela's undivided attention to her daughter began to waiver. She disliked the final phase of the sail training because it took place in the open ocean. The regime was too strenuous and she got seasick. She began to cut classes and sleep late. At the end of one long day spent in bed, she said to Alex, "Why don't you take her with you tomorrow? She can rinse test tubes or something."

They left before six. The lab was relatively inactive, so Alex quit early, packed a picnic, and took Philippa sailing in an old 5.5 metre wooden keelboat that wasn't being used.

Due to some extraordinary combination of circumstances, perception, and natural ability—perhaps her sense of space—Philippa understood the sailing process almost immediately. She responded to the wind as a tangible thing. She held her hands up and touched it. She saw where it came from, where it went, and what it did to the water. There were no shrieks when the wind brought spray aboard, just a sharp intake of breath, a small smile, and a lick to taste the salt.

They sped south across the choppy mouth of the Elorn River, south to the precipitous, Irish-looking cliffs and deep coves near Daoulas.

In the early afternoon, they hove to in the lee of the western peninsula and ate their lunch beneath a swirl of terns diving for theirs.

Downwind, on the way home, Alex poled the jib off to one

side and the mainsail off to the other. He pointed to a landmark ten kilometres away and gave Philippa the helm. He'd already demonstrated how the boat steered.

Philippa stood straight in the cockpit with her little feet wide apart, held the tip of the tiller behind her with both hands as she'd seen Alex do. She gazed up at the great curving wings drawing them along so effortlessly, and said, softly, "Coo, Alex, it's a glorybird!"

They reached the cottage just before sunset, Philippa bursting to describe this latest and best adventure. Angela had left a note: "Gone to the flicks." Philippa frowned. The Kawasaki was still out front. Without a word she walked into the bedroom and opened the plywood cupboard that served as a closet. She glanced briefly at the clothes hanging there, closed the closet, and busied herself straightening up the unmade bed.

Alex had begun rattling pans for supper when a knock came at the door. The neighbor, Madame Arthur, stood on the terrace with a bowl each of white mushrooms and fresh raspberries. "For the little girl," she said solicitously. Alex thanked her. She lowered her voice. "It is not my desire to precipitate an ambuscade," she whispered, "but the child's mother entertained a dark-skinned person for most of the day and then drove off with him in his noisy red roadster. I am as liberal as the next citizen, monsieur, but if I were you I'd fumigate the place!" She raised her eyes to heaven and disappeared.

The "dark-skinned person," Alex knew, was the son of an oil sheik of limitless wealth whose plan was to mount a challenge for the America's Cup in behalf of one of the Arab emirates as soon as he learned to sail. He'd brought his favorite Porsche with him from home.

Supper was sautéed mushrooms, another first for Philippa, followed by raspberries and cream.

At nine o'clock, Alex made hot chocolate and Philippa toasted slices of the morning's bread. When it was time for her bath, she became suddenly shy and declined his offer to help. But she allowed him to tuck her into bed. He felt her eyes examining his face in the dark.

He was in his cot by ten and slept soundly until daybreak, when Madame Arthur's rooster commenced its vocalise and the Porsche skidded to a stop in front of the cottage, its stereo demolishing the morning. Alex jumped up to deal with the noise, but heard a door open and close quickly and the car roar away. Angela, disheveled and wearing an irreducible cocktail dress, wobbled in on high heels. When she saw him she stopped and reached for the back of a chair for support. "What are you waiting up for, then?"

He closed the door to the bedroom. "Tell me about Wold Manor."

She groaned and slid into the chair. "Not now, for Chrissakes." She was quite drunk. She kicked off her shoes. "How did you find out about old Woldy?" Alex was silent. She peered at him unsteadily, trying to focus. "Old Woldy is where you leave your bastard kid when her teenage father runs off and gets himself fucking killed in an IRA roadblock in fucking Auchnacloy. It's where you leave your kid when their Lordshits cut you off without a fucking farthing, and when you finally face it that you're feckless, untrustworthy . . . and a harlot after all. I'm a harlot after all. It's the only work for which I have the slightest aptitude." She closed her eyes and sat still for a long moment. "I tried, Alex," she whispered. "I promised myself that I'd take her out of old Woldy for good this time. But I can't." She raised a hand from her lap and let it fall back. "I can't." She got up and started unsteadily for the bathroom. She opened the bathroom door. "Actually, it's your bloody fault," she said. "You didn't protect me. You protected her." She went in and closed the door behind her. He heard the tub running.

He put the coffee on, washed in the kitchen sink, and changed into a clean shirt. He peeked into the bedroom to see that Philippa was covered. The temperature had dropped. Outside, the sea was gunmetal gray and covered with white horses. The wind had backed into the northeast and the surf made up on the shingle. An early equinoctial gale seemed likely.

He drank his coffee black. It was bitter and he threw half of it out.

After he rinsed the cup and turned off the tap he realized there

were no splashing sounds coming from the bathroom. He knocked
on the door. "Angela?"

"What?" Very faint.

"Don't fall asleep in the tub."

"Nuh."

"I'll open the door a crack."

"You're a fucking prince."

He drove to the lab, determined to get Angela out of the cottage
by evening. He'd already decided to try to find Philippa's grand-
parents. But the gale broke in midmorning. The staff at Atmos
had to stop work and shutter the windows. Afterward, he drove
to SF to help careen the keelboats on land. By noon he was on his
way home.

The coast road, swept by horizontal rain, appeared ominous and
dark, as if an eclipse had taken place. He needed his headlamps.
The little Renault pitched and yawed in the tempest, the wipers
barely able to keep ahead of the torrent savaging the windscreen.

A mile from the cottage, on an upgrade after the final turn in
the road, the car's headlamps picked up a pale and minuscule
movement at the side of the pavement. He stopped. Philippa, white
as a fish fillet, sodden and purple-lipped, stood in the glare of the
lights, semaphoring. He opened the door. She fell across the seat
and clung to him, shivering uncontrollably.

"Alex!" She threw her arms about his neck and pushed her
nose into his cheek.

For a moment he imagined Angela drowned in the tub, or worse,
wrists cut, lying dead in her own blood. He held Philippa tight.
"Where's your mother?"

"Gone for good!"

Don't worry, angel, we'll find her."

"No!" She pulled back. "No! I don't want that!" The eyes
beseeched him in the reflection of the headlamps. "Alex! Please!
Buy me! Keep me!"

He was stunned. "Philippa, listen—"

"Oh, Alex! Please! *Please!* Alex . . . I *love you!*" And thus
relieved for the first time in her short life of the enormous weight
of that declaration, she collapsed, sobbing, in his arms.

He held her and drove one-handed to the cottage. That evening she did not let him out of her sight. Wherever he went, to the stove, to the sink, she clung to his hand or to the back pocket of his trousers or to his shirt.

When bedtime came, she would not leave him. They slept together on the cot. He lay in the early darkness with the sleeping child snuggled against his neck. The gale had blown itself out, leaving the landscape murky and the atmosphere heavy and dripping. Through the barely opened kitchen window, he smelled the damp, salt air, heavy with the odour of kelp. . . .

Place Diaghilev. The back of the opera house, scenery loading dock, main stage entrance. Alex checked his watch. Philippa would be finishing her last class. He had to speak to her. If Claudine was telling the truth, this was not something he could let go. He crossed Boulevard Haussmann and entered the building.

Philippa was nine when he first brought her here to see the Bolshoi. He remembered the evening as a long parade of old Russian war-horses with all the Cossack variations, garlanded peasant dances, and pantomime left intact. But Philippa had sat on the edge of her seat for nearly four hours, transported. When it was over, after the révérences, the curtain calls, and the bouquets of roses, after the chandeliered houselights came in, she turned to him with great awed eyes and said, "That's what I want to do."

Of course, chérie. At her age, Alex had wavering allegiances. He dreamed of being a fireman, a fisherman, or an acrobat. But Old Woldy had discouraged her dreaming. She saw the path to the moonlit stage not as a dream but as a perilous labor. And so she embraced the rigor, the discipline, the competition, even the pain. It brought her her first identity.

Two classes a day, six days a week for four years. At age thirteen, with Alex as her stage mother, she auditioned for the Opéra Ballet School. Her chances of success were one in fifty. She was accepted. The odds were then excellent that she might grow too tall or too fat or watch helplessly as her adolescent body changed into a sofa or a tree or that she'd become discouraged or injured or both. Finally, with sixty girls competing for a single opening in the corps, it seemed beyond expectation that she might be invited to join the company. But on her second attempt, she made it.

He climbed the familiar stairs that led to the rehearsal rooms, his ears assaulted by a dozen disembodied spinto-mezzo-tenor baritones practicing Verdi-Bizet-Mussorgsky-Delibes simultaneously behind closed doors and accompanied by old, hard-hammered pianos. He guessed the company class was in the big studio on three.

The chaos of sound seemed entirely appropriate to his frazzled condition. He stopped on the stairs for a moment and recalled Claudine's angry prediction: "Committed forever, Alex; next comes lover and husband . . ."

He stood motionless between the second and third floors and examined his reluctance to go higher, but at that moment, he was startled by the clatter of footsteps behind him. He turned as Philippa and Jean-Jacques, hand in hand, laughing, raced up the steps two at a time. Another couple followed. They wore muslin rehearsal vests and harem pants over their tights.

"Alex, come watch!" Philippa cried as they fled past. "We're doing 'La Bayadère'! It's hilarious!"

They were gone before he had a chance to reply. The sound of their steps and laughter receded. Alex felt a sudden lightness. The real world had returned. "La Bayadère." Philippa and Jean-Jacques in baggy pants. He turned and slowly trotted down the stairwell, satisfied that Claudine was wrong, that her outburst had been nothing more than the final door slam of a pissed-off Cassandra.

14

Varnas

ALEX had not returned to the Maison when Varnas sat down at his desk at 4 P.M. to write his report.

"Parc cleanup finishes someday but not yet," he wrote.

Heavy vegetation below basin, called "Broccoli" by cadets, discloses secrets reluctantly at extremely low temperature. So far, they fill plastic bags with empty matchboxes, candy wrappers, usual stuff plus very many discarded prophylactic membranes, some in three or more remarkable colours. Does colour make difference, Alex? Frozen cadets excused by two o'clock.

I speak briefly with inspecteur-trainees charged with identifying plaster cast of female boot print at murder site. Paris shoe outlets and department stores do not display unanimity. Opinions range from Papagallo to cowboy boot.

Afterwards, I visit Madame Roget, Andrew Wilson's concierge, with object of learning his daily activities, particularly his walking habits in Parc de Monceau as you request.

When I get to Rue Georges-Berger, she prepares flat for Madame Wilson who arrives tomorrow. She is too busy to see me. I ask if I may return later when she is finished. No. Later she must go for fresh flowers and to walk Étienne. Seeing opportunity, I offer to walk Étienne and get flowers while she cleans Wilson logement, which saves her time and provides me maybe few minutes for chat. She hesitates. But bourgeois pragmatism overcomes peasant suspicion and she agrees.

I take Étienne for what I believe will be extended stroll in parc. I have it in my head that he follows special itinerary from days when he walks with Wilson which may reveal monsieur's preferred promenade. Or maybe he sniffs out vital evidence like Lassie or Rin-Tin-Tin. Not Étienne. When we cross Boulevard de Courcelles and reach parc entrance, he sits down next to sign that says "No dogs in parc."

So, we go instead to Courcelles florist, pick up two dozen chrysanthemums and return to Wilson flat. Let me say that Madame Roget is more relaxed with me now than before. She is not in the mourning but dressed for work in blue cotton smock with hair drawn back in kerchief. Very nice. I don't say we are ready to dance. I don't call her "Clothilde" yet. But we speak easily, possibly because I do not press her and she is occupied with relatively benign task of snipping stems with scissors and arranging flowers in vases. So, like this we chat for nearly one hour. I get some answers to questions you pose to me earlier. More important, I learn we may be seriously mistaken about Wilson's intentions on evening he is shot. But to answer your questions first.

Q: Is Wilson's routine of walking in parc regular enough to be predictable?

A: No. But time of day he walks is predictable: every morning at 8:30 and every evening at 5:30, without fail, for one hour.

Q: Who, besides Madame Roget, knows this?

A: Everyone. Priest and curate from Église Saint-Augustin, grandmammas and grandchildren from neighborhood, Mayor of Eighth Arrondissement, lovers, tradesmen, etc. Professional people know that if they wish to see monsieur between 8:30 and 9:30 A.M. or between 5:30 and 6:30 P.M. they must make appointment with him in parc.

Q: Is it Wilson's habit to detour to basin bridge on his way to Musée Cernuschi?

A: No. Here Madame Roget gives me a look of disbelief. She thinks question absurd. No one, she asserts, goes to musée via basin from here.

But now I intervene. I say we know for fact that monsieur means to go to musée to pick up birthday gift for his wife when he is shot at basin bridge. Madame Roget stops arranging flowers. Very quietly she shakes her head. On afternoon of murder, she says, just after she collects tenant's refuse, she sees normally prompt monsieur leave apartment later than usual. How much later? *Too much later to*

reach musée via basin bridge before musée closes at 6 P.M. Madame
Roget says she does not believe monsieur intends to go to musée
at all Friday evening. Are you listening, Alexei? If this is true, is
crucial.

Look where it leads. Friday evening, later than his usual time—
which is in itself unusual—Wilson leaves Rue Georges-Berger, enters parc at Pavillon de Chartres, and goes directly to basin bridge.
Why? Because someone sets him up.

In premeditated murder, killer does not wish to guess where he
will encounter victim. He wishes to know precisely where he will
strike. So, someone sets up Wilson to be certain he is at prearranged
spot at specific time.

Who does this? Someone he knows and trusts, of course. Someone calls and makes appointment to meet him at basin bridge at,
say, ten minutes before six—or earlier, or later if he likes. No, no—
ten to six is fine. Good. Now with only short distance to go, he
leaves home later than is his custom and arrives at basin bridge at
ten minutes before six, feeling no apprehension but walking deliberately because refreshment kiosk is closed and parc lights seem to
be out. At nine minutes before six he is shot. At six minutes before
six, with Poirier looking on, he is dead. No traces, no gunshot, no
powder burns, few footprints. Very professional.

So, ignoring motive for now, who sets him up? Ignoring motive,
Alex, can be nearly anyone. Can be priest or curate. Anyone from
neighborhood, Mayor of Eighth Arrondissement, any of Wilson's
friends including Zeke or Bollekens or some member of Old Eagles.
Can be someone from W. W. Wilson Company, including Stevenson. Can be Madame Roget herself, or exotic, long-legged Brazilian
bird of rare plumage who recently catches your fancy.

Give this some thought, Alex. If you need me I am at Chez
Suzanne.

Alex returned to the Maison just before dinnertime and picked up
Varnas's report. He left the office and caught the number seven
metro home, hoping to make an early evening of it. On the train
he read the report straight through twice.

In spite of Madame Roget's assertion to the contrary, Alex
couldn't shake his conviction that Wilson intended to go to the

musée. Certainly his prime objective Friday evening was to pick up Millicent's gift and deliver it to Zeke.

But here was a new possibility. If between the time Anna called to tell him the snuff bottle was on her desk, and the time Madame Roget saw him leave his apartment, someone persuaded Wilson to alter his schedule and go directly to the basin bridge, then the Sûreté might be dealing with a conspiracy. And under that circumstance, their chances of success could appreciate in direct proportion to the number of conspirators involved. How many were there? Three? Person unknown to short the lights; person unknown, but known to Wilson, to finger him; and person unknown to pull the trigger.

The train pulled into La Villette. By the time Alex climbed aboard *Le Yacht Club* five minutes later, he'd decided that Varnas's theory, hypothetical as it was, was worth investigating. But tomorrow.

He put his key in the companion hatch lock just as the phone rang below. Thinking it might somehow be Claudine calling from Pau to announce her disengagement to Max, he took his time opening the hatch. But Claudine usually hung up after the third ring. Whoever this was was persistent.

Alex hurried below and picked up the phone. It was Hippo, politely asking if Alex would please be at the Ballistics Lab at 8 P.M.

So much for an early evening.

Chez Suzanne

Varnas finished his cassoulet and, as was the custom at Chez Suzanne, deposited the empty casserole dish in the dumbwaiter. He ordered a nightcap from the barmaid, waited for his change, and returned to his table next to the window and the electric heater.

The table faced front. Varnas sipped his drink and watched the pedestrians passing by, the tops of their heads just visible above the soiled café curtain. This mechanical procession kept him diverted until he noticed a small head with curly red hair slow and stop almost directly in front of him. The head looked up and down the street several times, then turned toward the café. A pair of light blue eyes peered over the curtain and surveyed the interior. Varnas thought the eyes looked familiar but slightly smaller than he remembered them and rather washed out. He realized what caused this. They were devoid of makeup.

The girl was a teenage hooker named Noëlle. Nice girl from Épernay. He'd kept her out of jail once. She beckoned to him to step outside. She knew better than to come into Chez Suzanne. Suzanne allowed pimps, murderers, embezzlers, and kidnappers in her place, but she drew the line at hookers. In fact, Varnas couldn't remember seeing a woman of any description in Chez Suzanne other than Suzanne or the barmaid. He finished his drink, satisfied himself that the propriétaire was in her kitchen, and went outside.

Noëlle was dressed in blue jeans, a down jacket, and running shoes. She looked like a school kid.

"Day off?" inquired Varnas.

She ignored the remark and took his arm, "Buy me a coffee," she said, "and I'll tell you an electrifying story."

They walked to a place in Rue Gabrielle where he bought her a café filtre and a strawberry-meringue tart. She nibbled for a moment. "Word reached me the other night in Rue Bassano that you were inquiring into the health of Simple Simon Dieudonné, the électricien," she murmured casually.

Varnas nodded slightly and purloined a crumb that had detached itself from the tart.

"As my line of work is a little depressed right now, Monsieur Varnas, I hope you will not take it amiss if I try to turn a tiny profit on the information I'm about to unload."

"How tiny a profit?" Varnas asked.

"Let's say a hundred U.S. dollars."

"Let's say three hundred fifty French francs."

She had a crooked smile and a chipped tooth. "Make it five hundred francs and I'll give you the information plus a phone booth special."

Varnas chuckled. "I give you four hundred without special, half in advance."

It was settled. "You're sweet," she said as he slipped the advance onto her lap under the table. "When I grow up I'm going to find a man like you. Not too big, not too handsome. Solid. And sweet. You Polish?"

"No. Tell me now about Simon, please."

"I'm half Polish," she said. She finished her coffee. "Simon was in Paris last week. He was in the Lucky Strip Thursday, with Madeleine. Friday he picked me up in Raspoutine. He actually bought me dinner. I don't get that very often."

"What time?"

"About six."

"And after?"

"Nothing much. We went to my place. He fell asleep during the overture. I gave him almost a discount."

"You are too good," Varnas said. "What then?"

"Saturday morning he walked to the Gare de l'Est and took the TGV to Lyon."

"Lyon? Is that where he lives now?"

"No. He lives in Besançon. He went to Lyon because he's mad for trains and Lyon is where the TGV goes."

"Does he say why he's in Paris?"

"No."

"Where does he live in Besançon?"

"He didn't say. But he runs an appliance repair shop there. He probably lives over or under it."

Varnas grunted. "Maybe." He slipped her the balance of her money plus a hundred francs. "Put bonus away for the rainy day," he said and got up.

"Thanks." She remained seated and lit a cigarette. "I thought Simon was straight these days. Is there a rap?"

"No, no. Nothing. We lose track of him, that's all. We try to update computer archives." He straightened his hat. "See you soon. Keep off street. Go to law school."

He stepped into Rue Gabrielle and hurried to the Abbesses metro. The kiosk clock read nine-thirty. He entered the phone booth, deposited a coin, and dialed the Maison.

César told him that Alex was with the Commissaire and Chef-Inspecteur du Temple at Ballistics.

"Okeh, César, listen. I'm in public phone booth. I wish Alex to call me. Page him at Ballistic Lab and tell him to phone me immediately. I don't move from here." He gave César the number, made him repeat it, and rang off.

Hippo

As was their custom, Hippo and the Commissaire were arguing. Old and devoted friends, they nevertheless made it a point to take opposing views on most subjects. The Value of Speculation, for instance.

Hippo, though he was a scientist with a doctorate in physics, felt that speculation was healthy, stimulating, creative, and nearly always productive. The Commissaire, on the other hand, was typical of most police bureau chiefs answerable to case judges and government ministers. He was interested only in facts, hard evidence, and discernible motives. He would not tolerate guesswork, visceral or otherwise, in any of his staff.

Aware of this doctrinaire inflexibility in his friend, Hippo sometimes deliberately baited him. Tonight, however, the Commissaire was not up to this approach, and, like Alex, he was not thrilled to have been dragged from the warmth of his hearth to the spartan cells of Hippo's Ballistics Lab, deep in the Palais de Justice.

Chef-Inspecteur du Temple, feeling a cold coming on, held a steaming mug of tea laced with brandy in one gloved hand while, with the other, he made energetic passes in the air to emphasize the points he wished to make to the Commissaire. Demonet growled and bristled like an old dog defending his patch of earth and its assortment of already chewed bones.

The quarrel dealt with the effectiveness of silencers on firearms. The Ballistics Chef held that no firearm could be completely silenced. He argued that while the explosive charge within the enclosed magazine of an automatic could be sound-suppressed to a degree with a device similar to an automobile muffler, nothing could silence the crack of a bullet as it left the barrel and traveled through space at a velocity greater than the speed of sound. He insisted that all bullets fired by conventional firearms with conventional powder charges traveled at supersonic speeds and created a sonic report that could not be eliminated.

The Commissaire's argument was simplicity itself: if silencers were ineffective, why the devil were they against the law?

Alex half listened to this exchange. The discursive rumble—
Hippo pastoral, the Commissaire acerbic—reminded him of
Grandfather's tales of old generals more interested in winning the
argument than the war.

The Commissaire was waving his arms. Alex guessed he'd for-
feited a round. "Did you drag me across town in the middle of
the night to deliver a ballistics lecture and to tell me what I already
know?" the Commissaire cried. "I know the blasted Czech automatic isn't the murder weapon!"

"Of course you do, Henri," Hippo replied. "And I did not ask
you here for that purpose, but to suggest that the murder weapon
is not only not the Czech, the murder weapon is not even a firearm."

Demonet's sore jaw hardened and his mouth imploded slightly.
"Not a firearm?" The Commissaire knew he was on Hippo turf
and discussing a Hippo specialty. He made no comment but his
expression was one of stubborn disbelief and warned of counter-
attacks to come.

"When I left 'stanbul," the Chef-Inspecteur continued, "I was
troubled by the contradictory information in your telex to me.
The absence of gunpowder in the wound, for instance, combined
with the fact that no shot was heard. The newspaper reported a
silencer. Since I know that silencers are successful only in gangster
films where the hit man fires blanks, and since there were no
powder traces in wound serology, I concluded that the murder
weapon was not a firearm at all and began, while en route to Paris,
to assemble an alternative weapons profile. What I sought was a
silent, nongunpowder weapon firing a bullet that was greasy enough
and dirty enough to leave traces of silica particles and a petroleum
derivative.

"The only weaponry that conforms to those criteria, Henri, is
one with a fascinating history that emerged in Europe about the
time of Mozart. Incidentally, there are some magnificent examples
in the Royal Danish Arsenal in Copenhagen and the Armory Franz
Josef in Vienna."

The Commissaire groaned and closed his eyes.

"Wakey-wakey!" Hippo admonished. "The weapon that killed
Andrew Wilson was an air gun firing a fifteen-gram, needle-nose
steel pellet."

The Commissaire opened his eyes. "What makes you so damn sure?"

"Process of elimination. Contact wound without powder burn. Clean exit. At air-gun velocity, a projectile lighter than fifteen grams would not have the centimetre-gram force to do the job."

"Hmph. Calibre 6.3?"

"Less. Much less. 6.0. The chief pathologist was good enough to admit that his estimate of 6.3 was made in haste and probably out of prior expectation of a common calibre. When I reached Paris I called him. He met me at the morgue and, together, we measured the wound portal of entry. Absolute accuracy was difficult under the circumstances, but we agreed the projectile diameter would be somewhere between 5.7 and 5.9 millimetres, not a commonplace calibre. Of course, positive ident is impossible without the bullet." He turned to Alex. "Find me a bullet near that calibre and I'll find you the weapon."

Demonet scowled and got up. Unwilling to lose to Hippo for the second time in one evening, he confronted his friend. "Are you quite finished?"

"No," Hippo said. He vouchsafed the Commissaire a twinkle. "I would like to indulge in a little conjecture at this time."

"Oh?" Demonet's slight smile was crooked and edged with danger.

Hippo removed his gloves. "If it can be said that clothing defines the man, then it can be said that the weapon defines the killer. I perceive this murder weapon as not only unconventional but one that suggests a killer of style and intelligence. The choice of weapon is eloquent, Henri. Our man did not chose it haphazardly. He selected his weapon carefully to implement a carefully orchestrated crime."

That was enough for the Commissaire. "Fine! I will now call in a police artist and ask him to create a composite portrait of a killer who has style and intellect to implement a carefully orchestrated crime!" He snapped his fingers under Hippo's nose. "Mud pies! You're making mud pies! Do you seriously expect me to walk up to the Minister of the Interior and announce that some nut killed Wilson with a BB gun?"

"Not a BB gun, Henri. An air gun."

"What's the difference? Farmers use them to control rodents. Game wardens use them to shoot tranquilizer darts at wild animals—including Hippos—before they truck them off to the zoo!"

Alex interrupted. "Commissaire," he said. "It's possible Chef-Inspecteur du Temple is right"—Demonet raised his eyebrows— "that the crime was carefully orchestrated."

"What the devil do you mean by that?"

"This afternoon, Inspecteur Varnas found evidence that suggests Wilson may have been the victim of a conspiracy involving two or more persons."

The Commissaire stepped back and stared at Alex. "Well, why in the name of God didn't you say so earlier?"

"Certain facts remain to be verified, Commissaire."

"I see." Demonet had heard that one before. He gazed suspiciously at Alex. "What evidence has Inspecteur Varnas that suggests a conspiracy?"

Alex braced himself. He had chosen to speak prematurely and would now be forced to elaborate on probabilities and assumptions, a dangerous practice before an intransigent boss. At precisely the moment he opened his mouth to undertake this perilous journey, his beeper went off. The Commissaire directed him to use the phone on Hippo's desk.

Alex spoke to Varnas for less than a minute. "Bless your sweet ass," he whispered before hanging up. He turned to his boss and relayed the information Varnas had obtained from Noëlle.

The Commissaire's response was immediate. He wagged a finger at Hippo. "BB gun, air gun, or water pistol, you trigger-happy acolyte, here's one we can verify!"

Hippo did the Christian thing always. He got out the good glasses and poured Benedictine all around. They drank a toast to Simon the Électricien, wishing him guilt. Alex and Varnas were ordered to Besançon.

15

Millicent

AGENCE-FRANCE PRESSE release for Wednesday morning, 17 November, 1982:

"Millicent Henry Wilson, widow of Andrew Wilson, slain directeur-emeritus of W. W. Wilson and Co., will arrive here today, according to David Stevenson, directeur of the Company's Paris bureau. Madame Wilson, who plans to remain in the city until Sunday, will be met at Charles de Gaulle Airport by Madame Poinsard, the President's wife."

The wire service release was reproduced in most Paris dailies without comment. The tabloid *Le Quotidien*, however, ran the release, printed an early photo of Millicent in a cloche hat, and added its own bit of spice.

> While M. A. Henry achieved prominence as a photojournalist during the war period 1939–45, she had not gone unnoticed in her earlier years.
>
> According to the late American social archivist, Elsa Maxwell, Millicent Henry, born and bred in Washington D.C., had already enjoyed a considerable reputation for brains, beauty and independence by the time she was 19 years old. In 1923, during a dinner party at the White House, she was seated next to President Warren G. Harding, who is alleged to have turned to her and whispered an indiscreet suggestion. Under the circumstances she did not hesitate to empty a pitcher of ice water in his lap before returning to her Consommé Madrilène.
>
> On another occasion, during a costume ball at the old Willard Hotel, she became so annoyed at the antics of Alice Roosevelt Longworth, that she set fire to the hem of that lady's antebellum

hoopskirt and compounded the deed by extinguishing the confla-
gration herself with a fire bucket filled with wet sand. As her husband later said, "She is not to be trifled with."

The islands of Jersey and Guernsey, pale molasses shapes tumbled
from a cookie sheet onto sparkling blue linoleum, slid by under
the starboard wing. The 747 decelerated and started down.

The news of the Arab's arrest had produced an effect on Millicent that was quite opposite to the one she might've expected.
She might've expected to feel relief. After all, the Arab was what
she had hoped for: the author of an unpremeditated, random
crime, unconnected to anything.

But when the New York office called and told her that a Libyan
sailor had confessed to both robbery and murder, she knew in her
heart that it couldn't be true. Her granddaughter, Laura, had had
the same reaction. Laura said, "It's inconceivable that anyone would
shoot Grandy just to rob him. If a man asked Grandy for money,
Grandy would hand it over cheerfully, together with his watch
and overcoat, and then take the man to dinner on his credit card."
Laura was probably right. In all the years that Pudge worked in
New York and Paris, he never turned down a panhandler, never
refused a hitchhiker a lift, day or night, never ignored a drunk
lying in the street, and never regretted any of it. Whoever shot
him shot him because he wanted to kill him. Millicent guessed
she'd known that from the beginning, in spite of her defense to
the contrary with Bollekens. Far from bringing her relief, the news
of the Arab had flushed out her denial and confirmed her fear.

But it was immaterial whether she believed the news about the
Arab. What was material was what the French believed. That
would tell her if they were hot or cold.

The airplane bumped slightly as it encountered traces of tur-
bulence over the Cherbourg Peninsula. France again, to be confronted in solemn circumstance, and alone. Well, not quite alone,
She'd have Anna to lean on. While Zeke and Jan were old and
loyal friends, she couldn't count on their unconditional support.
Jan's devotion to the law precluded his giving a complete endorse-
ment. And Zeke—well, what could you expect of Zeke when you
knew he'd loved Tom almost as much as he loved Pudge?

Anna, like Millicent, was not constrained by juridical principle or by the sentimental intricacies of male bonding. Anna was a friend, a woman friend, something Millicent didn't have too many of. In her phone call yesterday from Paris, wonderfully timed to give maximum support (it had come an hour before Millicent's shaky departure for Kennedy), Anna quite simply offered to put herself and everything she possessed at Millicent's disposal, to become Millicent's handmaiden, her protector, advocate, sister. "My grief does you no good, Mimsy," she said. "But I'm able-bodied, reasonably intelligent, and I love you."

Millicent realized that she could not, as she so often had in the past, wriggle around the gravity of the moment by being naughty or outrageous. Not this time. Anna would make that task easier. Nevertheless, Millicent already regretted an earlier decision to wear blue instead of black, a sartorial whim that would not be lost on the impertinent Paris press waiting for her at the arrival gate. She whispered, "Please God, grant me imperturbability," and glanced out the window at hazy Le Havre, looking like a broken waffle.

The young Air France steward came to her seat in the forward cabin. He announced they would be landing in fifteen minutes and that she'd be disembarked first. He asked for her passport, ticket, and baggage stubs so that the process of customs and immigration could be accomplished for her with the least amount of discomfort and inconvenience. He then stood very straight and dark-eyed and, on behalf of the captain and crew of the aircraft, expressed his profoundest sympathies. This thoughtfulness, not at all in the same league with the awful greeting card condolence, may have been mandated by the Élysée Palace, she knew. Nevertheless, it surprised and touched her and was, she realized later, probably the first of several incidents that led to the eventual demise of her imperturbability.

The plane landed, slowed, turned off, and embarked on what seemed like a tour of the entire airport. It finally stopped. Millicent felt the bump of the access ramp being attached. Seconds later the passenger door opened and Françoise Poinsard appeared, elegant and dignified as ever in a dark Chanel suit (not black, Millicent noted, as if the President's wife had guessed her friend would avoid widow's weeds).

Like the posters of La Liberté, Françoise projected an air of
defiant integrity and seriousness of purpose—she had served alongside her husband in the Résistance—but she also possessed an
unrestrained capacity for joy and affection. She held the normally
reticent Millicent in what seemed like a permanent embrace, until
they were interrupted by a secret-service man. Françoise murmured, "Come on, Mimsy. My troops and I will lead you out of
this mess."

They escorted her up the jetway but, instead of proceeding
directly to the arrival lounge, slipped through a side door used by
service personnel. This led to ground level and a large gray Citroën
limousine with the tricolor flying from its left front fender. This
deliberate diversion, planned by the President's wife, left an angry
press corps waiting at the arrival gate together with the new U.S.
Embassy Protocol Officer on his first assignment, David Stevenson
and his French wife, Jan Bollekens, and a blinking and bewildered
Zeke McKim wearing a tie and holding a bouquet of red, white,
and blue carnations.

Apart from Françoise's occasional instructions to the chauffeur,
the two women remained silent as the limo glided away from the
aérogare. Françoise was a notorious backseat driver and knew
every shortcut in France.

They had just passed Roissy when Millicent spoke up. "I understand that your police have apprehended the perpetrator," she
said, borrowing New York precinct phraseology.

Françoise shrugged. "Yes and no." She turned to Millicent and
spoke with her special, unblinking vitality. "On the one hand, we
have a young man who has confessed to the crime. On the other,
we have his interrogator, a sort of vestige of the bad old days, a
twenty-year veteran accustomed to getting the job done without
too much interference from the Prosecutor's Office. If I am the
suspect, Mimsy, and have familiarized myself with the largesse of
the Western legal system, I will cheerfully confess to anything.
Compared to what will befall me back home if I am deported, I
will view a year or two in the federal penitentiary as a weekend
in the country. Particularly if, at the end of my holiday in jail, I
am rewarded with parole and the opportunity to vanish into the
back alleys of Marseilles, a city with more Arabs than Marrakech."

Millicent looked out the window. So, the French didn't believe the Arab story either. The limo was passing through St. Denis. Off to the right she recognized the Basilica and the Maison of the Légion d'Honneur. "Well, it doesn't matter," she said.

Françoise Poinsard studied the older woman's profile. "What doesn't matter, chérie?"

"It doesn't matter who killed Pudge."

At that moment the limousine entered the short tunnel beneath the Boulevard Périphérique. They had picked up a police escort. For an instant the flashing lights of the escort, reflecting off tile and cement, illuminated the inside of the car. Françoise took her friend's hand.

"But Mimsy." Millicent turned and gazed at the strong hand holding hers. "Of course it matters."

16

Besançon

ALEX packed toilet articles and his miniature cassette recorder into a small duffel. For the first time since the beginning of the Wilson case, he slipped his Walther 6.35 into the side pocket of his corduroy jacket.

Before he left *Le Yacht Club* at 7 A.M., he emptied his change into Philippa's vacation kitty. This was in response to a note left on the refrigerator door in which she complained of his tightwad participation in the funding of their projected trip to Martinique. He counted the money in the brandy snifter—130 francs—and wrote a note on the back of her note: "At this rate, it'll take 2.5 years to reach Forte-de-France. Would you settle instead for a guided tour of the Ministry of Overseas Territories in the Rue Oudinet? I'm off with Varnas to sparkling air of Jura Mts. for couple days. Love you."

He erased "Love" and wrote "Bless," realized she'd notice the erasure, rewrote the entire note, and put back "Love." He then stuck the note under the pink flamingo magnet on the fridge door and went ashore. On the metro his thoughts strayed back to Anna Gutierrez.

Anna, whose alien charm made Claudine's inaccessibility seem almost affable, had re-entered Alex's consciousness this morning and left him wrapped in ambivalent gooseflesh.

He'd gone to sleep last night thinking of Grandfather. As was usual with Alex, light sleep brought on a dream. This time, Grandfather was somehow arguing with Hippo over the relative merits of the spring-loaded versus the reservoir type of air gun. Alex was standing with them in the basin promenade, recently plunged into darkness by Simon's wire-cutting pliers. In the dream, the pliers seemed to glow in the dark from within a sepulchre-like junction box suspended in air over the Pavillon de Chartres. The next moment it was morning and there was Anna in his face, Anna, with her onyx black Chinese haircut and green-gold eyes, Anna, close, looking straight into him, lips slightly parted, saying, "If I'd delivered the gift, that would've saved him."

She smiled then and Alex, sensing something magnificent about to happen, struggled not to wake up. But he did wake up, of course, and she dematerialized. Her presence, insubstantial and illusory as it was, still illicited a memorable response in his seminiferous tubes. He wasn't sure if the sensation was arousal or danger or both. He imagined he smelt jasmine.

These feelings did not entirely subside until he arrived at the Maison and learned, to his disappointment, that there was no reply to his São Paulo telex inquiry about Anna. Instead, there was a perfunctory note from the Commissaire: "Alex. To avoid scrutiny by local police, here or abroad, please maintain low profile. Besançon is small place. Good Luck."

Varnas, up since dawn, had drawn their expense money, procured their agenda, their info pack (including cover ID for a Monsieur Gris and Monsieur Varne, manufacturer's reps of a Belgian chemical supplier to the textile trade), and a city map of Besançon. He had, as well, made photocopies of the slim file on Simon Dieudonné, alias Simple Simon, alias Simon the Électricien. Alex struggled to empty his mind of Anna and to digest these sparse, new details.

DIEUDONNÉ, Simon, born Remiremont, 1920. Entered École Polytechnique, Franche-Comté, 1935. Dropped out June 1937, joined Loyalists, Spanish Civil War. Returned France 1940. Served 1941–45 Forces Françaises de l'Interieur (FFI). Wounded. Captured. Escaped. Decorated 1945 (C de G) Belfort.

"Emigrated Sénégal after war. Returned France 1960. Active Communist Party Politics.

No criminal record prior '65. Arrested four times Dijon, Lille, Colmar, Paris, industrial burglaries. Specialty: demolition, neutralizing alarm systems, etc. No evidence activities politically motivated. Imprisoned Mulhouse 1971, ten-year sentence. Paroled after

six. No subsequent record. Last known address from Fiat truck
registration: 5, Place du Marché, Besançon."

Alex looked at the black-and-white photograph. It was a gentle
face, really, but with the defiant gaze of the anarchist, a thin, bony
face framed by thick gray hair cut short on the sides and brushed
into a sort of coxcomb on top. He had a small, carefully trimmed
goatee and wore oval, metal-rimmed glasses. He looked like Leon
Trotsky.

The old Citroën, freshly washed, waxed, and lubricated, was
delivered from the Transport Pool. Alex drove.

He checked the rearview mirror as they left the city and coaxed
the vintage black sedan onto the Autoroute de Soleil and up to its
unexceptional cruising speed of 81 k.p.h. (50 m.p.h.). Varnas said,
"Time for coffee" and opened the containers of café au lait. He
passed one to Alex and settled into that semi-suspended state that
overtakes one in railroad stations, airport terminals, and at the
beginning of long auto journeys. Anticipating a few hours of
serendipitous reverie, he closed his eyes and allowed his mind to
free-float . . . to a long-ago July in the Lithuanian Baltic town of
Neriga, to window boxes of blue delphiniums, to bowler hats at
Christmas. His woolgathering terminated, however, when Alex
suddenly said, "I have an idea who may have fingered Wilson."

Varnas jumped and nearly spilled his coffee. "Very good, Alexei. Who?"

Alex drove in silence for a moment as if disinclined to continue.
"I think," he began, "that of all the people we know who were
close to Wilson—Bollekens, Zeke, Stevenson, Madame Roget—
the one who could've done it most easily—and it's no fun for me
to say this because I greatly desire to fall on her bones—is Anna
Gutierrez."

"Yes," Varnas said immediately.

Alex glanced at him. "You said 'yes' awfully damn fast."

"Because I agree, Alex. Reason I don't say so before is when I
see flame of passion flicker in your eye I shut up, hoping it will pass.
Now I'm proud of you. Tell me how you reach conclusion it is
Madame Gutierrez."

Alex stared at the road ahead. "I listened to the tape of her testimony and realized that we only have *her* word that Wilson planned to go to the musée to pick up the gift.

"We know she wrapped the snuff bottle and left it on her desk; but we have no proof she told Wilson that. If she had, it seems certain he would've left his flat earlier.

"Suppose, when she phoned him to tell him the bottle was ready, she offered to deliver it to him at the basin bridge? Save him some steps. Meet you there at ten to six, dear Pudge. She then leaves the gift on her desk, says nothing to the custodian because she knows Wilson won't show up at the musée, and goes off to the embassy. Meanwhile, Wilson keeps his appointment at the basin, where the killer is waiting.

"Four days later, she returns from her airtight weekend with the porcelain choirboy and does her interview with me. She tells *me* Wilson intended to pick up the gift at the musée before closing, which I swallow because of the gardener's testimony.

"The plot is pretty cute. She planned it so that only she and Wilson needed to know it."

Alex finished his coffee. "The spoiler to all this, though, is that it completely ignores motive. What possible motive could she've had? And how could anyone so magnificent do such a thing?"

"Alex, no one knows these things. But we got to start somewhere." Varnas finished his coffee and deposited the empty container in the plastic bag hanging from the squelch knob of the defunct police radio. "Cheer up. Maybe when we receive telex from São Paulo confirming Madame Gutierrez's excellent credentials, we find she is beyond reproach."

"That would be nice."

They drove on. Besançon, 370 kilometres to the southeast, was closer to Geneva than to Paris in both distance and style. At Beaune, they left the Autoroute and picked up the eastbound La Comtoise. It was here that Alex felt the mountains for the first time. Though they were obscured by low clouds off to the south, their presence was nevertheless tangible as the altitude increased and the air became saturated with the fragrance of evergreen and the cold, sharp odor of ozone and icy mist from distant flumes and cascades feeding the Doubs, the Rhône, and the Rhine.

At Dole, with forty kilometres to go, Varnas dug out the info pack and agenda. "Logistics engages Renault Le Car for us from local rental agency east of town." Rental of a local vehicle was essential in the circumstances. The Citroën, though unmarked, was a police model and displayed Paris plates. Varnas continued. "Messieurs Gris and Varne are booked into Palais du Jura across from Town Hall. This is appropriate second-class commercial hotel where stays business associates of textile mill, food processing plant, and tool factory. You will be interested to know that Besançon dates from Roman times, becomes part of France in late Renaissance, that University of Besançon is founded in . . ." He looked up. "Why are we stopping?"

Alex had pulled onto the shoulder of the highway. He stopped the car and backed up to where a battered pickup truck was parked. "Saw something," Alex said and got out.

The small truck's carrying capacity had been crudely enlarged by a homemade wooden structure of uprights and lathing lashed to the bed with wire and rope. It listed precariously under a load of household junk. The cab was unoccupied and there was a note on the tattered seat: "Gone for petrol."

Alex pulled up his coat collar and walked to the back of the truck. He reached through the lathing and extracted a dilapidated electric toaster. It was the old, nonautomatic type, with doors stamped out of tin in a rococo pattern. He left fifteen francs on the front seat and returned to the Citroën, where he handed the appliance to Varnas. "It's your mother's. It's the only kind of toaster she likes. She's lost without it. Otherwise you wouldn't be bringing it to Simon for repair."

They reached Besançon a few minutes after 3 P.M., bypassed the center of town, and, after some difficulty, located the car-hire agency. Varnas drove the Le Car. He carefully followed Alex back into town to a municipal parking area where they concealed the Citroën behind some road-repair equipment.

The diminutive buildings and narrow streets of the city seemed constructed of the same gray granite, although the building stone was square-cut while many of the streets were cobbled. An initial impression was of a model medieval fort painted a base coat of gray with other colors to follow. Even the parcometres were gray.

The Palais du Jura, colonnaded in front, towered over its neighbors by several floors. It boasted the best view of the mountains. Alex and Varnas were installed on the top floor, but the mountains remained invisible in the heavy overcast.

"It will snow tonight," the bellman said. "It's already snowing in Bern."

"Is there a telephone directory?" Alex asked as the bellman demonstrated all the faucets in the bathroom.

"In the closet, monsieur." Alex tipped the man and he departed.

They verified Simon's address. He still lived at 5 Place du Marché (near Église de St.-Pierre)—telephone 83.15.32.17.

The city map showed the Place du Marché on the same side of town as the car hire but closer to the river. "It's a cul-de-sac," Alex said, "with the church closing off the end. We'll park a block away and walk."

This was easier said than done. Except for the principal thoroughfares, nearly all the city streets were one-way, a detail not shown on the map. It was almost four-thirty before they found an empty space within walking distance. They fed a coin into the parcometre and set out on foot, Varnas carrying the toaster in the plastic bag that had held the coffee containers. The air was still and cold and an occasional snowflake floated in the lowering twilight.

Rue du Marché was a narrow cobblestone street of modest private dwellings and empty market stalls. It led beneath an arch into the Place, a small square dominated by a plain Romanesque church that stood at the top of a flight of stone steps.

On the left were a bakery, a greengrocer, and a butcher: across the square a dry cleaner, a watch repair, and Simon's small shop.

Alex checked his watch. Ten minutes to five. Simon probably closed at five. But tactical considerations demanded they take the time to do a complete surveillance of the shop exterior before Varnas entered the front door and submitted the toaster. What was in back?

They entered the church. Varnas removed his hat. The church was dark and the interior smelt of burnt candlewax and old book bindings. When Alex's eyes became accustomed to the placid but colorless obscurity, he noticed a transept in the west wall containing a single door. They picked their way through a maze of prayer chairs. The door in the transept opened onto an exterior iron platform from which a flight of iron steps descended into an alley. The alley, wide enough to permit the passage of a single automobile, ran behind the line of shops that included Simon's. Alex noticed a motorcycle parked behind the first shop.

"Wait here," he whispered. He moved quickly down the steps and up the alley. The motorcycle, parked at the rear of the dry cleaner, was half concealed in an indentation in the wall that constituted a small parking place. Alex saw that the other shops were similarly equipped.

He moved further up the alley to the back of Simon's shop. Oil stains on the pavement there were fresh. Simon's truck was out.

There was a window in the back door of the shop. A yellow paper shade covered all but a few centimetres at the bottom of the window. Through this grimy slit, Alex could just make out a light burning inside and, faintly, hear the rasp of a cheap radio playing rock music. He hurried back to Varnas and climbed the iron steps. "He parks the truck in the back. The truck is on the road but someone's in the shop, someone younger than Simon, judging from the music." They reentered the church. "I want you to do your best country avuncular. You're innocent, unmechanical, patient and devoted to your mother. Don't stay in there more than five minutes or I'll come after you. When I see you leave the shop I'll start walking down Rue du Marché toward the car. Be safe."

Varnas, who normally wore his homburg straight, at the diplomat angle, tipped it back slightly to give himself a tentative, sleepy look. Walking flat-footed and carrying the bag to one side as if it contained an alien substance, he slowly approached Simon's shop. A cardboard sign announced the shop was still open. Varnas grasped the bell pull. An electric chime sounded somewhere in the back.

The dimly lit front room was tiny: little more than a foyer with a counter on which rested a small calculator. Behind the counter stood a curtained doorway that probably led to a workshop and living area. From there came the sound of a radio and the smell of vegetable soup, homey touches that contrasted markedly with the temperature of the place. The shop was freezing. Varnas could see his breath.

A pale young woman, wearing a cheap cloth coat with a rabbit-fur collar, appeared. Varnas guessed her to be thirty, perhaps younger. She had the sharp, angular face of a prematurely aged child. Her short, exhausted hair, a sort of brown and too sparse to style, was pinned haphazardly behind her ears.

"Monsieur desires?" she asked softly, holding her coat tightly about her.

Varnas produced the toaster. "It is antique," he said helpfully.

She glanced at it. "Simon's in Valdehon rewiring a cream separator."

Having no idea where Valdehon was, Varnas considered and immediately rejected any thought of trying to intercept Simon outside the shop. "When does he return?"

She shrugged. "It's anyone's guess. Not before we close. Are you in a hurry?"

Varnas explained about his mother. "But," he added, "I like to have estimate before Monsieur Simon starts repair. Maybe I can leave toaster and come back tomorrow."

She nodded, wrote out a ticket, gave him the stub, and attached the other half to the toaster. "We open at eight," she said.

"Thank you, madame," he said, although he had not noticed a wedding ring. She acknowledged this without comment, put the toaster under the counter, and accompanied him to the door. She was barelegged and wore dirty fake-fur slippers. She opened the door and took in the sign.

Varnas smiled and tipped his hat. "Until tomorrow, then."

"Until tomorrow, monsieur." He heard her lock the door behind him.

Dinner at the Palais du Jura was remarkable only for the hour at which it was served. The pale stucco dining room with apricot ceiling lights opened its doors at 5:50 and closed them at 6:50. Alex and Varnas never learned the reason for this.

They sat near the back of the room and surveyed the menu. There were three choices of entrée: ragout of beef, calves liver, and fried smelts.

"How's the chef?" Alex asked the waiter.

"She does her best," the waiter said without emotion.

They ordered soup, bread, salad, and a bottle of ordinaire and were back in their room by 6:30.

Varnas unpacked his woolen pajamas while Alex rang the hotel switchboard and put through a collect call to *Le Yacht Club*. When he was out of town, he made a point of phoning Philippa each evening just before she left for the theatre. He let the phone ring a dozen times. There was no answer. Probably she'd taken a late class or was out with Jean-Jacques. He hung up.

For security reasons, he went down to the lobby to call the Maison from a direct-dial phone box. He left a brief report on the Commissaire's spool then switched back to César to collect his messages. César reported the receipt of the telex Alex had been expecting from Brazil. "I can read it to you if you like," César said.

The tape recorder was upstairs. Alex dug out his notebook. "Okay, César. Give it to me slowly."

César intoned:

"FROM: CONSULAT-GENERAL, SÃO PAULO, 1042, ZULU, 8217 NOVEMBER.

"TO: A. GRISMOLET, CI, OPERATIONS, SN, PARIS.

"SUBJECT: INQUIRY 1232 ZULU, 8216 NOVEMBER ANNELIESE GUTIERREZ.

"BREAK.

"ANNELIESE MARIA DOLORES DE MAYO GUTIERREZ, BORN SÃO PAULO 12-7-49. FATHER: CARLOS FEDERICO DE MAYO, CHAIRMAN/CEO BANCO DO SUL, SÃO PAULO. MOTHER: JUANA FERNANDEZ DE LA CORUÑA, DOCTOR OF OBSTETRIC MEDICINE, HOSPITALIS ST.-BENEDICTUS, SÃO PAULO.

"BREAK.

"BACCALAUREATE 1966, LYCÉE DE LA SALMONIE, MONTREUX. 1970—BA. CUM LAUDE, GEORGETOWN UNIVERSITY, WASHINGTON DC, 1973—MBA UNIVERSITY VIRGINIA, CHARLOTTESVILLE, VA.

"BREAK.

"MARRIED 17-6-78 JÕAPEDRO SANTIAGO GUTIERREZ, CHIEF TRUST OFFICER, BANCO DO SUL, SÃO PAULO. NO ISSUE. SIGNED, G. CASTAIGN, DEPUTY CULTURAL ATTACHÉ.

"BREAK. END."

César continued, "Chef, about an hour after we received the telex, Madame Gutierrez came into the office and asked for you."

"For me?" Alex's mind raced back to his early-morning fantasy. Perhaps Anna was telepathic too. "She asked for me?"

"Yes, sir. She wanted to pick up the note Wilson wrote to his wife."

"Oh."

"The Commissaire authorized the release."

Alex was irritated. He'd missed seeing her again and something on his beat had coalesced in his absence, which made him feel expendable.

"Has anyone spoken to Madame Wilson yet?"

"I don't think so."

"Is that all you have for me?"

César paused. "Euh, Chef-Inspecteur?'"

"What?"

"When I became an inspecteur-trainee, it was my thought that the trainee part would be diversified. As it is, I've been stuck on the Assignment Desk since I passed the exam. I was wondering if my work has been unsatisfactory?"

"On the contrary, César. It's probably been too satisfactory, which is why you're still there."

"Chef. If anything opens up in your department—anything: driver, waterboy, whatever—I'd appreciate it if you'd keep me in mind."

"I'll keep you in mind, César."

"Thanks, Chef."

Alex rang off. He hurried back to the room to show Varnas Anna's unimpeachable credentials. Varnas was asleep.

8 Rue Georges-Berger

Zeke could be obnoxious when thwarted, especially if fueled by a fifth of Old Crow.

He saw himself as Pudge's closest surviving friend, a surrogate figure now, Millicent's strong right arm when she came to Paris. Zeke expected and wanted to be needed.

Instead, he was stood up at the airport. And when everybody finally ended up at the Wilson apartment and Mims asked to see Pudge's letter, it was Stevenson, not Zeke, who called the Sûreté for it, and the damn Brazilian—she seemed to be everywhere at once—who ran over to pick it up before Zeke could find his topcoat. Now the damn Brazilian was taking charge and inviting everybody to supper—the President's wife, the Stevensons, even the concierge. Which put the kibosh on the confidential stuff he and Bollekens wanted to talk over with Mims. It was a certified pain in the ass. He thought he might tie one on. And since Stevenson's wife was eyeing the liquor cabinet, he went into his bartender's routine.

"This saloon is open for business, madame. We got bourbon, scotch, vodka, gin, rum, tequila, cognac, Strega, Kahlua, Applejack, and all the mixers. Name your poison."

Stevenson's wife had a small, private smile on her face, her blink rate was way down and she was weaving slightly. Zeke decided she was loaded. She must've started early, at the airport maybe, unless she packed a flask.

"Tomato juice, please, no ice," Stevenson's wife said demurely.

Zeke grinned. "One Virgin Mary comin' up." He guessed her to be in her middle fifties, although he couldn't always tell with French women, especially when they were plastered.

As he poured, she came closer. "Isn't it exciting?" she said confidentially.

"Beg pardon?"

"About the Arab."

He handed her the tomato juice. "Oh yeah," he said without much enthusiasm, but added, "Yeah, exciting . . . no flies on the security police, that's for sure."

She stood with the glass of tomato juice in her hand, smiling and gazing at Zeke as if she were about to make an important statement. Then, with the ermine coat she came in with still draped over her shoulders, she turned her back on the room and chugalugged the drink with a certain authority. She put down the glass, smiled again, and turned toward the room where her husband was in deep conversation with Millicent.

"Isn't he beautiful!" she exclaimed and stretched out her arms.

Zeke wasn't sure he'd heard. "Beautiful? Who? Mims?"

"No. My David," she said happily and, holding on to the furniture, slowly made her way toward him.

Zeke downed his Old Crow and poured another.

Bollekens was trying to start a fire in the fireplace. A trio of logs hissed and boiled on a flaming bridge of dry shingles. The shingles crackled, making more noise than heat. As he worked, Bollekens decided he would not trouble Millicent with the news that Charlotte may have seen his Wilson file. So far, nothing had come of it. Of the dozen phone calls he'd made to Louvain in the past day, only one had succeeded in reaching Charlotte. The rest had been taken by the practical nurse, who said madame seemed content to sleep. Bollekens was uneasy when Charlotte was this quiet, but he saw no reason to alter the agenda he intended to present to Mimsy. He moved the logs to allow more air to circulate.

Zeke walked unsteadily into the kitchen to see what was cooking. The damn Brazilian had chopped meat, peppers, onions, tomatoes, and garlic chugging away on one burner, black beans on another, yellow rice on a third, and sliced bananas on the side.

"What d'you call this mess?" Zeke asked.

Anna smiled. "Picadinho a Brasileira Frijoles Negros with saffron rice and green bananas sautéed in coconut oil."

Zeke sniffed the preparation. "Don't forget the ketchup."

Neither Madame Poinsard nor the Stevensons could stay for dinner. They said their good-byes in the foyer and departed. That left Madame Roget and Anna.

"When can we lose these two?" Zeke whispered to Millicent. "We got stuff to talk over Mims. Last night, me and Boli decided the time has come to suit up!"

"Really?" Millicent glanced across the room at Bollekens laboring over the fire. "We have nothing to say to each other, McKim, that we haven't said already, or that can't be said in front of Anna or Madame Roget. Jan knows that and so do you." She looked down at his half-empty glass. "And I'd ease up on the kickapoo juice if I were you, before you disgrace us all."

"Too bad you can't have a snort," he muttered. "It might melt that ice-maiden heart."

"I don't need a snort. I'm half in the bag already from standing near you."

Bollekens got the fire started as Madame Roget appeared in the hall. She signaled Millicent. She seemed pale and distracted. Millicent went to her.

"I have set the table in the dining room, madame," she said. "And now I would like your permission to be excused."

"You're not ill, Clothilde?"

"No, madame." She removed her apron. "Just very tired."

"Of course you may be excused. And thank you for everything."

"You are welcome, madame. Please convey my apology to Madame Gutierrez." She nodded and disappeared.

"Prob'ly she don't go for the fried bananas," Zeke said.

"No, that's not it." Millicent went to the piano and fussed with the vase of mums. "She disapproves of me. She believes I should be grieving and acknowledging God's master plan, the one that determines the road we're supposed to follow from birth to death. Clothilde believes there's a time to laugh and a time to cry, a time to live and a time to die. I wish I could believe that. Life would be so much tidier and unsurprising." She moved the vase a few inches. "Actually, I guess I could be a little more charitable under the circumstances. Clothilde was madly in love with Pudge."

Dinner was delicious if a trifle bawdy. Zeke, wanting attention, behaved badly (he asked for two extra helpings of Picadilly à la Brassière). Bollekens, by contrast, was uniformly gracious and complimentary to Anna. However, she demurred when offered an after-dinner aperitif and withdrew with Millicent to the foyer.

"Past my bedtime, darling," she said cheerfully. "But call me if you need anything. And don't forget, tomorrow we have to face the coroner." She waved to Zeke and Bollekens and left.

"I hope you're satisfied," Millicent said to Zeke when she came back into the living room. "I've seen you obstinate before but never revolting."

"Just tryin' to ruffle your feathers a little," he said.

"You put that wet glass down on the piano and you'll ruffle my feathers plenty." She turned to Bollekens. "All right. Let's get this over with. What's on your mind, as if I didn't know?"

"Sit down, Mimsy."

"No thanks."

"As you wish."

They stood in the middle of the living room in an awkward semi-circle. Millicent, outnumbered, warily faced the two older men. She looked combat-ready.

Bollekens cleared his throat. "Mimsy. In the days that have elapsed since we last spoke, I have done as you requested and remained silent."

Zeke nodded. "Me too."

"However, since then, circumstances have changed. It now appears that the police have fallen back on the robbery option, which I view as a tacit admission of failure. I see no other explanation for the Arab affair. For this reason, and for others which I will not go into here, I feel we have arrived at the point where we must act. Consequently, I shall inform the Sûreté that I am in Paris and available to them if needed."

"I see." Millicent raised her chin another notch. She felt anger rising in her throat like a clot. She turned to Zeke. "And what have you to say?"

Zeke scowled and scratched his nose. "I don't like bein' muzzled. I'm used to bein' protected by the First Amendment!"

That was enough for Millicent. "First Amend—!" She made an effort to keep her voice down. "Why you sanctimonious old fraud! You haven't stepped out of your house to vote in a primary or national election in thirty years! Yet you have the temerity to flog me with the First Amendment when you need it! You've lost what little sense you were born with, for God's sake, which wasn't much! You're nothing but a vigilante! Now that you're in Paris where the action is, you can't wait to raise a posse!"

Bollekens came between them. "Please, Mimsy . . ."

She whirled on him. "Don't 'please Mimsy' me! You cloister yourself behind your damn law books and insist that we endanger the public if we remain silent! Sorry, counselor! To me, silence is golden! And this meeting is adjourned!" She pointed to the foyer. "Now please leave."

"Mimsy, I beg of you."

"No! I've heard all I need to hear. It's the old story all over again. Back to the Western Front. Someone killed your pal and now it's an eye for an eye. You imbeciles! You've completely forgotten what vengeance can do to a civilized human being!"

She handed them their coats and opened the door. "Here! Do what you want! But count me out! The war is over! We've collected our wounded and buried our dead!" She closed her eyes. "If there's a time to kill"—she placed her hands over her ears as if to keep out a loud noise—"then there's a time to forgive and forget!"

The two men left without another word. Millicent leaned against the locked door, trembling, her imperturbability scattered. After a moment, she walked into the living room and turned off the lights. The flickering fireplace provided the only illumination. She moved to the windows that fronted on the street and looked down. When she was satisfied that Zeke and Jan were gone, she went to the piano bench, opened it, and took out the manila envelope that Clothilde Roget had brought up earlier.

She examined the London postmark, the canceled English stamps, and, in the upper-left-hand corner, the logogram of *Tarmac,* Great Britain. Turning the envelope over, she saw that the flap was heavily taped.

She took the envelope across the hall to her husband's study, where there was a letter opener. However, she decided the opener wouldn't do the job and walked down the hall to the kitchen, where she sliced open the heavy flap with a butcher's knife.

Returning to the living room, she removed the fire screen from in front of the fireplace, knelt, and withdrew the contents of the envelope. It was a photocopy manuscript of about fifteen pages. She carefully tore it into two-inch strips and fed each strip into the fire. When the manuscript was totally consumed, she split the envelope in half, tore each half into strips, and fed them into the fire as well.

The last strip to curl and burn contained the sketch of the ancient FE-2 biplane in the *Tarmac* logo.

When the envelope was gone, she mixed the ashes of the burnt paper with the wood ashes, replaced the fire screen, and went to bed.

17

Simon

ALEX got up as a church clock struck six. It was still dark. He hadn't slept well. The bed was too short and he was cold and hungry.

Snow had entered the open window and drifted onto the carpet. He cleared off the sill with his bare hand, closed the window, and, wearing only a dance belt and T-shirt, began his ballet exercises.

At some point during a difficult floor combination in which Alex struggled to keep track of his arms and legs, Varnas awoke and beheld the astonishing daybreak spectacle of an oversize Chef-Inspecteur of Police tying himself in knots on the freezing carpet of a provincial hotel room like some Celtic materialization of the mythic, many-limbed Hindu god, Shiva.

They showered, dressed, and went out into the silent, white street. The parcometres wore snow bonnets beside a queue of snug, quilted sedans. A plow rumbled somewhere in the distance. Else-where, a broken tire chain tapped arrhythmically. The snow had stopped.

Alex and Varnas followed directions to a workman's café near the textile mill where they ate a good breakfast and dawdled over third cups of coffee into which Varnas poured thimblesful of schnapps from a small pocket flask.

"Wakes up bladder and steadies nerves," he said.

They returned to the hotel for postprandial meditation and dry socks. Leaving the Le Car secure in its garage, they walked freshly made, narrow-gauge paths eastward to the intersection of Rue du Marché and the larger Avenue du Doubs.

The alley behind Simon's shop, which ran parallel to the Rue du Marché and emptied into the avenue, had not been plowed.

No one was presently at work there with a shovel, nor were there any tire tracks. The neighborhood seemed tranquilized by snow.

At two minutes before eight o'clock, Alex and Varnas separated. Varnas, who disliked guns, went unarmed. "Break leg," he said and headed for the Place du Marché. As Alex moved down the alley to cover the back door, he caught sight of Simon's truck parked against the wall. A few seconds later, the back door of the shop opened and a small, almost wizened man, engulfed in a leather jerkin and wool ski hat, stepped into the alley carrying a dustpan brush. The man noticed Alex and halted. It was Simon all right. The goatee had been shaved off but the round eyeglasses and craggy bones gave him away. With his wiry gray hair jutting randomly from beneath the ski hat, he looked more like a Sherpa guide than a revolutionary.

Alex heard the electric chime ring inside the shop. If Simon heard it he didn't acknowledge it. He turned away and started brushing the snow from the truck's windshield. Alex stopped at the front bumper.

The young woman Varnas had described threw open the back door and bawled, "Simon! Customer!" Then she spotted Alex and froze. "What's going on?"

"Flics," Simon said in a surprisingly low and cultured voice. He continued to brush snow from the truck. "Go upstairs, Marie."

The woman hugged her cloth coat to her body and moaned, "Aiyy, Simon!"

"Upstairs, chérie," he said quietly. "Call Michel and tell him to prepare a writ of habeas corpus."

"You won't need that," Alex said. "We just want to ask you a few questions."

Simon smiled faintly. "That's what the Czarist police told Dostoevsky before they sent him to Camp Evergreen for seven years." He turned to Alex. "I assume you have called the local prosecutor for a warrant?" He didn't wait for an answer. "Never mind. Please come in."

They moved through the back door. Marie vanished up the narrow flight of stairs. Varnas appeared in the curtained doorway that led to the front of the store.

"I apologize for the lack of heat," Simon said. "We can't afford the coal. Please, come into my shop."

His shop was, in fact, the kitchen. Here every available surface except for the tiny stove and a small sink was covered with electrical components, soldering irons, voltmetres, and other test equipment. As Simon cleared off a pair of kitchen chairs, he asked, "To whom do I owe the honour of this visit? Territorial Surveillance? Directorate for External Securité? Préfecture? Sûreté? Interpol?"

Alex showed him his ID.

"Ah. SN. To be sure." Simon drew up a metal work stool and started to sit.

"Permit me," Varnas said. Simon raised his hands cooperatively as Varnas patted his pockets. There was nothing. "Do you have gun, Simon?"

"I've never owned a gun."

"Not even air gun, Simon?"

"No."

"No weapons upstairs with Marie?"

"There's an old bayonet in the hall closet. It's a war souvenir, not a weapon."

"I believe you," Varnas said and nodded to Alex.

Simon sat on his stool, put his feet on the rungs, and took out cigarette paper and tobacco. His hands were rock steady as he started to roll a smoke. Alex and Varnas remained standing.

Alex asked Simon if he'd enjoyed his ride from Paris to Lyon in the Train of Great Velocity. Simon licked the cigarette paper and answered that if he couldn't afford a ton of coal he could hardly afford a seat on the TGV.

"How about a seat at the bar in the Lucky Strip or Raspoutine?"

"No."

"Or dinner for two at Charlot?"

Simon sniffed the unlit cigarette. "Of course not."

Alex glanced at Varnas, who lifted his eyes to the ceiling. Alex asked, "The woman upstairs . . . Marie . . . is she your wife?"

"No. She's my housekeeper and employee."

"You must pay her very generously, Simon. Or else, she's exceptionally loyal to put up with this bitter cold and these poor working conditions."

"She's loyal. And we halve the income from the shop after expenses."

"Very generous. Did you halve with her the income you received to short the junction box in the Parc de Monceau on Friday the twelfth of November at four twenty-two P.M.?"

Simon considered the question soberly while focusing his attention on the cigarette. When he finally responded he barely moved his lips.

"In my heart she is my wife," he whispered. "She is everything to me. And I am reflected in her as I wish to be, not as I am." He slid the cigarette behind his ear. "To her . . . " He searched for the phrase. "To her, I am not the lapsed Marxist you see sitting before you. To her, I am still the bold partisan whose vision of a just society conforms to her simple egalitarian views, and to her perception of the teachings of Christ. I am the good thief, the soldier-priest, the protector of the disenfranchised. Her protector."

Simon looked up at Alex. "So you will understand I had to do something to pay off the filth from Crédit Lyonnais who were going to foreclose on the shop!" He shrugged. "Of course, when I got back to Besançon, I imagined I saw flics everywhere: across the street, in every shop window, in the pissoir. I suppose that's only natural for an ex-con who has been clean for years and decides to do one more little job."

He glanced at Varnas. "Then, last night, after I examined the toaster of the mama of this monsieur, I realized something was coming down. The toaster, which he characterized as 'antique,' is the electrical equivalent of the Bic ballpoint. It is made in great quantity in the People's Republic of China and is readily available everywhere in France for less than thirty francs.

Moreover, when I plugged it in, it worked perfectly. So, naturally I smelt police. One never forgets the scent of stupidity."

Simon said this with such warmth and with such a total lack of malice that Alex was momentarily diverted. He imagined that, given different circumstances, he and Simon would be friends.

"When I realized you were actually on my doorstep," the électricien went on, "I became calm, the way one does before a great battle." He sounded like Grandfather. Soldier echoes. Different war, same echoes. "Of course I said nothing to Marie. I was now able to think rationally, not emotionally. I said to myself, 'Simon, the flics are here. You have three options.' " Here he chose to interrupt himself. He plucked the freshly rolled cigarette from behind his ear and began a prolonged search through his pockets for a match. Varnas, who himself did not smoke but carried an old Ronson as an ingratiating tool of interrogation, gave him a light. Simon's first puff reduced the loosely packed cigarette to nearly half its original length. He left the smoldering butt between his lips, got to his feet, and began to pace.

"Three options, Simon," he repeated quickly. "One, you can run. Two, you can give yourself up and cooperate. Or three, you can give yourself up and tell them to fuck off.

"The easiest option was to run. I could pack my tools, my equipment, and my Marie in the truck and, with the help of the snowstorm, get lost in the mountains. I know intimately the mountains, and the mountain people know me on both sides of the border. We could hide there forever. But I rejected the idea. It was absurd to abandon the shop after we risked everything to save it. Most important, to run did not conform to Marie's image of me."

He puffed, inhaled, and butted the remains of the cigarette with his fingers. "The second option was to give myself up and cooperate: to sing, to betray old alliances, to enjoy an uneasy freedom at the expense of honour. I rejected also this option not only because of the dishonour, but because the life of an informer is never secure, and because it too did not conform to Marie's image of me.

"The third was the most difficult: to give myself up to you and not to cooperate. Very difficult. With this option, I lose the shop. But not really, because I leave it for Marie. I lose Marie. But not really, because I am safe in her heart. I lose my liberty. But not really, because I retain my self-respect. Therefore, because it is my wish to die with my reputation intact, it is this option I chose, monsieur, the one that best conforms to Marie's image of me!"

Alex applauded. "Bravo, Simon! Now, let me ask you. Does it

conform to Marie's image of you that you engaged a teenage tart
while you were in Paris to satisfy the urgency of your . . . ah . . .
contemptible flesh?"

Simon snapped the cigarette butt into the kitchen sink. "Please!
I view the urgency of my contemptible flesh as I view hunger and
thirst! As an appetite! It has nothing to do with honour or self-
respect!"

"Will Marie see it that way?"

Simon lowered his voice and wagged his thumb at Alex. "If
you tell Marie about the tart, she will not understand you! In her
piety, she has no comprehension of the erotic drives that possess
men like you and me! She is totally ignorant of our search for
physical gratification! She is a virgin! She is pure and good! Like
a postulant nun! If you speak of these things, she will not understand you! Do you follow my meaning? Or is your flesh immaculate!"

Varnas cleared his throat. "Let's ask Marie to come down."

"By all means," Simon responded righteously. "I have nothing
to hide!"

They called her. She came in, frightened, hugging her coat to
her as always. Her bare knees were blue with the cold. She sat in
the kitchen chair Varnas arranged for her. Simon rolled another
cigarette, placed it between her lips, and sat next to her in the
other chair, his arm around her. Varnas lit her cigarette. She took
a few little puffs without inhaling. Her hand shook.

Alex explained to Marie that while Simon would be routinely
charged with vandalism and the destruction of public property,
his principal crime was that of being an accessory before the fact
in a premeditated murder.

Simon squeezed Marie's shoulder. "They won't prove that,
chérie," he said. Marie shivered.

Alex added, "I think mademoiselle should also know that, if
you chose to go to prison, you'll be over seventy years old by the
time you're eligible for parole."

Simon took his arm from Marie and leaned forward. "You are
frightening her," he said. "I forbid you to engage in this tactic of
intimidation."

Marie whispered, "Aiyyy, Simon," and leaned against him.

"Talk to me," Simon said. "Not to her." He hugged her. "It's all right, angel."

Alex shrugged. "I'm finished. I have nothing more to say." He looked over at Varnas. "Do you have anything to say?"

Varnas slipped his pocket watch from his waistcoat and glanced at it. "I say is getting late."

Alex turned back to Simon and waited. Simon left his arm around Marie. A snowplow went by in the square. They listened to it backing and filling.

"Come on, Simon," Alex said quietly. "Decide. Now. The longer you wait, the less you have to offer the prosecutor." Simon was silent. "You can go back to Mulhouse and weave pot holders for fifteen years, or you can tell me who hired you to short the lights and go free with a suspended sentence."

Simon peered up at Alex through his little round glasses. He smiled. "Go free? That's a laugh." Traces of the old anarchist reappeared around his eyes. "Informers are never free," he said. "I have experience with informers. During the war we called them collaborateurs. We cut out their tongues and nailed them to the bulletin board in front of the mayor's residence."

Marie began to whimper. Simon pulled her close and kissed her. "She's young yet," he said simply. "She can sell the shop. She will make a new life for herself." He kissed her again and got up. "And now, flic, this is for you." He spat symbolically on the floor in front of Alex. "I've never collaborated in my life and I'm not starting now!"

"As you wish," Alex said. He nodded to Varnas and turned away.

Varnas gazed sympathetically from Marie to Simon and back to Marie. She was trembling. He took a pair of handcuffs from his overcoat pocket, unlocked them, and faced Simon. "Simon Dieudonné," he said, "in the name of . . . " He got no further. Marie shrieked and fell to her knees.

"Aiyyyyyy, Simon!" She clung to his legs. "No, no, no, no!" she cried. "I do not permit it! He picked me off the street when I was fifteen! I owe my life to this wonderful man!"

"Marie! Marie!" Simon lifted her to her feet.

She faced Alex and Varnas. "No, no, no, no! I do not permit it! You have not my permission! If you take him, I kill myself!"

"Shit!" Simon said and began to cry.

The rest was on tape. Simon never knew who hired him.

A letter had come to his shop in mid-September:

> Simon: Lo-risk junkbox jump, Paris, November.
> Reply by 1 Oct. to Brunete, Bureau de Poste,
> Gen'l Delivery, 75005, Paris.

"Who's Brunete?" Alex asked.

"No one. Pseudonym. Brunete was the scene of a battle in the Spanish war."

"Go on."

Pressed by the threat of foreclosure on his shop, Simon accepted the offer, on condition that the money be sent in four equal installments payable to Marie's account in the Banque de Jura, Besançon. He specified the dates.

The terms were agreeable. The date for the jump was set for 11 November at 4:20 P.M., Pavillon de Chartres, Boulevard de Courcelles, Eighth.

Then on 10 November, one day before the scheduled jump, Simon described a phone call he'd received at approximately 8 A.M.

"Simon?"

"Who speaks?"

"Brunete. There's a change. Put the roast in on the twelfth instead of the eleventh."

"Same time?"

"That's exact. Is it agreeable?"

"Yes. It's better actually."

"Until later then?"

"Until later." They rang off.

Alex asked Simon if he'd recognized the voice. He hadn't.

"Was it a man?"

"A man, yes. Well spoken, no special accent."

"Where did he call from?"

"I don't know."

"This call came at eight A.M. on the tenth of November?"

"Yes."

"To this number?"

"Yes."

While Varnas took care of the hotel bill, Alex phoned Paris from the coin box and spoke to Commissaire Demonet. He ordered a Poste Télégraph-Téléphone tracer on all calls made to Simon's shop on the morning of 10 November. He also asked the Commissaire to arrange, through the Ministry of the Interior, to keep Simon and Marie under continuous protective surveillance until further notice.

Returning to Paris by late afternoon, Alex and Varnas encountered a Maison in some disarray.

David Stevenson had called to say that Millicent Wilson expected all documents and items removed from her flat by the police returned before her departure for the U.S. An hour later, Comcentre reported that the Random Access Memory (RAM) linked to the Primary Central Processor, known as Big Louie, had suffered a partial meltdown. More than half the encoded data in the Wilson case had been erased, including civil dossiers, transcripts of interrogations, memos, and encoded correspondence. The Commissaire and the Directeur of Comcentre were not speaking.

It would be days before Big Louie could be renourished. In the meantime, data would have to be served up by hand. While this seemed a great inconvenience to some, it hardly bothered Varnas. He never liked computers. He wasn't entirely comfortable with tape recorders or calculators either. He trusted paper and pencil and his memory. And the copier, when it worked. At least with the copier he could see with his own eyes what was going on.

He met this emergency in his own way. Since it was now academic whether all the material from the Wilson flat had been encoded on computer tape, Varnas dug out the handwritten list of everything he'd catalogued at 8 Rue Georges-Berger and carried it down to File. With the object of duplicating or making a memo of each item scheduled to be returned to Millicent Wilson, he requisitioned two unassigned inspecteur-trainees and pointed them at the Toshiba. "You have twenty-four hours," he said. "Two copies of everything."

It had been a long day. He trudged back upstairs to check in with Alex before retiring for the evening to Chez Suzanne. He looked forward to a few tumblers of vodka and Suzanne's unsurpassed Thursday special, the Blanquette de Veau. As he entered the tiny office, he encountered Alex standing in front of his desk with the phone pressed to his ear. Something about Alex's expression stopped Varnas in the doorway.

Alex said, "Yes," and then, "Yes, Joseph," listened for a moment, and asked, "Is there anyone there with you? What about the custodian? All right, Joseph, we'll be there in five minutes."

Alex hung up the phone and peered at Varnas. "It's Poirier, the gardener, calling from Musée Cernuschi. He's found something in the parc."

18

The Gardener

POIRIER had used his police line pass only once, and that was on the day it was issued. Since then, because of a new assignment, he'd been too busy to visit the parc. The chief nurseryman had put him to work in the mist house, rooting black willows for eventual transfer to the Île de la Cité.

Not that Poirier was concerned about his young arborvitae. He was satisfied that he'd insulated them against the cold. And as it was unlikely they would contract a disease this late in the season, he felt the only problem that could conceivably spoil an otherwise perfect performance might be one of insufficient nutrition.

He left Neuilly a little after five and drove to the parc. Leaving the truck inside the Ferdousi gate, he took his electric torch and trowel and made for the northwest end of the basin.

The twenty-odd young trees there seemed robust enough. The mulch and burlap were in place; he saw no evidence of damage or undernourishment. After a brief inspection of each tree, he left them and crossed the promenade that led to the stone bridge. The trees in this area had been mound-planted on the moist, north bank of the basin. He took out his flashlight and closely inspected bark and scale leaves. These seemed as alert as the others, but because they were slightly less mature and planted in relatively moist soil, he decided to return at the end of the week to stake some of the smaller ones.

He returned to the basin promenade and crossed the bridge to inspect the three trees below the basin.

He started with the two smaller specimens just off the prom, where he'd found the old man. Both were healthy and strong with typical, densely packed scale leaves that felt to the touch like fresh, rough-cut tobacco. After a few minutes' examination, he turned his attention to the single tree to the north.

Poirier allowed his gaze to linger on the classic lines of this individual. It was taller than the others, with a much more elaborate brachial system. The bark was more developed and the young tree already pumped out a wonderfully heady juniper fragrance. He moved up and felt the bark. It was sharp and scaly, as it should be. He reached up to the crown of the tree and gently rubbed one of the prickly leaves between his fingers. Here he paused. The leaf crumbled. He stared in disbelief, first at the dry fragments in his hand, then at the crown, where, with the help of his torch, he saw that the growth ends had turned brown and brittle. Methodically, he tested the vegetation below the crown. It was healthy. But the compressed scale leaves on the three crown branches above were dying. Were dead. This had never happened to Poirier.

He ran his hand down the branches to the trunk. No puncture, no leakage, no injury to the brachia. He fell to his knees and inspected the upper trunk down to the top of the burlap. It was sound.

He placed the torch on the ground to illuminate his work and carefully examined the burlap. What he saw then—saw and felt— made his heart move in his chest. The bottom third of the burlap wrapping was dark with fluid. Not animal fluid. Conifer fluid. Resin sap. The tree was hemorrhaging. He smelt turpentine.

Painstakingly, as if he were removing an errant tourniquet, he unwrapped the burlap. He laid the cloth aside and gazed at the base of the tree. There, just above ground level, in the exact center of the trunk, he saw a split. It extended into the mulch and oozed nutrients.

He touched the sticky wound and felt something like pain in his wrist. Endeavoring to remain calm, he rummaged through his experience for some hopeful prognosis. Perhaps the split was an accident to the phloem, localized and repairable, a superficial tear caused by a suppressed butt or a tuber that had escaped his notice. But this logic dissolved when he took his trowel and dug away the mulch and mound earth at the base of the young tree. The deeper he dug, the wider the split became. Then the blade of his trowel struck metal.

Poirier sat back on his heels. The singular sound and feel of this homely garden tool striking solid metal was alien to him. He was not able to connect the event to his experience.

He troweled the soil away from the trunk and directed the beam of his torch into the hole. There at the bottom of the shallow dig, no more than eight centimetres below the surface, he made out the faint gleam of a slender, blue steel shaft, no larger than a lead pencil, buried in the heart of the tree.

Poirier was dumbfounded. How had this happened? Who would do such a thing to a tree? Who indeed? His gardener's blinkered view prevented him from imagining that the tree might have been an innocent bystander instead of a target. The parc murder never crossed his mind. He didn't consider the possibility that the implement presently killing his tree had already engaged in earlier, dirtier business. Didn't consider it, that is, until he thought to remove the steel shaft from the trunk. As he reached into the hole, some memory jog, linked to the site and the circumstance, ignited a flash of recognition that returned him, with perfect clarity, to the night of the murder when he'd phoned the police from the Musée Cernuschi, when the police had said, "Touch nothing."

Poirier withdrew his hand. The consequences of the situation slowly became clearer to him. He began to feel light-headed and euphoric. He even experienced a moment of slight spatial disorientation, enough so that he had to place a knuckle on the turf for balance. His heart began to hammer.

All at once and unexpectedly, he saw that his life and career had been brought into intense focus by a series of fortuitous choices and accidents. Of all the tree men in the parc system, it was he who had been selected for Monceau, he who on his own initiative had chosen to winterize the trees on that fateful night, and was now the proprietor of vital information known to no one else in the world. He staggered under the weight of this knowledge.

He switched off the light and stuffed it in a pocket. In the semidark, he refilled the hole with earth, rearranged the mulch at the base of the tree, and got to his feet. Deliberately, like a man who saves string, he folded the burlap, picked up his trowel, and headed toward the Musée Cernuschi. He looked at his watch. Ten minutes until closing. He took his time crossing the turf. When he reached the lower promenade, he began to run.

Conventional police wisdom prescribes total crime laboratory participation whenever important physical evidence turns up. However, before Alex finished his phone conversation with the gardener, it was clear to him that the object Poirier described was not to be treated conventionally.

Since it was primarily a ballistics matter, Alex made the unilateral decision to process this new evidence through Hippo only. Later, if necessary, he would submit it privately to the forensic pathologist, Doctor Lupi. Both men could be counted on to keep the matter confidential. Moreover, by restricting participation to them he guaranteed that there would be no security leaks into the chatty corridors of the Palais de Justice, where the assigned press corps assembled daily to flatter and cajole young crime lab techniciens longing to read about themselves in the morning papers.

Alex's decision was sanctioned by the Commissaire, who, on his way to the Ministry, asked merely to be kept informed. Varnas made it unanimous.

All was quiet then when they met Poirier at the basin promenade. Alex's plan was to remove the evidence and take it to Hippo. The ballistics chef was at home nursing a head cold lately contracted in the city morgue. However, before Alex could remove evidence from the murder site, procedure required that he perform the work customarily assigned to Photolab, that of providing the prosecutor's office with measurements, diagrams, and photographic documentation in situ. He and Varnas spent an hour at this, calculating line of fire and trajectory and photographing the embedded projectile.

When the moment came to remove the shaft, Poirier politely refused to allow Alex to touch his tree. Using a small wooden wedge and mallet, the gardener slightly opened the split in the trunk, loosening the shaft. Two more gentle taps of the mallet, and the shaft dropped, untouched, into Alex's white cotton glove.

The slim, needle-nosed projectile was heavier than Alex expected. And it possessed that spare, functional lethality peculiar to instruments purposefully designed for killing, like the guillotine.

It was missile shaped, round in section forward but fluted from amidships aft to the tail, forming integral fins, possibly to enhance stability in flight.

He wrapped the shaft in a length of gauze and handed it to Varnas. "I have no idea what it is. Maybe Hippo will know. Let's go."

Varnas bagged it and carried it with the camera equipment to the Citroën. Alex went to the gardener and shook his hand.

"Will you be able to save the tree?"

The gardener shrugged. "With intensive care, maybe. The shaft didn't go all the way through."

"Well, bravo, Joseph," Alex said softly. "Please understand that this information must be kept in strict confidence. That is why I am obliged to praise you in a whisper."

Poirier saluted. "You can count on me, Chef."

"Good night, Joseph."

"Good night, Chef."

Hippo

Hippo had recently moved. He moved every ten years or so, or when the storage needs of the European Society of Antique Weaponry demanded it. Each move took him farther from the centre of Paris.

He'd always lived in a former something: a former police annex, a former gymnasium, a former firehouse. He now lived in Aubervilliers in a former discotheque whose owner was in jail for extortion. The place was huge and boasted an octophonic, multiple-track stereo system. It is said that, when the volume of this electronic marvel was turned up, the concussion from Fender bass and synthesizer stunned fish in the Canal de St.-Denis. When he became familiar with the control panel, Hippo turned it down and played tapes of fifteenth-century motets by Orlando de Lasso.

Though it had masses of space, the glitzy, chrome-and-plastic nightclub, with its slightly cobwebbed cerise walls and black, starry ceiling designed to simulate the night sky over Antibes in July, quickly became what Hippo's former homes had all become: a dump, a storehouse, a repository of antique arms bibliography— hundreds of books, periodicals, references, catalogues, drawings, posters, models, paintings, prints, and engineering drawings, all placed in unmarked piles on cocktail tables, bar, bandstand, and Eames-inspired contour chairs. Though Hippo knew precisely which pile contained what, he'd acquired a personal computer with the view to sorting out this mess someday. However, the P.C. was still in its original carton on the floor next to a Mongol siege gun, circa 200 B.C.

His living quarters were in the building's second-largest room, the former Powder Room. Here, in keeping with Hippo's meticulous persona, chaos ceased. All was serene, even cloistered. The pink walls were covered with reproductions of his favorite Impressionists. The six toilet stalls at the end of the room, decorated with soft-porn, purple-phallused satyrs, were concealed behind a pair of standing walnut bookcases containing his mother's uncut, leatherbound editions of the Great French Classics.

He'd transformed the full-length, mirrored vanity with its rows of bright, theatrical makeup lights into a work space. Hippo could make his home anywhere, and he was at home here. And here, in dressing gown and woolly slippers, he received Alex and Varnas.

"Where is your distinguished employer?" Hippo asked as he hung their outer garments in a cubicle formerly occupied by the ladies' room attendant.

"At the Ministry of the Interior," Alex replied, "bringing the Minister the news of Simon and hoping it will serve as an antidote to the news of the computer breakdown. Big Louie suffered a mild stroke this afternoon and is temporarily recognition-impaired."

Hippo placed the velvet-lined, mahogany box that contained his calipers, micrometer, watchmaker's loupe, and beam balance on the vanity. He opened the box and drew on a pair of cotton gloves. "It's not like Henri," he said rather mysteriously, "to pass up a ballistics analysis for a half-block ride to the Ministry in his new Simca." He then turned to Varnas and beamed. "Well, Inspecteur, let's see if the pearl is real or paste!"

Varnas deposited the small gauze packet on the vanity and unwrapped it. The shaft lay on the pallet of cloth, coldly gleaming under the bright makeup lights.

Hippo placed his watchmaker's glass in his eye and leaned forward. He breathed rheumily through his nose as he pored closely over the entire length of the blue steel projectile. "Sweet Mother," he whispered faintly. "It's a World War One aerial dart!"

Alex thought he felt a draft on his neck. He imagined Grandfather standing beside him.

Hippo picked up the dart and examined it in more detail. "The French name for this was *fléchette,* the German, *fliegerpfeile.* He turned it over several times. "Both the Allies and the Central Powers used them early in the Great War. This one is German." He returned the dart to the cloth and his jeweler's loupe to its box. "Nasty business," he said and picked up his outside caliper.

"What," Alex asked, "is an aerial dart?"

Hippo adjusted the caliper to the dart's length. "There were thousands, possibly millions of them in 1914–15, Alex. They were history's first air-to-ground missile; quite clumsy really, but effective enough before the invention of the aerial bomb. Dropped from slow-moving aeroplanes in clusters, they were usually targeted on unsuspecting troops in trenches or on soldiers bivouacked in the open, or on columns of horse cavalry not yet accustomed to attack from the air. They were released from sufficient altitude to achieve a velocity of two hundred metres per second by the time they reached the ground, quite enough to go completely through the body of a horse or a steel helmet." Hippo fine-tuned the caliper with its thumbscrew, noted the result on the calibrated scale, and marked the dimension in his notebook. "Survivors say that one moment you'd be sitting in the sun, vaguely aware of an aeroplane droning about, next you'd hear the approach of furiously swarming insects, and next, the screams of dying men and horses." Hippo put back the caliper and took up his micrometer. "If the notion of an aerial dart seems rude or medieval to you, you must remember that the military mind at that time was fixed in the technology of the Franco-Prussian War of 1871, a war of lances and sabres, cannon and grape.

Hippo fell silent and held his breath as he adjusted the micrometer to the width of the dart's rounded section. This was the critical measurement of calibre. When he was satisfied, he exhaled and entered the dimension in his notebook.

Working deliberately, he removed the micrometer and placed the dart on his beam balance ("Delicate enough to weigh a butterfly's wing, Alex"). After making a few adjustments, he entered a third figure in his notebook, returned the dart to its cloth pallet, and slid the notebook along the vanity to Alex.

Length: 12 cm.
Calibre: 5.87 mm.
Weight: 20 grams

Only when he saw that Alex had digested the dimensions did he vouchsafe a small twinkle of satisfaction. "The beast is heavier than I supposed. But its calibre is within our estimate of the wound portal of entry. Unless your trajectory calculations tell me the dart was not intended for Monsieur Wilson, I will start looking for a smooth bore, spring-loaded air gun of 5.90 millimetres."

Alex tapped the notebook with his forefinger. "Then it's possible to barrel-launch an aerial dart like this?"

"Certainly."

"But how can a mass of metal that depends on gravity for its velocity get up enough speed to kill a man when fired from a rudimentary weapon like an air gun?"

"My dear Alex, today's air guns shoot field pellets at over two hundred fifty metres per second."

"But this isn't a pellet. This is a piece of steel that weighs twenty grams."

Hippo smiled. "In the Armory Franz Josef the First, in Vienna, there is a Turkish air gun with a leather reservoir that was built in 1790. It shot a bullet twice the calibre of this dart and half again its weight and was capable of killing a soldier at a distance of two football fields. Does that answer your question?"

Alex studied the dart for a moment. He said, "If the Commissaire were here, I would not ask this question." He turned toward the older man. "Do you believe in ghosts?"

"Spectral or spiritual? I can make do with the Holy Ghost."

"When I was a kid, my grandfather was my close friend. He was a veteran of 1914. Since I've been on this case, I've had more vivid recollections of him, waking and sleeping, than at any time since the day he died. I've actually felt his presence. I attribute this to the proximity of ghosts. I feel them hovering." Hippo frowned. "I expect Wilson's letter to his wife first stirred them up for me when he described the Armistice Day thing at the Étoile, that anachronistic memorial to the obsolete virtues of innocence, honour and gallantry, celebrated by a handful of ancient former schoolboys. They're still astonished to be alive, those old men. They're almost ghosts themselves.

"But is was Zeke who stirred up Grandfather's ghost. Now Grandfather is after me, trying to get my attention, exhorting me with his old battle cries of Sedan, Alsace-Lorraine, and Glory! He never believed the war ended, Grandfather didn't. He believed it was always there, just beneath the surface like some monstrous numen, crouching and waiting to strike. He wouldn't have been the least surprised at this new material evidence. Because it links Wilson's death to the Great War."

Hippo's pious face turned skeptical. "I do not wish to appear insensitive," he said, "but I suggest you are suffering from either indigestion or nostalgia. Surely you don't attach any significance to the fact that the dart is German and that Wilson is American!" He paused. "Or do you?"

"Yes."

"That's gummy thinking, Alex. The presence of the aerial dart does not, per se, link Wilsons' death to the Great War. As I said before, there were millions manufactured on both sides. So many, in fact, that during the thirties, they were sold as souvenirs. You could pick up one in any flea market, brand-new, still in its paper tube. No, it's not the fact of the aerial dart that is unique. What is unique is that it was used in a role for which it was not intended, to be fired from a weapon. When we locate the weapon, you can consider the possibilities of a World War One link, if there is one."

"I feel ghosts, Hippo."

"Your distinguished employer would say that you were making mud pies. Much as I admire your intuitive powers, you cannot measure ghosts, Alex, nor submit them to analysis by that richest jewel in the forensic crown, the gas chromatograph mass spectrometre."

Alex was silent.

"Somewhere there exists an air gun, spring-loaded, calibre 5.90, give or take a hundredth, that was custom-designed to fire this dart because—and this is opinion—the projectile possessed the avoirdupois, stability, and penetrating characteristics to do the job, not because of some spectral, metaphoric connection to an old war. I'm reasonably certain the weapon is one of a kind. The calibre is unusual. And since the few custom gunsmiths left in the world would fit comfortably into this room, it shouldn't be difficult to trace.

"I will contact my spies at the Armory Franz Josef in Vienna and the Royal Danish Arsenal in Copenhagen. I will play a little Scarlatti on my stereo, look at some Monet trees and Renoir flowers, allow my mind to free-float and go into my research trance. Isn't it exciting, Alex and Varnas?" He smiled seraphically and raised a diminutive forefinger. "Once more unto the breach, dear friends. So to speak."

Part Three
SCHUMACHER

19

The Maison

ALEX, who had slept poorly Wednesday night in Besançon, slept
not at all Thursday. Indeed, he'd not been home yet. After leaving
Hippo's disco, he dropped Varnas at Chez Suzanne for the long-
awaited Blanquette de Veau, and drove the Citroën to Vincennes,
where Emilio Lupi, the forensic pathologist, conducted his private
practice. There, with the hollow-eyed but willing doctor, he spent
the night performing a chemical analysis of the fléchette. While the
process was less accurate than the gas chromatograph, it nevertheless detected the minute particles of Wilson's blood and tissue
necessary to incriminate the dart beyond question.

He returned to the Maison through a thin, gray morning light
that seemed to transform the city into a steel engraving. The cold
air only partially refreshed him. He typed up his report, placed it
with the dart and photos in the Commissaire's safe, and started
back to his office with the hope that he might steal away to *Le
Yacht Club* for a few hours' sleep. Instead he encountered a rumpled young inspecteur-trainee arranging stacks of folders on Varnas's unoccupied desk. The I-T explained that the documents on
the desk were photocopies and that the documents in the cartons
on the floor were originals.

"Originals of what?" Alex asked.

"Stuff from the Wilson flat. Inspecteur Varnas ordered everything
copied. He gave us twenty-four hours. We did it in thirteen."

"What's your name?"

"Biramoule, sir."

"You new?"

"No sir. This is my third week."

Alex nodded. "Okay, Biramoule." He gave the youngster a

handful of francs. "Get coffee for yourself and your partner and, while you're at it, bring two au lait for Varnas and me."

"Thanks, sir." The boy left.

Alex peered at the cartons on the floor, news clippings, correspondence, business reports, periodicals, manuscripts, and lists; the departmentalized refuse of the fastidious. On top of one carton, he spotted the elaborate blue, white, and red cover of the Élysée Palace Armistice program. It bore the Great Seal of the President and was elegantly decorated in a raised enameled pattern of wisteria and anemones. It looked like the cover of a Belle Epoque jewelry box. He picked it up and carried it to his desk. He turned to the first page and read the stylish calligraphy:

Élysée Palace, Paris, 11 November, 1982
Reception to Honour World War I Aces of All Nations

—ANDREW SPENCER WILSON—

The President of France
Requests the Favour of Your Company
At an Assemblage of Eagles
To Revere the Memory of Fallen Comrades
1914–1918
1939–1945

On the next page, engraved in gold,

Benediction
Victor Yves Boissière
Archbishop of Paris

Dedication
General Christophe du Moulin de Ribemont
Commander, Army of the Air

Salutation
Armand Francis Poinsard
President of the République of France

Prayer for Peace
Heinrich Oswald Husseren
Archbishop of Cologne

Toast
Captaine Jules Marie Poinsard, L d'H, C de G (4p), MM

. . . the President's ninety-two-year-old father.

On the succeeding pages, presented alphabetically by nationality, appeared the list of aces, each with two photographs next to his name, the one taken recently and the other taken when the ace was a young eagle.

There were three Austro-Hungarians, two Belgians, six Canadians, four English, three Germans, one Italian, and six Americans.

Alex stared at the photographs. Apart from the odd lantern-jaw of hawk-nose facial eccentricity that could not be erased by age, he saw little connection between the swank young faces of 1918 and their benighted, fossilized remains. Painstakingly, using his forefinger, Alex picked his way down the photographs, looking for . . . what? For a face that bore the mark of Cain? Was one of these ghosts a killer? But they were all killers. Or once were. Like Grandfather.

The phone rang. It startled him. Gooseflesh. The Commissaire had arrived. He dropped the program into its carton and moved slowly down the hall to his boss's paneled office.

Demonet back at his desk. Jaw back to normal. Puffing contentedly on his office pipe, a colossal meerschaum carved to represent Joan of Arc in full armour. The Commissaire studying the aerial dart lying on its pallet before him. He glanced up. "Any prints on this thing?"

"Leather gloves."

The Commissaire nodded and tossed Alex's report into his file box. He took a final puff on the meerschaum, and got to his feet. "Can you rely on the gardener?"

"Poirier's an old soldier," Alex replied. "And he wants to keep his wounded tree a secret from the parc superintendents."

The Commissaire smiled faintly. "Damn good!" he said. "Puzzling, but damn good. However, I will keep the news from the Minister until we see where it leads Hippo. In the meantime . . ."

The Commissaire walked to his worktable and snapped on a fluorescent light. A large detailed map of Paris's Fifteenth Arrondissement lay on the table. The light flickered, imparting a slight stroboscopic effect. Alex blinked and stared hard to stay awake.

He heard his boss say, "We traced a call from Paris to Simon's shop on the morning of ten November." He placed a finger on the map. "The call was made at one minute past eight from this public box near the Centre Sportif in the Square Albert-Bartholomé." He tapped the spot, which he'd marked with an x.

The Commissaire placed an acetate sheet over the map. The transparency contained a colour-coded, scale printout of the electrical grid, the sewer system, and the gas main routes of the Fifteenth. He pointed to a spot near the x. "Here's your inspection hole, Alex. Put a tent around it and park the Gaz de France caravan alongside. It's exactly across the street from the phone box. I'll take care of the permits. Meanwhile, put together your work crew and two shifts of inspecteur-trainees and techniciens to handle the sound and video equipment. I want that box kept under twenty-four-hour surveillance."

Alex focused on the map. The phone booth was tucked into a tiny corner of the physical education complex on the extreme southwest edge of Paris. Very remote but very visible.

Whoever called Simon had elected not to make his call from a safe, low-profile phone, the sort that might be found in a busy part of the city, a railroad station, for example. It followed, then, that this phone was probably one of many widely scattered instruments he'd chosen for his clandestine purpose. The question was, would he use it again? Tomorrow? Next year?

Alex arranged to transfer César from the Assignment Desk to Operations. César would be fitted with a yellow Gaz de France hard hat and be sent into the field for the first time as an audio-video technicien's assistant assigned to a remote phone tap.

Varnas came in at 9 A.M. Alex left the rest of the stakeout details to him and went home to get some sleep.

Le Yacht Club

Judging from the angle of the boarding plank, the barge was floating a little higher than usual. Maybe the lockmaster upstream had allowed a few extra litres of water into the canal.

Alex went aboard. A hand-printed sign was duct-taped to the aft companion hatch. "Wet varnish below. Enter forward." He moved up the deck and stumbled over the shore power line and phone cable. Someone had moved them from their accustomed place to an alternate fixture. He opened the forehatch and carefully descended the narrow companion ladder into the unfinished storage locker. It was hot below and the rich smell of tung varnish hung in the air. He walked aft. Philippa, wearing jeans and one of his old denim work shirts, stood on a box varnishing the mahogany trim of the skylight.

She looked up. "Shit," she said softly. "I meant to have this done before you got back. Welcome home, chéri. I'll be finished in a minute."

Alex looked around. She'd sanded and varnished almost the entire saloon deck. It was an enormous job for one person. "Did you do this all by yourself?"

"Sure."

"What's the occasion?"

"I cannot tell a lie. I invited my railroad workers here for their aerobic workout because the room in the union hall was being used for a meeting. Some of my girls are a little heavy in the hoof. But the deck needed varnishing anyway."

"What's wrong with the skylight?"

"Nothing. I had some varnish left and didn't want to pour it back in the can." She finished a last brush stroke and turned to him. "I'm glad you're back." She smiled. "Have you seen last night's paper?"

"No."

"It's on your bunk." She jumped off the box, kissed him on the cheek, and herded him into his cabin. A copy of *Paris Soir* was open with an item circled. He read:

Pau, 17 November. The industrialist Maxim Globus today announced his betrothal to the equestrienne Claudine Dominique Joubert of Paris. The June wedding will take place at the Globus estate in Funchal, Madeira.

Alex, struggling again to keep his eyes open, gazed heavily at the newspaper, then at Philippa. "I knew about the wedding," he said. "I'm glad about the wedding. But there's something Claudine told me about you that bothers me." Philippa returned his gaze. "Claudine told me you applied to the civil court in Douarnenez to discontinue my guardianship.

Philippa frowned. "I told Claudine that, according to the law, your guardianship ended in May, on my eighteenth birthday. Which it did."

"I thought it was twenty-one."

"Eighteen."

"And that's all you told her?"

"That's all."

Alex rubbed his eyes. "She said you no longer saw me as your parent."

"My parent?" Her eyes sparkled. "Alex, I chose you. Don't you remember? I never saw you as my parent. I saw you as my prince."

He lay back on his bunk, yawned, and closed his eyes. "What," he whispered, "are the duties of a prince these days?"

"First, to stay awake while I tell you." No response. "Alex?"

"Phnf . . ."

She touched the tip of his nose with the wet varnish brush. "To be my champion."

After a moment she covered him with the bunk spread and tiptoed back into the saloon.

Alex remained in a dead and dreamless sleep until exactly 3:15 in the afternoon, when something woke him. The something that woke him was that he knew the phone was about to ring. He sat up. The phone rang. It was Hippo.

"Alex. Can you come to the Bibliothèque Nationale right away? I've found the murder weapon."

"In the bibliothèque?"

"No. In a book. I'm in the Contemporary Catalogues and Manuals section on the first floor. Please hurry!"

20

The Rügen Castle Collection

ALEX reached the mammoth national library building in ten minutes and found the ballistics chef-inspecteur in a poorly ventilated room about the size of a cafeteria. It was filled with quotidien freeloaders, some reading, some just in from the cold. Hippo, tucked away in a dusty alcove at the far end of the room, was bent over a battered wooden table reading a catalogue, his pastoral head silhouetted in the pale glare of an institutional lamp with a green shade. The room vibrated with crowded silence. Only the attendant's voice could be heard, occasionally directing a patron toward the stack displaying his or her chosen obsession, *Apse* through *Zodiac*.

As Alex approached, Hippo looked up furtively. He was flushed and bright-eyed. His features were wreathed in little conspiratorial tics and smiles. In a continuous legato gesture, he touched his forefinger to his lips, pointed to a chair opposite, and slid the manual he'd been reading across the table to Alex.

"Read this," he whispered. "I'm off to the water to relieve myself."

Alex sat down. The book was a catalogue published by the Sotheby Parke Bernet Auction Gallery, London. It described an auction that had taken place there on 6 May, 1982—over six months previously—at which the $3.5 million Rügen Castle Collection of Arms and Armour was dispersed. An historical note characterized the collection as the finest in private hands to reach the market since World War II.

Assembled over many decades by the late Gustav Wilhelm von Niess, Graf Rügen, at his ancestral home on the east German Baltic island from which the title derives, the collection narrowly avoided capture by advancing Soviet forces in 1945. Thanks to prompt action by the Graf's son, Oskar von Niess, a convoy of wood-burning lorries was hastily assembled and the collection transported westward across the Elbe to the Hanseatic city of Lübeck only hours ahead of the enemy. The collection remained there in storage until the late seventies when it was purchased by Sotheby.

The catalogue, prepared by the auction-house staff with the assistance of the present Graf, listed over four hundred pieces. Included were ten suits of armour, numerous medieval swords, breastplates, battle axes, and helmets—several decorated with ornate panels of cloisonné enamel—a fifteenth-century matchlock musket, seventeenth- to nineteenth-century rifles, pistols, conventional daggers, and a rare seventeenth-century dagger-pistol that contained a cunningly concealed, breech-loading wheel-lock firearm.

Concealed weaponry remained a lifelong fascination for the Graf, a fascination that led to a collection of canes and cane weapons. While not all antique, the cane weapons were listed. They included a rare nineteenth-century stiletto swagger stick of ivory and gold, several rapier and sabre canes, and an unusual pair of modern ebony, bamboo, and silver walking sticks manufactured in 1937 by the London canemakers Swithen, Ordney, Bispham Ltd. One of the walking sticks was conventional, while the other concealed a barrel-cocking smoothbore, spring-loaded air-gun mechanism, of 5.91 millimetres.

Alex read no further. He looked up as Hippo returned. "A cane gun?"

Hippo nodded. "A Hapsburg toy!" He leaned across the table. "Alex, I wanted you to see the catalogue with your own eyes so you'd be able to defend yourself against your distinguished employer when he starts shouting 'mud pies.'" Someone shushed Hippo from the next table. He continued in a whisper.

"I wish I could say that the idea of the auction catalogue came to me in the middle of a felicitous Scarlatti duo. It didn't. It came from Vienna. Of course, I've been aware of the Rügen collection for years, but it took my curator friend at the Armory Franz Josef to apprise me of the air gun. The moment I mentioned the calibre of the dart, he made the connection to Sotheby. In fact, Armory

Franz Josef intended to bid on the walking sticks by phone until Sotheby confirmed that the bidding would start at seven thousand U.S., a bit dear for a state armory. Sotheby confirmed something else, Alex. Included in the sale but unlisted was a velvet-lined cherrywood and ivory box containing four matched steel darts."

Alex copied the auction date into his notebook together with the walking stick lot number and other pertinent information. They left the catalogue at the book drop, descended the broad marble staircase to the ground floor, and emerged into the chilly Rue des Petits-Champs.

Hippo double-wrapped his scarf around his neck. "As far as I'm concerned," he said, "the catalogue confirms the identity of the murder weapon. What now remains to be confirmed is the identity of the buyer. I will leave that task in your very capable hands." With that he nodded and trudged off in the direction of the Palais Royal metro.

Sotheby Parke Bernet, London, paradigm of discriminating acquisition and profitable disposal, were politely evasive when Alex called to enlist their help in tracing the cane gun. Their position was that unless a piece had historical significance or unusual resale value, a Rembrandt, for instance, it was frequently forgotten when gone.

The explanation sounded windy. But Alex showed forbearance. He rather liked the English, in spite of an enduring family legend that his great-great-great uncle had drowned at Trafalgar. When he explained the circumstances, the Sotheby man, an enthusiastic reader of P. D. James and Jonathan Gash, was quick to oblige.

After some delay to assemble the file, he established that the ebony/bamboo walking-stick lot was purchased by an anonymous buyer through the London office of Crédit Suisse. The bid had been accepted upon receipt of $15,000 U.S. cabled the same day from Zürich, together with a signed assent agreement binding the buyer's bid and indemnifying the gallery.

"Swiss funds?"

"Yes."

Dead end. A Swiss banker would sooner fling himself off the Matterhorn than divulge the name of a depositor, even if the depositor proved to be a terrorist. The fact of the Swiss bank account added new scope to the investigation, but Alex now experienced an early misgiving about tracing the buyer from this angle. "Who signed the agreement?"

"A representative of Crédit Suisse."

"Name?"

"Does it matter? Crédit Suisse will not identify the buyer."

The Sotheby man made a small, well-bred noise. "Chief-Inspector, buyer anonymity is not unusual in the antiques business." He paused. "May I make a suggestion?"

"Please."

"In my opinion there are two courses open to you. If time is not a factor, you can attempt to obtain the cooperation of Crédit Suisse through political channels . . . or you can contact Oskar von Niess."

"Von Niess?"

"The present Count Rügen. It was he who got the arms collection out of the east ahead of the Soviets, before they turned his father's castle into a fish processing plant. He helped prepare the catalogue. He knows every piece in the collection. He followed some of the bidding. If there is anyone who can help you it is he."

Alex thanked the Sotheby man and rang off. At that moment Varnas walked into the office.

"Do you eat yet, Alexei?"

It was nearly six o'clock. Alex was starved.

They spent an hour in an omelette place. Over the remains of a baguette and a bottle of Chenin Blanc, Alex brought Varnas up to date on the arms collection and Oskar von Niess, Count Rügen.

"Very good," Varnas said. "We go now to research."

They walked back to the Maison. Tucked away in the research reference room, they found a copy of the Almanach de Gotha, the genealogical bible of the noble families of Europe. Alex carried the volume into the office and looked up the von Niess lineage. It filled a whole column.

Varnas grunted. "Probably my ancestors fight some von Niesses when Lithuanians come to Tannenberg in fifteenth century and kick shit out of Teutonic Knights."

Oskar von Niess was listed as an architect living in Lübeck.

Varnas went to the teleflex phone. "I never speak to Count before. I tighten lips little bit to sound a high German."

Lübeck information had no residential phone number for von Niess, Oskar, but his studio was listed. It was after eight o'clock (after nine in Lübeck). It seemed unlikely that anyone would be working at this hour on a Friday night. Except possibly a count.

Varnas dialed. A cheerful bass voice answered, "von Niess." Varnas apologized for the lateness of the hour. He identified himself as an officer of French Customs and Immigration inquiring into the whereabouts of a cane gun from the Rügen Castle collection sold by Sotheby Parke Bernet in May to an anonymous buyer believed to be a French citizen who failed to file a C&I declaration for the weapon.

From across the desk, Alex heard the Count's surprised response. But he discerned no hesitancy or suspicion in the man's voice. On the contrary, von Niess seemed cordial and cooperative. And he was long-winded. The conversation rumbled on for several minutes, Varnas scribbling an occasional note on the back of an envelope. When it was over he tossed the envelope on Alex's desk.

"Nice man. He tells me his life story if I give him time. He knows walking sticks very well."

"Does he know where they are?"

"No. But he thinks that if anyone knows, it is his papa's gunsmith from Rügen Castle old days. Gunsmith makes barrel-cocking mechanism for cane gun. Also helps save collection from Bolsheviks.

"Gunsmith? Why would the gunsmith know?"

"Count says gunsmiths and armourers are artists, like painters and sculptors. They work with their hearts as well as hands and always seem to know where their babies are."

Alex glanced at the back of the envelope and read, *Andreas Blücher, Flugzeug und Waffen Museum am Alten Norddeutschen Flugfeld, Axtedtstrasse 11, Osterholz-Scharmbeck (Bremen).* "Translation, please."

Varnas turned the envelope around. "Gunsmith is Andreas Blücher. Address, Aircraft and Weapons Museum at Old North German Aerodrome in Osterholz-Scharmbeck, near Bremen. I have also phone number. Graf says Blücher is seventy-five now, stays always a little homesick but works well as weapons curator at museum. Graf says he still receives Advent calendar from Blücher every year, same as when he was a little boy in Rügen."

Alex picked up the envelope. "They always know where their babies are." He glanced skeptically at the name and address. "Are you saying that if this gunsmith knows where his baby is, he knows who the murderer is?"

"I don't say nothing."

21

Porte de Clichy

ANDREW WILSON'S body was not released by the Paris coroner until evening. Cremation took place later at the mortuary near the Cimetière des Batignolles.

Millicent, her imperturbability down another notch, left the operational details to Anna. Outside the mortuary, she sat in the dark in the backseat of her hermetically sealed rented limo, vaguely aware of its yellow parking lights flashing on and off like a buoy guarding a wreck.

While she waited for Anna to emerge from the shadowy brick and limestone gothic-style chapel with the chimney in the back, she occasionally glanced down at the invoices in her lap and reflected on the fragility of human existence. What a crock it all was, she thought. You subscribe to the illusion that things will last forever, and end up with a shaky collection of memories and a lapful of bills.

Inside the mortuary, Anna stood on a deep, pile carpet in the pale reflection of blue, yellow, and red stained-glass windows, indirectly lit from the outside by tiny electric bulbs. The athletic young mortician, appropriately clad in black with a dazzling white shirt and gray silk tie, smiled and handed her a leather-bound volume the size of a dictionary. Since Pudge's ashes were to be buried in the family plot in Watch Hill, a suitable container for his mortal remains had to be selected from this catalogue of caskets and urns and the other paraphernalia of eternity. As she turned the glossy, full-color pages, it occurred to her that the funeral business was probably more profitable than banking and a lot steadier.

The choices of urn were: bronze (2660 fr.), mahogany (for the mantel, 2520 fr.), concrete (700 fr.), and gold (14000 fr.).

"Does anyone go for the gold?" she asked.

"To be sure, madame."

"But why? What possible difference could it make?"

"To the bereaved for whom expense is not an obstacle, the gold represents a significant and reassuring alternative." He broadened his smile. "Like driving a Lamborghini instead of a Ford."

She chose the bronze.

Hôtel Fleury

Though they were guests on the same floor of the hotel, Bollekens and Zeke saw little of each other in the days following their confrontation with Millicent.

Zeke, stung by her attack, responded indignantly the same evening by reciting to himself a litany of stereotypical indictments against every tight-assed, ball-breaking, liberated bitch alive, including where the hell she could shove it. But his fury was cut short, first by a monumental hangover, and afterward, by remorse. Zeke reckoned that, except for the war, he'd never lost a friend. Since it was pretty late in the day to start now, he scared up a pint of Kentucky Pride (to give him perspective) and called Millicent to apologize.

She asked, "When are you going back to Misquamicut?"

"When the do-re-mi runs out."

"How about helping me fly Pudge home on Sunday?"

He was so delighted to be needed again that he went to the Galerie Lafayette and bought a dark blue suit.

Bollekens, dining alone in his rooms, recalled a discussion he'd had with Millicent years before in which she declared herself quite incapable of bias.

In fact, Bollekens knew she was entirely capable of bias against anyone who didn't agree with her on such fundamental issues as gun control, the clear-cutting of timber, tea with lemon, capital punishment, and the sacrosanctity of individual rights over the needs of society.

Although Bollekens never wavered in his view that compelling

public interest outweighed Millicent's right to privacy, he nevertheless decided on a strategic withdrawal to the damask perimeter
of his small suite at the Hôtel Fleury for the time being. With
Charlotte still comatose and unpredictable, he concluded that it
would be prudent to wait until circumstances prescribed a clearer
course of action in the matter of the Wilson case, or until the police
called him in. Both events came to pass sooner than expected, and
simultaneously.

22

Meudon

SATURDAY, a northeast wind, blowing *Le Yacht Club* off the quay and thrumming her spring lines, woke Alex before dawn. He got up noiselessly so as not to wake Philippa. Out of habit, he padded into her cabin to make sure she was covered. He performed this ritual, as he had for ten years, for his own comfort and security. He did not see it as an act of love. It was an instinct, an extension of the living process, like breathing.

He skipped his exercises, showered, dressed warmly, removed the Wet Varnish sign from the companion hatch, and went ashore to reach the Pâtisserie Mariette in time for early croissants.

He tucked a couple of the hot pastries inside his down jacket and trotted the five kilometres to the Maison through a damp, low-pressure atmosphere that smelt alternately of rain, winter earth, and sea. As he jogged, he thought about the gunsmith, Andreas Blücher, asleep somewhere four-hundred kilos to windward.

Blücher sounded like a loyal family retainer who'd found a pasture of refuge for his old age, a place in which he could ruminate and indulge his metier while supplementing a meagre pension. If, as suggested by the Graf, Blücher knew where the cane gun was, it did not necessarily follow that he knew who the murderer was or, indeed, that the weapon was used to commit a crime. If that was a naive characterization and it became apparent that he was somehow involved, then neither the French nor the German police could approach him directly without substantially more evidence than they now possessed. For this reason, Alex decided to create a diversion around the gunsmith and concentrate on the museum and the Old North German Aerodrome for possible links to Blücher's role in the affair, if any.

Alex picked up coffee for himself and Varnas and, as the low morning sun briefly tinctured the rooftops along Rue des Saussaies, entered the Maison and walked up to the office. Varnas had not yet arrived.

He went to his desk, opened his carton of coffee, and dialed the Army of the Air.

A young duty officer reported that the Old North German Aerodrome was not listed in the Army's Airport Directory for the FRG. However, a small airstrip was shown on the Hamburg-Bremen low-level sectional chart, five kilometres northeast of Osterholz-Scharmbeck.

"It's civilian and private," he said. "It doesn't show up on the display. Try the Museum of the Air."

"Where's the Museum of the Air?"

"Half of it is at Meudon," the D.O. said, "and the other half at Le Bourget. Try Le Bourget first."

Alex dialed. The museum opened at ten, but he managed to speak to a civilian volunteer, a young aviation freak who was giving up his Saturdays to paint lavatories in exchange for the privilege of being around old aeroplanes.

"I'm not into German airfields," the boy said in response to Alex's inquiry. "But the guy who'll know is Geoffrey. He's at Meudon. He's English. Do you speak English?"

"Yes."

"Then Geoffrey's your man. He's restoring the Santos-Dumont Demoiselle. Don't call him 'Geoff.'"

Alex took the Versailles bus.

Because of a nearly impenetrable bureaucracy, the French National Museum of the Air at Meudon, a single cavernous hangarlike building halfway to Versailles, had few paid professional staff and virtually no heat in the winter. But if it was inadequately funded and staffed and its boiler was cold, this stepchild of the Ministry of Defense enjoyed an abundance of attention from a group of enthusiastic amateurs who called themselves the Ancient Wings and volunteered their time, energy, and talent to help preserve and restore France's priceless national resource of historic aircraft.

Geoffrey was an Ancient Wing working in the restoration facility upstairs, Alex was told. A volunteer pointed him in the right direction. He walked through the silent, freezing hangar beneath antique flying machines suspended in semi-darkness from the ceiling. He paused under a huge, square, open biplane with its motor in the back. It hung dimly overhead, congealed in space, a fragile, mute, kitelike creature of varnished sticks, linen, and wire, with four bicycle wheels hanging down and a faded blue, white, and red cocarde painted beneath each wing. It seemed unimaginable that the thing had flown. A placard identified it: "Maurice Farman 20 (1912)." Grandfather, whose hand Alex had held so often, was thirty-one years old when the Farman was built. It seemed a sort of connection.

The workshop upstairs was heated, not for the workers, Alex discovered, but for the glue and other organic substances that required heat or else came unstuck or warped or sagged. He closed the door behind him and removed his jacket. A young woman mixing paint nearby called out and asked if he was the new rigger.

"I'm to see Geoffrey," Alex said without answering her question.

"He's on the wing jig," she said and went back to work. Alex walked across the shop to a brightly lit stand of benches and sawhorses at which several people were silently adjusting clamps. One of them, a stocky young man in a dirty British battle-dress jacket, torn jeans, and unlaced high-top sneakers, looked up as Alex approached. He had a large uneven baby face, a quantity of thin blond hair that hung to his shoulders, and an enormous walrus moustache with drooping tips. He resembled a large child playing at grown-up in clothes found in an attic hamper. Perhaps to compensate for this youthful appearance, he adopted an almost menacing expression.

"Are you the rigger, then?" he asked in appallingly accented Churchillian French.

"No," Alex answered in English. "I'm researching a Boche airfield and I was told you were the man to see."

"Hmm. Pity you're not the rigger. We could use a chap your size when the time comes to set up the bloody pylon." He stood up from his work and stuck out a dirty hand. "Geoffrey Howell," he said, scowling. "Which Boche airfield?"

"The Old North German Aerodrome at Osterholz-Scharmbeck."

"Ah," he said offhandedly, "the Museum of the Golden Knight." He turned to his associates. "Right. You lot carry on whilst I attend to this chap. And don't forget the bloody washout." He nodded to Alex. "Follow me."

Geoffrey led him past the wing jig into a sort of office. Actually, it was a storeroom lined with shelves that held boxes of fastenings, screws, bolts, washers, coils of wire, turnbuckles, pamphlets, blueprints, engine manuals, and a shelf of books on antique-aircraft design and history. In the centre of the room was a metal table and a couple of wooden chairs.

They sat opposite each other. Geoffrey scratched the backs of his hands for a moment and put on such a serious face that Alex had to anchor his lip to keep from smiling.

"Right," Geoffrey said. "Old North German Aerodrome. Flugzeug und Waffen Museum. Quite remarkable private collection of vintage autos, World War One aircraft, and the armament associated with them. Of course, some of the aircraft are repros." He glared terribly at Alex. "I assume you are familiar with the Shuttleworth collection in England and Old Rhinebeck in the States?"

Alex wasn't, but he nodded.

"Well, the F and W is rather similar to Old Rhinebeck in that the collection, while excellent, is secondary to the air show they put on each weekend during the season. The place is a living museum; that is, the autos, aircraft, and weapons are all in working order and used regularly."

He paused and closed his eyes. "Let's see. What are the features that set the F and W apart? Well, the extraordinary diorama, for one. And their strict adherence to a single point-in-time scenario for another." His eyes fluttered open. "For example, as soon as one passes through the gate, one enters a time warp. Never mind what day or year it really is; inside the gate the time is April, 1917. They chose that date because it was then that the Imperial German Air Service was temporarily ascendant over the RFC and the French.

"You pass through the gate and a museum attendant leads you into this bloody great glass-domed building that could pass for the Gare de Nord or the Crystal Palace. They call it the Atrium. Inside, they have built a diorama that is an exact replica of a 1917 front-line airfield in northern France—Douai, as I recall—complete with Bessoneau-type hangars, workshops, officers' mess, cookhouse, and so on. One can smell sausages cooking." He leaned forward and pantomimed with his fingers.

"All at once there are preparations for an early-morning patrol. Fitters and riggers scramble about and pilots run to waiting aircraft. This is followed by the takeoff of a flight of Albatros D IIIs, the gold one in the middle, accompanied by the roar of Mercedes one-sixties turning at full bore. It's quite realistic, actually. Of course, what one is viewing is a sight and sound show employing a hundred or more film projectors on multiple cinema screens installed around the diorama. Even the sky is accurately depicted with high, cumulus clouds slowly traveling east.

"By the end of the diorama show, one is convinced he has slipped his chronological time mooring and is breathing the very air of Douai on Monday morning, eleven April, 1917. This illusion is reinforced by the appearance and behaviour of the museum attendants and aerodrome personnel, all of whom are in costume appropriate to the period and have been trained, like actors, to limit their perspective to events on the single day in history. I mean, one can't expect an answer to a contemporary question like, 'When does the bus leave for Bremen?' It's rather spooky but effective.

"After the diorama experience comes the live air show at the aerodrome. Here, the performance is reminiscent of Rhinebeck, while the physical surroundings remind one of Shuttleworth at Old Warden in Bedfordshire. There is the Shuttleworth feeling of immaculate greensward and hedgerow. One is likely to see a spotlessly restored old Hotchkiss phaeton or a boat-tailed Hisso coupe purring along the white graveled drive. Like the Shuttleworth, where the flying field and hangars are constructed on the Shuttleworth family estate, the Old North German Aerodrome is built on the de Clovis estate."

De Clovis. The name reverberated. Alex wasn't sure he'd heard properly. "De Clovis?"

"Right . . . von Martel de Clovis, the Frankish ace."

De Clovis. The German pilot with the French-sounding name.

The headhunter Zeke had mentioned. The man who killed Tom Wilson. The effect of hearing the name in this context was bewildering. Alex took a moment to refocus. Finally, careful to keep the urgency out of his voice, he said, "I'd forgotten about de Clovis. What is known about him?"

Geoffrey reached behind him and pulled down a book approximately the size of a schoolboy's atlas. It was entitled *Air Aces of the 1914–18 War* and had a painting on the cover of biplanes maneuvering. One of them trailed black smoke. "Let's start with Harleyford," Geoffrey said. He opened the book and leafed through it to the back. "Here we are." He placed the volume on the table and read: " 'Hauptmann Christien Albert Frieherr von Martel de Clovis . . . the Golden Knight. Jagdstaffelführer. Thirty-seven confirmed victories, fifteenth on the German list; Iron Cross first class, Pour le Mérite, et cetera. Never wounded, never shot down, alleged never to have received a bullet in the fabric of his aircraft.' " Geoffrey grunted. "Bit farfetched, if you ask me. Still it might be true. He's a hardy bloke! Highest-scoring surviving scout pilot of the Great War."

Not yet a ghost, then. Geoffrey continued. "He's probably in his mid- to late-eighties now, like the rest of them. Bloody fool was still flying when I saw the show five years ago. He flew a gold lozenge-patterned Albatros D III, a repro series two fifty-three aircraft with the spinner removed to accommodate the larger Austro-Daimler two twenty-five engine. Shocking amount of speed for a dirty old bird! And I'll say, in spite of his age, he put on a smashing show! Strafing runs with live ammo demolishing a line of olive-drab dustbins. And then roaring back, flat out, a metre above the deck. The bastard could drive an aeroplane!" He slid the book across the table. "Here. Have a look."

Alex wiped the palms of his hands on his trousers. He skipped over several entries on the left, facing page—Leutnants Baumer, Jacobs, Menckoff. At the top of the opposite page he saw the carefully posed studio portrait of a slender, handsome young man with the friendly morning face of a college roommate. Apart from the old-fashioned stance, the rather aristocratic carriage of the head, the blond hair and clear eyes, there was nothing stereotypically Teutonic or arrogant about his expression, no Prussian snarl, no sabre scar. He looked, well, nice. Alex remembered what Zeke had said. "The Englishman was a murderer. The German was only doing his job. Pudge understood that." Nothing about the photo seemed to dispute the statement. Indeed, the portrait could've been hanging on Wilson's wall next to the picture of Bollekens ("No hard feelings, Pudge. All the best, Chris"). But it wasn't hanging on the wall. Instead, here were the gunsmith Blücher and de Clovis on the same turf. Was that a coincidence or was it the missing link to the Great War that Alex had been looking for? He felt Grandfather wave him on. He asked Geoffrey, "Do you know of any connection between this man de Clovis and an American named Andrew Wilson?"

"The ex–AEF chap gunned down in a parc recently?"

Alex nodded. Geoffrey fell silent. A bemused expression replaced his normally severe countenance. "We are not now talking about the Boche airfield are we?" he asked.

"No."

He studied Alex before answering. "Christ," he said quietly. "There was something about those two in the spring issue of *Tarmac*."

"Tarmac?"

"Aero-history journal. Printed in the U.K. for builders, restorers, blokes like me." He got to his feet. "Hold on. I think the copy's here somewhere." He shuffled across the room, his loose shoelaces clicking on the scuffed linoleum, and picked over a shelf piled high with pamphlets and cotton waste rags. He found what he was looking for and tossed it on the table. It was a tattered magazine. "Here," he said. "Have a look at the back cover."

Alex turned the journal over. On the back cover there was a reproduction of the same photo of de Clovis he'd just seen in the Air Aces book—the handsome young flying officer in uniform. It was captioned, "de Clovis, Berlin, 1917."

"Now look at the front cover."

Alex flipped the magazine. The front cover was torn, but by piecing the page together he saw that the photo reproduced there seemed to be de Clovis as well, but this time he was dressed in a deerstalker hat, tweed jacket, and plus-fours and carried a shotgun on his shoulder. The caption read "Ernst Schumacher, Silesia,

1921." Across the bottom of the page, in bold uppercase, appeared the question "WHO IS THIS MAN???"

Alex looked up. "Schumacher? What's the joke? Isn't it the same guy?"

"Possibly." Geoffrey reached across the table and opened the journal to the table of contents. He pointed to a boxed item at the bottom of the page. Alex read:

"Itching to learn the identity of our front-cover boy? Pudge Wilson's lively article, coming in your SUMMER ISSUE, tells all!! Stay tuned!"

Alex stared. "Do you have the summer issue?"

"Yes, But Wilson's article isn't in it."

"Why not?"

"Dunno. Apparently Wilson or *Tarmac* had second thoughts. Actually, there was a rumor. Something about a lawsuit if the article was published.

Alex sat back. It was Willoughby-Jones again. The article would be some sort of exposé. If it were published, de Clovis would sue Wilson and the publication for slander. "A libel suit?" he asked.

"That was the rumor."

Alex was so certain that a copy of Wilson's article would be in his office among the cartons of papers removed from the Wilson flat, and was so impatient to verify it, he spent 186 francs on a cab back to the Maison. He took the stairs three at a time.

Entering the office he saw immediately that the originals had been returned to Madame Wilson. Thanks to Varnas's foresight, the photocopies remained.

But he found no trace of the article. There was an essay on Romanian cabernet sauvignon, an article on trout fishing ("Remembering the Esopus"), and a short piece on Paris in the twenties for the Brown University Alumni Bulletin.

After an hour of sorting through receipts, bank statements, and tax information, he finally came to the indexed correspondence file. Under "B" he located a copy of the letter, dated 6 March, 1982, from Jan Bollekens to Andrew Wilson. It read:

Dear Pudge:

I beg you to reconsider my proposal.

You of all people understand that premeditated disclosure of these allegations could have destructive consequences. If you persist in this plan, you will publicly dishonour the man, which might lead to a retributive act.

Alex checked his watch. Nearly noon. He dialed Bollekens at the Hôtel Fleury. Reception answered.

"One moment for four fourteen, monsieur." She rang.

The judge answered on the first ring. Alex identified himself and, without waiting for an acknowledgment, asked "Judge Bollekens, does the name Christien von Martel de Clovis mean anything to you?"

After the briefest pause, Bollekens replied, "Of course."

"I have in my hand a letter from you to Wilson dated six March of this year." He read it aloud. "Do you recall writing that letter?"

"Yes."

"Did you write it because you wished to dissuade Wilson from publishing an article unfavourable to de Clovis in the summer issue of the aero-history journal *Tarmac?*"

"Yes."

"And was it published?"

"No."

"But there appears to have been a retributive act."

Bollekens hesitated. "Chef-Inspecteur, I would prefer to discuss the matter with you in person. Could you meet me here at, say, ten o'clock tomorrow morning?"

"I'd prefer to meet you now."

"Monsieur, I am a trustee. And, as trustee, I require the extra time to persuade my beneficiary that further confidentiality will be counterproductive."

23

8 Rue Georges-Berger

BOLLEKENS took the elevator to the lobby and ordered a cab. While he waited he tried to sort out his thoughts.

He was stunned by the Chef-Inspecteur's question. Still confident that the police were mired in the robbery option, he was not prepared to hear de Clovis's name. Now, his struggle to choose an honourable course between loyalty to Mimsy and his concern for the public interest seemed irrelevant.

The cab arrived. The driver, skillfully manipulating the lunchtime traffic, dropped him at the Wilson flat in less than ten minutes. Anna Gutierrez answered the door. She smiled amiably, took his coat, and ushered him into the living room. Millicent was there with Zeke, chain-smoking and irate.

Security guards had returned the items removed from the flat by the police but had failed to include Pudge's diary.

When Millicent called the Sûreté to complain, she was put through to the Commissaire. He told her that since the diary had not been on the list of items removed from the flat, he was at a loss to explain how the police could be responsible for its disappearance.

"Your people brought back the key, for God's sake!"

"The key?"

"The key to the diary. It's the small key on my husband's key ring."

The Commissaire seemed embarrassed. He assured madame he would give the matter his personal attention.

Millicent flicked her cigarette into the fireplace. "Was it Dickens who said that the two types of people permanently outside of society were criminals and cops?"

"Victor Hugo," Anna said quietly.

"Thanks. It's my view that if crooks blundered as much as cops do, there'd be no crooks left and the cops would be out of business."

Bollekens interrupted. "Excuse me, Mimsy. May I have a word with you privately?"

The way he said it got her attention. It was the tone her father employed when punishment was imminent. "Privately about what?" she replied rather cheekily. "Something about Zeke or Anna?"

Bollekens shook his head. "Not about Zeke or Anna."

"Then fire away, counselor. We're all family here." She was wearing her chin high and imperious.

Bollekens hesitated. "Very well. I have just received a call from the police." The chin rose perceptively. He hesitated again and looked from face to face before returning to Millicent. "They know about Ernst Schumacher."

It took her a moment to react. She reached for the arm of the sofa and sat down very slowly. When she found her voice it had lost its cutting edge. "How?"

"Doesn't matter. They called about the *Tarmac* piece." Her lavender eyes stared, unblinking. He took a step toward her. "It's for the best, Mimsy. The time has come."

Anna abruptly went into the kitchen. She could be heard turning on a tap and filling a glass with ice. No one spoke. In a moment she returned and offered the glass to Millicent.

Millicent peered at the crystal goblet. "What's this?"

"Ice water."

"Bugger ice water," she growled. "Make me a drink."

"No, darling."

She suddenly shouted. "Zeke! Fix me a double Absolut!"

Zeke said, "You have a drink now, Mims, and you'll miss your flight."

"The flight's tomorrow, you nitwit!"

"Yeah . . . and you'll miss it."

"Christ!" She grabbed the glass from Anna and emptied it onto the rug. She kicked the ice cubes and turned toward the liquor cabinet. Zeke stood there with his feet apart and his fists on his hips.

"Out of my way!"

He stood firm. "I made a promise not to have another drink till I got you safely back to Stonington. If an old scarfer like me can make a promise like that, so can you. If you want to do a swan dive when you get home, that's your business. But I think you oughta stay sober till we get Pudge planted, wherever it is."

The colour drained from Millicent's face and she began to shake. She raised the glass as if to strike Zeke. But the helpless, palsied hand holding it would not keep still. She tried to immobilize it with her other hand. That was not a success. She dropped the glass on the rug. Her head sagged and she leaned on the piano. After several minutes her breathing settled down. She straightened then, and placed her still-shaking hand on Zeke's shoulder. "You are a loyal old son of a bitch after all," she said and patted him. She turned to Bollekens and Anna. "I apologize."

Anna went to her, kissed her cheek, and disappeared into the kitchen for a rag.

Bollekens waited. Experience had taught him that Mimsy, when vulnerable, did not respond well to sympathy. He watched her thrust her hands deep into the pockets of her slacks and walk to the fireplace.

"Okay," she said, trying to return her take-charge voice. "How far is it from here to Poperinge?"

Bollekens guessed two hundred kilometres.

Zeke scowled and looked out the window.

"It was Zeke's whimsical notion that Pudge's ashes would be a whole lot happier at Poperinge than scattered over Block Island Sound or buried in Watch Hill. I absolutely rejected the idea. But now, with the cat out of the bag, I don't see what difference it makes."

Ferme Olivier, Poperinge

Late that afternoon, Millicent, Bollekens, and Zeke flew to Lille in northeastern France. From there to Poperinge, Belgium, was scarcely an hour's drive. Bollekens phoned ahead for a car and chauffeur to meet the plane.

As the Airbus reached its cruising altitude near Compiègne, Millicent, looking down, imagined the wintry landscape as Pudge had described it to her years ago. He called it the world's longest ditch, dug by desperate hands, first to protect their flanks, then to hide in.

Just holes to begin with, he said. Then ditches connecting the holes, then ditches connecting the ditches, then deeper ditches and redoubts with wire in front and wire in front of that. And mud: the trench system of the Western Front, stretching from the North Sea to Switzerland, a system of warrens and wire so impenetrable that neither side advanced more than twelve miles in four years. It was, Millicent knew, that epic scar which, if it had been eliminated from the landscape, had never been erased from the mind.

At the arrival gate in Lille the chauffeur, a short-legged, muscular woman in riding britches, led them to a Volkswagen bus of a certain age. The vehicle was clean, however, had freshly curtained windows, and performed flawlessly. Millicent and Bollekens sat in back. Zeke sat in front with the driver, guarding the hatbox that held the urn.

They crossed into Belgium from Halluin at dusk. Within minutes they were in Menen. Millicent had been here before. Early in their marriage, Pudge brought her to Menen to a certain plowed field where Pudge was certain Tom had fallen. They'd stood for an hour, gazing across the flat, Flanders field of ripening hops, Pudge cocking his head this way and that like a robin listening for worms. Later he located the farmer who owned the land and offered him a reward if he found anything. For years the farmer mailed Pudge old tractor fan belts, broken spark plugs, and horseshoe nails. Pudge paid up and sent him a Christmas card every year. The land was sold when the farmer died and the exact spot where Tom fell (that is, where his engine supposedly fell) was now occupied by a cereal-factory warehouse.

They turned west at Menen toward a faintly discernible horizon beneath a blue-black sky. A half hour later they passed through Ieper (Ypres), once known to tens of thousands of British soldiers as "Wipers." There they left the highway. The moon rose behind them.

After the liberation of Paris in 1944, a photo editor with irony on his mind sent Millicent to the Somme Valley to photograph a World War I cemetery. She refused the assignment, not because of her early experience with Pudge at Poperinge, but for aesthetic reasons. To her, a photograph of a military cemetery was as cliché as the words used to describe it: Final resting place—hallowed ground—row upon row as far as the eye can see—mute testimony to man's (interchangeable) patriotic-heroic-glorious capacity for sacrifice—the bivouac of the dead. May as well try to bring something to a photograph of a child with a new puppy. But she steered clear of the burying grounds for another reason. They seemed to confirm what she'd always suspected: that human life was of no more value than the life of a squirrel, that to view it as sacrosanct was an hypocrisy, the great daily lie we indulge in as a hedge against atheism and anarchy. She hoped that someday we'd all choke on our condolences and accept that death was simply the final fact of life, man or squirrel.

Bollekens had unerringly directed the driver. They stopped now in a nearly empty car park next to the British Graves Commission building at Ferme Olivier Military Cemetery. Millicent remembered that the air had smelt of wet hay. Tonight it smelt of burnt leaves and charcoal. A thin shroud of mist was beginning to settle on the ground.

Zeke had had the foresight to bring a flashlight. While the wooden signs identifying the names of the grass avenues separating the rows of gravestones were illuminated, the rows themselves were not. The avenues were named after well-known front-line locations: Hooge, Sanctuary Wood, La Bassée. They located Avenue Zillibeke. Tom was forty-fourth down Avenue Zillibeke on the right.

The hard winter sod crunched under their feet as they moved cautiously over the slightly uneven turf, walking three abreast, Millicent in the middle, Zeke on the right, carrying the hatbox and the flashlight and counting.

Millicent held on to Bollekens's arm and felt an old urge manifesting itself: the urge to laugh at a wholly inappropriate time. The corners of her mouth were inexorably turning up. Not now, Millicent Ann Henry, she told herself. Not here, for God's sake.

This urge to laugh was the product of a lifelong habit to trivialize moments of gravity, to conjure up mischievous and intrusive thoughts as a defense against solemnity. The naughtiness was involuntary, she thought. It was the devil in her. A friend of hers, whose lifelong habit was to spend three hours a week at the shrink, told her it was a denial of reality and a bulwark against growing up.

Despite her best efforts, a crooked smile materialized on Millicent's face in the dark. Get your mind on something else! Quick! Something other and opposite! What do the gravestones all in a row remind you of? Something trite and awful. Hurry! What does their rectilinear uniformity resemble? A housing development. Good. Which housing development?

Zeke intoned, "Twenty-nine, thirty, thirty-one . . . "

Which housing development? Um. The huge one in the Bronx. Or is it Queens? Le-something city. Le-A, le-B, le-C, le-D, le-E, le-F . . . le-Ffff . . . LeFrak City, she whispered, just in time. She stifled a giggle. Okay. LeFrak City. Or was she thinking of Co-Op City? Whatever. Bruckner Boulevard to Manhattan: straight on is the Throgg's Neck Bridge, right goes to the FDR Drive and right-right to the Cross-Bronx and the G. W. Bridge.

"Forty-two . . . forty-three." They stopped. "Here's Tom," Zeke said and shone his light on the next marker. The circular beam reflecting on the lowering mist created a nimbus that filtered the dark letters and caused the pale stone to appear suspended.

THOMAS DEXTER WILSON
AV 57934201
2nd Lt., Royal Flying Corps
Killed in Action 22-11-16

Millicent closed her eyes and bit down on her lower lip.

Zeke placed the hatbox on the ground and opened it. He took out the urn and handed it to Millicent. With her eyes closed she was unaware this was happening until Zeke said, "Mims."

She opened her eyes and stared at the urn. "I'll never get through this, McKim," she said, already feeling the guffaw rising in her throat.

"You'll get through it," Zeke said. He handed the flash to Bollekens. "We can't just empty the thing on the grass, Boli. When the goddam wind comes it'll blow the goddam ashes away."

Millicent gasped.

Zeke fished in his pocket and brought out an old, single-blade jackknife. With some difficulty he knelt beside the gravestone, opened the blade, and made a wide, rectangular cut in the turf. After a few minutes' work, he managed to fold back a section of sod that revealed the black, unfrozen earth beneath. He roughed up the dirt with his knife, struggled back to his feet, and faced Millicent.

She gripped the urn in both hands like a basketball. "You do it, McKim," she whispered. "Please."

Zeke scowled. "You gotta do it."

"I can't. You do it. Please."

Bollekens said, "We'll all do it."

There wasn't a breath of air. The mist hung waist high. As Bollekens removed the cover from the urn, Zeke circled round next to Millicent. They each placed a hand on the container and, Zeke and Bollekens controlling, poured the black dust into the white mist. The mist swirled gray.

When the urn was empty, Bollekens capped it and handed it back to Millicent. Zeke knelt again, stirred the small cone of ashes into the earth with his knife, and carefully replaced the sod, patting down the corners. He then stood, took Millicent's hand, and, in a rusty voice, began to sing.

"There's a long, long trail a-windin' . . ."

Millicent snatched away her hand, lowered her head, and strode quickly down the grass avenue.

" . . . into the land of my dreams."

Bollekens shone the light after her. "Mimsy! Be careful where you walk!"

She dropped the urn and started to run. Zeke stopped singing. Bollekens went after her.

Fifty feet from the grave she stopped abruptly, flung out her arms, and howled. When Bollekens reached her, she was doubled over retching.

Bollekens tried to hold her but she shook him off. She took a single step, stumbled and fell, rolling the mist. She landed on all fours, cried out once, and vomited.

Bollekens, at her side immediately, wrapped an arm around her stomach, dropped the flash, and supported her forehead as she dry-heaved. Zeke, hurrying over, put his coat around her shoulders.

After an eternity of breath spasms and choking, a great sob tore loose. "I . . . love!" she cried. Another sob came, another, and then tears. Zeke and Bollekens eased her back on her heels. She covered her face with her hands and wept, yielding finally to the grief so long disallowed, freeing herself at last from her ironclad imperturbability.

Part Four

THE INFLUENZA HOAX

24

Square Albert-Bartholomé

SUNDAY MORNING.

After four days in the Gaz de France caravan parked opposite the public phone booth, César was becoming nostalgic about his old job on the Assignment Desk. He had not imagined that field-work could be so tedious.

The job of his unit was to provide audio-video footage of all persons using the phone box between 8 A.M. and 4 P.M., the footage to be of a resolution and fidelity sufficient to satisfy the fastidious inspecteur-analysts back at headquarters who daily reviewed the outtakes.

César's wistfulness for the Assignment Desk was twofold. First, the phone users, nearly all athletes-in-training at the Centre Sportif d'Éducation, shared a certain homogeneity that, in César's view, made a mockery of the surveillance process, and, two, César suffered from reverse age discrimination.

His crew were all older, gimlet-eyed provisionals who actively sought stakeout work precisely because of the inactivity. They were not about to have their repose disturbed by a serious, service-motivated inspecteur-trainee.

There was the engineer, disguised as a Gaz de France worker, whose responsibility was to keep the generator running. He had two assistants who moved sacks of tools in and out of the caravan from time to time and made a daily run for generator fuel, a half-hour trip that took much of the afternoon. Finally, there was the camera/sound technicien, a man in his late fifties who claimed to be a documentarist and feature-film cameraman. When he was not napping, he complained about ambient light, depth of focus, poor equipment, amateurism, and César.

The characters from the Centre Sportif, whom the unit repeatedly taped, consisted of a homesick Alsatian weight lifter who phoned his mother every day, a female gymnast who played the horses, and a bantamweight boxer who made obscene phone calls to the nurses' residence at the Hôpital Saint-Joseph at lunchtime. The boxer was finally picked up by the police after César reported him to the Commissariat. The crew complained bitterly. The boxer had been their midday entertainment.

Also taped daily was a young American woman, a masseuse who used the public phone as her office. Each day from 9 to 10 A.M. and from 2 to 3 P.M. she scheduled her house calls.

When no one used the phone, which was often, the cameraman (if he was awake) indulged in minimalism, photographing pigeons in flight, pigeons puffed up and walking in circles, male pigeons endeavouring to copulate with scruffy, often crippled females who remained just out of reach.

Time passed gradually.

Hôtel Fleury

Charlotte Bollekens's unpredictable silence ended at 8 A.M. when Jan received a call from the practical nurse in Louvain. Charlotte had been taken to the University Hospital for psychiatric evaluation. She'd swallowed a handful of Seconal tablets, left the empty bottle by the telephone, and rolled over onto the buzzer, summoning the nurse.

Charlotte had given this performance before. It was a role straight out of *Contemporary Romances* and meant she was on her way back to normalcy.

Bollekens gave instructions to the nurse to send a dozen yellow roses and a small bottle of anisette to the hospital. The liquor was strictly forbidden, a deception Charlotte would enjoy.

He'd no sooner hung up than the phone rang again. It was Millicent.

"Jan, dear," she said rather shakily, "good morning. I've postponed my flight home." He heard her strike a match, light a cigarette, and inhale. "Would you mind terribly if the meeting with the police was held here, at my place? I think I should be in on it."

"That's excellent, Mimsy."

"Tell Zeke."

"I will, Mimsy."

The Maison

As he walked down Rue La Fayette to meet Varnas, Alex examined the morning sky for omens. This was, he knew, a chancy business, like risking the success of a love affair on whether he made the next traffic light.

Still, the morning's events had so far augured well: the osprey landing on the barge's stemhead, larger croissants than ever at Mariette's, and the fact that Madame Wilson wished to see them.

The morning was mild and windless. Church bells encircled him haphazardly as he walked. Nothing irked. He picked up his pace.

Varnas munched a pastry and studied the grainy photocopies Alex had made at the Musée de l'Air.

"Who is Ernst Schumacher?"

"We'll see."

The Commissaire popped his head into the office. Dressed for traveling in a fashionable double-breasted tweed topcoat, he was on his way to Villefranche to attend a meeting of law-enforcement officials.

"Do me a favour, Alex," he said. "Find that diary for Madame Wilson before she returns to the U.S. It's of vital importance to her. Do that for me, will you? I'll be at the Hôtel Vauban. Keep me informed." He left.

Alex did not inform him that they were finally to meet the sheltered and heretofore forbidden Madame Wilson in person.

25

The Influenza Hoax

MILLICENT answered the door herself. Alex, who had been exposed only to the ambiguous Christmas photographs in the bedroom, noted now the seamless delicacy of her features and the wide, vulnerable lavender eyes, slightly puffy under a light dusting of powder. She was smaller than he expected, and slimmer, and younger looking.

She glanced up at Alex and down at Varnas and said, "You two ought to be in vaudeville."

"We are," Alex replied.

She smiled. "I think I'm going to like you. Give me your coats and go right through that door. You'll find coffee, tea, and scones. Help yourselves."

They walked directly into Wilson's study. Zeke, clinging to a mug, waved to Alex from across the small room.

"Hiya, Lootenant! What'll it be? Caffyolay? Caffyfilter or tea? We got So-Long-Oolong-How-Long-Ya-Gonna-Be-Gone and Tetley. I'm buying!" He scurried over to serve them. Alex and Varnas took café au lait. A moment later, Bollekens and Millicent walked in. Zeke said, "Oh-oh, here come de judge." But there the bantering stopped.

Everyone shook hands and took seats, Bollekens at Wilson's desk, where books and documents had been set out, Millicent and Zeke on the small couch opposite the desk, and Alex and Varnas on a pair of Louis Quinze chairs brought in from the dining room.

Alex placed his tape recorder on the desk and switched it on. Millicent glanced at the machine, hesitated for an instant, and spoke.

"Before we start," she said evenly, "I would like the Sûreté to know that my pals, Bollekens and McKim, were prepared to co-operate with you long before I was. That they held off was out of their deep loyalty to me. Rather late I have realized that my demands on their loyalty were motivated by self-indulgence and a notion of privacy and privilege that really has no place in today's society." She paused and passed a hand over her hair. "Dear me, I sound like a Democrat. I certainly don't mean to. But enough already. This meeting may now come to order. I move we dispense with the treasurer's report."

"Second!" Zeke said. "And let's not beat around the bush! The Lootenant wants to know who killed Pudge. Let's just tell him and all go to lunch!"

Bollekens held up a hand. "Zeke," he said softly, "there are to be no personal opinions."

Zeke scowled. "Why the hell not? We know who bagged Pudge as sure as I'm sittin' on this davenport!"

"*I* know no such thing. We are not here to conduct a poll from which a majority sentiment can be projected to declare who is or is not suspect. Guilt is for the police to prove and a court to adjudicate." He looked around the room. "We are here to answer questions." He turned to Alex. "Chef-Inspecteur, at your service."

"Thank you," Alex said and put down his coffee cup. "Actually, I have no objection to your personal opinions now that we're all on the same side. I have a personal opinion; it is that Andrew Wilson was not satisfied he vindicated his brother's death by joining the air service and destroying fourteen enemy planes."

Zeke studied the backs of his hands.

"Eight years after the Great War, Wilson found it necessary to hunt down Major Willoughby-Jones, contributing to that officer's suicide. And now, sixty-four years after the war, Wilson seems to have attempted to repeat the process by writing an exposé of the Baron de Clovis for an aero-history journal. But this attempt boomeranged. The article was not published and, somehow, Wilson, not de Clovis, became the victim."

He turned to Zeke. "I gather you think de Clovis murdered Wilson."

"You're damn tootin'."

To Millicent: "What about you, madame?"

"Probably."

To Bollekens: "And you, judge?"

"We have no hard evidence that de Clovis was the murderer, but there is evidence that he had a motive. First, however, let me say that your attempt to draw a parallel between the Willoughby-Jones affair and de Clovis is flawed. De Clovis is not Willoughby-Jones. Willoughby-Jones sued for libel. Nineteenth-century aristocrats, as a rule, do not go to court. They prefer to settle disputes discreetly, among themselves. De Clovis was a man compelled by honour to redress an injury."

"What injury?"

"In the *Tarmac* article, Wilson called de Clovis a liar."

"But the article wasn't published."

Millicent interrupted. "Jan, perhaps I should explain this part." She turned politely to Alex. "Chef-Inspecteur, it didn't really matter that the article wasn't published. To begin with, there were only two copies. *Tarmac* had a copy, which they returned to me and I later destroyed so you wouldn't see it, and Pudge had a copy. When *Tarmac* informed him they wouldn't publish because they found the final draft unsuitable for a serious journal of aero-history, Pudge was furious. You must understand that he was just as compelled by the nineteenth-century code of honour as de Clovis was. He was absolutely furious. He took his copy of the article, entitled 'The Influenza Hoax,' put it in a fibre strongbox, and, without informing any of us, hired a pilot to fly it to Osterholz-Scharmbeck and drop it, complete with red, white, and blue streamers, onto the airfield next to the museum. I daresay this old war movie parody of delivering a challenge was not lost on de Clovis.

"To add insult, Pudge autographed the copy and inscribed a sort of Robert Service epigraph on the title page. He wrote,

'Here is the Sword of Damocles
Hung by a human hair.
Lost in the purblind sun
It waits
To plunge down the blazing air!' "

Zeke cleared his throat. "Pretty good metaphor for a head-hunter if you ask me! Damn sight better than Robert Service!"

Alex said, "The epigraph sounds more like a threat than a challenge. What did Wilson have on de Clovis?"

Bollekens answered, "He had proof that de Clovis lied about his final aerial battle of the Great War."

Alex wasn't sure he'd heard correctly. "Lied about his final aerial battle? That's all?"

"Essentially."

"Are you saying that because Wilson accused de Clovis of falsifying the result of a fight between two aeroplanes in 1918, de Clovis shot him?"

"Possibly."

"But surely the fight was a matter of record."

"Wilson disputed the record."

"Oh." Alex glanced at Varnas, whose features belied nothing at all. Alex had never learned the trick of wearing a completely empty expression. Varnas could do it and remain in disguise for hours. Alex's disappointment was already spreading to his arms and legs. He looked at Bollekens. "Am I missing something? Or is what we have here simply a controversy? An old controversy, subject to partisanship and conjecture?"

"I don't think so. If the flight was a matter of record, it is also a matter of record that de Clovis claimed to be invincible, never to have been shot down, never to have received a bullet in the fabric of his aeroplane, much less to have been wounded. In fact, Wilson had proof that de Clovis was seriously wounded in his last fight and deliberately concealed the fact."

Alex grunted. "Judge, at this moment there are old men somewhere arguing about a referee's call in a soccer match that took place sixty years ago. They all have proof the referee was wrong and they'll go to their graves with it. I'm looking for a motive for murder here. You'll forgive me, but I can't take what you're saying seriously."

Bollekens reddened slightly. "Then you'll forgive me. Whether you take it seriously or not is immaterial. What is material is whether de Clovis took it seriously."

Alex couldn't imagine it.

"We are talking," Bollekens continued, "about a time when western society held Character to be the criterion of judging a man. Today, Personality has replaced Character . . . especially in America. Today, except in some military schools, certain rural areas, and, possibly, the Moslem world, a man accused of lying can simply deny the charge, or ignore it. Not so in that vanished age when de Clovis was a young man, when a trivial slight could provoke, if not a duel, at least a demand for honour restored. To understand, Chef-Inspecteur, it becomes necessary to go back a bit, to a time of primary colours, easily perceived truths, and passionately held convictions."

Alex recalled Zeke's recitation of the Victorian virtues and prepared himself for another stroll among the ruins.

"Andrew Wilson's compelling reason for going to war in 1918 was to kill the man who killed his brother, not just to shoot down Germans. He wanted to take the life of this one German. Luckily for Wilson, who had only fifty hours in the air to de Clovis's fifteen hundred, they never met and the war ended.

"But the fact of the armistice presented no obstacle to Pudge's avowed purpose to kill his brother's killer. It made no difference to him that civilization did not now sanction murder on a daily basis. He still had a score to settle. It was something he counted on." Bollekens hesitated and glanced at Millicent. "What he did not count on was the sudden appearance of Mademoiselle Millicent Ann Henry."

Millicent leaned forward and rested her elbows on her knees. "I was at a State Department reception on the hottest day in history in May of 1919. My job was to keep track of diplomatic children. I was fifteen and serving lemonade when I looked up and beheld this deity enter the hall. His halo lit up the place, I swear it. Knowing immediately that it was this man for me or a nunnery for life, I excused myself and went straight at him. I don't remember what I said, but I got his attention. Somehow, when my knees stopped shaking, I led him on a prolonged tour of the gardens and balconies, during which we discussed Rabelais, Flaubert, and Diderot. Actually, I did all the talking. I told him I intended to go to the Sorbonne and become a writer. I told him other lies as well before declaring that he'd completely stolen my heart. We then returned to the reception where, before the startled French ambassadeur, I kissed him full on the lips and announced our engagement.

"Pudge, poor dear, never had a chance. He was probably in shock. But eventually, the reality of a precocious, not-bad-looking platinum blonde madly in love with him sunk in. He was no longer the unencumbered warrior. Of course, unknown to me at the time, his love for Tom and his need for retribution remained steadfast. But Jan says that, in the interval between our engagement and marriage three years later, the civilized man triumphed over the instinctual. Anyway, he altered his agenda.

"We were married in Paris in 1921. I was eighteen, blissfully happy but utterly ignorant of his obsession until the day I went with him for the first time to the military cemetery at Poperinge on a cold, rainy November twenty-second, the fifth anniversary of Tom's death.

"I'd never seen a man cry. I didn't know what to do. Perhaps I'd inherited some puritan denial of tears. Or maybe I was jealous of Tom. Pudge clutched my hand and wept. I remember the warm tears and the cold rain. It tore at me that I couldn't weep with him. Because my heart was as heavy as the stones in the box buried beneath the new white marker at our feet."

Millicent became silent then, but gazed at Alex with a remarkable, glistening intensity. After a moment, she stood. "Excuse me," she said and left the room.

Bollekens rose halfway out of his seat at her departure. When he settled back, Alex asked, "How did he alter his agenda?"

"Very simply. After the first aero-history began to be written in the years following the war, names like Bourjade, de Clovis, Baracca, and Moissinac emerged. It was then that Pudge started his de Clovis file and became the world's leading authority on the man he intended to destroy. This was in the firm belief that, for a nineteenth-century German aristocrat, dishonour would prove to be a greater pain than death."

Millicent returned with a fresh pot of coffee. Everyone stood. While his cup was being refilled, Alex glanced at the documents on the desk and recognized two leather-bound volumes he'd seen on his last visit to Wilson's study: *The Wartime Diary of V. C. Moissinac* and *Mirror and Shadow,* the medical biography of Richard K. Douglas, M.D. He took Varnas aside.

"Do you understand this man?"

"Bollekens?"

"No. Wilson. I can understand a man who goes to war to vindicate the death of a brother. But I can't understand one who makes the destruction of another man's reputation a lifetime priority. First Willoughby-Jones, then de Clovis. It's pathological!"

"It is vengeance, Alex."

"That's too simple. Vengeance is a Mafia motive. Vengeance is a murder committed by some Corsican to settle the theft of a goat sixty years ago. Vengeance needs Mediterraneans with long memories, short tempers, and sharp knives."

"Beware stereotype, Alex. No one is exempt from instinct for revenge."

"But this is Andrew Wilson, the great reconciler, the champ of private diplomacy, the civilized man triumphing over the instinctual."

"Sure. But remember, Man of Peace keeps Browning in sock drawer."

"I remember." Alex went back to the desk, checked the tape, and sat down. When Bollekens resumed his seat behind the desk, Alex abruptly asked, "Who's Ernst Schumacher?"

"Schumacher was the name de Clovis used to conceal his identity while he underwent plastic reconstruction of the face."

"Then there was an injury. A real injury, I mean."

"Oh yes."

"When and how was he injured?"

Bollekens smiled. "That is the essence of the . . . ah . . . controversy, as you call it. According to Pudge, de Clovis's injuries were inflicted on 30 October, 1918, during the last aerial encounter with the Frenchman Moissinac."

"And according to de Clovis?"

"Wounded in a hunting accident in Silesia in 1921."

"Is there medical evidence?"

"There is no medical record of the hunting accident, although de Clovis's private physician provided an affidavit we believe is false. The medical records of de Clovis's evacuation to hospital in 1918 are inconclusive.

"But we won't speculate. Instead we will cite documentation

to establish conditions as they were on the afternoon of 30 October, 1918. Try to place matters in perspective: it's a Wednesday, the armistice is only twelve days away, the Argonne has fallen to the Allies, the German Army is demoralized and in retreat, three hundred thousand soldiers on leave in central Germany refuse to return and fight.

"In de Clovis's report of his last flight, taken from the *Luftfahrt archiv*, Berlin, he states that, at approximately four-thirty P.M., he made a single, diving pass at a French scout monoplane near Moyenvic, firing a four-second burst. The enemy was seen to falter and descend in a shallow dive to crash-land in no-man's-land near the Nomeny road.

"His victory was confirmed by a Jaeger regiment. They took the pilot prisoner and later destroyed the aircraft with a trench mortar when the enemy was observed attempting to dismantle the wreckage.

"The encounter was officially de Clovis's thirty-seventh and final victory of the war. That evening he was evacuated from his aerodrome at Moyenvic to a field hospital at Saarbrücken with P.U.O. (Pyrexia of Unknown Origin), later diagnosed as Spanish Influenza, then widespread in Europe.

"De Clovis's opponent on that day was the French Adjutant, Virgil Constant Moissinac. His report of the same encounter sharply contrasts with de Clovis's. The details of the fight are contained in this volume of Moissinac's memoirs, which you are welcome to examine, if you wish.

"In brief, Moissinac states that the attack from the gold Albatros only slightly damaged his right wingtip, nothing more. Moissinac was flying a brand-new aeroplane, a Morane-Saulnier XXIX C-I, with untested guns. Nevertheless, after he recovered from de Clovis's diving attack, he saw his opportunity to respond. From an altitude advantage, he hurled his aircraft at his opponent, firing a burst of perhaps twenty rounds. He saw his bullets strike the enemy just beneath the upper wing and move aft to the windscreen. Then he saw no more, for, in firing the untested guns of his new aircraft, he caused some failure of the gun synchronizing gear and shot off his propeller.

"Now defenseless and powerless, he banked to the west and prepared himself for the enemy's coup de grace that he knew would come in a matter of seconds.

"But the coup de grace never came. The only sound he heard was that of the wind in his flying wires. The sky around him was empty. The German had broken off the engagement, not out of chivalry, Moissinac was certain, but because the burst of gunfire had either disabled him or his aeroplane so that he was unable to press his advantage.

"Moissinac crash-landed without injury, destroyed the monoplane himself to prevent it falling into enemy hands, and was taken prisoner.

"De Clovis, in the meantime, was evacuated to Field Hospital Number Seven at Saarbrücken. While the few hospital records filed in the *Bundesarchiv* are indecipherable due to water and rodent damage, an ambulance evacuation ticket was clearly marked 'P.U.O., probable influenza,' and stated that medical personnel, including the Hauptmann's orderly, 'took the precaution of wearing gauze masks.'

"De Clovis was flown home on 6 November and placed in the care of his family physician. There, he virtually dropped out of sight.

"Following the war, everyone on both sides, particularly generals and other senior officers, rushed into print, publishing their memoirs to justify their actions in battle. Many airmen wrote of their exploits as well. They were, after all, the first to experience aerial warfare in its most rudimentary form, and probably the last to practice combat by consent.

"But from Schloss Scharmbeck came only silence, until 1924, when an item appeared in the newspaper *Berliner Taggblatt*." Bollekens referred to a memo.

" 'Schloss Scharmbeck, Osterholz-Scharmbeck, 18 April, 1924. The wedding of Eugénie Gabrielle von Mai to the air ace, Hauptmann Christien Albert von Martel de Clovis, took place today at the bridegroom's ancestral home. The bride was attended by her sister, Erika Maria, and the groom by his young brother-in-law, Karl Friedrich von Mai. The wedding, which was private, had been delayed to give the Freiherr an opportunity to recover from a hunting accident.' "

"Hunting accident," Millicent repeated. "Pudge went wild when he read 'hunting accident.' He was all set to contact the *Berliner Taggblatt* and expose de Clovis as a fraud. But Jan talked him out of it for lack of proof. Jan and I had our first fight over that. I wanted Pudge to get it over with, proof or no proof. Cooler heads prevailed." She glanced at Bollekens. "The result is that we had to wait until last year to find the medical evidence that proved de Clovis was a liar."

Bollekens nodded. "As someone once said, 'Time is the Great Detective.' And Time brought us Doctor Douglas and Ernst Schumacher.

"You already know who Schumacher was. Douglas, a Scot, had been an orthopaedic surgeon experimenting with bone and tissue transplant in the early days of the war. By war's end, he was a chief proponent of the restorative procedures now known as plastic reconstruction.

"In the spring of 1922, a 'luminously beautiful young woman'—those are Douglas's words—came to his surgery on the Firth of Forth near Inverness. She said her name was Gabrielle Schumacher. She was Swiss, she said, and had come on behalf of her husband, who'd suffered a facial disfigurement in a hunting accident the year before."

"Who was she really?" Alex asked.

"Eugénie von Mai, de Clovis's fiancée. In brief, Douglas agreed to treat Schumacher. The treatment was successful, but, in the end, Douglas was persuaded that Schumacher had not been wounded in a hunting accident the year before. The calibre of bullet needed to bring down the game Schumacher described—bison—was not the calibre of bullet that had injured him. The round that had struck him was a standard .303 calibre bullet used by the Allies in World War One. Nor was the wound a year old but more like four years old, and bore the unmistakable stamp of rudimentary army field surgery.

"I should add that Douglas believed Schumacher may have received a cranial blow, either as a consequence of his injury or subsequently, for he displayed mild symptoms of epilepsy. By that Douglas meant that the seizures were not violently convulsive. There was no pupil dilation or excessive elevation of blood pressure. Nevertheless, he recommended to Frau Schumacher that she place her husband in the care of a neurologist should the attacks persist. He recommended the Freud Institute, Vienna.

"Wilson was now satisfied that Schumacher and de Clovis were the same man, that the wound was inflicted by a .303 round from the guns of Adjutant Moissinac on thirty October, 1918, and that the influenza hoax was devised to preserve de Clovis's myth of invincibility. That was the Sword of Damocles Pudge delivered to the man who killed his brother. It may have provoked a retributive act. We have no proof that it did." Bollekens seemed to have finished.

Varnas spoke for the first time. "Excuse me, judge. World War One ends now in less than fortnight. Even if we accept that de Clovis is wounded and returns to aerodrome despite shock and loss of blood that someone manages to conceal, how or why does he continue such deception after war, particularly as there is no dishonour to be wounded?"

Bollekens answered without hesitation. "The epilepsy. Or what Frau Schumacher . . . that is, Eugénie von Mai . . . believed was epilepsy. You must realize that the popular view of epilepsy held by the public at the time was that it was a form of insanity, hereditary and transmittable to offspring. De Clovis's profitable marriage, postponed for two years, would have been out of the question had Eugénie's parents known he was epileptic."

"Was he?" Alex asked.

"Actually no. He suffered from what was eventually diagnosed as psychomotor epilepsy. It's a condition that, unlike conventional epilepsy, is curable by intensive psychotherapy, much as post-traumatic stress is treated today."

"What became of Eugénie?"

"She died in an Austrian sanatorium two days after the Nazi Anschluss. She was the same age as the century. Thirty-eight. We know little about her. There is a portrait of her in the schloss."

"And when," Alex asked, "did Wilson locate this final evidence? Was it last autumn?"

"Yes. Douglas's biography came to his attention in late summer. He flew to Edinburgh in November."

"I gather, then, that this was his 'epiphany' whose anniversary you celebrated after the Élysée Palace reception?"

Bollekens made a barely perceptible smile and glanced at Zeke. "Yes. If I evaded the question when you first asked it, you will understand that I was uninformed at the time and felt my first duty was to my friend's memory and to his widow."

Zeke coughed. "Me too, Lootenant."

"Okay, Zeke," Alex said. He turned to Millicent.

"Madame Wilson, although this material hasn't been made public, your husband, in his epigraph to de Clovis, left no doubt that the sword could drop at any moment. For de Clovis, if he is the nineteenth-century man you describe, the threat of disclosure—and dishonour—was therefore unequivocal. There seems little doubt that he had to respond. What puzzles me is that your husband, having finally thrown down the gauntlet, didn't behave like a man expecting a response. He went walking in the parc alone. He planned to drive to Poperinge alone. Did he expect a response or not?"

"*I* expected a response," Millicent said. "That's why I bought him the Browning. I made him carry it. I made him practice with it. When the firing pin wore out I made him replace it. But when I went back to Connecticut to get the house ready for Thanksgiving, there was no one here to badger him. I'm sure he didn't take the gun with him on the NATO round. And he obviously wasn't carrying it in the parc."

Zeke said, "He wasn't carryin' it because he didn't think the Kraut had the guts to come out and fight. Pudge thought he had the bastard by the short hairs, too chicken to respond because a response would acknowledge the damned truth!"

Bollekens waved this away. "Zeke, as we've already seen, de Clovis wasn't remotely interested in the truth, only in matters of honour. If you're saying that Pudge underestimated his opponent, I will agree. After all, Pudge was ambushed, just like Tom."

Millicent placed her hands lightly over her ears. "That's an irony I can do without." She sighed and dropped her hands to her lap. "I haven't said this before to anyone, but, in the end, I don't think Pudge cared if de Clovis responded or not. That remark, I realize, makes him sound arrogant. But he wasn't. He was exhausted. He'd been furious for so long, he was worn out." She shook her head slightly. "In the end, I think he was ready to join Tom."

"Mimsy!"

"That's what I think, Jan. I have the credentials to say that. I remember all those Tom dreams . . . when I'd wake before dawn to find Pudge silhouetted against the oval window at the top of the stairs, or the bedroom window, or downstairs in the kitchen, fast asleep on his feet and talking to Tom in that half-comprehensible, ruminating, chuckling language of perpetual boyhood. He was sick with grief. He never got over his loss. Nothing replaced it. Not wife, children, or work." She blinked at the ceiling and whispered, "His dying word was no surprise to me."

She touched her cheek with the back of her hand and rose to face Alex and Varnas. "Gentlemen, I'm sure that at some point in your investigation, you will conclude that you are dealing with the bizarre spectacle of a man of exceptional character and reputation who nevertheless persisted, for sixty-four years, in a blood feud against a former enemy who was only doing his duty. I realized that fact in my first pregnancy.

"If I could've found a reason to loathe Pudge, it would've been simple. But I loved him. I didn't intend to live without him. Which was probably why, for about half those sixty-four years, no one called after five P.M. because they knew Mimsy was too loaded to make it to the phone. So maybe you can understand now why I wasn't exactly bending over backwards to help you find your man. The road that leads the press to Schloss Scharmbeck will lead them to my front door as well. Nevertheless, I hope you find your man." She smiled. "Shall we warm up the coffee?"

Alex decided he liked Millicent Wilson. He had stood and reached out to turn off the tape when he heard Varnas say, "Madame Wilson, may I ask how long you know Anna Gutierrez?"

Alex stared.

"Anna?" Millicent replied. "Let me see. Since the spring. We met in April or May. Why? Do you think Anna killed Pudge?"

"Certainly not, madame. I am only interested how you meet

Madame Gutierrez. Are you formally introduced? Do you know her parents?"

"Her parents?" Millicent made a little laugh. "I fail to see that the question is . . ." She glanced at Bollekens. "What's the courtroom term, judge?"

"Relevant."

"Relevant, yes. I always have trouble with that word. It usually comes out 'revelant.' " She turned back to Varnas. "How did we meet? Let's see. Actually, Pudge met her first. In the Parc de Monceau. He was doing his constitutional."

"Is that morning constitutional or evening?"

Millicent frowned. "Morning. Does it matter?"

"Do you recall circumstances of meeting?" Varnas noticed Alex was becoming annoyed.

"Circumstances. Yes. Anna had just come to Paris. I think Pudge found her standing in the middle of one of the promenades, holding a Michelin guide or a Taride or something, and looking helpless. Pudge adored those opportunities, especially if the lost child was young, female, and beautiful. She was looking for the musée. She said she was interested in oriental porcelain."

"Monsieur walks at eight-thirty. Musée does not open until ten."

"It was a Monday. The musée was closed. Pudge bought her an ice cream at the kiosk and made a date for me to show her the porcelain next day."

"Then at this time she is not working as receptionist?"

"No. That came later."

"With your help?"

Millicent raised her chin. "I don't see where this is leading, Inspecteur."

Alex cleared his throat to speak, but Varnas turned to Bollekens. "Judge, can you locate news item of de Clovis wedding in 1924 and repeat name of best man?"

Bollekens leafed through the pages on the desk. After a moment, he read, " ' . . . the bride was attended by her sister, Erika Maria, and the groom by his young brother-in-law, Karl Friedrich von Mai.' "

"Karl Friedrich von Mai." Varnas repeated the name and wrote it down. "Thank you, judge." He turned to Alex. "I have no more questions, Chef-Inspecteur."

The meeting was over. But Varnas's unsolicited questions about Anna had ruffled the surface civility that had prevailed. It was uncharacteristic of Varnas to make what amounted to a gaffe, and Alex found himself in the awkward position of minding the Sûreté's manners, a job that usually fell to the Commissaire. Attempting to acknowledge everyone's cooperation, he felt cumbersome and arch. At the door, he reassured Millicent about the diary.

"No hurry," she said. "If it turns up after I fly home, you can leave it with Stevenson. He'll see that I get it."

Varnas was already in the Citroën, warming up the motor. Alex slid in the passenger's side.

"What the hell was all that?"

"Shh, Alex," Varnas replied and steered out of Rue Georges-Berger.

"I don't understand! I thought we agreed there wasn't enough evidence to involve Anna. You nearly turned Millicent Wilson into a hostile witness!"

Varnas drove into Boulevard de Courcelles and handed Alex a scrap of paper. "Read name written there."

Alex read, " 'Karl Friedrich von Mai.' So what?"

"Now try to recall telex we receive from São Paulo in response to inquiry about Anna Gutierrez."

"What about it? She went to school in Montreux and earned an MBA from the University of Virginia."

"What is name of her father?"

"I don't remember."

"I refresh your memory. Anna's papa is CEO of prestigious Banco do Sul in São Paulo. His name is Carlos Federico de Mayo."

Alex stared at the slip of paper.

Varnas glanced over. "Does not take unusual linguist to recognize that Carlos Federico de Mayo is exact Spanish equivalent of Karl Friedrich von Mai."

The *Almanach de Gotha* supplied the rest. Von Mai, Karl Friedrich, born 2 December, 1916, emigrated to Rio 1939. There was a parenthetic "See 'de Mayo.'"

Varnas capped it. Anna's father is still de Clovis's brother-in-law. Anna is de Clovis's niece."

Alex stared at the office wall. The gaffe was his.

"Don't feel bad, sweetheart," Varnas said, "but time is now to come in out of rose garden."

26

Villefranche

THE COMMISSAIRE had not finished unpacking at his hotel when he received the message to call Paris immediately. The message contained a supplementary cipher that indicated classified material. He groaned slightly, went down to the lobby, and located a public phone.

Alex gave him a detailed report of the meeting and added the suggestion that they detain Anna Gutierrez for questioning.

"What sort of questioning?" the Commissaire replied coolly. "She could be Hitler's niece and you wouldn't have enough to hold her for questioning. Everything you have is circumstantial. If you bring her in for questioning now, it will do two things right away. It will instantly transform our covert investigation into an overt investigation. It will bring the Brazilians down on us, followed by the media. And if the media come in, it will alert the suspect, if he is a suspect. Isn't she under a restraining order?"

"Yes."

"Then you can detain her if she tries to leave Paris. But for no other reason. Alex, do what you have to do. Keep track of her. Stake out her flat. But don't touch her unless you have tangible evidence that she's an accomplice. Did you find the diary?"

Alex's first impulse after Varnas's disclosure was to call Madame Wilson and alert her to Anna's new identity, to preclude her sharing further confidences with the woman whom she considered her closest friend. But knowing Millicent as he now did—as a fiercely independent, even combative individual—he feared that if she learned of the de Clovis connection she might deliberately confront Anna, the consequences of which could be damaging. Instead, he called Millicent and urged her not to discuss the case with anyone, not even with Anna or the President's wife.

"That'll be no hardship," she said. "Zeke and I plan to fly home tomorrow, provided you have no objection."

"No objection whatever." He'd miss her, he realized.

By midafternoon, there was a surveillance team at Anna's apartment building on Rue des Grands-Augustins; another at the Musée Cernuschi, and a third at the Brazilian Embassy. Alex ordered a twenty-four-hour tail to be undertaken by four female inspecteurs, two to a vehicle, working twelve-hour shifts. They were in place by lunchtime. Finally he ordered photographs distributed to the Préfecture, to Territorial Surveillance, Interpol and Customs, and Immigration, as well as to the Transport Police at Orly, Charles de Gaulle, and all S.N.C.F. stations.

Anna

"Hairdresser?" Madame Seńkowska trilled. "If I had hair like yours I wouldn't allow a hairdresser within a kilometre of my head!"

Anna giggled. "I need my bangs trimmed and to feel slightly gussied for the embassy theatre party tonight."

She left the musée at 2:15 and walked the hundred metres to the Villiers metro, where she bought two first-class tickets. She took the number three to St.-Lazare and changed there for the number twelve for Porte de Versailles. Since this would be a voyage of forty minutes or more, she settled into the nearly empty coach and took out her paper edition of Barzini's *The Europeans*.

This kept her marginally occupied until Station Pasteur, where even the first-class carriages suddenly filled. Well, it was a sunny Sunday afternoon and the petit bourgeois were out in their scarves and mittens for Montparnasse and the Parc des Expositions.

She disembarked at Porte de Versailles. The station clock read 2:47. She hurried up the stairs and walked along Boulevard Lefebvre with her long muscular stride, reaching the Square Albert-Bartholomé at 2:55. There was a young woman in the phone box. Anna stood in the cold sunshine near a Gaz de France caravan and waited.

*   *   *

The young American masseuse, wrapped in sweaters and a long wool scarf, finished her business at two minutes before three and before the Centre Sportif afternoon break. However, a woman wearing a mink coat, dark slacks, and designer dark glasses entered the booth the moment the masseuse departed.

She busied herself with the contents of a large shoulder bag. Looking for change, César guessed. The bitch probably didn't have anything smaller than a hundred-franc note. The bag, he noticed, was embroidered with green and gold monkeys..

The phone in the booth rang. The woman immediately slung the bag over her shoulder and picked up the receiver. Obviously she'd been expecting the call. César adjusted his headset. He checked that his audio level was in the green and banged on the partition to alert the camera operator. "You awake?"

"Yeah."

"And rolling?"

"Yeah, yeah."

César's interest was mildly piqued by the woman's appearance and by the fact that she'd chosen this out-of-the-way phone for a prearranged call. But at his briefing he'd been told the target would be a man. Consequently, when she hung up after a few minutes he thought no more about her until his transceiver went off. His caller was a Roving Remote (female) who instructed him to remove the footage of the woman in the mink and deliver it to the Maison immediately.

The Maison

Alex and Varnas were in Comcentre checking on Big Louie's progress when Varnas was summoned to the projection booth to translate some German from the latest outtake in the Square Albert-Bartholomé.

Expecting more of the weight lifter who spoke to his mother every day in Alsatian, Varnas didn't hurry. Consequently, when the analyst rolled the tape, he was unprepared for what he saw and heard. His response lagged. But his sense of outrage developed quickly as the phone conversation progressed.

Tape:

(Anna Gutierrez enters phone box. After phone rings, she picks up.)

ANNA: *(In French)* Five-four-two-three-zero-zero-six.

WOMAN'S VOICE: Anna?

ANNA: Yes. Frieda? *(Closes phone box door, switches to German)* Hello. What's going on?

FRIEDA: The French Police know about the électricien.

ANNA: *(Pause)* What?

FRIEDA: The police know about Simon. They have him under surveillance.

ANNA: How do you know?

FRIEDA: His phone is tapped. Keck wants to do something.

ANNA: That's stupid. The électricien knows nothing.

FRIEDA: Then why is he under surveillance? Listen, Anna. It's time for you to go. *(No response)* Anna?

ANNA: Yes?

FRIEDA: It's time for you to go.

ANNA: What about the transfer?

FRIEDA: The transfer is done.

ANNA: When?

FRIEDA: Since two days.

ANNA: How?

FRIEDA: As planned.

ANNA: A million shares?

FRIEDA: Yes. Your father confirmed it yesterday.

ANNA: *(Exhales)* Well. That's it then. I'm finished here.

FRIEDA: Yes. You are finished. Now go.

ANNA: I can't go just like that. I have a theatre party tonight. Besides, the police have restricted me to Paris.

FRIEDA: Are they watching you?

ANNA: No.

FRIEDA: Do you have your passport with you?

ANNA: Yes.

FRIEDA: Credit cards?

ANNA: Yes.

FRIEDA: Then go. Forget the theatre. Don't return to your flat.

Never mind even your toothbrush. By the time the police miss
you, you will be past the Canaries.

ANNA: You sound frightened.

FRIEDA: I am. Only go, Anna. If Keck does something about the
électricien, you are not safe.

(*She hangs up. Anna holds the receiver for a moment, hangs up,
and hurries from the phone box.*)

"Rewind and run again," Varnas said and called Alex.

He watched Alex watch the tape and felt compassion as well
as apprehension.

But in less than an hour, Alex had the call to the phone box
traced. To no one's surprise, it had come from Osterholz-
Scharmbeck in the FRG. The call had been placed by Frieda Keck
from a phone listed in her husband's name. The address was Ax-
tedstrasse 11, same as the de Clovis estate.

Alex called César, secured the video tap on the phone box, and
ordered the caravan back to Transport to be repainted and fitted
with alternative surveillance equipment. Assuming Anna would be
out for the evening, he assigned the Sûreté's best "ear," a diminutive electronic elf named Primo, to wire her apartment in Rue
des Grands-Augustins.

"Delighted," said Primo. "Do we get to dress up?"

They assumed the white overalls of EDF (Électricité de France)
employees. A pair of Operations inspecteurs would accompany
Primo upstairs in the apartment while a trio of techniciens kept
the building superintendent busy in the basement inspecting the
power cable.

Just before six, Alex went down to Telex and wrote a message
to the consulate in São Paulo: "Check transfr 40,000 unspecified
shrs 20-11-82 to Carlo Federico de Mayo, Banco do Sul, São Paulo.
Urgnt. End."

He went back to his office and filled out another wiring permit
to be filed with the case judge. Finally, he contacted the Security
Police in Besançon and ordered them to place Simon and Marie
in protective custody.

27

Rue des Grands-Augustins

THE TWO female inspecteurs, in their dark blue Renault, spotted Anna as she and a pair of middle-aged men departed the Brazilian Embassy at 2005 in a late-model gray Mercedes sedan driven by a chauffeur. The tail followed the sedan to the Theatre de Rond Point in the Champs-Élysées, where Anna and the men got out and entered the theatre. The Mercedes drove off.

One of the two women went into the theatre while the other remained in the Renault in transceiver contact. Anna and her companions checked their coats and remained in the lobby sipping aperitifs until 2020, at which time they entered the auditorium and took seats in the fifth row of the centre section of the orchestra. Anna sat between the two men. At 8:31, the house lights dimmed and the curtain rose on Jean Louis Barrault's *Christophe Colomb*.

At 8:45, Primo parked the caravan, newly sprayed with quick-drying enamel and now bearing the logo of EDF, on Rue Christine just off Grands-Augustins. While the apartment building super was kept occupied below watching the techniciens check the power-cable splice and insulation, Primo installed an omnidirectional listening device in the chandelier at the centre of Anna's parlour and another behind the bureau in her bedroom. While he was at it, he bugged the phone.

At the same time, his associates carefully screened every item in the apartment without disturbing either the dust on the bureau or the flecks of toothpaste on the bathroom mirror. They removed only one item from the premises, an object carefully hidden beneath sheets and pillowcases on the top shelf of the bedroom closet. It was a highly incriminating industrial espionage device known as an Electronic Handkerchief. Its function was to transform a woman's voice into that of a man. They completed the entire operation by 9:50, at which time Primo and two assistants returned to the caravan to occupy the listening post while the others returned to the Maison.

During the intermission, Anna and the two men left their seats. The men returned to the lobby to smoke. Anna headed for the ladies' room but did not go in. Instead she placed a call from an adjacent coin box. The call took less than a minute. She then returned to the lobby and engaged in conversation with her companions. From her gestures, the young inspecteur got the impression Anna was not feeling well. The men appeared solicitous. One seemed to offer his help. She declined, shook their hands, and walked to the checkroom. She recovered her coat, waved across the lobby to her friends, and left the theatre.

The inspecteur reactivated her transceiver and alerted her partner in the Renault. Anna hailed a cab on the Champs-Élysées. The tail followed her southeast around the Place de la Concorde, to the Quai des Tuileries, and across the Pont Neuf to Rue des Grands-Augustins. The cab stopped in front of her residence. She paid the driver and entered the building at 10:20.

Both the tail and the stakeout reported her arrival to Primo in the caravan and to Alex monitoring the operation from Comcentre at the Maison.

"Alone?" Alex asked.

"Affirmative."

When Primo heard her key in the door, he rolled the audio tape. He sat in the dimly lit caravan with two assistants and tuned his perfectly pitched ear to the faint hiss of the high-fidelity speakers.

222200NOV82

TIME	AUDIO	COMMENT
2223:00	Key in door. Door unlocked. Door open. Light switch on (push type), door closed, locked	

TIME	AUDIO	COMMENT

	(triple). Heels on bare floor, heels on carpet. Second door open. Single step on bare floor. Rattling sound.	
		PRIMO: Closet. Hangers.
	Clothing movement. Hangs up coat. Single step. Door closed.	
2223:30	Heels on bare floor, heels on carpet. Single step. Interval. Picks up, dials parlour phone.	
		PRIMO *(As she dials):* Two-two-two-zero-seven-zero-seven.
2224:00	Bug picks up two rings. Someone answers.	
		WOMAN: Zero-seven-zero-seven.
		ANNA: Gutierrez.
		WOMAN: One moment, Madame Gutierrez.
	Interval	WOMAN: Yes, madame. One message. Madame Seńkowska called at seven-thirty. She has changed her mind about the obsidian bowl.
		ANNA: Am I to return her call?
		WOMAN: No, madame.
:30		ANNA: Anything else?
		WOMAN: No, madame.
		ANNA: Very well. I'm turning the phone off until nine A.M. Please take any calls.
		WOMAN: Yes, madame.
	Hangs up. Heels on carpet; heels on bare floor receding. Light switch. Heels on bare floor approaching. Heels on rug.	
		PRIMO: She's in the bedroom.

TIME	AUDIO	COMMENT
2225:00	Heels on bare floor; heels on tile. Light switch.	
		PRIMO: Bathroom.
	Bathwater on. Running water.	
:30		
2226:00		
:30	Bureau drawer open.	
2227:00		
:30		
2228:00		
:30		
2229:00	Bathwater off. Enters tub. Splashing, washing.	
:30	Soaks. Interval.	
2230:00		
:30		
2231:00		
:30		
2232:00		ALEX: Primo?
		PRIMO: Yeah, Chef?
		ALEX: What's happening?
:30		PRIMO: She's in the tub, Chef.
2233:00		
:30		
2234:00	Runs additional bath-water.	
:30		
2235:00	Bathwater off. Interval.	
:30		
2236:00		
:30		
2237:00		
:30		
2238:00		
:30		
2239:00		
:30	Splashes.	
2240:00		
:30		
2241:00	Opens drain. Exits tub. Toweling. Atomizer spray.	

TIME	AUDIO	COMMENT

PRIMO: YSL cologne on window shelf.

:30   Door squeak, clothing movement.

PRIMO: Green terry-cloth robe behind bathroom door.

Sink faucet on. Bathroom cabinet door open, closed; interval, teeth brushing.
2242:00   Cabinet door open, closed. Water off. Light switch off. Barefoot steps. Barefoot steps approaching. Soft sound, click.

PRIMO: She turned down the bed and switched on the bed-table lamp.

:30   Sits on bed. Opens table drawer. Interval. Unidentifiable sound.

PRIMO: Emery board.

2243:00
:30   Bed-table drawer closed. Gets up. Barefoot steps. Bureau drawer closed. Brushes hair.
2244:00
:30
2245:00
:30   Places hairbrush on bureau. Barefoot steps on floor, on rug, on floor receding. Light switch off. Barefoot steps approaching.

PRIMO: She's back in the parlour.

Steps recede slightly, stop. Silence. Clothing movement. Silence.
2246:00

ALEX: What's now?
PRIMO: I think she knelt down. In the parlour there's a sofa with a

TIME	AUDIO	COMMENT
		coffee table in front, a small desk, and a TV and phonograph against one wall. She's on the bare floor by either the TV or phonograph.
	Floor creaks.	
:30		PRIMO: Parquet floor. The whole flat is parquet except for the bathroom and the kitchen. Oriental rug in parlour, throw rug in bedroom.
	Floor creaks again.	
		ALEX: Are you sure she's alone?
		PRIMO: Nobody in there with her, Chef. She's safe.
	Swish.	
		PRIMO: Phonograph record. She just pulled one out of its envelope.
2247:00	Click. Record drops. Pickup contact. Music too loud. She turns it down. Symphonic. Violin.	
		PRIMO: What piece is that, Chef?
		ALEX: Mendelssohn Violin Concerto.
:30		PRIMO: Class.
2248:00	Barefoot steps recede. Distant light switch.	
		PRIMO: Kitchen light.
	Unidentifiable sound.	
:30		PRIMO: Fridge. There's a bottle of skimmed milk, a container of yogurt, a bottle of Perrier, and two ice trays.
2249:00		STAKEOUT IN FRONT OF BUILDING (Interrupts): Chef. There's a couple walking up to the front door.

TIME	AUDIO	COMMENT

ALEX: Describe.

STAKE: Man in late sixties, well-dressed. Looks like businessman. Woman approximately same age, carries bouquet of flowers.

:30

ALEX: Okay. Be ready to move if they ring Gutierrez's bell. The parlour mike will pick it up.

2250:00

Interval.

STAKE: Affirm.

STAKE: The guy just took out his keys. He's holding the vestibule door open for the woman. She's in. Now he's in. The bells and house phones are on the right wall. He's not going over there, Chef. He's letting himself into the foyer. They're tenants.

ALEX: Okay.

:30

PRIMO: Chef?

ALEX: Yeah?

PRIMO: She emptied the ice trays into a bucket and put the bucket on the coffee table. If you ask me she's expectin' a guest.

ALEX (Whistles into mike): Now everybody listen good. No one visits Madame Gutierrez tonight. Is that clear? No one. Not her mother or her maiden aunt. Anyone who attempts to see her has to be

2251:00

TIME	AUDIO	COMMENT
		considered dangerous. You guys got that?
		PRIMO, STAKE, etc.: Yeah, Chef . . .
	Music plays.	
:30		
2252:00		
:30		TECHNICIEN IN CARAVAN: What was Flaubert's first name? Seven letters.
		ALEX: Gustave. Primo, anybody screws up tonight he's headed for French Guiana in the morning.
		PRIMO: Gotcha, Chef.
2253:00		ALEX: Primo?
		PRIMO: Chef?
		ALEX: What's she doing now?
		PRIMO: Listenin' to music.
:30		
	Music.	
2254:00		
:30		
2255:00		STAKE (Quietly): Chef?
		ALEX: Yes?
		STAKE: Little old guy in floppy jeans and leather jacket.
		ALEX: Where?
:30		STAKE: Heading for the front.
		ALEX: Describe.
		STAKE: White hair, earmuffs, glasses, walks with short quick steps. Meek and mild. Nonthreatening. Pigeon-feeder.
		ALEX: Is he going in?
		STAKE: Yeah.
		ALEX: Be ready if he . . .

	(Suddenly shouts) HOLD IT! Is this guy wearing scarves? STAKE: He's wearing a scarf. ALEX: Stop him!
2256:00	STAKE: Huh? ALEX: STOP HIM! STAKE: What stop him? He's already in. He let himself in with a key. ALEX: Shit! Primo. PRIMO: Chef? ALEX: Can your mike pick up the elevator? PRIMO: If it opens on her floor, yeah. ALEX: What about footsteps in the hall? PRIMO: Depends on the shoes. ALEX: Stake. What's your name? STAKE: Maurice. ALEX: You got a picklock? MAURICE: Yeah. ALEX: Get into the building now. Walk up to the second floor and stay in the stairwell. And stay on the air.
:30	MAURICE: Okay. ALEX: Primo. This guy may be her sissy friend from the Musée Cernuschi. That doesn't eliminate him as a threat. If he goes to her flat and she lets him in, monitor every word and movement for any sign of trouble. Acknowledge. PRIMO: Got it, Chef. ALEX: Maurice?

TIME	AUDIO	COMMENT

MAURICE: Chef?
ALEX: You hear that?
MAURICE: Affirm.
ALEX: Where are you?
MAURICE: Just picked
    the lock.

Unidentifiable sound.

2257:00

PRIMO: The elevator just
    stopped on two. Door's
    openin'. I don't hear no
    . . . wait. I hear a
    squeak. He's wearin'
    runnin' shoes and
    comin' down the hall.

Door buzzer.

ALEX: Maurice?
MAURICE: I'm going up
    the stairs.
ALEX: If Primo gives the
    word, it's apartment 2F,
    wooden door, easy
    break-in.
MAURICE (Whispers):
    Okay. I'm in the
    stairwell.

Door unlocked.
Door opened.

:30

MAURICE (Whispers): He
    just went in.

Door closed, door locked
(triple), door chain in
place.

ANNA: Hello.
MAN: Hi.

Interval.

ANNA: Let me take your
    jacket.
MAN: Wait. There's a
    going-away present in
    the pocket.

Clothing movement. Rustle
of paper.

2258:00

MAN: Here.
ANNA: Do I know what
    this is?
MAN: Yes.

TIME	AUDIO	COMMENT

		ANNA: I can't believe it!
		MAN: Nevertheless.
	Tearing paper. Interval.	
		ANNA *(Gasps):* Ohhh! Lucien! It's exquisite!
		LUCIEN: Eighteenth-century portrait bottle with your very own frozen Aveyron carp in the style of Chien Lung.
		ANNA: I'm speechless! I've never . . . My God, I'm shaking! Let me put it down before I drop it! *(Voice recedes)* I'll put it on the desk.
:30	Barefoot steps recede. Interval.	
		ANNA: There! Chéri, it's magnificent! *(Voice approaches)* It will never be out of my sight!
		LUCIEN: I'm pleased you're pleased.
		ANNA: Pleased? I'm incoherent! *(She is standing directly under the chandelier. We can hear her breathing.)* And now, monsieur, your jacket, please.
	Clothing movement.	
		ANNA: No, no. Let me. I want you to save your strength.
2259:00		ALEX: Primo.
		PRIMO: Chef?
		ALEX: I can't believe this is the same guy from the musée. The cadence of his speech is roughly what I remember, but he's gone from alto to at least second tenor. And what does she mean "Save his strength?"

TIME	AUDIO	COMMENT

COMMENT column:

For what?
PRIMO: Dunno, Chef.
TECHNICIEN: For
   charades, backgammon,
   paperdolls. Whatever.
   What's a six-letter word
   for the alloy of copper
   and tin?
PRIMO: Bronze. *(On
   mike)* Maurice?
MAURICE: Yeah?
PRIMO: Do you copy?
MAURICE: Yeah.
PRIMO: Keep in touch.

ANNA *(Voice recedes)*:
   Make yourself a drink,
   chéri. There's cognac
   and rum and I think
   Triple Sec.
LUCIEN: Perrier for you?
ANNA: Yes, please.

ANNA: Cheers.
LUCIEN: Cheers.

ANNA *(Exhales)*: Sit
   chéri. I just want to
   stand here and look at
   you.

ANNA: Eyeglasses, off.

ANNA: Shirt . . . off.
   No. no. Let me.

TIME column:
:30
2300:00

AUDIO column:
Clothing movement.

Closet open, hangers,
closet closed. Clink of ice
in glasses. Cork removed,
liquid poured. Sound of
fizz, liquid poured.
Barefoot steps return.
Clink of glasses. She's
under the chandelier again.

Interval.

Faint movement of
upholstery.
Interval.

Interval.

Unsnapping. Clothing
movement.

TIME	AUDIO	COMMENT

ANNA: There. That will do. For the moment. Are you warm enough?

LUCIEN: Yes.

ANNA: You are too beautiful. Your shape is exquisite. And your skin is like translucent calcite. What a pity you're not a necklace so I can take you home with me.

LUCIEN: What . . . and shut me up in your dark little jewelry box with all that fake Inca shit?

:30

ANNA *(Giggles):* I'd wear you around my thigh.

Interval. Clothing movement.

LUCIEN: Around your thigh? Where? Here?

A breath slowly expelled.

ANNA *(Whispers):* Lucien. Easy. This night has to last me for the rest of my life.

LUCIEN: How about here? Or here? Or here?

2301:00

ANNA: Lucien. I'll fall . . .

LUCIEN: Shhh. How about here? Mmm. Crème au Caramel.

Interval.

ANNA *(Faintly):* Ohhhh . . . God. *(She wimpers.)* Luc-ien . . .

The soft crumple of cushions and fabric. A cry. Moist sounds of dalliance.

That was only the beginning. When it became clear to Alex, after an unendurable hour, that the bug on Anna's apartment would produce nothing of value to the police except prurient entertainment (the surveillance personnel had already made book on how many times the participants would debauch), he ordered Maurice back to his stake post outside the building and left Primo in charge with instructions to activate the Maison frequency only if the situation deteriorated.

"What if he fucks her to death?" Primo asked.

"I'll talk to you in the morning," Alex said and started up the stairs to his office. Either by accident or by mischievous design, Primo hit the amplifier rheostat at that instant. As Alex climbed the stairs, the corridors of the Maison rang momentarily with Anna's proliferating cries of joy. This final ignominy caused him to vault up the last few steps and into the office, where he slammed the door. He closed his eyes in the sudden silence, pressed his forehead to the back of the door, and waited for his foolish heart to stop hammering.

"Alexei?"

He turned. Varnas sat on the edge of his desk with a document in his hand.

"This is for you." He held out the paper.

"Not now, for Chrissakes," Alex said and went to his desk.

"Now," Varnas said firmly.

Alex slumped in his chair and accepted the document. It was a telex from the French Consulate in São Paulo. His hands shook.

It read:

CARLO FEDERICO DE MAYO AQRD 1,000,000 SHRS TAGUS INDUSTRIES CMN STK WIRED CRÉDIT SUISSE, ZURICH, 19 NOV, ENDING HOSTL TAKEOVER ATTEMPT BY CONSORTIUM JÕAPEDRO GUTIERREZ. GUTIERREZ DISMISSED. MAY FACE CRIMNL CHGS INSIDR TRADING. END.

Alex looked up. "Anna's husband?"

"Anna's husband. She arranges transfer of shares to Banco do Sul, enabling father to thwart takeover of Tagus Industries by ambitious spouse. Please note that shares are wired from Crédit Suisse, same as funds used to pay for walking sticks."

"Where did she find a million shares of Tagus common?"

"From Uncle Christien."

Alex pressed his temples. "Explain."

In the small space between the desk, Varnas did his imitation of the Commissaire's promenade.

"This is how I see transaction, Alex. Anna does not go to Europe to learn Chinese bric-a-brac but to obtain shares her father needs to regain control of large, but narrowly held, corporation. This occurs in late March. Do you recall visa for West Germany in Anna's passport? She pretends to visit old school chum from Montreux when, in fact, she visits Uncle Chris in Osterholz-Scharmbeck. Already by now, Uncle Chris receives Wilson's copy of 'Influenza Hoax,' together with Sword of Damocles epigraph that we agree is explicit threat to his honour. During this time, he decides on what Bollekens calls 'retributive act.' But he does not yet make definitive plan.

"When beautiful niece comes to visit and makes pitch for controlling stock in Tagus, he sees a way. Wily old eagle makes simple condition for transfer of shares. Drawing on proven wartime tactic of engaging enemy, his condition is this: in return for million shares that he agrees to sell to Banco do Sul below market, she must agree to go to Paris, to meet, to charm, and eventually to set up Andrew Wilson so de Clovis can attack his adversary from a position of advantage."

Alex was silent.

"Do you need more, Alexei?"

Alex got up. "No. Even if your fanciful summary will never get past the Commissaire, we have enough to pick her up, especially if she tries to leave Paris."

Varnas beamed. "Thank you, my dear."

28

The Maison

MONDAY.

At 7:15 next morning, Primo reactivated the Maison frequency. Alex and Varnas, who'd spent most of the night checking details of the computer link with German security, were already downstairs in Comcentre.

"Go ahead, Primo."

"She's getting ready to leave," Primo said. "They climbed out of the sack at six, showered, and she started packing. They have an agenda.

"At eight, he goes to de Gaulle with her suitcases and checks them through to São Paulo on Varig. At nine an embassy car picks her up and takes her to the airport. He sees her off at eleven-ten and the embassy car takes him back to Musée Cernuschi."

"Do you have that on tape?"

"Yeah."

"Then we have proof that she intends to jump her confinement order."

"Yeah. That's the good news."

"Oh?"

"She knows we wired the house."

Alex sat down. Primo said he first realized something was wrong when she started throwing things around in the linen closet. When she finally saw that the electric hanky was missing, she called the super and asked if he'd let anyone into the flat last evening. Of course he hadn't. But he reported that Électricité de France had been in the basement while she was out. She then dialed the Brazilian Embassy. She spoke briefly to some guy in Portuguese and hung up. "That was ten minutes ago. Since then she and her trick haven't said a word that I could pick up."

Alex phoned the Commissaire just back from Villefranche. With a sense of foreboding, he briefed his boss on the situation.

Demonet asked, "Is she connected to the embassy?"

"Socially, yes. She hosts the IMF when they're in town. Stuff like that."

"You're sure she doesn't have diplomatic immunity?"

"She didn't have a diplomatic passport when I checked it. Commissaire, we have proof she called Simon! We have proof she's related to de Clovis and that she probably fingered Wilson!"

"None of that will matter if she has diplomatic immunity. I'll check the Foreign Ministry. Do you have an arrest warrant?"

"Yes."

"Then you'd better get moving."

At 7:45, the female inspecteurs in the blue Renault across the street from Anna's apartment reported the gray Mercedes speeding up Grands-Augustins. It skidded to a stop in front of the building. Three men, one dressed in overalls and carrying a tool box, hurried inside.

Primo heard the buzzer sound in the apartment. Anna rang back. Minutes later, the men were at her door, which she opened immediately. They spoke in Portuguese. There was a sound of running footsteps, shouted instructions, windows being opened and closed and furniture being moved. Within ten minutes they'd located both microphones.

In heavily accented French, one of the men, presumably a spokesman, stood under the chandelier mike and announced, "This premises has been retained by the Brazilian Legation for the private use of its diplomatic and consular personnel. My government will issue a formal complaint through the appropriate channels for this outrageous violation of international protocol!"

A second later, Primo heard the pliers cut the wire. The bug went dead. To Primo it was like having a vein opened.

Alex and Varnas careened into Rue des Grands-Augustins just

in time to see the Mercedes make a shrieking U-turn and speed past them with the blue Renault in hot pursuit.

Anna Gutierrez spent four hours in the Brazilian Embassy, or just long enough to enable consular personnel to secure a reservation for her on a Paris–St. Louis flight with a connection to São Paulo.

During her brief sanctuary, she was officially expelled from France for "activities inimical to the republique." This was a diplomatic two-step choreographed by the Foreign Ministry to save face and to provide an analgesic for the Sûreté's headache.

Lucien Violet, apparently ignorant of Anna's complicity, was questioned by the Sûreté and released. The Commissaire said, "We cannot hold him for impersonating a homosexual."

8 Rue Georges-Berger

Millicent handed Madame Roget an envelope containing ten new hundred-franc notes.

Madame Roget blushed. "It is not necessary, madame."

"Of course it's not, Clothilde. But you know monsieur would have wished it."

Madame Roget buried her face in her apron and burst into tears. Millicent held her until the sobbing subsided.

"We all loved him, Clothilde," Millicent said, surprising herself at this straight-arrow banality but feeling better for it. The sobs stopped. Madame Roget finally disengaged herself, abruptly kissed Millicent on both cheeks, and fled.

Millicent walked into the living room and left the envelope on the piano. Zeke poked his head in.

"Limo's here. Got everything?"

"Yes. Is Anna in the car?"

"Nope. Just Boli and the President's wife. Let's go." He left.

She glanced at her watch. How very strange. Anna was to have been here over an hour ago to discuss the porcelain pieces Millicent intended to donate to the musée. And to accompany her to the airport. It was not at all like Anna to alter her plans without calling.

Millicent took a deep breath, looked around the living room once, and walked to the foyer. She was putting on her duffle coat when the phone rang. With one arm in the coat she went into

Pudge's office and answered. It was not Anna calling about being late but the young Chef-Inspecteur calling about Anna.

Millicent listened without comment. Finally, she asked, "You're quite sure of your facts?" He was. "Well," she said, "I guess that explains why she's not here to see me off." She noticed that her voice was trembling and wondered if the policeman noticed. "Thanks for not telling me sooner. You might've had another homicide on your hands."

She hung up and stood by Pudge's desk, gazing at the two boys holding the string of trout.

"Mimsy?" Bollekens at the door.

"Yes. I'm coming."

29

Aérogare 1. Charles de Gaulle

THE GRAY Élysée Palace limousine deposited them at Pan Am departure. David Stevenson was waiting on the curb. For a second, Millicent didn't recognize him. Then she realized he was letting his beard grow. She wondered why. Could he be embarking on some new virility? Hang gliding? Or a love affair?

She half-listened as he apologized for his wife's absence. "Jeanne is on the altar guild at Notre Dame de Grâce, and Monday is fresh flowers and linens. I couldn't let you go without saying good-bye." He squeezed her hand and bowed to the others. "Good-bye, good-bye," he said, waved, and disappeared.

Zeke placed himself in charge of the luggage while Bollekens and Françoise Poinsard accompanied Millicent to the VIP lounge.

Here they encountered an exotic mélange: a pair of turbaned sheiks surrounded by veiled wives and relatives, watchful servants, and beautiful jet-eyed children; a group of leopard-capped diplomats from Djibouti with paprika-coloured robes and mahogany fly whisks; a few Japanese businessmen in dark suits; an Indian woman wearing a purple and gold sari over white Reeboks; an animated group of elderly Hasidim in black hats and prayer shawls; and, in a far corner, attended by a Transport Policewoman and a trio of expensively dressed, deeply tanned men, Anna in dark glasses, knitting.

Millicent saw her first. Her instinctual response was to turn away, to avoid the face of her betrayer, to deny her. Millicent turned quickly toward Françoise.

"You're white as a sheet," Francoise said. "Are you all right?"

"Certainly not. I've just seen a witch. How do you kill a witch? With water? Fire? Stake through the heart?"

"Mimsy, what is it?"

Millicent turned then and pointed across the lounge at Anna. Françoise followed her finger. "Turn around, chérie. She is in police custody."

At that moment, Anna stood and, accompanied by the policewoman, marched briskly across the far end of the lounge toward the ladies' room.

"I've ordered us some tea," Bollekens said and took Millicent's arm.

Millicent gently removed his hand. "In that case I'll need to freshen up," she said quietly and set off in the direction of the ladies' room.

Françoise started after her. Bollekens intervened. "Let her go. She is a woman of principle with something on her mind. She'd never forgive us if we meddled."

The policewoman had stationed herself outside the door. Millicent smiled affably at her and went in.

Inside, on the left, a plaza of sinks and mirrors. Beyond, left and right, a lane of toilet stalls. In front of a mirror, a young Japanese woman renewed her lipstick beneath the inscrutiny of her mother. Farther along, a sheik's servant waited on station outside a stall, guarding with her life the child within.

Millicent roamed along the lane of toilets, looking for the feet beneath the aluminum closures that would identify Anna. She moved low to the ground, like Groucho. She had no strategy. She didn't know what she would do when the moment arrived, only that she would confront her adversary face to face, achieve warfare in its most rudimentary form.

Halfway down the lane on the left, she spotted the perfectly polished cordovan boots encircled by an ankle ruff of black gabardine. Millicent stopped so suddenly that her bag slipped off her shoulder and thudded onto the tile. The heavy brown paper envelope that contained Pudge's Browning automatic, wrapped according to airline specifications and to be surrendered before boarding, slithered out of the bag onto the floor with her hand cream and nail file.

A strategy immediately presented itself. With the file, she pierced the tape sealing the parcel, tore it open and carefully removed the gun. She then backed into the stall opposite Anna's and waited. She noticed that Anna was sixth down water-closet lane. Tom, she recalled, was forty-fourth down Avenue Zillibeke.

The sheik's daughter finished and departed. After a short interval, the gabardine ruff opposite stirred and smoothly ascended in parallel columns of immaculate tailoring. Anna flushed the toilet. Millicent stepped out of her enclosure.

Millicent saw that all the stall doors opened in, which meant that Anna would have to pause and wait for the door to clear before she could exit. And, as Anna's door opened, Millicent noticed that her toilet seat was up. As every woman knows, women are divided into two public toilet groups: those who cover the seat with paper and sit down, and those who leave the seat up and suspend themselves over the bowl. Anna belonged to the second group, a fact that provided Millicent with a tactic to enhance her strategy.

As the door now opened fully, Anna had time to take but a single step before Millicent lunged. The force of her attack knocked off Anna's dark glasses and caused the backs of her legs to buckle against the toilet bowl. This jackknifed her into a sitting position. She fell backwards into the bowl with her knees stuffed under her chin.

Millicent slipped into the stall, closed and locked the door, and placed the muzzle of the gun against Anna's throat.

"Well, well," Millicent said. "Live and learn. I always thought that if someone was reasonably attractive and reminded me of me they couldn't be all bad. Guess I was wrong. Do I remind you of you?"

Anna exhaled unevenly. "A little."

"Then you must know I'm entirely capable of killing you."

Anna met the lavender gaze. "I don't think you'd be that stupid, Mimsy. There's a policewoman outside."

"Why is that?"

"Why is there a policewoman outside?"

"Yes."

"She's guarding me."

"Why?"

"Something about espionage, the Foreign Ministry said."

"Something about hiring an electrician, more likely. Something about telling Pudge to meet you at the basin bridge so he could pick up my birthday present. Something about a phone call from a woman named Frieda confirming a stock transfer—your Big Payola, as they used to say in the old gangster movies. The policewoman is out there because you're a criminal. And as for my getting away with murder, it is a matter of complete indifference to me whether I do or don't. I've already lived ten years longer than my mother and eighteen years longer than my father. Indeed, I can think of no better way to cap off a rich, full life than to perform an unselfish act like this that will benefit all mankind."

Anna tried to pry herself loose. "This is insane! You know perfectly well I had no more to do with Pudge's death than you did!" She managed to raise herself a few inches. Millicent pushed her back. The displaced water in the toilet bowl slopped onto the floor. Anna shuddered. "Have you lost your mind? Mimsy, for God's sake, I'm your friend! I was *his* friend! You've been horribly misinformed! The police have nothing on me! They're expelling me to cover their embarrassment! Can't you see that? Mimsy, please, you're hurting me!" Millicent pressed the gun barrel into the flesh of Anna's throat. "Owww! Oh God! What do I have to do to convince you?"

"Make me an offer."

A tear had started down Anna's cheek. But at this remark, Millicent, remembering an old joke, imagined the tear to hesitate, to stop, then to travel purposefully back up Anna's cheek and back into her eye. Such was the 180-degree change in her expression. She leaned back as far as she could and crossed her arms over her chest. "What sort of offer?"

"A business offer, of course."

"You mean money?"

"I mean a business offer. You understand business. The business of business is profit and acquisition, which includes the removal of obstacles to profit and acquisition. Your husband's attempt to take over a certain company was an obstacle to profit and acquisition. You removed the obstacle by acquiring a controlling share of the company's stock. But there was an obstacle to acquiring those shares which you removed by agreeing to the conditions of sale imposed by your uncle. Well. Now here's Mimsy with a gun to your head, an obstacle if I ever saw one. How will you remove it? Simple. By making me an offer."

Anna uncrossed her arms and looked directly into Millicent's eyes. "There was no condition placed on the sale of my uncle's shares. He's a major depositor in the Banco do Sul. He's my father's brother-in-law. What kind of family do you imagine us to be?"

"A business family. Make me an offer."

Anna stared. Without blinking she said, "A hundred thousand dollars. U.S."

Millicent smiled. "Dear me, even I think you're worth more than that. Where's your self-esteem?"

"Five hundred thousand."

"That's better. Do I hear seven-fifty?"

A nearby lavatory speaker interrupted. It boomed the announcement that TWA's nonstop flight to St. Louis was now boarding first-class passengers and passengers with young children. This was followed immediately by the sound of the ladies' room door opening. A stern woman's voice echoed along the tile. "Madame Gutierrez?"

Anna tensed and opened her mouth as if to cry out. Millicent cocked the hammer of the Browning. Anna exhaled and closed her eyes. "Yes?" she answered feebly. "What is it?"

"They are calling your flight. Do you need help?"

"No."

"Then please hurry." The door closed.

Millicent nudged the throat. "Do I hear seven-fifty?"

Anna sighed. "Seven-fifty."

"Say your prayers."

"Mimsy, I'm innocent!"

"Pray!"

"I don't know how!"

"Then I'll pray for you. Now I lay me down to sleep, pray the Lord my soul to keep; if I should die before I wake, pray the Lord my soul to take. God bless Mommy, Daddy, and Uncle Chris. Good-bye treacherous bitch!"

Anna's jaw dropped. "MIMSY!"

Millicent pulled the trigger. There was a click. Anna recoiled and covered her face with her hands.

Millicent dropped the gun in her bag and opened the stall door. She stepped out, turned, flushed the toilet, and left.

The gyros on the Pan Am 747 were already spooling up as Millicent and Zeke boarded. Flight attendants were checking carry-on luggage and seat belts. Had it not been for Françoise Poinsard and the Secret Service, Jan Bollekens would not have been allowed on the aeroplane.

Millicent and Zeke were shown seats in the rear of first class. Everyone stood in the aisle.

Zeke and Bollekens, with the accumulation of 172 years between them, pumped hands. Zeke said, "I got a free lunch comin' next year from that young Lootenant. You're invited."

"I'll be there," Bollekens replied and patted Zeke's arm.

"You be there, Boli!" Zeke said.

Françoise Poinsard held both of Millicent's hands. "You'll be back in the spring, Mims?"

"If I'm still among the quick and can talk my grandkid into coming. I can't imagine being anywhere else in the springtime."

The two women exchanged kisses on both cheeks. To Françoise's surprise Millicent gave her an extra squeeze and kiss on the forehead.

The engines started. Françoise withdrew to the jetway, turned, blew a kiss, and left.

Bollekens held Millicent at arm's length. "Call me when you get in so I know you're safe."

Millicent smiled. "My daddy always said that when he sent me off to camp. I can't remember if that was slightly before or after the War of the Roses. Call you where, Jan?"

"Louvain."

She hesitated. "Louvain. You know you haven't told me how Charlotte is."

"Charlotte is the same."

"Still clinging tenaciously to the riverbank?"

"Yes."

She straightened his bow tie. "She will not go gentle, will she, Jan?"

"No."

She kissed him on both cheeks. "You be well, my dear friend."

"I will, Mimsy. And you too. I'll keep you up to date on developments here." He kissed her hands, gazed at her face for a moment, and hurried away.

Six hours later, a short time before Millicent's flight landed at Kennedy, Sûreté headquarters in Paris received a teleflex call from Security Police HQ, Besançon. A plastic explosive device placed in Simon's truck by persons unknown had detonated, killing Simon and Marie instantly and leveling the row of shops adjacent to the allée.

30

The Maison

MIDNIGHT.

The Commissaire toyed with Joan of Arc's visor. He remained silent for a minute or so before snapping the meerschaum helmet shut. He glanced up and spoke softly, almost regretfully.

"Well, the murderer has finally acknowledged us. It could not have happened at a worse time. This is a poor season to be a flic. The General Directorate for External Securité is undergoing a public scandal and personnel restructuring due to its failure last year to correctly anticipate the Libyan invasion of Chad. The Surveillance Territoriale have been criticized in the press for alleged strong-arm tactics in their confrontation with suspected members of Direct Action.

"Now here comes the Sûreté, the jewel of French law enforcement. So far, its investigation of the Wilson murder had been impeccable and out of the newspapers. But soon it will risk becoming the next target of police bashing by, one, allowing Simon's death, and two, by publicly committing the indelicacy of summoning France's extradition treaty with the FRG in order to arraign Germany's oldest surviving aerial ace of World War One for the murder of an American octogenarian at precisely the moment the Élysée Palace is attempting to nurture a mutual defense policy with Bonn."

Demonet performed what is known, outside France, as a Gallic shrug. "Very well," he said, "you worry about the evidence. I'll worry about its effect. I will return to the Foreign Minister and do my best to argue your case."

       *   *   *

During the week that followed, Alex and Varnas learned that Simon had refused to be taken into custody. He and Marie had recently married and planned to drive to Lausanne for their honeymoon.

"Instead they spend it in Paradise," Varnas said.

The Commissaire traveled between the Maison and the Ministry of Foreign Affairs. He attended two meetings at the Élysée Palace. It was only after the second of these that low-profile negotiations with West Germany commenced.

Extradition was ruled out from the beginning. The Baron de Clovis was a relic of a Germany most Germans preferred to forget. Nevertheless, he was considered a hero who'd served his country with distinction. Out of consideration for this and for his advanced age, the negotiators referred the matter to the Bremen prosecutor.

After several days of reviewing Sûreté material, the prosecutor concluded that the case against de Clovis had merit. He agreed to issue a search warrant giving police access to the aerodrome, the museum, and the schloss. If subsequent evidence proved conclusive, the suspect and his accomplices would be placed under house arrest until a hearing could be arranged.

The French, now out of their jurisdiction, wished to guard against the possibility of collusion to exonerate and insisted that Sûreté personnel accompany the officers issuing the warrant and that they be present in court, with counsel, at any hearings.

Alex and Varnas were told to pack.

Le Yacht Club

The day before they were to leave, Philippa took the afternoon off to shop and prepare dinner. She had just placed the rack of lamb in the oven when the phone rang. It was Alex's mother, calling from Douarnenez.

"Philippa? Is everything all right?"

"Of course, Nana. Why?"

"I don't know. I just had a feeling something wasn't quite right."

Philippa made no attempt to humour her. Madame Grismolet had country woman instincts. "I can't imagine what it might be,

Nana. Nothing new here, except . . . I broke up with my boyfriend."

"Ah, that's too bad, chérie."

"Not really. Oh. And Alex and Varnas are off to Germany."

"To Germany?"

"On a case."

"Perhaps that's it. Will it be dangerous?"

"I don't know, Nana. I hope not."

The older woman hesitated. "Philippa, how would you like some company while Alex is gone? I can bring a couple of lobsters and some fresh butter."

Philippa didn't need the company. But she couldn't disappoint Alex's mother. And if she was going to fall off the anorexigenic wagon, what better way than with Brittany lobsters and fresh country butter?

"I'd love the company, Nana."

An hour later, Varnas arrived bearing chrysanthemums and daisies.

"How long will you be gone?" Philippa asked as she arranged the flowers in a water pitcher, the ship's only vase.

"Three days . . . five . . . hard to say."

"Three days is okay. Five would be better."

"Better for what?"

"For my surprise. Let me show you."

She walked to the centre of the saloon and removed the hooked rug that covered the hatch to the barge's engine compartment. She leaned over to pull the recessed lifting ring but hesitated. "Can I swear you to secrecy, Varnas?"

"Of course."

"Promise. Cross your heart and hope to die?"

Varnas grinned. "Hope to die."

She pulled up the twin hatches and locked the hinges. Varnas gazed into the engine compartment. It was newly painted in white enamel but was empty except for a battery box and some cables and wires.

"Where is engine?" Varnas asked.

"That's the surprise. I made a deal with my lady railroad workers to give them a year of aerobics plus a few thousand francs for engine parts if they'd remove the old Buda and repair it in their workshops. Turned out the engine wasn't that different from the ones in their small locomotives. When you were in Besançon, we took out the saloon skylight, borrowed a mobile crane, and pulled the engine out through the overhead. Since then we've cleaned up the rust, put in a new main bearing, a new connecting rod, new injectors, and new hoses. We fired it up yesterday and it runs like a clock. Now we need time to put it back, get it aligned, and fix the stuffing box."

Varnas looked at her with admiration. "Does Alex know that future prima ballerina becomes also diesel mechanic?"

"No. He thinks I'm raising the money for us to fly to Martinique, a trip he could care less about. Alex's big dream is to take *Le Yacht Club* down the canals to the Med."

"And what is Philippa's big dream?"

She closed the hatch. "To dance Giselle someday. Not to break a leg. Maybe to choreograph when I'm older. Or teach. To work on diesels. You know . . . what most dancers dream about."

"Philippa never dreams about love and marriage?"

She straightened the rug over the hatch. "Not marriage," she said soberly. "I just went over that with Jean-Jacques. He asked me to marry him. I think he did it partly as a challenge to Alex, partly to prove to himself that he's straight, and partly because he's one of those dancers who believes he can be at his best only when he's experiencing a *grand passion*. For a boy from Bordeaux, J-J can be very Russian.

"I'm the opposite. I can only handle one passion at a time, and dancing is my passion. Alex understands that. He's like me. J-J understands nothing. He basically wants me in the kitchen."

Varnas nodded. "Probably you make right decision. But Philippa, nobody dances forever."

"I know. And when my time comes I'll transfer my passion to something else. Or someone else." She smiled and kissed Varnas on the cheek. "You're a sweet old fart. But the answer to your question is no, Philippa doesn't dream about marriage. Love sometimes. And food." She patted his arm. "Be sure to let me know when you'll be back. It takes forever to get that skylight in. Oh shit!"

"What?"

"Alex's mother is coming. Well, she'll just have to cope."

Alex arrived with three bottles each of Spanish champagne and red Bordeaux. They devoured Philippa's rack of lamb, Belgian carrots, and rosemary potatoes. They drank all the wine. After dinner they drank a bottle of Armagnac.

Varnas sang "The Passing Lighter" with tuba accompaniment. Philippa danced a soft java.

Varnas spent the night on board. He slept on the sofa in the saloon fully clothed with his hat on.

Next day, Wednesday, 1 December, badly hung over, Alex and Varnas flew to Bremen.

Part Five
THE GOLDEN KNIGHT

31

Bremen

THE Lufthanza Airbus landed at Lemwerder airport, west of the city, in a howling snowstorm. The flight had not been pleasant: neither for Varnas, who urgently needed a glass of warm bicarbonate of soda (not on the menu), nor for Alex, who imagined he was being taken away from the sea. Creatures of the littoral become uneasy when moved inland.

"You are closer to sea in Bremen than in Paris," Varnas muttered.

"Not my sea. The birds will be different. And the smell. Bremen will be cold and dark and buffeted by Icelandic lows." With that the Airbus descended into a snowstorm that persisted until touchdown.

Inside the terminal, they were met by a welcoming committee of one, an affable, dark-haired man in his early forties. He was slim and of medium height and wore a well-cut tweed jacket and bow tie under an open trench coat. He possessed the easy, compact assuredness of a TV correspondent. Alex expected he was a liaison or protocol officer running interference for the remote chieftain of a sprawling municipal law-enforcement bureaucracy whom they would never meet. It came as a surprise, therefore, when, in excellent Oxford English, he introduced himself as the Bremen Prosecutor and hustled them out of the building.

"Sorry to rush you chaps," he said, "but we have a meeting practically immediately. I'll see to your billet later."

The chauffeur of the black Mercedes limo saluted and stowed their bags. The prosecutor got in front with the chauffeur. Once clear of the terminal building, he turned and said, "I've got to tell you something straight away. This is a warrant that no German prosecutor is anxious to serve. It will please no one. Neither those old conservatives in government who insist the Freiherr should be immune from prosecution, nor those more liberal who have little sympathy for him but fear that any move against him will be viewed as a victory for the Greens, or worse, the peace-movement activists who gather each spring with songs and placards demanding that all weapons of war be destroyed.

"In any case, the government wishes no publicity. To that end, we will move quickly and discreetly."

"When?" Varnas asked, thinking of Philippa's schedule.

"Tomorrow morning. We have already stationed a police van with two men outside the gatehouse, the sole entrance to the de Clovis estate. As well, we have a police helicopter and crew parked on the hangar ramp to discourage anyone who might wish to leave by air. We ourselves will move just before sunrise with three vehicles and six men, plus the two of you. That's twelve on our wicket versus seven on theirs; four on theirs really. You can't count the Freiherr, who is eighty-seven and confined to a wheelchair, or his cook-housekeeper, who is nearly as old, or his nurse. Actually I *would* count the nurse. She outweighs us all."

"Is that Frieda?" Alex asked.

"Frieda Keck, yes. We should also count her husband, who is the aircraft custodian and reputed to be bad-tempered, plus an air mechanic or two and, of course, the gunsmith Blücher. Incidentally, the sheer bulk of Frieda suggests she may have done your boot prints in the parc."

"Do we anticipate trouble tomorrow?"

"I doubt it. But I'd like to be assured of de Clovis's cooperation ahead of time. That's what the meeting is about."

In the high-ceilinged office, a rococo, marzipan, and nougat candy-box affair with pink plaster cupids, gold acanthus leaves, and a crown-shaped chandelier, the prosecutor perched on the edge of his cherrywood and mother-of-pearl desk and eyed the court-appointed advocate, a formal old-world lawyer whose starched wing collar and black tailcoat perfectly matched the decor.

"May it please the court," the old gentleman began.

"This is not a court of law, Herr Hopke," the prosecutor interrupted, placing a tasseled loafer on a gray-flanneled knee. "This is simply a hearing to determine your client's willingness to co-operate with a court-ordered search warrant. Will he cooperate or not?"

The old man lifted his arms to his sides and let them drop. "Herr Prosecutor, the Freiherr does not accept my services. He has never employed an advocate, he says. Always a handshake and a man's word is enough, he says. Always enough is the concept of private settlement to resolve disputes, a different and dignified law, he says, that has nothing to do with the law under which you seek to judge him."

"Does he understand that if he resists the court order he will be placed under house arrest?"

The advocate sighed. "I'm not sure, Herr Prosecutor."

"Did you tell him?"

"Of course, Herr Prosecutor."

"And?"

The old man shrugged. "The Freiherr said, 'Let them come.' "

Alex and Varnas were installed in a suite of rooms at the Hotel Weser, a few blocks from the Criminal Court Building and within walking distance of the Bremen Rathaus, a gothic and gabled edifice of fairy-tale magnificence.

The suite had a small kitchen with a refrigerator temptingly stocked with liquor and delicacies. Included was an engraved list of prices so appallingly inflated as to demolish any desire to snack on even the small can of peanuts.

They went out to dinner and ate sauerbraten with sweet-and-sour cabbage. The view from the restaurant included a houseboat moored in the river. Back at the hotel, Alex called Philippa. It had not snowed in Paris. "What's on tonight?" he asked.

"La Belle Hélène."

"Ah."

"You sound wistful."

"I'm homesick."

Philippa smiled into the phone. "Home is waiting," she said. "Hurry back before nostalgia drives you into the arms of some compliant fräulein. By the way, a friend of yours wants to say hello."

Alex's mother came on. "Alexandre, I invited myself to Paris. I'm sure it's a great inconvenience to Philippa. But she's taking marvelous care of me. I am installed in your stateroom with all the comforts, and tonight I go to the ballet. When will you be back?"

"Not sure. We make the pinch tomorrow."

"Please be careful, chéri. Here's Philippa."

"Alex? You be safe."

"I will."

"And take care of Varnas."

"I will. Hold on. He wants to talk to you."

Varnas picked up. "So sweetheart, how are the things?"

"Ahead of schedule. Got the engine in this afternoon. Only took an hour. Took another hour to clean up Alex's mother. Listen, Varnas. Try to give me a little warning when you arrive back so I can crank the thing up. I want to see his face when he walks up the quay and hears . . . and sees . . . and smells this wonderful thing running. It goes pouf-pouf-pouf-gurgle-pouf-gurgle-pouf-pouf and smells like the Saint-Malo ferry. It's beautiful."

"That's good, Philippa."

"Take care of my friend."

"I take care of him, sweetheart." He rang off.

They began to get ready for bed. "She is so fine, Alex," Varnas said. "Someday she makes the wonderful mama."

"She doesn't need kids. She's got us." It was the sort of gratuitous wisecrack Alex had been making for years. Tonight it sounded stupid. "Sorry."

"And I'm sorry to sound always like matchmaker. Philippa doesn't need my help. She knows what she wants."

"What does she want?"

"Love, food, to dance Giselle, not to marry. But I say she gets married someday and when she does it is to you."

"You sound like Claudine. Varnas, I'm sixteen years older than Philippa."

"Sure. When you are twenty-four and she is eight, you are sixteen years older than Philippa." He carefully hung up his trousers. "When you are thirty and she is fourteen, you are still sixteen years older. But then she starts getting older faster than you. Ask any woman and she agrees. When you are fifty, Philippa is already thirty-four and beginning to get the crowfoot. Before long you are sixty-four and she is already forty-eight. For a man like you, sixty-four is nothing. But nobody wants a single woman of forty-eight. She is already over a hill."

They completed their toilet, left a call for six, turned off the light, and crawled into bed under bruising eiderdowns. The darkened room blinked pastel pink from an electric bar sign across the street.

Just before sleep, Varnas said, "Alex?"

"Hm?"

"I understand de Clovis."

"Hm."

"I understand him like I understand Wilson. When written law does not provide opportunity to redress violation of honour, family, or homeland, person in distress turns to unwritten law. Do you know what is Justice Commandoes of Armenian Genocide? To avenge massacre of Armenians by Turks in 1915—that's already more long ago than Wilson and de Clovis—third- and fourth-generation Armenians today murder third- and fourth-generation Turks in Paris, Los Angeles, London . . . wherever they can find them. They don't forget. And they don't forgive. Like your grandfather never forgives the Germans.

"You say you don't understand revenge, Alex, unless it is Mafia. Never mind. Try to feel it. It is instinct. Like sex. You understand sex?"

"Hm."

"Maybe you are too civilized. Maybe not enough happens to you in your young life. I understand revenge. If I think I can liberate ten hectares of Lithuanian soil by crawling on my belly to Moscow, I leave tomorrow. Good night."

Alex opened his eyes and peered at his friend's profile silhouetted against the flashing windowframe. Brave men, Varnas and Grandfather: impassioned, enraged, committed . . . the indispensable ingredients of heroes and scoundrels. Too civilized? Maybe.

32

Grandfather

ALEX slept soundly until 2 A.M., when he awoke, covered in gooseflesh and thinking he smelt smoke. He raised up on one elbow, peered into the darkness, and clearly saw him sitting on the foot of the bed, lighting his great, curved calabash.

But this could not be a Grandfather dream! The hotel room was exactly as it had been before sleep. Nothing had changed except that the bar across the street was closed and the snow had stopped. It couldn't be a dream! Varnas lay in the next bed, snoring. Alex shivered.

"You shiver, Alexandre," Grandfather said, "because you are afraid." He took a few puffs of his pipe. "Soldiers always shiver when they go into battle. But when they begin to fight they overcome their fear. They stop shivering when they find they are less afraid of death, which they do not comprehend, than of cowardice, which they do."

"I'm not a coward," Alex said.

"Of course not! You are my grandson, Alexandre!" Grandfather puffed. "So what will you do tomorrow, Alexandre?"

"Stay in bed, if I can," Alex heard himself say.

"Very wise, my boy. Very civilized, Alexandre!"

Alex was suddenly overcome by languor. He heard the whistle of a tugboat on the river and the low, unidentifiable hum that every large city makes at night. He adjusted his pillow, rolled over, and closed his eyes.

When he opened them a moment later, the lights in the room were on and Varnas was shaking him.

" 'To chase your precious sleep away
Is lousy way to start a day!'

"That's Guillaume d'Artois on morning before Battle of Crécy,
26 August, 1346."

"What time is it?"

"Six. Rise and shine." Varnas went into the bathroom, where
the shower was already generating steam.

Alex turned over and went back to sleep.

Varnas was fully dressed when he shook Alex the second time.
He proffered a bowl of café au lait. "Time for coffee. Prosecutor
picks us up at seven. You have twelve minutes."

The Golden Knight

The autoroute from Bremen to Osterholz-Scharmbeck was dry
and clear of snow. The convoy of three black Mercedes sedans,
traveling easily at 120 kilometres per hour, left the city in the
leaden predawn. As they approached O-S, the crimson pod of a
bloated, amoeba-like sun ignited the crowded cloud base along
the eastern horizon. The north German plain stretched away, snow
quilted, an occasional wrinkle casting shadows longer and more
fanciful than Alex had seen before. Something to do with high
latitude.

He and Varnas occupied the rear seat of the lead vehicle. In
the front seat, next to the driver, the prosecutor checked the frequency and squelch knobs on his transceiver. As the convoy slowed
and entered the darkened town at the edge of the Teufels Moor,
he established contact with the police van and helicopter on station
thirteen kilometres up the Axtedt road to the north. The time was
7:40. Estimated time of arrival at the gatehouse was 7:50. However, after they turned onto the secondary Axtedt road and saw
that it had been plowed for a single lane of traffic only, the prosecutor extended his ETA.

When this was confirmed the convoy yawed up the narrow,
drifted track, leaving a turbulent trail of blowing snow crystals.

Clear of the town, the prosecutor pointed into the near distance.
There, rising out of the moor like some remote volcanic island
rising out of the sea, was the great glass-domed atrium of the

museum. The topmost panes and bronze cap caught the low sun and cast rockets of red and gold over the sombre, thinly wooded plain.

Varnas nudged Alex. "Look . . . like Bishop's mitre at Christmas."

Alex cracked the window for air. To him the scene was anything but benign. There was something hallucinatory about the way the patterns of red and orange were being flung about inside the dome. Why was the reflected sunlight *inside* the dome? The rising sun had reached the low cloud layer and left the surrounding moor in darkness. Yet the domed atrium remained alight. Why? The bright glow rose and fell like the aurora borealis. He sniffed and smelt smoke. At the same moment the prosecutor shouted, "Christ! He's torched the place!"

The radio began to babble as the other vehicles became aware of the fire. The prosecutor ordered them to stand by as he attempted to raise the helicopter crew. No answer. He tried the van at the gatehouse. No answer there either. He'd spoken to both less than five minutes before. He pressed the Tx button. "Stay off the air and follow!"

The convoy accelerated and plunged into the woods bordering Schloss Scharmbeck to the west.

At the gatehouse, all was serene. A gray cat sat on the roof of the van, washing itself. Both doors of the van were open. There was no damage or sign of a struggle. The keys were in the ignition. But fresh jeep tracks led under the padlocked entrance gates and snaked up the unplowed drive toward the museum and airfield.

They sliced the lock with chain cutters, threw open the gates, and raced through. To avoid becoming mired in the deep snow, they kept to the narrow-gauge jeep tracks. These led past the museum at a safe distance, though the heat from the building was now sufficient to melt the heavy snow on the evergreens surrounding it. As a consequence, they plowed through an avalanche of falling slush while skidding past the burning, ominously crackling atrium. There was no one about. No firemen, no one.

A hundred metres beyond, they encountered a fork in the drive marked by signs bearing the Eurostencil symbol for Castle (Schloss), left, and Airfield (Flugfeld), right. They stopped and saw that both drives were freshly plowed. What remained of the jeep tracks seemed to favour the left fork. However, to the right, they saw the backs of aeroplane hangars and, beyond the northernmost hangar, the unmistakable blur of the twirling red and white rotor blades of the police helicopter. The prosecutor ordered a right turn. The convoy plunged down the steep access road and circled round the north hangar directly to the chopper parked on the partially cleared ramp.

They slid to a stop before an eerie sight: ahead, an unmanned helicopter, virtually poised for takeoff, fidgeted in the wash of its own rotor, while fifty metres away, before the dark mouth of the open hangar, the varnished wooden propeller of an antique gold biplane turned slowly, casting pointillist shards of pale morning light over the tarmac. Alex recalled Geoffrey's description . . . *repro D III with the larger Austro-Daimler engine, shocking amount of speed for a dirty old bird.* A black-helmeted pilot sat deep in the cockpit.

The prosecutor pounded his driver on the shoulder. "You're going to ram that aeroplane! Now! Get going!"

The driver, whose sole responsibility it was to keep this particular Mercedes in mint condition, simply did not comprehend the order. In the lapse between word and deed, the biplane's engine roared to life. It surged forward. Within seconds, its tail was off the ground and, in less than fifty metres, it was airborne and climbing. On the ramp, where the aeroplane had been, all that remained was an empty wheelchair, which, caught in the propeller blast, backed sedately into the hangar unattended. Seconds later, the roof of the atrium collapsed in a roaring cataract of glass and steel.

Inside the car, the air seemed to disappear, to be sucked out, leaving a vacuum. The atrium flames, no longer constrained within the great conservatory, shot up hundreds of metres. When the air returned, it returned with the impact of a tornado followed by a heat storm of wind.

The prosecutor ordered his vehicles out of the area. They were completing a half turn around the helicopter when Varnas, inspecting the horizon through the rear window, shouted, "Air attack!"

No one had noticed the biplane. It had leveled off beyond the airfield, turned, and now rocketed toward the defenseless helicopter at ground level.

Doors flew open and bodies dove out of the still-moving vehicles onto the ground. Varnas landed on top of Alex as the biplane opened fire.

Alex felt the impact of a nearby explosion followed by a chaotic shower of snow, frozen mud, and twittering birds. The plane boomed overhead leaving a cyclone in its wake. He opened his eyes. The helicopter was burning and the vehicle they'd occupied seconds before was now a hissing derelict of punctured tyres and shattered windows. The other cars seemed intact. Dazed men were scanning the sky and drawing weapons. Alex tried to move but Varnas was heavy on top of him.

"Varnas?"

A gasp.

"Varnas?"

No response.

Alex's stomach turned to ice. "Varnas?" He took a breath. "Alphonsas?" The word expired in the baking air. He'd never used Varnas's Christian name before.

Snow was melting under him. He tried to free an elbow. Varnas groaned.

Oh Jesus. He edged left and emptied his lungs to make himself smaller. The hot air was becoming heavy with the noisome odour of burning kerosene. He pried, edged sideways, and wriggled free.

Varnas lay facedown, his heavy black overcoat shredded from the left shoulder to below the shoulder blade, woolen fibres wicking blood, engorged, fabric and flesh indistinguishable.

Alex, his heart thundering in his chest, thought he would never get his anorak off, never get the lining out and folded and placed over Varnas's brimming wound.

Events now moved in slow motion. Varnas had saved his life. If events continued to move in slow motion, Varnas would die. Keeping pressure on the wound, Alex sat back on his heels and shouted for help.

Men swam in from somewhere with a stretcher and blankets.

The prosecutor knelt beside Alex. "I have radioed the Emergency Medical Unit."

"How long will it take them?"

"Fifteen minutes. Maybe twenty. One of my men is dead," he added. Slow motion.

To make it easier for him to breathe, they turned Varnas over and, with the anorak poultice beneath him, placed him on the stretcher between doubled layers of blankets. As they lifted the stretcher, Alex stroked the bare head.

Very faintly. "Alex?"

"Don't talk. Doctor's on his way. Tons of pretty nurses."

"Alex, I like my hat, please."

The black homburg lay a metre away. The prosecutor retrieved it and brushed off the snow. Alex carefully put it in its accustomed place.

"Thank you." The stretcher bearers began to move. "And Alex . . ."

"Yes?"

"If it is not too much trouble, I like to see Catholic priest."

They placed him in the hangar away from the fire. His face, beaded with sweat, was the colour of library paste. He mildly complained of thirst. Alex moistened his lips with a wet cloth.

How long this vigil continued, Alex never learned. He was aware of police coming and going, of the prosecutor speaking into a dirty white telephone perched on an oil drum. A Protestant clergyman appeared, the only cleric they could locate. Varnas received the last rites of the Lutheran Church. He didn't seem to mind. Sometime later he smiled benignly and began to jabber in Lithuanian. All the symptoms of shock were in place. Alex was certain they were going to lose him.

But at some interval, the light and sound in the hangar altered; Alex felt a hand on his elbow and heard a quiet voice, *Bitte*. He looked up. The EMU helicopter whined on the hangar apron . . . a wheeled stretcher, figures in blue nylon moving very quickly, slow motion terminating, arm of the overcoat, suitcoat, shirt cut away, tubing, massaging the forearm, no vein, massaging, needle, elevated bottle, lactated Ringer's solution . . . Varnas's homburg receding beneath IV bottle slung from metal rod shaped like a question mark, Alex powerlessly following, homburg into the chopper, blue figures in, acceleration before even the door is closed, blur of rotors, bird away.

Please God, thy beloved servant.

The prosecutor gave Alex a shot of kirsch and said, "We have learned that de Clovis is headed for the town of Havnbjerg in Denmark, a distance of about 220 kilometres. He has a vacation chalet there with an airstrip. I have spoken to the Federal Aviation office in Brunschweig. They believe there is time for the Luftwaffe to intercept."

Alex closed his eyes. He experienced a moment of extraordinary clarity: he would reach up and snatch the gold biplane out of the sky with his bare hands, crush it with his bare hands! The thought exhilarated him and made him dizzy.

33

The Dogfight

A PAIR of aging Luftwaffe F-4F Phantoms from Jagdgeschwader (JG) 71, Wittmundhaven, smoked along north of Schleswig at 5,000 metres. Code-named Adler 27 and 28, the two-plane formation was on routine Perimeter Patrol. Wired to Ground Control Intercept (GCI) near Leck, 50 kilometres to the west, the two-seaters carried four Aim-9 Sidewinder missiles apiece. The pilot of each aircraft and his weapons system officer (WSO, also known as GIB, the guy in back) busied themselves with the tasks and checklists appropriate to this daily defensive patrol during which nothing whatever happened. The chief task was not to lose concentration. Lost concentration led to distraction, which led to screwup. In the absence of an enemy, screwup was the enemy.

At 0942 local time, the unimaginable happened. Ground control reported a possible airspace violation vicinity Brunsbüttel. Course and distance information were punched into their visual display indicators, and both birds rolled left and hauled high ass. A shock wave from the afterburners startled cows as far away as Sønderborg, Denmark.

The WSO in Adler 27 tuned his radar and fiddled with the crosshairs as the F-4, traveling at 760 knots, leveled off at 2,000 metres and headed southwest toward the Elbe.

In 4.4 minutes the river flashed by below.

"Slow to two hundred," ground control ordered. "Bogey at fifteen hundred near village of Hochdonn, heading north-north-east, speed one twenty-five."

The pilot of Adler 27 whistled. "Speed one twenty-five! What is it?"

"Single-engine tractor biplane."

"Damn. Propeller and everything?"

"Roger. Pilot wanted by police. We are to intercept."

A moment later the WSO reported a weak radar target, distance 4 kilometres. "Do we arm?"

"Negative. You'll have to talk him down. How slow can you go?"

The pilot answered, "About one-fifty. The generals deleted the boundary layer control on these birds so we can't float low and slow."

"Do your best."

Both pilots throttled back and deployed landing gear and full flaps. They mushed along, nose high, at 160 knots making smoke.

"Say when you have visual," GCI commanded.

Adler 27 reported the biplane a minute later at twelve o'clock, distance 1,000 metres. "He's old and gold," the pilot said. "What do we do? Talk him down on a unicom frequency?"

"Negative. No radio. Adler twenty-seven, go alongside. Adler twenty-eight remain in reserve. Adler twenty-seven, try to make him understand he is to land at the small civilian airport south of Rendsburg. Draw him a picture if necessary."

Adler 28 stood off to the west as Adler 27 descended 200 metres and approached the biplane from the rear. As the large, black-on-white Maltese Cross came into view on the gold fuselage, the jet pilot chuckled into the intercom: "I know that aeroplane. Built a model of it when I was a kid. World War One Albatros. Monocoque fuse, balsa and Jap tissue, rubber-band motor. Flew it into a tree."

"We're too fast," the WSO said as he dug a grease pencil out of his kit and, in large letters, wrote on the inside of the canopy:

⟨ƆƎWWI ⅁ЯႮႻ8ᗡИƎЯ ᗡИA⅃

They came level with the biplane and quickly drew ahead, executing S-turns in a futile effort to stay with the slower aircraft.

The helmeted pilot of the Albatros glanced over but did not otherwise respond.

Adler 27 executed a 180. The formation was now north of Rendsburg airport and approaching Schleswig. The pilot contacted Ground. "He understands but will not coop."

"Can you fire a burst?"

"A burst of what? All I got is missiles."

"Can you do a flyover and bump him with your legs?"

"I can try." The pilot eased back on the stick and lifted the F-4 a few metres. He concentrated on maintaining a stable, nose-high altitude at minimum controllable airspeed. He was flying the tiny-winged fighter on the edge of a stall.

The biplane was still 500 metres ahead when it abruptly nosed up, appeared to go into a loop, rolled instead into an Immelman turn and dove at the F-4. The pilot of the jet thought he saw sparklers. A second later, his cockpit canopy disintegrated.

Adler 28, a kilometre to the west, saw it all: saw the attack, saw the Phantom falter and roll left, saw it enter an inverted spin and begin to tumble. He screamed, "Eject! Eject! Eject!" There was no response. Adler 27 tumbled out of control for 1,000 metres, impacting the earth in a huge fireball.

Adler 28 retracted everything, firewalled the throttles, and yo-yoed straight up.

The twenty-two-year-old pilot shakily reported to Ground Control. The pilot of Adler 27 was his cousin.

GCI replied, "Stand by."

The WSO of Adler 28 fiddled nervously with the radar. This was his first combat experience.

GCI came back. "Bogey approaching Boklund." He gave course and distance. "Arm," he said. "Prepare for radar lock-on."

Adler 28 punched in. The steering needle on the Visual Display Indicator edged to the right. The pilot reduced speed to 270 knots and centered the needle.

The WSO turned on the master armament switch and divided his attention between the radar screen and the VDI.

"Tallyho," he whispered as he adjusted the radar and got a target. "Three kilos." He checked the arming switches. At one kilometre he hit the auto-acquisition. "You're locked on," he said.

The pilot waited four seconds for missile matchup, then squeezed the trigger. He waited another 1.5 seconds for electrical sequence. After what seemed an eternity, the Sidewinder snaked out in front of the F-4, swinging her hips like a tart in high heels, and growled in their headsets as she sniffed the heat.

34

Sörup

VARNAS underwent thoracic surgery for a shattered scapula, contusion of the upper left lung, and the fracture of ribs three, four, and five. He would remain in the Hospital for Special Surgery, Bremen, for the foreseeable future. Given his age and physical condition, the thoracotomy did not include an estimate of his chances for recovery.

In Osterholz-Scharmbeck the Flugzeug und Waffen Museum was completely destroyed. Nothing from its rare collection of antique aircraft and weapons could be saved.

On the other hand, the schloss was undamaged. Indeed, it was to this turreted seventeenth-century Mansart château that the missing crews of the police van and helicopter were earlier taken by jeep at gunpoint and kept until de Clovis's escape was assured. The crews were then served breakfast on Limoges china, after which the schloss and museum staff, with the exception of the gunsmith, Blücher, who was off playing Saint Nicholas at a local children's hospital, surrendered to the police and, predictably, declared themselves innocent victims of intimidation and coercion whose only crime had been to follow orders.

The prosecutor, his political opponents and a newly electrified press corps now howling for accountability, sequestered himself and his assistants in the great salon of the schloss, where he accepted no incoming calls except those from the police and military.

In late morning, after Varnas's surgery was confirmed, the prosecutor summoned Alex to his beleaguered headquarters and showed him the highly confidential air force combat report just received. It was maddeningly incomplete, so much so that Alex, seized now by a fury that was alien to his emotional repertoire, accused the Germans of stalling.

The report was explicit enough concerning the loss of a modern jet fighter to the guns of a World War I biplane. It included the location of the F-4 remains and its crew, but included no details of the fate of the Albatros or its pilot. Alex slammed down the report and turned on the prosecutor.

"You're stonewalling! You're withholding information! You're unwilling to verify the bastard's death because it's a national embarrassment! You're closing ranks until you can figure out some Nietzschean argument to sanitize this murderer for the greater glory of the fucking fatherland!"

The prosecutor, to his credit, kept his temper. "We are withholding nothing, Chef-Inspecteur, nor are we trying to deceive you out of some dark, Teutonic perversity. I remind you that I've lost one of my men. I want de Clovis as much as you do. It's not that we are unwilling to verify his death. We are unable to verify it. The air force is still conducting reconnaissance over an area three hundred kilometres square."

"Maybe they need the practice. Give me a road map, a piece of string, and a schoolboy's compass, and I'll lay out de Clovis's line of flight and locate the crash site, if there is one, within a kilo! Don't you think the goddam air force, with its inertial navigational systems and loran could do the same?"

"Yes," the prosecutor replied, "unless the crash site is too remote for quick confirmation."

An aide across the room wigwagged and held up a phone. The prosecutor excused himself.

Alex stuffed his hands in his pockets and stalked around the salon. The enormous room was designed in the French classic spirit with gilt molding and trompe l'oeil and baroque architectural detail. At the far end, he came to a pair of life-size portraits hanging side by side over the mantel.

The portrait on the left showed a young, idealized de Clovis in dress uniform, complete with crimson sash, decorations, and ceremonial sword. The other showed a slim, darkly beautiful woman standing in a shadowy wood with pale sunlight filtering through the trees behind her. She wore a luminous Empire gown of ivory satin. A tiny coronet glistened in her hair, and she held a single red rose in one hand.

Alex stared and felt his face flush. The woman was Eugénie von Mai, the Baroness de Clovis, smaller-boned and lighter-skinned, but otherwise an eerie preincarnation of Anna Gutierrez.

The prosecutor reappeared and touched Alex on the elbow. "Chef-Inspecteur, we've received confirmation that the air force have located the Albatros crash site near the village of Sörup, just south of the Danish border. There is no sign of life." He paused. "Will you take their word for it? Or will you want to see for yourself?"

Alex gazed at the crimson sash and ceremonial sword. "I want to see for myself."

In late afternoon, Alex and a German TV film crew climbed aboard a five-place police helicopter. They lifted off and flew northeast, away from the sun. As they crossed the sparkling waters of the Schlei and the city of Schleswig, Flensburg traffic control came on the air and vectored the chopper to a frozen lake between Satrup and Sörup, course 022, distance 11.3. The landing area was at the southwest end of the lake, identified by a cluster of ice-fishing huts and a parked blue Chinook. A Chinook was a large cargo helicopter and sky blue was Luftwaffe. The pilot acknowledged the transmission.

While finding a northern lake on a summer afternoon is one thing, finding a frozen lake in winter with the entire landscape hidden under a uniform blanket of snow, with daylight fading, is quite another. However, within minutes, they spotted a single lane road below that wound through a narrow gorge to a village of tiny lights and whispy ringlets of chimney smoke. Stretching away from the village to the southwest was a flat, unobstructed plain surrounded by trees. The sudden flatness and the trees identified the lake.

Alex's eyes ached as he tried to take in the entire scene at once. He strained to spot the telltale slash and bits of debris that would quiet his soul. But it was getting dark. He saw only blue snow, black trees, and inhospitable terrain.

They circled once and settled onto the ice behind the big, twin-rotor Chinook.

As they shut down the chopper, a moon buggy with giant, deep-tread balloon tyres appeared on the shore, bounced down a ramp onto the ice, and rumbled toward them. Sky blue, like the Chinook, its square military canopy and three blazing pod-mounted amber headlamps gave it the curious look of a battle tank crossed with a blue crab. Alex noticed a cargo sling folded on the roof and realized that the moon buggy had been flown in beneath the Chinook.

They transferred the video equipment from the chopper to the buggy. A young sergeant greeted them. "We are pleased to co-operate with the police and media," he said. "Sorry for the delay. We knew the area where the bipe went in but couldn't pinpoint the point of impact until the Flensburg police gave us the coordinates. Actually, it was a dairy farmer who saw the crash. He was repairing a fence at the time."

"What happened to the pilot?" Alex asked.

"You'll see."

The moon buggy began to move. It clambered off the ice, rumbled into the woods, and immediately began to climb. As they pushed farther into the hills above the lake, the snow became opaque and the buggy's shadow danced in front of them. The sky had cleared. The moon was up.

Higher still, they entered a shallow ravine. On the opposite slope stood a farmhouse and barn in a grove of birch saplings black-etched on the moonlit snow.

The sergeant parked the buggy near the barn as a large, taciturn-looking farmer emerged from a side door carrying a milk pail and lantern. He raised the lantern in greeting and immediately withdrew into the barn.

Meanwhile, the sergeant led Alex to the edge of the barnyard and pointed across the shallow ravine to a slight rise. Alex stared at the spot a hundred metres away. The stillness was palpable. Was this desolate spot to be the end, finally, of the long journey begun so precipitously, and noisily, in the sky over Belgium so long ago?

The farmer returned with the lantern. He wore a battered leather jacket and a cap with earflaps. "Ready?" he asked. Alex nodded. "Come."

The film crew held back. "After you," they said and lit cigarettes.

In single file, then, Alex and the sergeant followed the farmer along a trail of deep footprints that pockmarked the rising moonlit field. From the snow-covered pattern of shadowy furrows along which they walked, Alex saw that this field had been plowed for crops. As he trudged along in the wake of the farmer's bulky figure, he found himself counting footsteps as he had behind Grandfather in the beet field outside Vailly.

After ninety-six steps, they came to a slight gradient and stopped. A newly wired section of fence stood beyond. The farmer stepped aside and held up his lantern. At his feet was a shallow, discoloured crater in the snow. Nothing more. Alex walked to the edge and looked down. There, just below the frozen surface, rested the charred engine block of the Austro-Daimler.

"Only the engine reached the ground," the sergeant said. "We identified the aircraft and pilot from the serial number."

35

Lemwerder

ALEX called the hospital from the airport. A young, English-speaking nurse told him that Varnas was still in intensive care but, as no empyema had developed, as was originally feared, his condition was currently being upgraded from grave to serious.

"Does that mean he's—" But she'd already hung up.

Since his presence in Bremen was of no use to Varnas, Alex reluctantly booked a Sabena flight home. This included a layover in Brussels. It was all he could get on a weekend with no reservation.

For him, the Wilson case was over. The interrogation of Andreas Blücher and the Kecks was scheduled for the following week in Bremen Criminal Court. It would not involve Alex. The Sûreté intended to send an observer.

Paris

From the airport coffee shop in Brussels, he called the Maison and left his arrival time with the Assignment Desk. The DC-10 landed at Charles de Gaulle just at sunset. As he exited the jetway Alex glanced around to see if anyone from the office had come for him. Seeing no one, he slung his pack over his shoulder and walked through the automatic passenger gate. Philippa waited on the other side.

She took a step forward and buried her face in his jacket. She clung to him and wept. Eventually, she dug a tissue out of her pocket and blew her nose.

"When we heard Varnas had been shot, Nana went immediately to church. I cleaned house. I didn't know what else to do, Alex.

I felt that if I made the barge shine it would somehow help Varnas get well. Is that too weird?"

Next day, which was Sunday, Alex, his mother, and Philippa went to midday mass at the Église Saint-Augustin, one of the more or less unofficial churches of the Sûreté, attended by Maison personnel only at those infrequent intervals when, no longer able to rely on pure science to guarantee the recovery of an injured colleague, they put themselves temporarily at the disposal of the Almighty.

In attendance were the Commissaire, Hippo, César (newly promoted to Inspecteur), and a cross section of patrons from Ajaccio and Chez Suzanne, including Suzanne herself.

After the service, those members of the demimonde well known to the police, finding themselves outside and no longer on sanctified ground, dispersed quickly. The Commissaire drove César and Hippo home in his Simca. Alex, Nana, and Philippa walked slowly up Boulevard Malesherbes toward the parked Citröen. A half block from the church, Alex sensed someone close behind him.

She was small and pale and dressed in black from head to foot. She wore an old-fashioned pillbox hat with a veil and carried a paper bag. She attempted a smile.

"Do I speak with Inspecteur Varnas's police associate?"

"At your service, madame."

"I am Clothilde Roget, propriétaire of eight Rue Georges-Berger."

Alex introduced his mother and Philippa. Madame Roget acknowledged them but, after the introduction, appeared apprehensive. "May I speak freely, monsieur?"

Alex had no idea what she meant to speak freely about, but he said, "Certainly."

She lowered her voice. "I have something here that I intended to give to Inspecteur Varnas. Will you accept it for him?" Seeing Alex's hesitation, she quickly added, "What I wished to give him is Monsieur Wilson's journal."

She reached into the paper bag and withdrew a red and gold Florentine leather diary on which were engraved the initials A.S.W. A tooled leather strap held the book closed by means of a bronze hasp and lock.

Alex asked, "But madame, how did you come into possession of this?"

Without hesitation she said, "I took it from monsieur's desk at the same time I removed the brown envelope. I did it because I knew monsieur cared for me." She hesitated and gazed down the street. "Out of loyalty to madame and respect for propriety, Monsieur Wilson could not permit himself an expression of his feelings to me directly. Nor would I have wished it. However, I was certain that, at some point, he could not help but confide his secret feelings for me to the pages of his journal. A journal is, after all, the folio of the heart. I know these things."

She turned back to Alex. "And so, out of my deep respect and devotion for monsieur, and to protect madame's sensibilities, I placed the diary . . . beyond public scrutiny, so to speak." She returned the diary to the paper bag and, with her free hand, patted the sides of her hair. The hand strayed across her cheek and stopped at her throat, where it remained.

"However," she added softly, "after I took it I began to have doubts. After all, I had taken something that was not mine. Some might have called it stealing. Suddenly, I needed someone to confide in. Then, out of the blue, Inspecteur Varnas telephoned."

"When was this?" Alex asked.

"Last week. He said he needed the answer to a question he thought only I could supply. We met at the refreshment kiosk in the Parc de Monceau. He bought me a limeade. Then after a few pleasantries, he asked me if I knew what had become of monsieur's diary. Well, I was so astonished at his prescience that I was speechless. But I could see that there was no point in denying that I had taken it, so I blurted out the truth and immediately felt better.

"Inspecteur Varnas was the soul of tact. He said that taking the diary had been a mistake; not that it had been wrong, mind you, given my reasons, merely a mistake. He said that if Monsieur Wilson had not permitted himself an expression of affection for me directly, he would certainly not risk committing any but the most proprietous thoughts to the pages of his journal. Monsieur, was, after all, a public figure whose journal might one day be published. Indeed, the inspecteur said, it was probable that my name did not appear in the diary at all . . . because monsieur preferred . . . he preferred to carry me in the sanctuary of his heart, where our mutual devotion would be forever safe from public scrutiny." She smiled slightly. "Isn't that beautiful?"

"Yes."

"The inspecteur's judgement on my behalf seemed so sweet, so logical, that soon after our meeting, I resolved to return the diary. But since madame had already left Paris, I decided to entrust it to the inspecteur's care."

Her dark eyes glistened under the veil. "I am very triste that he has suffered, my little inspecteur. He is every day in my prayers." She sighed. "So, monsieur. Under the circumstances, will you take it?"

"Of course."

"Thank you." She smiled at Nana and turned to Philippa. "You are a lovely couple, mademoiselle." With that she handed Alex the paper bag and was gone.

Philippa watched her meticulous, mincing retreat. "Do you think she's rowing with both oars in the water?"

"I think so."

"Actually, she's kind of cute in a frayed sort of way. I wonder if the old fox was trying to get it on with her."

"I think the old fox knew exactly how to get the bird to open her beak and drop the cheese."

They drove back to *Le Yacht Club*, where Nana's memorable late-lunch preparation, the periwinkle-crayfish-codheads-mussels-squid-and-scallop chowder, a sort of northern bouillabaisse, simmered on the galley stove. Below, the barge smelt like low tide. But the soup, eaten with sourdough bread, was sublime, and Philippa's last indulgence before her return to tofu and gelatin.

After lunch, Nana packed while Alex and Philippa cleaned up the galley. They performed this task wordlessly in anticipation of what they knew would be a difficult farewell. Apart from an elderly cousin in Rennes, Nana's only family in the world was Alex and, by extension, Philippa. She could not bear to say good-bye but knew she must and always wept.

They were therefore not prepared for the dry-eyed woman who emerged from Alex's stateroom, carrying her suitcase rather casually and wearing an enigmatic expression. She put down the bag and hugged Philippa.

"There's no need for us all to go to the station, chérie, so I'll say good-bye here."

That seemed plain enough. There were no tears. Just hugs and pats. Philippa, misty-eyed, waved from the cockpit as the Citröen rolled up the Quai de la Charente.

On the way to the Gare St.-Lazare, Alex's mother made small conversation. She spoke of the declining Biscay fishery and the failure of the famous ceramic works at Quimper. She said she would pray for Varnas's recovery but thought he should retire. She would send him a rum cake in hospital.

Alex found a space near the station. He was about to park when she stopped him.

"You don't need to come in, Alexandre. I can find the train." She reached into her purse. "I have something here for you." She handed him a tiny box covered in imitation ivory leather. He opened it. Two small pearls in a gold setting gleamed on a bed of gauze. "It's my engagement ring," she said. "Your father gave it to me in 1946. I want you to have it."

"Maman—"

"Someday you'll need it, Alexandre. There. That's settled." She opened her door. Alex fetched her bag from the back and circled round. They embraced on the curb. She reached up and smoothed his hair. "And Alexandre, you must encourage Philippa to get baptized. Good-bye, chéri." She walked purposefully into the station.

He drove to the Maison, locked the ring in the secure drawer of his desk, and phoned the Commissaire at home to report the return of Wilson's diary.

"Where was it?" the Commissaire asked.

"Cleaning lady found it behind Wilson's safe," Alex lied.

"Good. Tell Stevenson to tell Madame Wilson that when you deliver it into his hands."

Alex walked to his office and called the Stevenson residence. It was almost six o'clock. A servant answered. After a longish interval, Stevenson's wife came on. She seemed a little drunk.

"So, first it's an Arab and now it's a German," she said. "Are you sure you've got it right this time?"

"Reasonably sure."

"Oh dear! I thought you were Commissaire Demonet. Do I know you?"

"I don't believe so, madame."

"Well, you sound lovely and brave. I envy you. I could never be a flic. I'm too polite. I suppose you want to speak to David. He's dressing. We're expecting guests. I'll call him." After a moment, Stevenson picked up.

"I'm to place the diary in your hands," Alex said. "Commissaire's orders." Stevenson was entirely agreeable.

"I'll leave the side-door light on. Just ring when you get here."

Alex drove through the picture-postcard Sixteenth via the Étoile. Stevenson owned a house off the Place du Venezuela. A maid answered his ring. Monsieur would meet him in the study. She opened a carved mahogany door and disappeared. Music and voices filtered in from the front of the house.

The study was a cheerful and informal room of comfortable chairs and small sofas facing an open iron hearth in which a fire crackled.

The maid reappeared with two glasses of Kir on a tray. Alex accepted one and, after she deposited the tray and withdrew, relaxed and looked around the room.

One wall was all bookcases filled with leather-bound volumes, mostly in English: Robert Louis Stevenson, Henty (*With Clive in India*), boys' books. There was some poetry—Masefield, Tennyson—a 1950 *Encyclopaedia Britannica,* and an entire shelf of military history and theory: Clausewitz, French, Haig, Jellicoe, Foch, Churchill, Montgomery, Freyberg.

Another wall was covered, floor to ceiling, with flamboyant art deco posters advertising the cinema, mostly old films Alex had never heard of: Anna Sten in *Monte Carlo Madness; The Prince of Bohemia,* starring Joseph Schildkraut; Ernst Lubitch's *Love Parade,* introducing Jeanette MacDonald. Apparently there was a playful side to Stevenson, unless the posters were the whim of some interior decorator.

Stevenson thumped in finally, beaming hospitably and wearing a smoking jacket of crushed crimson velvet. "Well!" he exclaimed, "I hear congratulations are in order! Case finally closed. Splendid! Is Henri crowing?"

"The Commissaire is pleased that it's over."

Stevenson raised his glass. "Cheers! I daresay the police force is not unlike the army, where the front-line troops do the job and HQ do all the press interviews!" He did his hearty laugh and chugalugged his wine. "Well. You mentioned something about a diary."

Alex handed it over. "Madame Wilson said you'd know what to do with it."

"It'll go straight into the daily airmail sack to New York. She'll have it day after tomorrow." He stood there blinking for a moment, then snapped his fingers. "Hallo. Nearly forgot." He reached behind him, opened a cabinet, and withdrew a small parcel. "This is *English* tobacco, acquired at great expense and effort to change your boss's foul pipesmoker's palate. If he likes it, tell him I shall become his pusher and supply a pound per month. Care for another drink?"

"No thanks."

Stevenson shook hands with a too firm, too prolonged grip. "Well! Splendid! Congratulations again, Chef-Inspecteur! And all the best!"

Alex hadn't remembered Stevenson being such a bore.

Le Yacht Club

Due to circumstances, Philippa had postponed Alex's surprise. Relying on Nana to keep the rebuilt diesel a secret, she'd put the rug back over the engine hatch and concealed the newly installed instrument panel behind a dance calendar.

Now she placed Milt Hinton on the stereo and positioned Alex's captain's chair in a strategic spot in the saloon. When he finally came home, halfway through the second side, she handed him an aperitif and made him sit.

"What's this?"

"Are you comfortable?"

"Very."

"Close your eyes."

"Philippa!"

"Shh. Close your eyes."

He did. She removed the dance calendar from the instrument panel, turned the bulkhead-mounted master switch to BOTH, and pressed the glow button. The glow button had to remain depressed for thirty seconds to preheat the engine.

As she counted down the seconds, she felt a tiny heart flop of doubt. Would he feel threatened that she'd restored the engine without consulting him? After all it was his boat. Fifteen, fourteen, thirteen. Screw it! It was *their* boat!

Eight, seven, six, five, four, three, two, one, zero. She pressed the starter button. The old Buda fired off and rumbled pleasantly beneath them, vibrating the cabin sole and breathing life and mobility into the somnolent old barge.

At the first murmur of the diesel, Alex's eyes flew open. He shot out of his chair and instinctively reached for the grab rail in the overhead.

Philippa smiled proudly. "Welcome to Martinique!"

36

The Maison

DURING the next week, Varnas's condition was upgraded from serious to stable to satisfactory. Alex spoke with him by teleflex.

"There are a million cards here for you."

"Very nice. How is my Philippa?"

"Misses you."

"Alex, do you ever hear of drug Demerol?"

"I think so."

"It is worth to be in pain just to get Demerol. Not only does pain immediately disappear, but is replaced by journey to heaven. Heaven is blue and orange, Alex, and smells of rosewater and roasting coffee. While I am in heaven I see Simon the électricien and Marie. They are well and send best wishes. For first time I understand drug addiction. Because, starting yesterday, I am on a cold turkey."

His bonus in the banque, Alex now had time off, which he spent assembling lists of needed supplies, canal pilot books, and charts. He made arrangements for *Le Yacht Club* to be hauled and painted prior to her first trip down the canals as a private vessel. With Varnas out of danger, he and Philippa planned to start their vacation the day after Christmas. It was an exciting time for them, filled with anticipation and pride of voyage.

But, with another week still to go and a huge list of things left to do, Alex was abruptly summoned to the Commissaire's office.

"I'm sending you back to Bremen," Demonet said, without preamble.

Alex was stunned.

"The man appointed to represent us at the hearings can't make heads or tails of the interrogation. He's been recalled. You're the only one who can straighten it out."

"Straighten what out?"

"The Germans are saying that de Clovis didn't kill Wilson."

Bremen 2

He caught a Lufthanza flight next morning and found he had to make an effort to be pleasant to the young German flight attendant when she asked to see his boarding pass.

Since Osterholz-Scharmbeck he'd become less sure of his ability to bar emotions from colouring his judgement and behaviour. Now he tried to forestall a mounting resentment at what he perceived to be a German attempt to launder facts and bowdlerize history.

A car and driver met him at Lemwerder. Before he boarded the limo, he called Varnas at the hospital. "I won't have time to see you."

"Nothing to see, my dear. With these bandages I look like logo for Michelin tyre."

They drove out of the airport. No new snow had fallen, and the drifts were black with soot. The city looked like a dirty shirt.

At the Criminal Courts building, Alex took the elevator to the fourth floor candy-box office. The prosecutor greeted him hospitably. Alex said, "I brought an overnight bag. But there's a four, a six, and an eight o'clock Paris flight out of here, and I'd like to be on one of them."

The prosecutor smiled without enthusiasm. "I'll do my best. Coffee?"

"No thanks. Let's get on with it."

They sat down. The prosecutor placed a dossier and a large attaché case on his desk. He leaned back in his chair. "You'll recall that the purpose of our original search warrant, which we never delivered, was to substantiate allegations made by the Sûreté that de Clovis, the Kecks, Blücher, and Anna Gutierrez were all part of a conspiracy to murder Andrew Wilson."

"Right."

"It's hardly necessary to add that events seem to confirm the allegations."

"Hardly."

"I wish it were that simple. Subsequent testimony has produced some glaring inconsistencies. For example, Frieda Keck. We placed considerable emphasis on the notion that she did the boot prints in the parc. She says not. She freely admits her part in coordinating the activities of de Clovis and Anna, but emphatically denies she accompanied the Freiherr to Paris. The housekeeper at Schloss Scharmbeck confirms her denial. Added to that, we have the testimony of a registered podiatrist affirming that Frieda must wear specially made orthopaedic shoes to support her weight and that there is no way her foot could've fit into the heeled boot represented by the size ten B plaster cast you submitted. She wears a size twelve double E."

Alex waved this away. "All right. For the moment, the boot prints are not Frieda's. But didn't I just hear you say that de Clovis went to Paris?"

"Yes."

"Why did he go to Paris?"

"To kill Wilson."

"Premeditated."

"Premeditated."

"And now you say he didn't kill Wilson."

"That's right."

The prosecutor opened the attaché case and turned it toward Alex. The plush interior contained a disassembled gun. There were three parts: a barrel fitted with a silencer, a breach with a telescopic sight, and an aluminum stock.

The prosecutor removed the components and assembled the gun. It took him about fifteen seconds.

"We found this firearm in the gate house. Blücher identified it as the murder weapon. De Clovis ordered him to build it in September. It's a 6.3 millimetre semi-automatic with a silencer and a night scope. It fires a low-charge, subsonic, hollow-nose lead slug. It is absolutely silent, the tradeoff for silence being low velocity and accuracy reduced to only thirty-five metres. It was designed that way." He put the gun down. "Now look at this."

He opened the dossier and withdrew a pen-and-ink drawing, which he handed to Alex. Executed on heavy bond paper and done in the flowing, elliptical oriental brushwork style of Lucien Violet, it was a gracefully detailed map of the basin bridge, the bridge steps, and the promenades immediately below the bridge. An accurate scale had been included. Thirty metres below the bridge steps, the artist had reproduced three trees, each with a fancifully enlarged leaf designed to identify the species. There was a maple, a ginkgo, and a walnut. Next to the centre tree, the ginkgo, appeared a sketch of a human eye from which a flight of arrows flew directly to the bridge steps.

"Anna Gutierrez supplied the map. There can be no doubt as to its significance. As you can see, she assigned de Clovis a front-row seat. Wilson was to arrive at five minutes to six. She wanted de Clovis in place no later than seven minutes to six. But Wilson must have arrived early. For when de Clovis was in place and ready to fire, he saw Wilson through his night scope, lying on the promenade below the bridge. He was dead."

Alex closed his eyes.

"And a small person, undoubtedly your Arab, was already going through his pockets."

"Prosecutor," Alex said with exaggerated patience, "de Clovis killed Wilson with the cane gun and left the scene. The gardener came next. The Arab came later."

"Chef-Inspecteur, Blücher and Frieda swear they know nothing about a cane gun or a small calibre aerial dart connected to this event. They believed de Clovis killed Wilson with Blücher's 6.3 millimetre weapon. That is, they believed it until after de Clovis's death, when the truth came out."

"What truth?"

"De Clovis never acknowledged that he failed to kill Wilson. Only Keck, who accompanied him in the parc, knew . . . and he kept it to himself for as long as de Clovis was alive." The prosecutor hesitated. "We know that de Clovis was skilled at creating the official truth about himself. The official truth after the so-called influenza hoax in 1918, was that he was invincible in war. The official truth this time was that he successfully defended his honour." The prosecutor picked up the weapon. "And officially, he did it with this, the calibre of which was verified in the *Paris Soir* article of Monday, fifteen November. No one doubted it at the time."

"You can't seriously expect me to believe this!"
"But Chef-Inspecteur, I don't see that you have a choice."
"You're still trying to acquit the bastard!"
"Nothing of the kind!"
"I want to see Blücher."

Alex had once interrogated a woman whose friendly, open gaze and direct manner seemed to signify an appealing and honest personality. Later he learned that whenever she was being open and direct she was lying. It was only when she appeared evasive that she was telling the truth. He wondered if Blücher was like that.

The gunsmith was a slight, avuncular old gentleman of cheerful countenance, jack-o'-lantern eyes behind rimless spectacles, a stack of short white hair, and a carefully trimmed moustache.

The eyes twinkled. He wrinkled his nose. He made passes in the air with a finger. He told anecdotes that, at first, seemed to have no connection with the matter under discussion but always managed to circle back to the subject in the end. Like the story of transporting the Rügen Castle collection to Lübeck during the last war when wood was so scarce they were forced to trade a twelfth-century two-handed sword to a woodcutter for enough birch to keep the trucks running. Which led to the moment when Blücher realized the collection was to be sold, and rather than say good-bye to a life's work, turned his back on it forever. Which led to the fact that he hadn't seen the walking sticks in forty years.

"But you kept in touch," Alex suggested.

"No, sir. Out of sight, out of mind." Smile. Twinkle.

Alex didn't believe him so he tried a test broadside. "Herr Blücher, we have evidence that traces the walking sticks to the Flugzeug und Waffen Museum."

Blücher blinked and looked mildly offended. "You must be mistaken, sir. No offense. I'm sure you were misinformed. The weapons in the F and W are weapons of war dating from 1905 to 1918. No curator of a war collection would acquire a 1937 curiosity, even if the curator himself smithed the piece. Except to collectors of unusual air guns or fanciers of concealed weapons, the piece is merely a novelty. Certainly it has no place in a military collection."

Whereupon he went off on an anecdote about the old Count's fascination with concealed weapons of all kinds: stiletto canes, rapier canes, a dagger that shot bullets, and a walking stick that shot daggers. Which led him to how he happened to build the cane-gun mechanism in the first place.

"The Count fancied the cinema," Blücher said, "especially ornate films that glorified the past. During the twenties and thirties he had films shown at the castle on many occasions. One, in particular, featured the actor Schildkraut in the part of a central European prince who dispatched an unscrupulous armed rival with a dart fired from a small-bore air gun concealed in a walking stick. What especially appealed to the Count was that the dart, at least in principle, was recoverable, thereby eliminating the ballistic evidence that would precipitate police meddling in what was essentially a private affair. The Graf fancied the cane gun so much that he ordered me to make him one like it."

Schildkraut. Alex waited for his antenna to align itself with this new signal. Schildkraut . . . the long-dead film star known now only to film buffs, anthologists, and collectors of the poster art that once bedizened the trams, billboards, and alleyways of the world. Schildkraut. The unexpected name embellished Blücher's fanciful tale with a new resonance.

Alex asked, "What was the name of the film?"

Blücher frowned. "Can't remember. It was about the Hapsburgs, all puff pastry and epaulets."

"Was it *The Prince of Bohemia?*"

37

Avenue de Wagram

ALEX caught the 4 P.M. flight back to Paris. The office of the orthopaedic surgeon, Roscoe Fielding, was still open at 6:20. Indeed, the waiting room was packed.

"We're running a little late," the nurse said, "as usual." She punched some keys on an old IBM computer and waited for the information to fall into place. "Yes. David Stevenson had a six o'clock on 12 November. Nothing special. Regular checkup for what he calls his Long John Silver blisters."

"Do you remember if he was on time for his appointment?" Alex asked.

"No. But if he was, he would've had to wait. Doctor loves to chat up the patients." She nodded at the crowded waiting room. "Look at this mess."

Doctor Fielding's office was no more than 800 metres from the Parc de Monceau. Stevenson, even on foot, could've kept his appointment if the doctor was running late as was his habit. Still, ownership of an old film poster was hardly evidence. Alex drove to Rue des Saussaies.

The Maison

Commissaire Demonet's eyes were dark with suspicion and doubt. "Two days ago I was satisfied that de Clovis was the murderer. Now you tell me David Stevenson killed Andrew Wilson."

"Yes."

"Alex, this is a shocking accusation. I've known Stevenson for as long as I've known you. Longer. We belong to some of the same clubs. Please think carefully. What possible motive could Stevenson have to kill Wilson?"

"I don't know. Yet."

"Didn't you verify his activities and whereabouts on the night of the murder?"

"Yes. He had a doctor's appointment. But according to the nurse he could've kept his six o'clock appointment at six-thirty, or later."

"That's not evidence."

"There's more. Stevenson is a collector. He collects kitsch, including old cinema posters that feature trivia-game names like Anna Sten, Jeanette MacDonald, and Joseph Schildkraut. I can't believe that I never connected his disability to the walking sticks, but now I have a strong feeling that when we go in there, we'll find he collects canes as well as posters."

"We're not going in anywhere yet, Alex."

Next day, Alex placed Stevenson under twenty-four-hour surveillance. He assigned the task to his new temporary assistant, César. Two cars, four men alternating. He then dove down the back stairs of the Maison to Comcentre.

While Alex was away, Comcentre had passed dozens of memos across his desk, most of them out of date. Example:

> TO: A Grism
>
> FR: CC
>
> CASE: Wils
>
> RE: McKim, Lewis (Zeke), testimony p. 24, ln 4.
>
> DATE PROG: 16 Nov.
>
> DATE MEMO: 18 Dec.

☐ Confirmed   ☐ Unconfirmed

☑ Error   ☐ Ambig

☐ Contradict   ☐ Omission

MEMO: Zeke McKim did not win Pulitzer Prize for garden piece as stated.

SOURCE: 1. *Providence Journal*, 14 June, 1938.
        2. *International Herald Tribune*, Pulitzer list, 1938.

The fact that the computer was only now getting around to processing old information like this led Alex to conclude that pertinent background material on David Stevenson was probably backlogged somewhere in Big Louie's scarred memory. But Comcentre said no. They said that source material on Stevenson had been extremely thin from the beginning. Consequently, very little had been processed apart from Stevenson's record at W. W. Wilson and Co., his business relationship with Wilson himself, some few charitable activities, his marriage to a Frenchwoman in '45, and his decision to become a French citizen in '48. Stevenson was a private person with an impeccable civil dossier and, of course, no criminal record, not even a speeding ticket. So, almost nothing had been processed.

When questioned about the dearth of material, Data Processing did what it always did. It blamed Research.

Research said it had done nothing on Stevenson because he was understood to be a witness for the prosecution (see Testimony, Ministry of Interior, 14-11-82). Moreover, subsequent events made inquiry into his background superfluous.

"Nothing is superfluous," Alex said. "I want to know what he ate for lunch in 1930."

The Research worker bees buzzed and groaned, returned to their honeycomb, and rescheduled Christmas week.

Two days later, César submitted his first report on Stevenson's activities. "Watching him is like watching ice melt," César said. "He leaves the house every morning at eight-twenty and arrives at the WWW office at eight-forty. He doesn't go out for lunch, doesn't stop for a drink on the way home, and doesn't have a mistress. He gets home at five-twenty, except Wednesday he left the office early and went to a livery stable in the Bois de Boulogne, where he rode a horse around a ring for an hour."

Alex dug back to his days with Claudine. "What style of riding? Hunter? Jumper? Dressage?"

"I dunno. The horse was brown and white. Guy who works there called it a pinto. I though a pinto was a Ford."

"What about his wife?"

"She has a full schedule. She goes to mass every morning and to the liquor store every afternoon."

Alex considered the information. He took down his *Petite Larousse* and looked up "pinto." The word wasn't listed in the French dictionary, so he dusted off his battered copy of *Webster's Third International* and flipped through the pages. *Pinpoint, pins and needles, pintle, pinto.*

pin·to/ pin·tō/ n, pl *pintos* also *pintoes* (AmerSp, fr. *pinto*, adj., spotted); chiefly western US: a spotted or calico horse or pony.

Alex frowned at César. "Western U.S."

"Something wrong?"

"What did Stevenson wear when he rode this pinto?"

"Leather pants, blue denim shirt, black Stetson hat . . . cowboy boots."

The Commissaire listened soberly. Finally he said, "Have you done your Christmas shopping?"

"No."

"You may as well do it, Alex, because I will not go public with this until you place evidence on my desk that is irrefutable."

"If he still has the boots, I'll need a search warrant to match them against the plaster cast. That'll be evidence that is irrefutable."

The Commissaire hesitated. "If I request a search warrant, I go public. And I don't go public until you bring me a motive."

Alex decided not to press the point.

On Thursday, 23 December, Alex lashed a small Christmas tree to the wireless mast of *Le Yacht Club* and strung it with tiny lights. He bought another tree for the saloon that he and Philippa planned to trim after the performance Christmas Eve. He bought her a new down jacket, a string of pearls, an Irish wool hat, a leather skirt, and a pair of boat shoes, all in less than an hour. He had no idea when he'd find time to wrap them.

Christmas Eve day, Alex haunted Comcentre all morning to no purpose and kept in touch with César by radio during the afternoon. Stevenson's routine did not change. He left his office at 3:30, drove to the Bois and rode the pinto. He was back in his house by 5:35. César radioed Alex.

"He's home. Do we have to work Christmas Eve?"

"We who serve the public—cops, waiters, hookers—all work Christmas Eve."

Alex sent out for Chicken Egg Foo Yung and ate it with a plastic fork. A few memos drifted up from Comcentre. Most of them contained biographical information on tenants in Rue Georges-Berger. Alex tossed them in the wastebasket.

At 10 P.M., church bells and carillons began to sound. Église Saint-Augustin, Église de la Madeleine, and, far away on the Île de la Cité, the great bells of the Cathédrale de Notre Dame.

Varnas never worked Christmas Eve. "I don't catch thief this night, Alexei, even if he has hand in my pocket."

César radioed at 10:15. "They've gone to bed. The lights are out."

Alex told César he planned to go home at 11 and to have the Maison beep him there if anything came up.

"Think of me when you are snug in your warm bed."

"Merry Christmas."

There were no more calls. Operations had virtually shut down and Comcentre seemed moribund. Alex left the Maison and caught the number twelve metro at Miromesnil. His car was empty except for some churchgoers who got off at St.-Lazare. When the train slowed for Pigalle, his beeper went off like a factory whistle. He got off the train and called in.

Inspecteur-trainee Biramoule was on the desk. "Yes, Chef. Comcentre wants you."

He rang the extension. The Directeur himself came on.

"Alex? Where are you?"

"Pigalle."

"We've got something. Confirmation just came in. Hurry!"

Alex reached the Maison just before midnight and went directly to the basement. The Directeur took him into his office, closed the door, and placed a memo in his hand. It read:

TO: Grism
FR: CC

CASE: Wils

RE: Stevenson, D.

DATE PROG: 21–23 Dec.

DATE MEMO: 24 Dec.

☑ Confirmed   ☐ Unconfirmed

☐ Error   ☐ Ambig

☐ Contradict   ☐ Omission

MEMO: 2nd Lt. David Scott Stevenson, M.C., 23rd Battalion, 2nd Division, New Zealand Expeditionary Force (NZEF) was killed on Sangro River near Atessa, Abruzzi, Italy, 4 Dec., 1943, while attempting to rescue Staff-Sergeant Nigel Willoughby-Jones whose leg had been shattered in a land mine explosion.

Stevenson's remains returned New Zealand where he was awarded Military Cross posthumously.

Willoughby-Jones reported MIA, 1944, near Monte Cassino.

SOURCE: 1. Imperial War Museum, London.

2. Public Records Office, London.

3. Office of Military Historian, Wellington, N.Z.

38

Place du Venezuela

THE STEVENSON RESIDENCE was dark except for a night-light shining somewhere in the back. Alex and the Commissaire sat in the Commissaire's Simca and waited for César and the weapons officers to get into position. When everyone was ready, the Commissaire picked up his car phone and dialed Stevenson's number.

After half a dozen rings, a light came on upstairs. Stevenson's wife answered. Her speech was slurred and guttural from either sleep or alcohol or both.

The Commissaire said, "This is Henri Demonet. I'm sorry to call so late, but it is extremely important that I speak with David."

"Can't it wait till morning, Henri? We're a bit fragile tonight. Got on to the eggnog."

"I'm sorry, no."

She said nothing for perhaps fifteen seconds. Then the Commissaire heard her gasp and whisper, "Oh David!"

Stevenson picked up. "Hallo? Henri? What's this, then?"

The Commissaire said, "I want you to listen carefully and do exactly as I say."

Alex held a light for the Commissaire as he read the London Public Records Office report on the death of David Stevenson. When he finished, the Commissaire said, "Nigel Willoughby-Jones, you are under arrest for the murder of Andrew S. Wilson in the Parc de Monceau on twelve November, 1982. We have your house surrounded. There are men on the roof at the back. I want you and your wife to dress immediately and come downstairs. When you reach the ground floor, you will turn on the lights, open the front door, and, together, come out on the veranda with your hands behind your heads. Is that clear?"

A chuckle. "Very clear, Henri. I take it you did not like the tobacco?"

"You have ten minutes."

As they waited, the Commissaire turned to Alex and said, "I owe you an apology. In recent weeks I've been distracted by a political game devised by the Élysée Palace to unnerve a handful of candidates hungry to become the next Chef of the General Directorate of External Security. The position pays approximately twice my current salary. Yesterday I was informed the job was mine . . . if I wanted it." He glanced at Alex. "How would you like to replace me as Commissaire?"

"Not at all. I'm not even sure I still want to be a flic."

"In that case I'll turn down the offer. I very much want to be a flic."

With three minutes to go, Alex, already impatient, became uneasy; not out of fear, out of apprehension. He had not agreed with the Commissaire's gentlemanly tactic of offering Stevenson/Willoughby-Jones the opportunity to surrender.

But lights began to appear on the ground floor. "Here we go," Alex said. They slid out of the car and moved quickly across the street to be joined at the iron gate by César and a squad of weapons officers.

The veranda light flickered on. Alex thought he heard the heavy lock tumblers of the paneled door fall. But the door didn't budge.

Alarmed, Alex vaulted the gate and started up the steps. The door swung open. He heard a sob. She crawled onto the veranda wearing an ermine coat over her nightgown. She held one hand behind her head and supported herself on the other like a three-legged dog. As she attempted to crawl forward, she repeatedly tore the nightgown.

"Where is he?" Alex asked.

She moaned and shook her head.

Alex raced past her into the empty foyer. He took the steps of the curved staircase three at a time. At the first-floor landing, he paused to orient himself. Seeing a lighted door frame to his left, he ran down the hall.

Master bedroom. Twin four-posters, rumpled bedclothes. Vanity. Two chiffoniers. Open closet. Open bathroom door with the light on. Artificial leg lying on the floor with straps. He ran into the bathroom.

Willoughby-Jones lay on his back in the marble Jacuzzi in a swirl of blood. The handle of the ebony and ivory walking stick was supported by the gold faucets. The other end was in his mouth.

Stevenson's Wife

They placed her on a chaise longue in the library with the ermine coat over her legs. Her face was swollen but she was dry-eyed and sober. A police matron handed her a red plastic cup of black coffee. The Commissaire, who'd been a guest in this house so many times, disqualified himself from the interrogation. He sat to one side and left the questioning to Alex.

She took tiny sips of the scalding coffee. "I didn't think he would do it," she said in her depleted voice.

"But that isn't the question, madame. The question is, did you know he planned to kill Wilson?"

She thought for a moment, took another sip, and said, "When I was a little girl, I planned to run away to East Africa. My mother and father knew I planned to run away, but they didn't think I would do it. That's the way I felt about David. I didn't think he would do it."

"But you knew it was his intention?"

"I knew he had a plan."

"When did you know?"

"Years ago."

"You knew, years ago, that your husband had a plan to commit murder and did nothing about it?"

"That's right."

"But why?"

"Because I didn't think he would do it. *Plan* it, perhaps. But not do it." She put down the coffee cup. "David had a plan to rob the Paris branch of Barclay's Bank," she said matter-of-factly. "He showed me the blueprint of the bank building with all the entrances and stairways labeled, a wiring diagram of the alarm system, an engineering drawing of the vault mechanism, complete with a combination. It was his hobby: to plan the perfect bank robbery, the perfect murder, the perfect theft . . . to place a priceless gem in a surgical incision over his old appendicitis scar, to allow the incision to heal and, that way, to smuggle the jewel out of the country. His aim was to plan the crime, not to do it."

"Did he ever tell you his real name?"

"No."

"Never spoke of his father?"

"No."

"So you were not aware of a motive?"

"No. Except that he wanted to make a perfect plan."

"Do you believe his joining the Wilson Company was part of the plan?"

She shrugged. "I suppose. And I suppose marrying me and becoming a French citizen was part of the plan as well. But I didn't know it then." She stroked the fur in her lap for a moment and almost smiled. "He seduced me with his English eloquence. I saw him as utterly romantic, with his military bearing and his war hero's limp. I thought him incapable of any sort of malice."

Alex asked, "What took him so long?"

She exhaled. "Well, as I said, David was a planner, not a doer. When he made a plan, he put it together like a quilt, square by square. He loved to luxuriate. He was a perfectionist. And it takes ages to make a quilt."

"What do you think changed him from a planner to a doer?"

"I'm not sure. This is a guess. Sometime this spring, he mentioned an article Wilson wrote for an English aero journal."

Alex glanced at the Commissaire. "That article was supposed to be confidential."

"Oh? Well, it was typed on the office word processor. Everything Wilson wrote was typed on the office word processor. Copies were made and the tape erased, but David was always involved and fully informed. He knew Wilson had been urged not to publish the article because of possible consequences. And when Wilson insisted on having it delivered to Germany, I believe David felt the old man's life might suddenly be in jeopardy, that someone else might kill him. Of course this is hindsight, but I think that possibility may have been what changed David from a planner to a doer."

"And none of this aroused your suspicions?"

"No. But I'd become frightened of him. He was obstinate and obsessive . . . even abusive." She picked up the coffee and finished it. "I have a small annuity from my father. In the spring, David withdrew nearly all of it to pay an outrageous price for what I thought was just another pair of walking sticks for his collection. If I had known that one of them concealed a gun, I think . . . I hope I would have done something. In any case, we had a terrible row over the money and he hit me." She put down the cup. "He hit me, and I hit the bottle.

"I don't remember much after that, except the luncheon we gave on the day David received the call from Wilson's grand-daughter in New York. I also remember he phoned the propriétaire in Rue Georges-Berger to learn that Wilson had not slept in his bed for several days. And I remember that he called you for advice, Henri," she said, not looking at the Commissaire. "David seemed genuinely concerned that Wilson had gone missing. And when he identified the body that afternoon, he was quite inconsolable." She shook her head in silence. "I knew he had the doctor's appointment the night of the murder. I knew he couldn't be in two places at once. Under the circumstances, it was impossible for me to imagine he'd actually committed the crime. And, in spite of everything, I still loved him. So, when the police arrested the Arab, you will understand that I was happy.

"I concluded his obsessiveness was somehow related to his bad experiences in the war. And then . . . he suddenly seemed better. We started seeing people again." She stroked the fur. "I never knew I was married to a murderer until tonight."

39

Bollekens

THE DAY Millicent Wilson left Paris and Jan Bollekens returned to Louvain, Charlotte abandoned her fake coma. She discharged herself from hospital, redecorated her bedroom, and made plans to celebrate her ninety-second birthday for the second time.

Charlotte's actual birthday fell on Christmas Eve. But when she was very young, her parents, regretting that their only child was deprived of her own celebration because of the proximity of Christmas, decided to mark her anniversary on the first of May. After that, Charlotte's birthday took place on 1 May until sometime following her seventy-fifth year—Bollekens could not pinpoint the actual date—at which time she began celebrating it twice a year, on 1 May and 24 December.

This Christmas Eve she was particularly gay. Jan had bought her an exquisite museum reproduction of a fifth-century B.C. Etruscan pin decorated with tiny gold rams. She spent the day humming and bustling about, dividing her time between the cook in the kitchen and a seamstress in the sewing room. Everything seemed fine until she came down to dinner wearing her satin and lace wedding dress from 1930.

The gown, brittle and brown with age, had been split up the back and oddly gusseted to force itself around a poitrine, hips, and belly it was never expected to accommodate. Added to this, she wore on her head a chestnut-coloured wig fashioned by a Brussels peruquier at great expense to simulate the Empire hairstyle she'd worn on her wedding day.

After dinner Charlotte, looking like Frederick Ashton dancing one of the ugly sisters in *Cinderella*, lurched about on cloglike heels and flooded the salon with sentiment and nostalgia to the uneven strains of Paderewski playing Chopin from a stack of old seventy-eights on the parlour gramophone.

She danced, she drank champagne, she flirted, she rolled back the years. And, as the heavy wax-coated records dropped one by one onto the labouring turntable, the music became slower and slower. She laughed, she wept, and, inevitably, passed out on the large divan.

Bollekens fetched pillows and a comforter and made her as comfortable as the circumstances would permit. He then went to bed. Next morning at seven, when he brought her her breakfast tea, he found her lying serenely on the floor alongside the couch. She was inert. Both her eyes were closed and she had no pulse. He called the coroner. The diagnosis was that some time during the night her heart had simply stopped.

While the coroner prepared the requisite documents and the body was removed, Jan walked through the salon French doors onto the terrace of the huge stone mansion. There, in the clear, cold sunshine of that Christmas morning, he experienced the ambivalent exhilaration of the dissident who, having never wavered for a moment in his loyalty to his homeland, learns, to his astonishment, that his visa to emigrate has been unexpectedly approved.

Hospice de Ste.-Anne

Varnas was flown back to Paris and transferred to a nursing facility near the Bois de Vincennes. He had limited use of his left arm but was ambulatory to the extent allowed by the slow-healing scapula and ribs.

He spent Christmas and the week following in a solarium surrounded by flowers and gifts, including a dozen toy pandas ("Hot animals, Alex, from informants in Eighteenth Arrondissement").

After Varnas's discharge, the Maison, not wishing him to return unattended to his cramped fourth-floor walkup in Pigalle, arranged to lease one of the smaller transient flats at 8 Rue Georges-Berger, where he would complete his convalescence under the sheltering eye of Madame Roget.

40

Le Yacht Club

PHILIPPA had read somewhere that promiscuity was a narcissistic hedge against old age and death. She hadn't understood the phrase. Her mother was promiscuous not because it was a hedge against anything, but because it felt good and provided the excitement of love without the commitment.

If Alex was not exactly promiscuous, Philippa knew he was wary of love. But unlike Claudine, she didn't find his wariness a selfish refusal to commit so much as a form of openness. When his father stopped loving his mother and he grew up in a house of polite strangers, Alex learned that love could end. He decided then that if the price of loving was that it could end, he would be careful before offering it. So he courted adventure, danger, and casual sexual liaisons to avoid what he called "the siren song that lures unsuspecting assholes onto the rocks of conventional marriage."

Philippa, as she had confided to Varnas, held no exalted opinion of marriage herself. But never having felt anything like love before Alex, she had no experience of love ending. And while she had no specific emotional strategy in mind for the future (apart from a reflexive instinct to protect Alex from those perfumed and lotioned Lorelei forever lining up on the love rocks), she knew she wanted things to remain as they were.

She and Alex celebrated Christmas on the day after Christmas. She put on her Irish wool hat, her pearls, her down jacket, leather skirt, and boat shoes and kept them on all day. She wore them to the theatre. The régisseur said she looked like a teenage bag lady. She danced one of the mice in *The Nutcracker* and hurried home, expecting to find Alex stowing gear. Instead, he was lounging in his captain's chair in the saloon, wearing the new Cardin dinner jacket and vest she'd given him, playing the tuba.

She stopped at the bottom of the companion ladder. "What's this? I thought we were leaving tonight?"

Oom-oom-oom-pah-oom, doodle-oom. "I've decided to cancel the cruise," he said. *Oom-oom.*

She put down her dance bag and came into the saloon. Something had happened, she decided, something outside, that had nothing to do with her. "Any special reason?" she asked as casually as she could manage over the ooming.

He deposited the horn on the floor. "Too dangerous," he said, "especially for a man who has only lately come to maturity. Plus, I've been looking over the canal pilot book. There are seven locks in the first six and a half kilometres of the Canal St.-Denis. It gets worse later. We have two weeks. With all those locks we'll barely get out of town before our vacation is over."

She looked at him sitting there, splendid and shining in his new tuxedo. She'd never seen him look more beautiful. And then it occurred to her that perhaps the real reason he'd canceled the cruise was that some siren had nicked him after all. Maybe he had a new trick waiting in town to help him celebrate solving the Wilson case. He'd done that once before. She said, "So where are you going all duded up like that?"

"Out." She held her breath. Was this the bullet with her number on it? So soon? "I've reserved a table for us at Le Rivage. They won't let you in there in a down jacket and deck shoes."

She changed into her only formal dress, a silver and black floor-length sheath of remarkable form and lustre, created originally by the company costumier for *Der Rosenkavalier,* but returned to wardrobe because its style was more 1982 than 1911, more Karl Lagerfeld than Gustav Klimt, and because it was impossible to waltz in. Philippa cajoled it from a wardrobe mistress in exchange for an old Edith Piaf record. She wore it with four-inch heels and looked like a young goddess.

Alex had ordered ahead. They dined at midnight, by candle-light, on Caviar Vilnius en Croûte (for Varnas), Clams Breton au Beurre Noir (for Villa Philippa-by-the-sea), Shrimp Marseilles

(for Shafik, for whom Alex hoped to get early parole), and, after
a salad of endive and tomato, a Tarte d'Ananas Martinique (for
the trip to the Lesser Antilles not taken). When, nearly two hours
later, they finished their coffee, Philippa carefully folded her napkin and said, "This is a fat lady you have here." She patted her
stomach. "My career is finished. I'll never dance again. Let's get
married."

Without looking up from the bill, Alex said, "But chérie, I can't
have you sitting around the boat in a caftan, eating chocolates
and watching TV all day. Who'll support me when I'm old and
gray?"

"I can get work as a diesel mechanic."

"That's true enough. Well, I'll think about it." He handed the
waiter his credit card.

While they waited for the bill to come back, she put an elbow
on the table, rested her chin in her hand, and gazed at him. Her
eyes shone in the flickering light of the nearly expired candle. "Will
you really?"

"Will I really what?"

"Think about it?"

He met her gaze. "I thought you were making a joking reference
to imagined obesity."

"Well, I was and I wasn't." She wiggled her hand. "If I think
you're joking, then I'm joking. If you're not, I'm not. It's called
ambiguity. It's the latest thing. It can get you out of trouble." She
smiled. "I just wanted to be sure you didn't think I was promiscuous, like my mother."

"Now you *are* joking."

"Not really. I get horny when I'm full."

The waiter, already in his street clothes, returned. Alex signed
the invoice and left the tip in cash. The waiter bowed and left.
Pocketing the receipt, Alex said, "Well, first things first, chérie.
During our vacation you have to work off this dinner and get back
to class. I have to practice my tuba and decide whether I want to
be a flic. And next week, or the week after, I think we ought to
plan a circumnavigation of Paris in *Le Yacht Club*."

"And take Varnas."

"If he has his sea legs."

Outside, the air was soft and still. There were no cabs. Philippa took a deep breath and, feeling beautiful, slipped a hand around his waist and into his jacket pocket. They walked that way, in step, down the Champs-Élysées to the metro.